GALACTIC BOUNTY

A traitor is on the loose. A treacherous navy captain plans to sell military secrets to the alien Il Ronn. The only man who can stop him is Sam McCade. Betrayed by his friends, stalked by his enemies, McCade is the only one standing between a terrifying alien threat—and the unimaginable devastation of the Terran Empire . . .

IMPERIAL BOUNTY

Since her brother's absence, Princess Claudia has seized the throne and brought the Empire to the brink of war with the Il Ronn. Only the missing Prince Alexander can stop Claudia's plans—and Sam McCade has only three months to find him. But Princess Claudia controls the Imperial Fleet and will stop at nothing to keep McCade from bringing in his imperial bounty . . .

McCade for Hire

WILLIAM C. DIETZ

ACE BOOKS, NEW YORK

An Ace Book
Published by The Berkley Publishing Group
A division of Penguin Group (USA) Inc.
375 Hudson Street
New York, New York 10014

McCADE FOR HIRE

PRINTING HISTORY
Ace trade paperback edition / January 2004

Library of Congress Cataloging-in-Publication Data

Dietz, William C.
    [Galactic bounty]
    McCade for hire / William C. Dietz.
        p.   cm.
    Contents: Galactic bounty—Imperial bounty.
    ISBN 0-441-01129-2
        1. Human-alien encounters—Fiction.   2. Space warfare—Fiction.   I. Dietz, William C.
Imperial bounty.   II. Title: Imperial bounty.   III. Title.

PS3554.I388G35 2004
813'.54—dc22

                                                              2003060508

PRINTED IN THE UNITED STATES OF AMERICA

10   9   8   7   6   5   4   3   2   1

CONTENTS

GALACTIC BOUNTY

To Grace Dietz who taught me to love books,
To Marjorie Dietz who believed I could write one,
To F. M. Busby for his advice and support,
And to Sue Stone, who found this story, read it,
and improved it.

ONE

From his vantage point at the bar, McCade could watch the entire room. It was saturated with smoke and noise and filled to overflowing with people. Cadien was there somewhere. McCade could feel it. An evil presence. A hunted animal gone to earth. But where? All sorts of people mixed and mingled in a swirl of movement and color. There were miners just in from the asteroids eager to live out fantasies devised a million lights away. There were long-haul freighters, the stink of their sweat still on them, celebrating the end of a three-month run. Navy men drank and laughed, trying to forget the fear and boredom of patrol along the frontier. And yes, there were also those like McCade himself. Hunters of men, watching and waiting for one of the many faces they'd memorized, hoping that tonight they'd make the big score. Among them moved drug vendors, thieves, and prostitutes, all plying their various trades. All were welcome in Floyd's Pink Asteroid Bar and Grill. All helped make Imperial Earth possible. None were welcome among its more refined pleasures.

McCade slid off his stool. His stained leathers creaked slightly as he stood. Alien suns had darkened his skin and etched deep lines around his gray eyes. Under thick black hair, his features were strong and even. A muscle twitched in his left cheek. He moved with the smooth confidence of a man well aware of his own ability. His right hand brushed the grip of the slug gun worn low on his right thigh.

He felt the familiar flutter of fear low in his gut as he began to circle the room. Cadien scared the hell out of him. Psychopath. Professional assassin.

Butcher. Cadien was all these and more. On New Britain he'd fulfilled an illegal assassination by blowing up a yacht along with its owner. In the past he'd committed many lesser crimes and gotten away.

But this time Cadien had gone too far. Among those who died on the yacht was the Emperor's favorite niece. A price was placed on Cadien's head. One million Imperial credits, dead or alive. Every hand was turned against him, so Cadien ran. From planet to planet and from system to system. Bounty hunters followed—men like Sam McCade.

Since the cost of creating and operating an Imperial police force was considered prohibitive, interplanetary law enforcement was carried out by bounty hunters. They were a strange breed. Both hated and feared, loners mostly, they were forever excluded from the society they served. Planetary law enforcement officers resented them, and placed them on a par with those they hunted. Citizens often romanticized them, imagining their lives to be both glamorous and exciting. But no one wanted them around for longer than it took them to do their job. So bounty hunters were constantly on the move.

For a few credits at any public terminal, they could punch up a current list of Imperial fugitives, including their names, known histories, habitual weapons, and most important of all, the reward offered for their capture or termination. Occasionally the reward would be conditional, specifying that the fugitive must be brought in alive, but most often dead or even proof of death was just fine. Having picked a fugitive, the bounty hunter could request and receive a hunting license for that particular person. Capturing or killing a fugitive without a license was considered fortuitous, which meant no reward.

A record number of bounty hunters had requested licenses on Cadien, including Sam McCade. One million credits was an unusually high reward. But time passed and Cadien had proved to be both cunning and elusive, so most of his pursuers gave up, turning their attention to other less difficult prey. But McCade was tenacious, and a million credits was a lot of money—enough to buy a ship of his own.

For a bounty hunter a ship was both a status symbol and a tool, a means of catching more fugitives. But at times that goal seemed distant in-

deed. Expenses had consumed most of his money, and the trail was growing cold. But finally, just when McCade was about to give up, a paid in-
former led him to Cadien's mistress. It took time, and the rest of McCade's
money, but the information she provided had led him to the Pink Asteroid.
He was broke, and liners were notoriously expensive, so to get there he'd
been forced to ship out as third mate on an ore freighter. It had touched
down on Imperial Earth three days before. Each night he'd waited for Cadien to show. Maybe tonight would be the night.

As he moved, McCade's eyes continually scanned the crowd, comparing each face with the memprinted image of Cadien burned into his mind.
Some eyes met his in open challenge. Those he ignored. Others slid away.
Those he followed, checking and comparing. Toward the center of the
room he noticed a miner who looked a lot like Cadien. Casually he moved
between the tightly packed tables to get a better look.

He had just decided it wasn't Cadien when something tugged at his
arm, and the miner's head exploded. He turned, dropping to one knee.
His gun roared three times. The heavy slugs tore Cadien's chest apart. A
woman screamed. Suddenly everyone wanted to be somewhere else. The
crowd pushed toward the doors and streamed outside.

McCade's left arm hurt. Cadien's slug had passed right through it before hitting the miner. He clutched it as he walked over and looked down at
the miner's crumpled body, dully wondering who he'd been, why he'd died,
and whether anyone else would care. A trail of red dots followed him over
to Cadien. He'd seemed larger than life, almost superhuman, as McCade
had tracked him across the stars. But dead, he looked small and empty.
McCade would have preferred to bring him in alive. But sometimes they
didn't give you any choice.

His arm hurt more now and was covered with blood. The bastard had
nicked a vein or something. His vision was fading. He was falling. He heard
distant voices. They didn't seem to make any sense. "Tourniquet . . . under
arrest for . . ." Rough hands grabbed and lifted. There was an explosion of
pain and then nothing.

He struggled to clear his vision. Gray ceilings and walls swam into focus. Wherever he looked he saw surveillance sensors. Made obvious to intimidate? McCade smiled wryly. If so it was working. His left arm was numb. Turning his head he tried to see it, but couldn't. From the shoulder down it disappeared into an automedic. The machine hummed softly as it speeded the healing process along. It was a standard, navy model. As was the bed, the room's single chair, and everything else in sight. No doubt about it, somehow he'd wound up in a navy brig. The Pink Asteroid was located in Santa Fe. So they'd probably taken him to Earth Fleet Base, which sprawled across most of New Mexico. But why? McCade didn't know . . . but somehow he felt sure that he wouldn't like the answer. He felt very tired, or was it just that the automedic was pumping a sedative into his system? He decided it made very little difference and fell asleep.

When he awoke he felt better. The automedic was gone. His left arm was bandaged and sore but seemed able to move normally.

Silently a section of wall slid back. A man stepped into the cell. "Hello, Sam. It's been a long time."

He was strongly backlit, and it took McCade a moment to recognize him. Walter Swanson-Pierce. A little older, hair dusted with gray, but still trim and fit. Never a friend, but not exactly an enemy either. More like a friendly adversary. But that was a long time ago. While time had passed, it had done nothing to change the smile that rang slightly false, the eyes that reflected vain arrogance, or the face still a shade too pretty for a man. Still, some things had changed. The gold rings on Swanson-Pierce's immaculate, space-black sleeve were those of a full captain. Lieutenant to captain in ten years. Not bad. Good old Walt had done well for himself. McCade felt sorry for those who'd been in the way.

Squinting into the light, McCade replied, "Hello, Walt. Since you're in, I might as well ask you to sit down. You will anyway."

The other man crossed the room with a smile. "It's nice to see you've retained your sense of humor." He lowered himself gracefully into the skeletal form of the chair. "Yes, it's been a long time. Those were the days, weren't they, Sam? The old *Imperial* wasn't much compared to today's battleships. Still we showed the pirates a thing or two, didn't we? By god we were bright-eyed and bushy-tailed back then!"

"Cut the crap, Walt," McCade replied. "The *Imperial* was a stinking old tub that could barely lift off-planet, and you know it. And we weren't bright-eyed and bushy-tailed. More like hungry, tired, and scared shitless. Let's get on with it. . . . What're you doing here? Or, more to the point, what am *I* doing here?"

"Why, Sam," Swanson-Pierce said. "I see your charming directness hasn't changed a bit! In answer to your question, you're the guest of the Imperial Navy, recovering from wounds suffered while ridding the empire of a dangerous criminal. Or so it says in this morning's news. By the way, the Emperor sends his thanks." Swanson-Pierce leaned back, the hint of a smile touching his lips.

McCade grimaced. "Walt, you know where you and the Emperor can shove it. I don't want your hospitality. I just want out. Now."

Swanson-Pierce frowned in mock concern. "Sam, you really must be more circumspect. Imagine! Telling the Emperor to shove it. Why some would call that treason. Fortunately I know you jest." His look hardened. "As for leaving, wherever would you go?"

McCade sighed. Swanson-Pierce clearly enjoyed toying with him, and for the moment there wasn't much he could do about it. It reminded him of junior officer's mess when they'd both been aboard the *Imperial*. As the most senior lieutenant—his commission had predated McCade's by a week—Swanson-Pierce had always enjoyed playing games with those junior to him. Not so much with McCade, who refused to be intimidated, but especially sub-lieutenants and midshipmen.

McCade forced a smile and said, "I'll tell you what, Walt, you let me out of here, I'll toddle off, collect the reward for killing that dangerous criminal you mentioned, and then I'll check into a nice hotel." McCade smiled hopefully.

"Well I'd like to Sam, I really would," Swanson-Pierce replied gravely. "But there is the matter of the Imperial Claims Board."

"The Imperial Claims Board?" McCade asked, dreading the answer.

"Why yes," the naval officer replied innocently. "All claims for reward stemming from the death of a fugitive from Imperial justice must be dully considered and approved by the Imperial Claims Board," he recited. Swanson-Pierce watched to see if McCade would take the bait—just as he had taken it so long ago.

"Since when?" McCade asked through clenched teeth, unable to resist.

"Since yesterday," Swanson-Pierce answered happily, the game won.

For a moment the two men stared at each other. Swanson-Pierce with barely disguised glee, and McCade with disgust verging on hatred. Now he remembered why they'd never been friends. Straining for control, McCade asked, "How long will it take for my claim to be approved?"

"That's really hard to say," the other man replied thoughtfully. "The Board's just getting organized, and of course they'll want to agree on some rules and what not, why I suppose it could take months!"

"In that case," McCade said grimly, "I'll just leave and wait for my claim to clear." He sat up and swung his feet over the side of the bed. A wave of dizziness and nausea swept over him.

Swanson-Pierce summoned up a look of fatherly concern. "I really couldn't allow it, Sam. You're obviously not up to snuff." He paused judiciously, regarding McCade through steepled fingers. "I hesitate to bring this up, considering your health and so on, but there is one other small difficulty. It seems you're under arrest. Something about discharging firearms within the city limits."

McCade allowed himself to fall back against the pillow. Obviously Swanson-Pierce still wanted something, and he'd have to provide it before he could go. "All right, Walt," McCade said wearily. "You've had your fun. Now cut the bull. Exactly what do you want?"

The other man smiled as he rose from his chair. Walking toward the door he shook his head in pretended amazement. "Sam, you'll never change." He turned in the doorway. "Get some rest, Sam. We'll talk again soon." He stepped out of the cell and the door slid silently closed behind him.

For some time McCade lay there, rigid with frustration. He'd done it.

He'd tracked Cadien halfway across the empire, damn near got his ass blown off, and earned a million Imperials in the process. Right now he should have been getting drunk, getting laid, and getting ready to pick out his ship. Roughly in that order. Instead, a naval officer with a sadistic sense of humor had gone to a great deal of trouble to lock him up. Why? Nothing came. One by one he ordered his muscles to relax. Gradually they obeyed and finally he sank into the oblivion of sleep.

He awoke with the sun in his eyes. The wall in front of him had become transparent. Outside, the huge naval base sprawled to the horizon. In a way, it symbolized the entire planet. As the center of a vast empire, Terra was almost entirely dedicated to the various branches of government, the military, scientific research, and of course the pleasures of those so engaged. He sat up and swung his feet over the side of the bed. He felt better. His arm was still a little stiff, but the pain had almost disappeared. There were clothes draped over the chair. Moving gingerly he stood and shuffled over to them. His worn leathers had disappeared and been replaced by a new set in navy black, without insignia of course. Everything fit perfectly. Except the memories. Those belonged to someone else, someone younger. Someone who'd believed what they taught him.

The door slid open. McCade accepted its unspoken invitation and stepped outside. Two Imperial marines stood waiting in the corridor. Both snapped to attention. McCade smiled. The hand of steel within the velvet glove. Just Walt's way of letting him know where he stood.

The larger of the two marines wore the chevrons of a section leader and the confidence of a professional. Bright brown eyes looked straight ahead from under bushy brows. When he spoke, his lips barely moved. "Will you accompany us, sir?"

McCade almost laughed. As if he had a choice. He nodded, and together they moved off. One marine fell in ahead and the other behind. Down corridors, through halls, along autowalks and, on one occasion, two hundred feet straight up a vertical shaft using some kind of new anti-grav field. He was impressed. He hadn't been to Terra for years and had forgotten what it was like. Everywhere, he saw purposeful activity and new technology—little things, many of them, but still new.

In spite of the empire's vast size, Terra was still the principal source of new technology. That fact had helped her remain at the center of human endeavor instead of being relegated to its past. In 3,112 years of recorded history, man had inhabited hundreds of worlds. Many had never seen Terra and never would. But for the most part all still thought of Terra as home.

By the time they arrived in front of huge, ornate doors, McCade was tired. They'd come a long way and his arm had started to ache. As they approached, two more marines snapped to attention. They seemed to come in pairs, like bookends. To McCade's surprise they opened the heavy doors by hand to let him pass. Their deference indicated the status of whoever he was about to meet. Or the ego, he reflected sourly.

As he entered, he noticed that the room was simply but elegantly furnished. A long walk across plush carpet carried him to a large desk. The chair behind it stood empty. The top of the desk was bare. But deep in its black surface a star map could be seen, accurate in every detail. He recognized many systems and planets. Imperial stars were colored silver, and, in spite of the empire's size, they were few against the immense backdrop of space. Between them tiny red sparks flew, which McCade supposed were navy ships, continually striving to bind the empire together.

"Impressive isn't it?" Surprised, McCade looked up into amused blue eyes. The sound of the man's entry had evidently been lost in the thick carpet. His white hair suggested age, but his movements retained the quick precision of youth. His face was round and unlined, yet there was a profound weariness in his eyes. His simple white robe bore no mark of rank. He needed none. The feeling of power surrounding the man was almost palpable. His smile seemed genuine and McCade found himself responding in kind. "Please be seated, Citizen McCade," the man continued. "I'm Admiral Keaton."

The floor behind McCade extruded a formless-looking chair. As McCade sat down, the chair quickly molded itself to the shape of his body. He'd never seen one like it. He was amazed.

Admiral Keaton! The man was a legend. He'd helped build the Imperial Navy under the first emperor. Then he'd shaped it, molded it, and used it to further expand the empire. Later he'd commanded the fleet that defeated the pirates near the planet Hell. McCade knew because he'd been there, aboard the *Imperial.*

"First allow me to apologize for the considerable inconvenience we've put you through, though, as you'll see, this is a matter of grave concern to the Empire." The Admiral's tone was that of one equal addressing another on a problem of mutual concern. In spite of his distaste for the military, McCade couldn't help feeling complimented. "I'm aware, of course," Keaton continued smoothly, "that your separation from the navy wasn't entirely voluntary."

"A court martial rarely is. . . . Voluntary, I mean," McCade replied dryly. He remembered the cold empty feeling as he entered the enormous wardroom of the *Imperial.* Facing him from behind the semicircular table were nine senior naval officers. One for each planet in Terra's system. Each had commanded a ship in the Battle of Hell. Their verdict was unanimous. Guilty. McCade could still see the grim satisfaction deep in the eyes of his commanding officer, Captain Bridger. He felt the familiar surge of anger and hatred sweep over him and pushed it back as he'd done a thousand times before.

Admiral Keaton nodded knowingly. "For what it's worth . . . I would have favored a less severe punishment than dishonorable discharge. I think we both realize that Captain Bridger's personal feelings may have colored his judgment. However you did choose to disobey a direct order. As I recall, you admitted that. And once Captain Bridger brought formal charges, the Court had little choice." Keaton paused, regarding McCade with a thoughtful expression before going on. "Of course, no one but the Emperor can change such a verdict after the fact."

McCade's thoughts churned. Had he just heard a veiled hint? If so, at what? His commission reinstated for services rendered? If so, why the heavy-handed approach from good old Walt? Surely the Admiral must be aware of the kind of leverage Walt had used to get him here. Of course he was. The carrot and the stick. He was being expertly conned. He didn't know what was coming—but he felt sure it would be a real lulu.

"I'll get to the point," Keaton said. "There's an important service you could render. Though I realize you may feel little loyalty to the Empire . . . I think you know it's necessary. The alternative is anarchy."

McCade didn't know if he believed that or not, but he certainly knew the theory. The Academy instructors had hammered it home day after day. It was the basic tenent underlying the Emperor's rule. There had been a confederation once. But there were too many stars, too many systems. Each had a point of view, special needs and special problems. Each saw itself as the center of the human universe. An entire planet had been set aside as a capital. It was populated with millions of representatives sent to vote on behalf of thousands of worlds. But the democratic process constantly broke down into endless bickering and squabbling. Nothing effective was accomplished because decisions always called for sacrifice by one or more special interest groups. Eventually a coalition of systems seceded from the Confederation. A bloody civil war followed. Finally after years of conflict a strong and brilliant leader emerged. He amassed a great armada and used it to conquer all the planets then held by man. His supporters proclaimed him emperor . . . and the Empire was born. His rule proved reasonable and consistent, preferable to the profitless anarchy of war. Eventually, most became willing subjects. However a stubborn few fled to the Empire's frontiers. There they eked out a marginal existence on uncharted worlds, or raided the Empire's commerce as pirates. Now the first emperor's son ruled, and little had changed.

Admiral Keaton paused as though gathering his thoughts. "We can also offer what we think is generous compensation for your services."

McCade would've sworn there was a glint of humor deep in the Admiral's eyes. "In addition to helping you resolve your legal difficulties, we are prepared to offer you a first-class ship. I believe such a vessel is central to your future plans." Admiral Keaton allowed himself an amused smile.

Blast them! McCade thought. They were leading him around like a child. He knew it, they knew it, and right now there wasn't a damn thing he could do about it. Forcing an even tone and sardonic grin, McCade said, "You're too generous, Admiral. You offer to pay me what's already mine, and throw in the ship I could have bought with it to boot. Terrific. It's a great deal. But before I agree . . . I'd like to know what's involved. So let's skip the bull and get on with it. What do you want? And why me?"

For a second McCade saw anger flicker in the other man's eyes and wondered if he'd pushed Keaton too far. But then the anger vanished to be replaced by a grim smile.

"All right, maybe I deserved that, McCade. . . . So, as you put it, I'll skip the bull. As for what we want, well, you did the Empire a service when you tracked Cadien down. We want you to find another fugitive for us and bring him back." The Admiral paused for a moment and said, "Failing that, we want you to kill him."

McCade experienced a sinking feeling. Whatever the game was, it obviously involved high stakes.

Keaton looked at him appraisingly. "As for why we picked you, well, you have quite a reputation in your, ah, chosen profession. I'm told your peers hold you in very high esteem. What's more important, however, is that you know the fugitive, how he thinks, what makes him tick. And that may well give you an edge in finding him. And last but not least . . . you just happened to be in the right place at the right time."

"Or the wrong place at the wrong time," McCade replied sourly. "Who am I supposed to find?"

"Captain Ian Bridger," Keaton replied grimly. "Ironic, isn't it?"

Totally insane is more like it, McCade thought. Find Bridger and bring him back dead or alive. Deep down he knew a part of him would enjoy tracking Bridger down. And they knew it, and were counting on it. But what had Bridger done? Whatever it was must be big.

"I'm already starting to feel underpaid," McCade said. "I want the bounty for Cadien, plus the ship, plus let's say, half a million for Bridger." He was as much interested in Keaton's reaction as in getting what he'd asked for.

The Admiral smiled crookedly. "The offer stands as is. If you succeed, we'll consider a bonus. Otherwise, I suggest you prepare for a long stay while the Claims Board gets organized and then considers your case."

For a moment McCade just sat there, wishing he could see some way out, but finding each possible door closed to him. With a sigh he said, "All right, you've got a deal. What exactly did Bridger do?"

"Swanson-Pierce will fill you in," Keaton replied, his face remote now, already considering the next item on his agenda for the day. "Good hunting, McCade." And with that, the Admiral shimmered and disappeared, leaving only an empty chair.

Suddenly McCade realized Keaton had never been there at all. Some kind of holo? If so, it was the best he'd ever seen. Thoughtfully he got up and made his way across the plush carpet to the massive double doors. They opened on silent hinges, and as he stepped out of the room, the four marines snapped to attention.

"Ready sir?" asked the section leader who'd brought him.

McCade nodded. "Yes, thanks, Section."

Together the three men started down the corridor. McCade noticed it was busier now. Glancing at his wrist term, he saw it was almost noon. People were heading for lunch. Moments later, as McCade and the marines rounded a corner into a crowded hallway, the assassins made their move.

TWO

There were three assassins, one ahead, one to each side. They were positioned to place McCade and his two escorts in a deadly cross fire. In keeping with Imperial law, they threw off their cloaks to reveal bright red jump suits. The word "assassin" flashed on and off in lights across each man's chest. The one in the middle delivered the formal warning.

"Attention! A level-three, licensed assassination will be carried out on Citizen Sam McCade five seconds from now." His amplified voice boomed down the corridor. People scattered and dived for cover in every direction. The lead assassin drew his blaster.

McCade dived for the floor and rolled right. Blaster fire splashed the floor where he'd just been. A wave of heat rolled over him, filling his nostrils with the stench of burned plastic. He looked up to see the lead assassin hurled backward by a blast from the section leader's energy weapon. Then McCade was hit from the side as the body of the second marine fell on him. There was a hole the size of a dinner plate burned through the man's chest. McCade rolled out from under the body, grabbing the marine's energy weapon as he did so. He fired as soon as his finger found the stud. Swinging left he punched a line of incandescent holes into the far wall before coming to bear on the lefthand assassin. As soon as the assassin filled his sights, McCade held the stud down. Pieces of the man flew in every direction.

McCade swung his weapon right, searching for another target. None remained. The assassins were dead. The section leader had killed two before being hit himself. McCade moved quickly to the marine's side. To his relief he saw the man was still alive. A blaster beam had grazed his right thigh. Fortunately it had cauterized the wound on its way by, so there wasn't any bleeding. McCade was something of an expert on wounds and had the scars to prove it. It looked like a stint in an automedic would make the leg as good as new.

The marine grinned at McCade through gritted teeth. "Glad you made it, sir. . . . For a moment there I thought we were all goners. Level three, for god's sake. . . . They must want you awful bad. . . . Woulda' been my ass if they'd got you though. . . . How's Reynolds?"

Slowly McCade became aware of the pandemonium around them. People caught in the cross fire screaming, others yelling commands, the smell of burned flesh, and the distant sound of approaching sirens. Good, someone had called the medics. McCade glanced at the other marine's crumpled form and then back to the section leader. "I'm afraid he didn't make it, Section."

The marine nodded unhappily.

"I'm sorry," McCade said, knowing it wouldn't help.

"Not your fault, sir," the section leader said. "You did your part." With a motion of his head he indicated the assassin McCade had killed.

"So did you, Section," McCade replied soberly. "I owe you one."

The marine shook his head. "No sir, that's what they pay me for. . . . But damn . . . level three . . . I can't believe it."

The marine's words still echoed in McCade's ears as he moved among the other wounded, doing what he could to help. A few minutes later he was brushed aside as the medics arrived, followed closely by a ground car loaded with marines.

"Level three . . ." McCade said to himself. Level three meant assassins could kill not only their intended target, but any bystanders who happened to get in the way as well, all without fear of official reprisal. It was legal, of course. Legal but expensive. First you bought a license from the government. A nice source of revenue for the empire, by the way. Then you hired a member of the Assassin's Guild. Both were expensive. A level-three license, plus three Guild assassins would cost a small fortune. To have the hit carried out on a naval base would cost several more small fortunes. He'd never even heard of such an attempt before. But chances were, it was all legal and aboveboard. Otherwise, Guild assassins would never have gotten involved.

Of course every now and then there was someone stupid enough, or greedy enough, to try and cut both the government and the Guild out. Cadien was a good example. But for every Cadien there was a McCade. A bounty hunter willing to track a man across the empire for a fraction of what an effective Imperial police force would cost. And if McCade hadn't caught up with Cadien, the Guild eventually would have. They took illegal assassinations very seriously indeed. Particularly ones which offended the Emperor personally. Not only did such acts rob them of revenue, they gave assassins a bad name, and the Guild was already quite aware of its negative public image. The public rated assassins even below bounty hunters. What if assassination was made illegal? The very thought must send their blood pressure soaring, McCade thought sourly. Assuming, of course, they had blood in their veins.

Anyway, the section leader was right. . . . Someone did want him awfully bad. It wasn't a pleasant thought. McCade returned the section leader's wave as the marine was loaded into a ground vehicle that promptly disappeared in the direction of the base hospital.

"Citizen McCade?" The voice belonged to a tall, serious-looking marine captain.

"That depends," McCade replied. "Who are you?"

"My name is Captain Rhodes," the officer replied levelly. "My men and I are here to protect you." There was something superior about his expression and condescending in his tone. He put out an open hand for the energy weapon still tucked under McCade's arm.

McCade ignored the hand by taking a long slow look around. The marine was forced to do likewise. The wounded were still being loaded into ambulances. Reynolds was being zipped into a black body bag, and robot repair units were starting to arrive. McCade turned back to the captain without saying a word. He didn't have to. The message was clear. In spite of a valiant effort to protect him, his previous bodyguards had nearly failed. The marine flushed a dark red. McCade handed him the weapon and allowed himself to be ushered aboard an open ground car. He noticed they weren't taking any chances now. The marines surrounding him were heavily armed and the car mounted twin automatic weapons.

As the car eased into motion, McCade said, "Do I get to know where we're going?"

"Captain Swanson-Pierce has requested your presence," Captain Rhodes answered stiffly, as though unable to understand why anyone would request McCade for anything.

McCade turned away from the resentful marine and looked out the side of the speeding vehicle. The faces that passed by merged into a blur, along with his thoughts. He remembered the screams of those caught in the cross fire. Strangers had been hurt or killed because of him. Why? It made no sense. Of course he'd made enemies as a bounty hunter. But most of them were dead, or sentenced to a prison planet for life, if you could call that life. Friends or relatives were always a possibility. But why now? And why in the middle of an Imperial Navy base? It didn't make sense . . . unless of course it was somehow connected with the Bridger thing.

McCade put those thoughts aside as the vehicle left the confinement of the building and emerged into bright sunshine. Lush green grass, still slightly moist from the rain programmed to fall at exactly 0500 every morning, reached out to touch a bright blue sky. The air smelled fresh and clean. Pollution and crowding were things of the past. At least on Terra they were. For hundreds of years, Earth had exported her problems, including both heavy industry and excess population. As a result, much of Terra's surface was dedicated to vast forests and parks. Cities were designed for beauty as well as function. Even naval bases had been made easy on the eye, so that visitors from off-planet couldn't imagine the crowded, polluted misery of a thousand years before. In the distance, the neat symmetry of a spaceport could be seen shimmering in the early heat, surrounded by concentric rings of navy ships. Thunder rolled as the slender needle shape of a destroyer rose toward the sky.

The ground car stopped in front of a black building which soared a thousand feet upward. The building bore no sign announcing its purpose. There was a momentary wait as Captain Rhodes issued orders to his men. McCade used it to read a small gold plaque set into the permacrete at his feet. It read:

> *The first to see,*
> *The first to hear,*
> *The first to know,*
> *The first to die.*

The motto of Naval Intelligence. Those who worked within were the Emperor's eyes and ears. From here they wove an invisible web between the stars. A network of information that touched every planet held by man . . . and quite a few that weren't.

As McCade and Rhodes approached the building its black surface grew blacker. Evidently the entire building was protected by a force field. The area directly in front of them shimmered and disappeared, leaving an opening just large enough for them to pass through.

Inside, both men were invisibly but thoroughly scanned by hidden security sensors as they waited by a lift tube. The captain's sidearm was detected immediately, its serial number checked against the one issued to him, his entire personnel file quickly reviewed, all in a fraction of a second. McCade was identified by his retinal patterns and also checked. A moment later computer approval flashed back, allowing the lift tube doors to open. They stepped aboard the waiting platform, and it moved smoothly upward. McCade followed the marine off at level eighty-six. They went a few steps down a gleaming corridor and into a roomy reception area, where they were greeted by a very attractive lieutenant, who looked stunning in navy black and, from her slightly amused expression, knew it.

"Citizen McCade reporting as ordered," Captain Rhodes said.

McCade winked at the lieutenant, and to his surprise she winked back. She nodded to the marine and murmured into a wrist mic before turning away to tap something into the terminal on her desk.

"Sam, you've been at it again. You really must stop shooting people in public places. . . . It's so messy." Swanson-Pierce had appeared in a doorway. He also wore an amused expression and another perfectly tailored uniform. "Come on in," he said, turning and disappearing back into his office.

As McCade entered he noticed the office was quite luxurious, resembling more the working quarters of a successful businessman than the spartan day cabin of a naval officer. After dropping into a chair facing Swanson-Pierce's highly polished rosewood desk, McCade reached to pluck a cigar from an open humidor, and settled back. Puffing it alight, he watched Swanson-Pierce through the smoke. "Speaking of shooting people in public places, Walt . . . you wouldn't happen to know why I'm suddenly so unpopular, would you?" McCade allowed some white ash to drift down toward the plush carpet.

Swanson-Pierce laughed. "Why Sam, considering your vast wealth of personal charm, I must admit I'm surprised. Old, ah, clients perhaps?"

McCade regarded the naval officer soberly and shook his head. "I don't think so. It takes a big bankroll to swing a level three . . . especially in the middle of a naval base. If I'd offended somebody with that kind of clout, I'd remember. No, I think it's something else, maybe connected to this Bridger thing."

Swanson-Pierce nodded in agreement. "Our people are looking into that possibility at this very moment. It's too bad all three assassins were killed. It would have been interesting to talk with one of them." He frowned at McCade disapprovingly.

"Yeah, that was too bad. I'll keep it in mind next time," McCade replied dryly.

Swanson-Pierce shook his head in mock concern. "Sam, what'll I do with you?"

"Let me go?" McCade asked hopefully.

"That hardly seems wise right now, does it, Sam?" the other man said, his brow furrowed in apparent concern. "What with all those nasty types looking for you? Not to mention your regrettable financial situation. No, I think not. And besides . . . you did agree to undertake this little chore for Admiral Keaton."

"Yeah," McCade said. "Let's talk about that little chore." He tapped his cigar, sending an avalanche of ash toward the expensive carpet. "First, I didn't 'agree' to take this Bridger thing on. I was forced, as you very well know. Second, I think it's about time you told me what this is all about. Since when does the navy need a bounty hunter to find their officers? Especially dead or alive. Come to think of it . . . why bother? Is there a shortage of war heroes or something?"

Swanson-Pierce frowned as he watched the last of the cigar ash on its journey toward the carpet. "For one thing, Captain Bridger is AWOL, but you're right, if that were the only concern, we wouldn't need you. Needless to say we don't normally send bounty hunters after errant naval officers. But this is a special case." Swanson-Pierce touched a series of buttons in the armrest of his chair. The room lights dimmed as a section of wall to McCade's right slid aside to reveal a holo tank. Color swirled and coalesced into the face and upper torso of Captain Ian Bridger.

As the sound came up it was apparent Bridger was lecturing a class at the Naval Academy. He was every inch the naval officer. He stood ramrod straight. His rugged features radiated confidence. The Imperial Battle Star hung gleaming at his throat. Rows of decorations crossed his barrel chest. And when he spoke, his voice carried the authority born of years in command, and the confidence of a man who has lived what he's teaching. In spite of himself, McCade had to admit the lecture was good. Bridger's thoughts were well organized, and delivered in a clear, distinct manner. He gave frequent examples, and skillfully extracted an occasional laugh from his audience.

As he described the Battle of Hell, however, his commentary became increasingly heated. He grew more and more agitated. His pupils dilated.

His eyes took on a strange look. A vein in his neck began to throb. He called the pirates "vermin and filth in the eyes of God." He described in gruesome detail how a pirate cruiser had blasted an Imperial lifeboat out of existence. A reaction shot of the audience showed hundreds of shining eyes. They believed every word.

Picture and sound dissolved together as the room lights came up. Swanson-Pierce swiveled his chair toward McCade, and regarded him through steepled fingers. "What you just saw was a routine audit taken a few days before Bridger disappeared . . . about six weeks ago."

"Practically yesterday," McCade said, blowing a perfect smoke ring.

"Bridger gave himself a four-week head start by taking a month's leave," the other man replied defensively. "And unfortunately it was a week after that before his disappearance was taken seriously."

McCade raised an eyebrow quizzically. Swanson-Pierce responded angrily.

"Damn it man . . . we don't check captains in and out like children at a boarding school."

"What makes you so sure he took off of his own volition?" McCade asked. "How do you know he wasn't abducted or murdered?"

"We don't," Swanson-Pierce answered, frowning down at the surface of his desk. "But we've received no ransom demand and his body hasn't turned up anywhere." His eyes came up to meet McCade's. "So we're forced to assume he's disappeared voluntarily . . . and we've got to act on that assumption." McCade nodded and the other man continued. "As you saw in the holo, Bridger still feels a pathological hatred for pirates, which is hardly surprising. What happened to his wife and daughter is common knowledge. The liner *Mars* found drifting, its drive sabotaged by the crew, stripped of cargo, lifeboats still in place, but no crew or passengers aboard, except for the bodies, of course."

Swanson-Pierce fell silent for a moment, possibly thinking about the fate of those passengers and crew who had survived. It was said the pirates were always short of women. And then there was slavery. And Bridger's daughter had been very pretty, even beautiful. Both Swanson-Pierce and

McCade had admired her from afar during her frequent visits to the *Imperial*.

Swanson-Pierce resumed his narrative. "And there's Bridger's career. It didn't prosper after the Battle of Hell, and I imagine that too fed his hatred of the pirates."

The naval officer stood and began to pace back and forth.

"After you, ah, left the *Imperial*, we, along with the rest of Keaton's fleet, chased the pirates as far as the frontier. Then they split up and took off in all directions. Rather than divide his forces, Keaton decided discretion was the better part of valor, and we returned to base. Chances are the Il Ronn got quite a few of the pirates in any case."

McCade knew the other man was right. Of all the alien species Man had encountered, the Il Ronn were the most dangerous. Not because they were the most intelligent or advanced. There were many alien races more advanced than either Man or the Il Ronn. But because the Il Ronn were the most like Man, they were a constant threat. They too had built a stellar empire at the expense of less aggressive races. They too had almost unlimited ambitions. Now only a thinning band of unexplored frontier worlds provided a buffer between the two empires. Fortunately the races had physiological differences which were expressed in a desire for radically different kinds of real estate.

The Il Ronn preferred the hot dry planets avoided by Man and shunned the wet worlds humans liked, in spite of the fact that water held tremendous religious significance for them. Occasionally, however, both would desire a single planet regardless of climate, usually due to its unique mineral wealth. When that happened, conflict usually followed. But so far one or the other had always backed down short of all-out war. Nonetheless the Il Ronn considered any ships straying into their sector fair game, and both Imperial and pirate craft alike frequently disappeared along the frontier.

Swanson-Pierce continued. "As you can imagine, we returned to a hero's welcome. There were medals and promotions all around."

"I trust you weren't left out," McCade said dryly.

"No I wasn't," the other man replied evenly. "However, Bridger was.

Oh, he received the Imperial Star all right. It isn't every day a commander personally leads a boarding party, and then wounded, returns to command his ship for the rest of the battle. Usually such a man could expect automatic promotion to admiral. But not Bridger. Nothing was ever said officially of course, but it was whispered that Bridger was too unstable, too fixated on pirates, for promotion." Swanson Pierce stopped pacing long enough to remove an invisible piece of lint from the left sleeve of his immaculate uniform before dropping into his chair.

"About the same time, Bridger became more and more outspoken about his religious beliefs. Apparently he told anyone who would listen that the pirates were the 'spawn of the devil.' A view which became increasingly unpopular as it became obvious that killing pirates was counterproductive. So Bridger was appointed to the Academy, there to serve out his days in academic obscurity. And that's what he did . . . until six weeks ago . . . when he disappeared."

McCade stubbed out his cigar in a small porcelain candy dish which sat just inches from an ashtray. Swanson-Pierce winced. "Since when does the navy consider killing pirates to be counterproductive?" McCade asked.

Swanson-Pierce allowed himself an amused smile. "Sam, you never cease to amaze me. In some ways you're incredibly naive. Haven't you ever wondered why we didn't just wipe them out? We could, you know, or at least we think we could. Anyway, in the period right after the Battle of Hell, we tried to patrol the frontier worlds. Our ships were constantly ambushed by both pirate and Il Ronn raiders. So we sent more ships. But it didn't do any good. In that kind of conflict a fleet simply makes a bigger target." Swanson-Pierce paused dramatically. "Then Admiral Keaton had a brilliant idea."

"I'm surprised his staff was able to recognize one," McCade said innocently.

Frowning, Swanson-Pierce continued. "Keaton's idea was to pull all our ships out, except for occasional scouts, and let the pirates and Il Ronn go to it. Hopefully they'd keep each other in check. That's exactly what we did, and it works very well. So now we try not to kill too many pirates. We just keep them confined to the frontier. Someday we might even have to step in and save them . . . if it ever looks like the Il Ronn are getting the upper hand. In the meantime the pirates are holding their own quite nicely. So as you can see, it wouldn't do to have someone like Bridger running around killing pirates."

McCade shook his head in disgust. "And the settlers, and merchant ships the pirates take just inside the frontier . . . what about them?"

There was silence for a moment as the naval officer stared off into space. When he answered his face was devoid of all expression. "Everything has a price, Sam . . . . Including peace. Imagine the cost of a navy large enough to do the job alone. Taxes would be astronomical. . . ." He left the thought unfinished as his eyes slid away to the star map decorating one wall.

"Bridger's out there somewhere right now. Among other things he's a highly trained naval officer, a combat veteran, an expert in strategy and tactics, and quite knowledgeable about our current defensive capabilities." Swanson-Pierce met McCade's eyes. "Think about it, Sam. . . . What if he offered that experience and knowledge to the Il Ronn, in return for their assistance in destroying the pirates, something they've got to do anyway in order to defeat us?"

"I don't believe it," McCade replied. "Bridger may be a few planets short of a full system, and god knows he's a total bastard, but he's no traitor."

"Basically I agree," Swanson-Pierce said. "But try to see it from his point of view. The Empire has two enemies. The pirates and the Il Ronn. Of the two he believes the pirates are the worse. So if he can use the Il Ronn to destroy them . . . he's halved the enemy . . . performed a great service for the Empire . . . and satisfied his own desire for revenge."

"What you're saying," McCade said thoughtfully, "is that the Il Ronn might allow themselves to be used . . . and in doing so . . . learn enough from Bridger to give them an edge in a war with the Empire."

"Exactly," Swanson-Pierce replied. He paused for a moment as though considering his next words carefully. "And there's one other small item to consider."

"Uh-oh," McCade said. "I've got a feeling I'm not going to like this."

Swanson-Pierce shook his head. "It's nothing really, but I suppose it could have a bearing, so I'll mention it just in case. Since Bridger's disappearance our people have gone through his personal affairs with a fine-tooth comb."

"God knows they've had plenty of time to do it," McCade interjected sweetly.

"And," the naval officer continued, pointedly ignoring McCade's jibe, "they inform me Bridger may have stumbled onto something. He was forever poking around the artifact planets while on leave, publishing articles on his pet archeological theories, and boring everybody to death at the officers' club. Anyway there's the possibility that he's come up with something of military value . . . and is planning to hand it over to the Il Ronn in order to gain their cooperation."

"Is that possible?" McCade asked, one eyebrow raised.

The other man shrugged. "Anything's possible, I guess. But people have been messing about with those planets for years and never discovered anything useful in the military sense. It's probably a good idea to remember the man's a bit eccentric, to say the least. Anyway, I'll get you access to what information we've got, and you can decide for yourself if it means something."

Both men were silent for a moment. McCade tried to sort out his feelings. On the one side was the Empire's cynical balancing of forces and the ruthless sacrifice of innocent lives. On the other was a single renegade officer whose desire for revenge might touch off an interstellar conflict that would destroy billions of lives. The whole thing was sick.

McCade's thoughts were interrupted as an autocart rolled into the room on silent treads. "I took the liberty of ordering a late lunch for both of us," Swanson-Pierce said.

As the cart rolled up to the naval officer's desk and began disgorging dishes of food, McCade said, "All right, I'm convinced. But how am I supposed to succeed where your spooks and gumshoes haven't?"

"Well," the other man replied mildly, helping himself to a cup of fragrant New Indian tea, "it's true we haven't found Bridger yet, but I remain confident we will. You are by way of, ah, insurance. A weapon, if you will, that happened to be in the right place at the right time. Besides, from what I hear, you're reasonably good at what you do." Swanson-Pierce blew steam off the surface of the dark blue tea with evident satisfaction. Looking up, he said, "Actually our people have learned quite a bit. It occurred to Admiral Keaton that their knowledge, combined with your rather gruesome talents, might very well lead to success. Quite frankly your, ah, profession should provide a perfect cover, allowing you to pursue paths of investigation not open to our personnel." Swanson-Pierce sipped his tea delicately, gazing at McCade with an innocent expression.

"And of course if I happen to get killed, it's no great loss . . . and nobody's likely to complain," McCade said, selecting three of the four sandwiches on the autocart.

"Well, yes, there is that of course," Swanson-Pierce replied serenely. "Though I suspect any number of creditors would grieve your passing." He picked up the remaining sandwich and examined it critically prior to taking a tentative bite. The Lor Beast had been cooked rare the way he liked it, and had traveled well from Asta II.

With his free hand he punched a button in the armrest of his chair, and once again the holo tank swirled into life. This time it displayed the likeness of a young woman dressed in the uniform of a cadet squadron leader. She was cute, rather than pretty. Short black hair cut in the style approved by the Academy framed an elfin face. Brown eyes regarded the camera with indifference.

"I give up. . . . Who is she?" McCade asked, his mouth full of the second sandwich.

"Cadet Squadron Leader Marsha Votava," Swanson-Pierce answered. "When Bridger left, he evidently took her with him."

"She left of her own accord?" McCade asked, studying the face that stared back at him from the holo.

Swanson-Pierce nodded. "It would seem so. There's no sign of violence in her quarters. Six weeks haven't turned up her body, or for that matter, any information about her whereabouts."

McCade finished the last sandwich and washed it down with coffee. "A love affair then?" he asked.

"Perhaps . . . ," the other man replied, placing his empty dishes on the cart, "but we're not sure. It could also be hero worship."

Swanson-Pierce touched the "dismiss" button on the autocart. As it trundled toward the door, it blew up with a deafening roar.

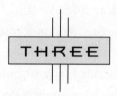

THREE

The force of the explosion hurled both men to the floor. McCade found himself sprawled across the wreckage of an antique oriental table. He staggered to his feet. His ears were ringing, and he was bleeding from numerous small cuts. Otherwise he seemed to be in one piece. Across the office Swanson-Pierce pushed some fallen ceiling panels off his legs and, using his scarred rosewood desk for support, stood up. His right arm hung limply by his side.

The office was a smoking ruin. McCade noticed that the areas nearest the cart had suffered the most damage, especially the ceiling. Apparently the top of the cart had blown off first, directing the blast upward and probably saving their lives.

A squad of marines burst in through the blackened doorway, weapons at the ready. Finding no current threat, the squad leader motioned, and men dressed in fire-fighting gear entered to spray foam over the smouldering debris.

A muscle in McCade's left cheek began to twitch as he made his way over to Swanson-Pierce. The naval officer was bent over, sorting through the rubble at his feet. He straightened up with a smile on his face and a fistful of cigars in his left hand.

"Might as well salvage something," he said, clenching a cigar between his teeth. "Here, Sam, help yourself."

"Don't mind if I do," McCade replied, taking most of the cigars, and puffing one alight. "How's your arm?"

Swanson-Pierce glanced down ruefully. "It doesn't hurt yet . . . but I suppose it's going to." He looked thoughtfully at the blackened autocart. "It wasn't assassins this time."

"Nope," McCade agreed, adding a stream of cigar smoke to the already polluted atmosphere. "This one was unlicensed all the way. No official warning of any kind."

"How fortunate you ate our lunch so quickly," Swanson-Pierce said dryly. "Otherwise it would have blown up right next to us."

"A good point, Walt. You should have a word with the chef. His idea of dessert leaves something to be desired," McCade replied.

Just then a doctor and two medics appeared and took charge. Mc-Cade's cuts were quickly disinfected and covered with nuskin. Swanson-Pierce was helped onto a power stretcher. The pretty lieutenant McCade had met earlier materialized at the naval officer's side, and they spoke in low tones. McCade did his best to eavesdrop but couldn't make out more than a word or two. As the medics began to guide the stretcher through the door, Swanson-Pierce said, "Lieutenant Lowe here will take care of everything, Sam. Don't give her too hard a time, and good hunting!"

Lieutenant Lowe was very efficient. Swanson-Pierce was barely out of sight when she went to work. Questions were asked and answered. Forms prepared and signed. Calls were made, demanding or pleading, whichever would get the fastest results, so that by evening McCade found himself standing on the blast-proof surface of the spaceport looking up at the long, graceful lines of his ship. She was beautiful.

He resisted the temptation to call up her registry on his wrist term. He knew it by heart. Her name was *Pegasus*. Three hundred and fifty feet long, she'd begun her career as a navy scout. Decommissioned during the budget cutbacks a few years ago, she'd been purchased by a wealthy businessman for use as a yacht. He'd lavished considerable love and money on her. Unfortunately during a routine customs inspection, officials had found a small quantity of yirl hidden aboard. Rumor had it the illegal substance was planted there by rival merchants, but whatever the truth of the matter, the businessman was sent to a prison planet, and *Pegasus* was returned to the navy. Now she was McCade's. According to official records, he'd made a down payment of five hundred thousand credits for her. Money supposedly paid him for killing Cadien. The same records indicated that a final payment of twenty-five thousand credits was due in six Terran months. Just Walt's little way of keeping a handle on him.

McCade smiled crookedly as he walked up the ramp and palmed the panel next to the entry port. The lock cycled open and then closed behind him. Inside he paused for a moment as the inner hatch opened, allowing him to enter the ship.

An hour later he sat relaxing in the small lounge just aft of the ship's four cabins. He'd toured her from bow to stern and liked what he'd found. She was strong, fast, and well armed. Thanks to her previous owner, she was also quite comfortable. Just the kind of ship a successful bounty hunter would choose. Plus, he'd requested additional equipment from Lieutenant Lowe, and was pleased to see she'd granted about half of it. He'd been kidding about the swimming pool anyway. He reached over and punched a request into the ship's well-stocked bar. As he settled back with a drink in one hand and a cigar in the other, McCade asked the ship's computer for an update on the first assassination attempt.

After considerable effort, he'd convinced Lieutenant Lowe to grant him direct access to the Naval Intelligence computer. She'd finally agreed— but restricted his access to those matters directly related to Bridger's disappearance. He wondered idly if the computer would consider her personnel file to be directly related or not. A soft tone chimed as information flashed onto the screen opposite him. For some reason the ship's previous owner had preferred text, and programmed the ship's computer to use voice only in emergencies. McCade saw no reason to change that policy.

He wasn't surprised to find the report contained little more than a garbled account of the action. However, he was relieved to learn that, in spite of his fears, all the bystanders had survived, though some would be hospitalized for some time. The section leader's name was Amos Van Doren, and he was doing well. Judging from the nurse's notes, McCade guessed he'd be released soon. He got the feeling the nurses couldn't wait. Van Doren was evidently a difficult patient. As McCade read on, he learned that routine autopsies hadn't revealed anything useful about the three assassins. Each bore prints, retinal patterns, dentition and vocal cords they hadn't been born with. All standard for assassins. Inquiries to the Assassin's Guild had been met with the usual refusals on grounds of Guild-client confidentiality.

A request for the most recent report on the bombing in Swanson-Pierce's office was met with a notice reading "Investigation in Progress." With a snort of derision he asked for the intelligence summary on Bridger's disappearance. It wasn't very helpful either. They didn't know why Bridger went, where he went, or how he got there. They thought Cadet Votava was with him . . . but they couldn't prove it. The only thing they seemed sure of was where Bridger wasn't. According to "reliable sources," which McCade doubted, Bridger wasn't on any Imperial planet enjoying regular inter-stellar commerce. All arrivals and departures from such worlds had been carefully screened since Bridger's disappearance. They'd even checked the records of arrivals and departures for the last standard month. Nothing. Of course that didn't mean much, McCade reflected as he ordered another drink. He'd arrived on and departed from more than one planet without bothering to notify customs. Plus there were all the frontier worlds to con-sider. And to top it all off, Bridger had a six-week head start. But still . . .

He requested Bridger's service file and sipped his drink as it came up on the screen. Most of it was boring and routine. "Lieutenant Bridger was transferred to such and such a vessel on a particular date. Commander Bridger completed a Headquarters course on logistics with honors." And much later, "Captain Bridger will go aboard the ship *Imperial*, there to take command of said ship, and all personnel aboard, conducting himself with honor and in accordance with Imperial naval regulations." It was all there. The thousands of entries which mark off the predictable path of a military career.

Just out of curiosity he ran the file forward to where the first annual psych profile after the Battle of Hell should have been. It wasn't there. The screen lit up with "For Imperial Eyes Only. Enter access code." McCade leaned back, an amused smile tugging at the corners of his mouth. So they didn't want him reading what the shrinks had to say. No sweat. It didn't take a bulkhead full of degrees to know Bridger had been operating on about half-power. And at least he knew what they weren't telling him. But what if they'd simply deleted information? He'd have no way to know it was missing. And it would be Walt's style. The old "just tell 'em what they need to know" routine. Grimly he turned his attention back to the screen. He'd have to assume some things were missing.

The next regular entry recorded Bridger's assignment to the Academy as an instructor. He taught mostly naval history. And the regular evaluations by the head of the history department suggested Bridger was good at it. His interest in history even extended to his own time. This was the part Swanson-Pierce had mentioned. McCade read the subsequent information with interest. After the loss of his family, Bridger often used his leaves to make one-man expeditions to the artifact worlds.

Many of the artifact worlds were discovered during the early days of space exploration. They were empty of intelligent life, except in a few cases where other life forms native to that particular planet had gained sentience after the disappearance of the original builders. The fact that they'd had time to do so suggested the Builders had been gone a very long time indeed. In any case, the fantastic ruins and artifacts the Builders had left behind gave mute testimony to an advanced civilization whose people had occupied and ruled many systems. The similarities between artifacts found on different worlds left no doubt as to their mutual membership in the same empire.

But archeologists discovered little more than that. Oh, they had plenty of theories, but very little to base them on. For one thing, the evidence was so ancient that the ravages of time had reduced most of it to little more than enigmatic hints at what must have been a magnificent race and culture. But, every now and then, some lucky person or group would stumble onto a hidden cache of artifacts protected, by luck or happenstance, from the elements. Over time all sorts of things had been discovered in this manner, including a variety of machinery, art works, precious stones, written documents, and a great deal of thus far unidentifiable, but nonetheless interesting junk.

So each year countless academic and private expeditions were launched in an effort to find a hidden chamber deep inside the ruins of some artifact planet which would reveal the nature of those who preceded both man and Il Ronn into space. Some sought knowledge, and others sought the riches knowledge can bring, but so far no one had really succeeded. But while none had yet managed to strip bare the secrets of the Builders, quite a few did find something for their trouble, and McCade was intrigued to learn that Bridger was among them.

At the time, the press made quite a fuss over it, probably because Bridger was a war hero more than anything else. Then too Bridger's find turned out to be quite controversial, or at least the centerpiece of it was.

What made Bridger's find special was a large metal plate. Its composition was similar to durasteel. Inscribed on its surface was writing in what was clearly two different languages. One was the language of the Builders, examples of which had been found in many locations, but the other was a complete mystery. No one had yet managed to decipher the language of the Builders, though many had tried, so attention quite naturally centered on the new, and heretofore unknown second language. Bridger swore it was a form of ancient Il Ronn, so old that even the Il Ronnians had lost track of it. To support his thesis he pointed to various similarities between its characters and modern Il Ronnian script. Some experts supported Bridger, especially those who believed the Il Ronn preceded man into space by thousands of years. Others scoffed at his claims, pointing out that the characters were also similar to the pictographs used by ancient Chinese, and did he think the Chinese had somehow left Earth to meet with the Builders?

In spite of such criticism Bridger continued to claim that the plate could be the modern equivalent of the Rosetta Stone, which offered the first clue to understanding ancient Egyptian hieroglyphics more than a thousand years before. He argued that the layout of the metal document suggested a list of some kind, the decoding of which might provide an understanding of the Builders' language, or provide insights into what they were like. He even referred to it as the "Directory."

Had they chosen to, Il Ronnian scholars might have been able to confirm or deny Bridger's thesis. However, the on-again, off-again state of hostilities between the human and Il Ronnian empires made such cooperation impossible.

Nonetheless, Bridger continued to search the artifact worlds as his time and funds allowed, looking for evidence which would prove his theory. To that end, he also used a great deal of Academy computer time, running programs he hoped would unlock the secrets of the metal plate.

And there it seemed to end. McCade pulled out and lit a cigar. It was interesting stuff. Partly because it offered new insights into Bridger's personality, and partly because the naval officer's theory involved the Il Ronn, thus creating still another link between Bridger and that alien race. Walt had played down the importance of Bridger's hobby . . . but McCade wasn't so sure. Curious, he asked for the date of the last computer run prior to Bridger's disappearance. What he got surprised him. Bridger's last run occurred more than a month before he vanished. A long time for someone who made use of the computer almost every day. A quick check revealed Bridger had also wiped all memory assigned to him. Why do that unless you've got something to hide? Positive he was on to something, McCade asked for the last date on which someone else had requested the data he'd just received. When it flashed onto the screen he saw it coincided with the start of Swanson-Pierce's investigation. So they knew, but either felt it wasn't important, or didn't want him to think it was. The possibilities made his head spin.

So what did it all mean, if anything? McCade inhaled deeply as ashes from his cigar tumbled unseen down across the arm of his chair. It could mean any number of things. But his favorite theory by far was that Bridger cracked the mystery of the metal tablet on that last run. Somehow he'd found the key that eluded everyone else. He'd figured out the language of the Builders and learned something. Something valuable. Something he could use for his own purposes. Something Swanson-Pierce was trying to play down. So Bridger had recorded or memorized whatever it was, and then wiped the memory. Then he'd taken some time to plan his next move.

It all made sense and fit together logically. Of course that didn't make it true. But it would explain something that had bothered McCade all along. Why now? After all these years, why take off now? The answer might be that Bridger's discovery had provided him with leverage. Enough leverage to convince the Il Ronn to do his bidding? If so it would have to be something military, as Swanson-Pierce had suggested. Nothing else would interest the Il Ronn sufficiently to enlist them in Bridger's cause. A hidden cache of Builder-designed super-weapons perhaps? There was no way to know, but the theory felt good, and McCade had learned long before that a successful hunter often relies on intuition.

Putting Bridger mentally aside for the moment, McCade turned his attention to Cadet Votava. Where did she fit in? When her Academy file came up on the screen, he wasn't surprised to see she'd taken leave at the same time as Bridger. What was surprising was the routine personality profile the Academy shrinks had prepared on her the year before. For some reason McCade imagined her to be insecure, emotional, and dependent. Hungry for an authority figure to worship and follow. Nothing could have been further from the truth. It seemed she was intelligent, confident, and extremely independent. So much so her life seemed to lack significant personal relationships of any kind. She had no close friends, lovers, or enemies among her classmates. They described her as "smart but distant." Out of curiosity he scrolled back to her pre-enrollment personality profile. His eyebrows rose with surprise. It sounded like a different girl. Her instructors on Mars had described her as "warm, sociable, and expressive." Of course people change as they grow older ... but it still seemed strange. He shrugged and read on.

It soon became apparent there was a notable exception to Votava's self-imposed isolation. Captain Ian Bridger. Her transcript and personal calendar indicated either a close personal relationship with Bridger, or a fixation on him. She'd taken every class Bridger taught—many of which weren't even required for her sequence. She wrote him notes. She sought his advice. She met with him for counseling. She attended his church. A quick check of Bridger's daily schedule confirmed that the two were in daily contact. And because their meetings all took place within the framework of an appropriate instructor-student relationship, no one had noticed or objected. It all seemed to point toward an impressionable young woman pathetically in love with an older authority figure. Except according to her most recent profile she was neither impressionable nor dependent.

McCade scanned the reports and research papers she'd written searching for something, anything, that might hint at where she and Bridger had gone, or what they planned to do. They all seemed routine except for two. Those he read with great care. The first dealt with the Empire's strategy regarding the pirates and the Il Ronn. Votava did an excellent job of demonstrating the Empire's use of the pirates to counter the aliens. In fact, she made it seem so obvious that McCade squirmed in his chair. She went on to suggest that with each passing year both the Il Ronn and the pirates became stronger, while the Empire grew weaker and more complacent. It all sounded very familiar, McCade thought, and he wasn't surprised to see that Bridger had given her a very high grade for it. Here then was something both of them had in common.

In fact, the more he read, the more Cadet Votava sounded like Bridger. Or did he sound like her? There's an interesting thought. . . . Which came first, the chicken or the egg? In any case she was quite persuasive. McCade began to wonder if she and Bridger were right . . . maybe the pirates were too strong . . . not that it made much difference to him.

The second document to attract McCade's attention was a research paper on methods used to transfer bulk cargo over interstellar distances. He read the paper with great interest, taking particular note of the marginal comments added by Bridger. Why would Votava's history instructor comment at all? The paper was for another class. Long after he'd finished reading, McCade continued to stare at the screen, lost in thought.

The computer chimed softly, and the image before him changed to reveal the head and shoulders of Lieutenant Lowe at the main entry port. She looked very pretty. Dark brown hair cascaded down to surround a heart-shaped face. Her eyes looked tired. To McCade's annoyance the ship's computer let her in as she palmed the lock. He wondered what other liberties she'd granted herself. Moments later she arrived in the lounge and tossed a navy-style duffle bag in his direction.

"Your stuff's in there," she said, wrinkling her nose in distaste.

"Hello to you too," he replied as he opened the bag and rummaged through it. Inside were the things he'd taken along as he chased Cadien from one system to another. He'd last seen them in a cheap hotel near the Pink Asteroid. It was mostly dirty laundry now. At the bottom, his hand encountered the familiar feel of his slug gun. As he pulled it out, he saw someone had cleaned and oiled it. "Thanks, Lieutenant. By the way, did the navy issue you a first name?"

When she laughed it was warm and open. "My friends call me Laurie . . . although it's actually Lauren. May I call you Sam?"

"I wish you would," McCade replied. "Drink?" He motioned toward the autobar.

She shook her head. "No thanks. Not just now. Is everything squared away?" She glanced around the lounge.

"I think so . . . ," McCade answered, taking another sip.

"So what happens now?" she inquired.

"I try to bring Bridger in," McCade replied with a slight smile.

"Just like that? You just go out and pick him up?"

"No . . . I think a squad of marines might come in handy," McCade answered dryly.

"You're serious, aren't you," she said, leaning forward eagerly. "You know where he is."

"Correction," he replied. "I *think* I know where he is."

Laurie frowned thoughtfully, drumming her fingers on the armrest of her chair. "Obviously you think he's close. . . ." Suddenly her face registered surprise. "You think he's right here—on Earth!"

McCade smiled as he shook his head. "No you don't. We're doing this my way. Your people had their chance. Besides, if I'm right we don't have much time. Certainly not enough to waste trying to convince your superiors to get off their butts. Now here's what I need—"

"What *we* need," she interrupted. "Where you go, I go. Besides, if it's like you say, you'll need some help, and I was top of my class in hand-to-hand combat." Her features were set in hard, determined lines.

"I'll bet you were," McCade said reflectively as he pretended to think it over.

Six hours later McCade sat next to Laurie as she expertly nudged their small troop carrier out of Earth's atmosphere and into high orbit. She'd insisted on piloting the craft herself, pointing out that without her, he wouldn't be able to get either the ship or the marines. Unless of course he wanted to go through regular channels. He had reluctantly agreed. Going through channels would take forever, plus he'd probably end up with Walt looking over his shoulder, and that would be even worse. Whether he liked it or not, he needed help, and allowing her to run this part of the show was a price that had to be paid.

He glanced back, and received an answering grin from Section Leader Amos Van Doren. McCade had approached the marine, looking for some volunteer help. Van Doren quickly agreed to round up some "off duty" buddies. They all turned out to be friends of Reynolds, the marine the assassins had killed. They were eager to even the score. Van Doren himself had refused to remain behind, in spite of his wound. When McCade started to insist, the marine gently suggested that if he didn't go, the others wouldn't either. McCade knew when he was beat. Maybe they weren't doing it his way, but at least they were doing it. So the section leader sat behind him, wearing full space armor, and an ear-to-ear grin.

As Laurie skillfully maneuvered the troop carrier through the maze of satellites, orbiting ships, defense installations and cast-off junk which circled the planet, McCade popped a stim cap and hoped he was right. Still, it seemed like the only possibility that made sense. What if Bridger and Votava hadn't left Earth? What if they'd holed up somewhere waiting for the search to die down? But they'd still need transportation off-planet. How could they get it without alerting the authorities?

Votava's paper had suggested a possible answer. She'd written about a whole new generation of cargo carriers. They'd be huge. Each would carry what it presently took ten freighters to move, and as a result, shipping costs would be greatly reduced. The key to their design was that, except for central power-control modules, the giant vessels would make one-way trips. That meant many systems required by conventional ships could be simplified or eliminated. The result . . . even more savings.

But more important from McCade's point of view was that the ships would be unmanned. Computers already did most of the work involved in piloting ships anyway. Except for atmosphere landings or emergencies, human pilots were little more than expensive back-up systems. So the ship's computer would take it into hyperdrive and then out in the vicinity of the destination. All without aid of a human pilot.

Nonetheless Votava's paper indicated that cramped living quarters were included in the power-control modules for use by emergency repair crews. She'd been very specific about that. So much so that McCade had begun to wonder. What if Bridger and Votava were aboard one of the huge ships? Hidden away in the emergency living quarters which no one would think to examine. Waiting until the search died down. Sweating out the days and minutes until the giant vessel hurled itself into hyperspace. It made a great theory, McCade reflected as the tiny troop carrier skimmed along the flanks of a mighty battlewagon, bristling with turrets and launch tubes. And he was going to feel damn silly if it was wrong.

Bright sunlight poured into the cockpit as the troop carrier emerged from the battleship's shadow. Ahead, the huge cargo carrier gleamed in the sun. It wasn't pretty. Built to voyage only in deep space, it had none of the streamlined beauty common to ships designed to negotiate planetary atmospheres. It was long and cylindrical. The hull was not a proper hull at all, but comprised of thousands of cargo pods, each connected to those around it by standard fittings. As a result the ship had a bumpy, textured look. Their angle of approach hid it, but McCade knew from the diagrams he'd studied that the power-control module was suspended in the center of the hollow space running the length of the cylinder.

They were closer now. He could see four tugs, dwarfed by the freighter's tremendous bulk, cautiously starting to tow it out of orbit. It was the largest ship he'd ever seen. No wonder they'd christened it *Leviathan*.

There wasn't much time left. His foot tapped out an impatient rhythm until he became conscious of it, and forced himself to stop. Being a passenger was driving him crazy. As soon as the vessel was clear of other traffic it would enter hyperspace, where the little troop carrier could not follow. Days or weeks later it would emerge in the vicinity of Weller's World, a relatively primitive planet just inside the frontier.

"Sam . . . look." Laurie pointed to the main detector screen. It showed a luminescent outline of the cargo carrier and the four tugs. Now a sixth ship appeared. Its outline suggested an atmospheric shuttle, a guess confirmed moments later when the computer inserted "AS Type IV" in the lower right-hand corner of the screen. Until moments before, it had been hidden on the far side of the *Leviathan*. Now it had cleared the larger ship and seemed headed their way. At first McCade was unconcerned. Chances were it was on a perfectly innocent errand. In any case it was an unarmed model, and there wasn't much it could do short of ramming them.

However, as it got closer, it became increasingly apparent that the shuttle intended to intercept them. The com screen came to life with an excellent likeness of Cadet Votava. He noticed with amusement that she'd promoted herself to lieutenant commander. Nonetheless she was quite convincing. Her voice carried just the right mix of bored authority and arrogance.

"This is a restricted Naval Operation Area under code one-niner-zero-two alpha. Reverse course immediately or be fired upon." Her image faded to black before McCade could reply.

"We've got 'em," McCade said with grim satisfaction.

"Maybe," Laurie replied, turning up the magnification on the detector screen. The shuttle had slowed and opened its cargo bay. A dozen tiny figures dressed in space armor spilled out. One maneuvered a space sled. On it rested the unmistakable form of a recoilless energy cannon.

McCade felt his pulse begin to race. The energy cannon was designed for surface action against enemy armor. Its use in space was extremely unconventional. But it would work. One of Bridger's ideas no doubt. Walt was right—the man was dangerous. That kind of creativity applied to an entire battle could be devastating. Meanwhile the cannon was a very real threat. It had its own integral tracking system, and more than enough power to vaporize the small troop carrier. A fact not lost on Laurie, who hurled the troop carrier into a series of gut-wrenching, heart-stopping, evasive maneuvers that made the hull creak. She seemed to enjoy it. McCade didn't, but was determined not to show it. If he'd been at the controls himself, it wouldn't have bothered him, but just sitting there watching, it made him feel queasy.

Laurie switched on the suit coms and her voice boomed into his helmet. "Attention all personnel . . . button up and stand by for cabin depressurization. Section Leader . . . by the numbers please."

McCade went over his gear, checking seals, power supply, oxygen and so forth, while behind him Van Doren and his men did the same. McCade glanced up to see the shuttle getting uncomfortably close. It appeared the energy cannon would be operational any moment.

"Section One, combat ready, Captain," Van Doren said formally. "On your command."

Out of the corner of his eye McCade saw Laurie was pleased by the honorary "Captain."

"Roger," she replied with equal gravity. "Ejection and enemy contact in approximately four minutes. Secure the energy cannon by whatever means possible. Take prisoners if you can . . . but don't risk your men unnecessarily. I don't know who they are, but one thing's for sure, they don't look friendly."

"Aye aye, Captain," Van Doren answered calmly.

McCade flinched as a pulse of blue light raced by in front of them. A ranging shot. A vise closed on his chest as they went into a tight turn and raced straight toward the cannon. The troop carrier shuddered as an energy pulse slid down its side. A red warning light blinked on in front of McCade. The cabin was fully depressurized. Laurie's gloved hands danced over the controls. The troop carrier began to zigzag in a random pattern. The little ship shuddered and groaned under the strain. McCade felt the tug of the facial tic that always plagued him in moments of stress. He hoped Laurie wouldn't notice it and desperately wished for something to do.

Laurie touched a button and the top of the carrier split down the middle as the sides were retracted into the hull. McCade felt momentary vertigo as she put the small craft through another series of acrobatic maneuvers.

"Five, four, three, two, one," Laurie counted, and hit the ejection control. Together Van Doren and his marines were blasted out of the troop carrier in perfect formation. As the ship raced away, McCade watched the rear screen on full magnification. Laurie had placed them slightly above and behind the cannon. Once clear of the troop carrier, each marine released his seat and used his suit jets to blast down toward the enemy.

Van Doren was in the lead. His men were spread out in V formation behind him. Lines of blue light rippled and flared as both sides opened fire. A marine disappeared in a yellow-red explosion. Then the cannon and two figures near it flashed incandescent as they were hit by a shoulder-launched missile. "Got the sonovabitch," an exuberant voice shouted over McCade's suit com, followed by a scream as a marine was hit.

"I want radio silence, goddamnit!" Van Doren bellowed.

After that the battle was silent, men moving as though part of an eerie, slow-motion ballet which someone had forgotten to score. Shoulder weapons lashed out, slicing through armor as if it weren't there. Then, as the combatants got closer to each other, hand blasters came into play. Their less powerful beams often failed to penetrate the heavy armor, causing many to draw older and more effective weapons. McCade thought he could make out Van Doren swinging an enormous battle axe as he led his men into hand-to-hand combat. While difficult to use in normal gravity, the axe would be lethal in zero G, especially in the hands of an expert. And Van Doren was undoubtedly an expert. Then the screen went blank as the little ship passed out of high mag detection range.

The enormous bulk of the freighter loomed ahead. The tugs had cut their tractor beams and started to move off. Laurie frowned in concentration as they skimmed the side of the large ship.

"The lock's just ahead," she said. "Get ready."

The lock was located about halfway down the ship's length. A long tunnel running through the center of a support strut connected the lock with the power-control module suspended in the center of the hollow cylinder. McCade was thinking about the length of the tunnel.

"It's gonna be real fun trying to get down that tunnel if there's someone at the other end shooting at us."

"A cheerful thought," she said grimly as she brought the troop carrier down in a graceful arc, killing thrust, and gliding smoothly toward the other ship's lock. She flicked a switch activating a light tractor beam which locked onto the larger vessel and began to reel them in. Moments later they were snuggled up a few feet below *Leviathan's* lock.

McCade hit his seat release. His stomach lurched as he floated free of the ship. An eternity of emptiness stretched away in every direction. He felt the moment of panic that always accompanied free fall for him. They'd almost washed him out of the Academy for it. Forcing himself to concentrate, he fired his suit jets, and moments later was clinging to the other ship's lock, happy to have his hands on something solid again.

Meanwhile Laurie was using the troop carrier's com unit. "Merchant ship *Leviathan* . . . Merchant ship *Leviathan* . . . This is naval vessel MTC four-niner-two. Terminate departure immediately. Imperial Navy authorization code four-five-one delta zero . . . I repeat . . ."

McCade decided the lock had either been purposely jammed or shorted out.

There was a burst of static over his suit radio followed by a male voice which could only be Bridger. "Naval vessel MTC four-niner-two. Cut your tractor beam and depart at once. Make no further attempt to board this ship. I repeat . . . depart at once. This vessel will shift into hyperspace ten standard minutes from now. Repeat . . . ten standard minutes and counting. End of transmission."

McCade swore under his breath and struggled even harder with the lock mechanism. Laurie appeared at his elbow. She held a ship cracker cradled in her arms. It was intended for rescue work on damaged ships and could cut through almost anything. The ship cracker wasn't heavy in zero gravity, but it was bulky and awkward. Normally operated by a crew of three, it took both of them to hold and aim it. As Laurie pulled the trigger, a ruby red lance of energy leapt from the device's nozzle and bit into the ship's durasteel hull.

McCade began to sweat. He felt his recycling unit shift into a higher speed. He could just barely make out Laurie's face through her darkened visor. Sweat rolled off her face and her teeth were bared in a grimace. A dark comma of hair had fallen across the whiteness of her forehead. McCade thought she looked beautiful.

Moments later the beam cut through the lock's mechanism and the hatch swung open. There was no rush of atmosphere into space. The tunnel had been depressurized. McCade wondered why. He didn't like the possibilities. Motioning Laurie to stay back, he entered the tunnel. It stretched off into the distance, ending in another hatch which provided access to the power-control module. The tunnel was evenly lit and empty. The walls covered with a maze of pipes and electrical conduit. It looked too easy— too inviting. McCade took a few cautious steps forward, gesturing to Laurie for radio silence. Bridger could easily monitor their suit radios. McCade pulled his blaster and began to move swiftly down the tunnel. He noticed the weapon had none of his slug gun's comforting weight. He'd have to compensate for that.

He soon reached a junction where two smaller maintenance shafts joined the main tunnel from the left and right. Cautiously he peered into each. Both were dark beyond the first twenty feet. He signaled Laurie, and together they hurried forward. McCade figured they had five minutes at most before the ship hurled itself into hyperspace, taking them with it.

A figure dressed in space armor dropped from the ceiling. Apparently he'd been hiding in a vertical maintenance shaft. He fired his blaster before his feet hit the deck. That was a mistake. His bolt went wide. Smoke and electrical sparks poured out of a section of pipe and conduit to McCade's right. McCade fired his blaster in reply. A white-hot hole appeared where the man's chest had been. He was slammed back against the tunnel wall.

"Behind us, Sam!" Her voice was shrill. Instinctively he dropped to the deck, and sensed more than saw the energy beam that passed over his head. Scrambling on all fours he turned to see Laurie go down. Beyond her lay a headless figure in space armor. Next to the body knelt another man who had a blaster centered on McCade's chest. McCade began to bring his own blaster up knowing he'd never make it. As he waited to die, some remote part of his brain reproached him for not checking the side tunnels more carefully. If he'd only had more time. . . . Then the man's left side disappeared as Laurie blasted him from the deck. McCade moved quickly to her side. She seemed so small, even in bulky space armor. Behind the visor her face was terribly white and drawn. A quick check revealed no sign of a wound, and her armor seemed intact.

"Laurie?" he said.

Her eyes blinked open, and she managed a weak smile. Wordlessly he picked her up as gently as he could and started down the tunnel toward the lock. He'd taken only a few steps when a tremendous jolt threw them both to the deck. The lights went out, and a moment of total darkness passed before dim emergency lights flickered on. McCade knew he should get up but couldn't find the energy. The half-healed wound in his left arm began to throb. The pain cleared his head. He felt the deck move erratically under him. Then he understood. Bridger had detonated the explosive, emergency fittings connecting the power-control module to the cargo pods—and disappeared into hyperspace. Evidently he didn't want to take the boarding party with him—especially since they were winning.

The force of the power-control module's departure, plus the loss of its mass, put the remaining part of the ship into an erratic spin and tumble. As he struggled to his feet McCade wondered if the cargo pods would hold together. Awkwardly he gathered Laurie's inert form into his arms and started toward the lock. He'd taken only a few steps when the emergency lights flickered off and the artificial gravity disappeared. Somewhere an emergency generator had failed. Naturally the main field generators had vanished into hyperspace along with the power-control module. After a brief moment of dizziness, McCade managed to shift his grip on Laurie to use only one hand, so he could use the other to activate his helmet light. He pushed off the nearest bulkhead in the direction of a handhold. As he moved from handhold to handhold, he quickly decided weightlessness was an advantage rather than a problem. By towing Laurie behind him he could make fairly good time.

Occasionally, forward motion stalled as the hull tumbled, and they were thrown into the nearest bulkhead. McCade worried that the violent motion of the ship might break the light tractor beam securing the troop carrier to the hull. If it did it would be one helluva walk home. Which reminded him of the marines. Their air would be running low. He tried to move even faster. Finally he made it to the lock. To his relief the troop carrier was still there. He paused, calculated, hoped for the best, and jumped. They damn near soared right by the smaller ship before he managed to grab an antenna with his free hand and haul them in.

He strapped Laurie into the copilot's seat, slid behind the controls, and plugged his suit into the ship. Fresh oxygen squirted into his helmet, and there was a burst of static as the radio came on, followed by an exchange of conversation between Van Doren and a navy shuttle. The marines were being picked up. He started the engines, cut the tractor beam, and plunged recklessly down into the atmosphere.

FOUR

McCade sat staring at the green wall, wondering why hospital walls were always green. "Of all the colors you could program a wall to be, why choose bile green? Ah! There's the connection," he mused wryly. "It's obvious, once you put your mind to it."

Wearily he swung his feet over onto the floor. He made an ancient gesture of derision toward the nearest scanner. Only Walt would put surveillance sensors in a hospital room. He stood slowly, and then shuffled over to the wash basin in one corner. He splashed cold water on his face and looked up into the bloodshot eyes which stared balefully back from the metal mirror. He watched in the mirror as the door behind him slid open. He wasn't surprised to see Swanson-Pierce. The other man's right arm was in a cast and sling. Somehow he made it appear dashing and elegant.

"Well, Sam old boy, you've been at it again, haven't you?" Swanson-Pierce said, settling himself into one of the room's two ugly chairs. "Bodies everywhere." He shook his head sadly. "Unauthorized use of a naval vessel, not to mention half a dozen Imperial marines, illegal boarding of a merchant ship, and a re-entry that broke every regulation in the book. It's quite a list. I've spent the entire morning trying to sort the whole thing out. God help us if the press gets hold of it."

"Blow it out your tubes, Walt," McCade said angrily, walking painfully over and sitting on the edge of the bed. He remembered the frantic plunge through the atmosphere, way too fast for the shields to shed enough heat, the emergency landing, confusion, and arrest. But nothing about Laurie. Trying to appear casual, McCade asked, "How's Laurie?"

Swanson-Pierce raised an eyebrow and replied, "The lieutenant is fine . . . no thanks to you. I left her moments ago in the base hospital. Evidently she suffered a mild concussion. She says someone bounced her helmet off a bulkhead." There was curiosity in the naval officer's look which McCade chose to ignore.

"I'm glad she's okay," McCade said. "She's a good kid. . . . She did all right up there." He remembered looking into the blaster and waiting to die. He fumbled through his pockets for a cigar. "And the marines?"

"One dead, four wounded, and one of those probably won't make it," the other man replied soberly, his eyes on the deck.

McCade winced. One dead and maybe another. For nothing. Bridger had escaped. His searching fingers found a cigar butt which he lit with a trembling hand. He sucked smoke deep into his lungs and blew it toward the deck. "And Van Doren?"

Swanson-Pierce's expression changed to amusement as he said, "Corporal Van Doren is fine." He paused for effect. "His Captain's Mast adjourned about half an hour ago. It seems he pleaded guilty to drunkenness on duty, issuance of illegal orders, theft of a navy vessel, illegal dueling, and interference with a merchant ship. All things considered, I think he got off easy, don't you?"

"You really think the press'll buy that?" McCade asked.

Swanson-Pierce shrugged. "They have so far. It's preferable to censorship, which always makes people even more interested."

McCade stared wordlessly into the naval officer's gaze, his thoughts still on the marine who had died and the other who probably would.

After a moment Swanson-Pierce said, "Don't do it, Sam. It won't help. These things just happen sometimes, that's all. Besides, we've gained quite a bit actually. It's true they got away . . . but at least we know they haven't made contact with the Il Ronn. So we've got a chance." He paused. "You'll be interested to know your marine friends took a prisoner." He watched McCade expectantly.

The silence stretched out. Finally McCade gave in. "And what did you learn from that prisoner?" McCade asked through gritted teeth.

"I thought you'd never ask," the other man replied with evident satisfaction. "It seems he, along with his stalwart companion, were all port-trash of one kind or another. Ex-mercenaries, beached spacemen, laid-off miners and the like. I'm sure you know the type." His expression made it clear that he thought McCade probably knew the type intimately.

McCade ignored it. "Then they weren't assassins," he said thoughtfully.

"Exactly," Swanson-Pierce replied smugly. "Apparently Bridger hired an ex-mercenary named Iverson, who then recruited the rest. Unfortunately Iverson met an untimely end recently while operating an energy cannon. Clever idea that. Anyway it may interest you to know Iverson made the bomb which concluded our luncheon in such a dramatic fashion." He made a microscopic adjustment to his sling.

McCade frowned thoughtfully. "So let's see, these . . . what did you call them? Port-trash? They infiltrate Naval Intelligence Headquarters, plant a bomb on exactly the right autocart, and then make their escape. All without your fancy hardware and highly trained spooks noticing anything suspicious. I don't know, Walt. . . . It's not the kind of report I'd want to file." He shook his head in mock concern.

Swanson-Pierce recrossed elegantly clad legs nervously. "Well, ah, yes, naturally we're quite concerned. Unfortunately our prisoner doesn't know how the bomb was placed or detonated. He swore, however, that he helped Iverson put it together. We have our best investigators on the problem."

"Terrific," McCade said, crushing the cigar butt under his heel. "If Bridger knew, he'd be terrified. While they're at it maybe they can find out where everybody's getting little items like energy cannon, high explosives, and navy-issue space armor."

Swanson-Pierce coughed and looked slightly embarrassed as he studied the gleaming toe of his right boot. "Actually I think we know the answer to that one. Our prisoner says they all came out of the *Leviathan*'s cargo. Evidently part of a shipment for the marine detachment on Weller's World."

McCade shook his head in disgust. "Well tell me this. . . . If Iverson's men worked for Bridger . . . who sent the assassins? And why?" Both men stared at each other and silence filled the room.

Swanson-Pierce broke the silence. "You'll know when we do." He paused as he turned to leave. "They say you'll be discharged in the morning. I trust you've got everything you need?"

McCade nodded silently.

"Well, good hunting then." When the other man didn't answer, Swanson-Pierce slipped out of the room closing the door behind him.

McCade sat in the darkened control room staring at the viewscreen. Around him, *Pegasus* hummed and vibrated gently. The air was cool and dry, carrying the faint aroma of cooking. He watched, fascinated, as constellations wheeled slowly along their eternal paths and stars shimmered across the unimaginable distances of space. Of course they weren't real. As long as the ship remained in hyperspace, normal space wasn't visible. These were computer simulations. But they looked real, and he never tired of their beauty. The flickering light of the screen brought back memories of boyhood campfires when the dancing flames had captured his eyes and set his mind free to roam a sky full of mysterious stars. Now the stars no longer seemed mysterious. Just beautiful points of light, none of which were home.

"Hi, Sam!" Laurie dropped into the seat next to him. He turned, and the brightness of her smile washed away his somber thoughts. Her hair had fallen across her brow again and her eyes flashed as she shook it back into place. "Why so serious?" she asked.

He smiled. "Just remembering how things were when I was a boy."

"And how were they?" she asked, drawing her knees up under her chin, regarding him seriously.

McCade shrugged. "Pretty good actually. I spent my early years on Dorca III, and then my parents were transferred to Terra, and naturally I went with them. They were electrical engineers. They must have been good, because they both taught at the Imperial Academy of Arts and Sciences. Dad died a few years ago of a heart attack, and Mom went a year later. I wasn't surprised. She wanted to be with him." He stared at the viewscreen for a moment before speaking again. "I don't think they were very pleased about the way I turned out." He looked across at Laurie. "How 'bout you?"

A veil fell over her eyes as she replied. "Oh nothing special. . . . I never knew my parents. . . . They were killed in some kind of accident out near the frontier. So I spent a lot of time in various kinds of schools and academies. I did well, and managed to enter the Academy. . . . End of story."

McCade didn't believe it. Oh, what she'd said was probably true enough, but he felt sure she was leaving a lot out. Why? There was no way to tell.

Laurie sniffed the air dramatically, her eyes flashing once more. "Smells good! Wait till you see what Amos made for dinner! Who'd of thought a stuffy old marine could cook?"

"Lucky for us he's an expert with the ship's weapons too," McCade replied dryly.

"Phooey," she said. "I'm an expert with the weapons. . . . What we needed was a cook!" She made a face and disappeared toward the lounge.

McCade smiled after her. Swanson-Pierce had insisted she come. She'd volunteered, probably at Swanson-Pierce's request, and the medics had given their approval, also at the naval officer's request no doubt. In any case she'd been sent along to keep an eye on him. McCade had given in with a tremendous show of reluctance.

The main control monitor buzzed softly. He looked up to see that they would emerge from hyperspace in six standard hours. He punched the "acknowledge" button and began a routine scan of the major system readouts. Of course the ship's computer did the same thing thousands of times a second, but it made him feel better. And once in a while over the years he'd even found something wrong.

They'd been in hyperspace for three weeks. During that time they'd traversed a distance it would've taken pre-empire ships years to cross. That hadn't stopped the early colonists, though. They'd risen from Terra and disappeared into the blackness of space. Some won through to habitable planets. Many didn't. In time the colonized worlds broke free of Earth and formed their own governments. The Confederation followed. Some said it was the lack of hyperdrive, as much as constant bickering, which caused the Confederation to disintegrate. It takes speedy communication to hold a stellar government together. And since no one had managed to punch a com beam through interstellar distances, ships remained the fastest form of communication.

It was certainly true that the rise of the first emperor occurred about the time a workable hyperdrive was discovered. In fact most historians agreed that the first emperor couldn't have won without it. Even though they were vastly outnumbered at the start, hyperdrive enabled his ships to travel vast distances in a fraction of the time required by the Confederates, a tactical advantage he exploited brilliantly. Even so, he'd been forced to amass a great fleet, and fight battle after battle. The empire he'd built was founded on hyperdrive and the blood of those who didn't have it.

McCade's thoughts were interrupted as the intercom buzzed, followed by Van Doren's basso saying, "Chow's on, sir. . . . I mean boss."

"Thanks, Amos." McCade grinned. Van Doren was supposed to be his bodyguard, not an Imperial marine. But old habits die hard and Van Doren was still having trouble ridding himself of his military mannerisms. McCade had asked Swanson-Pierce to restore the marine's former rank, and the naval officer had agreed—but only if McCade would take the man along on detached duty. All the marines who'd been in the fight with Bridger's men were being reassigned far from Terra's inquisitive press— except for the two buried with full honors, McCade thought soberly.

For his part Van Doren was eager to go along. He wanted to be there when they caught up with Bridger. But by way of an added incentive he'd been told that otherwise his next duty station would be on a planet called Swamp. A small detachment of marines was stationed there to protect resident scientists from their specimens.

After an excellent meal of smoked Fola on a bed of steamed Zuma, with chocolate torte for dessert, courtesy of the ship's stasis locker, the three of them relaxed over coffee in the lounge. McCade rolled rich cigar smoke off his tongue filling the air with an evil-looking blue haze.

"Remind me to renew my anticancer treatments," Laurie said, wrinkling her nose in disgust and turning the lounge's air scrubber up a notch.

"If there *are* twelve torpedoes waiting at the nav beacon," McCade replied, "there isn't much chance we'll die of cancer."

She stuck out her tongue at him but knew he was right. They'd gone through *Leviathan*'s cargo manifest together before launch. Besides explosives, energy weapons and space armor, the huge ship carried five hundred Interceptor-class torpedoes bound for the Naval Arms Depot on Weller's World. After the giant hulk was caught and towed back to Earth orbit, a quick inventory revealed that twelve of the torpedoes were missing.

McCade considered the torpedoes as he sipped his coffee. Each needle-shaped black hull would be ten feet long. Aboard would be a very sophisticated minicomputer, an array of sensors, and a tidy little nuclear warhead. Usually they were carried and launched by Interceptors, small one-person fighters like the one tucked away in the bay where *Pegasus* normally carried her lifeboat. Trading the lifeboat for the Interceptor was a calculated risk. The lifeboat could save their lives in case of trouble, but so could the fighter; it all depended on which way things went.

To make matters worse, before they had left, naval armorers had confirmed that an expert could rig the torpedoes for an ambush. It had been done once or twice before. Was Bridger an expert? No one knew for sure—but they'd have to assume he was. He'd certainly had access to the necessary information.

If Bridger laid an ambush, the nav beacon would be the logical place to do it. Though technically a ship equipped with hyperdrive could enter and depart hyperspace anywhere, doing so entailed an element of risk. What if you happened to pick an exit point right in the middle of a large asteroid, for example? No one ever lived to report such incidents, of course, but there was little doubt they occasionally happened. As a result, a far-flung network of nav beacons had been established along the Empire's main trade routes. Each emitted its own distinctive code while entering and exiting hyperspace at one minute intervals. That way the beacon could be located by ships traveling in either normal space or hyperspace.

So while scouts and prospectors took pride in playing cosmic roulette and rarely had the luxury of using nav beacons, ships using established lanes always did. Therefore Bridger could expect his pursuit to emerge from hyperspace soon after he did and in proximity to the nav beacon. They'd considered sending an unmanned drone through first, but naval experts had agreed the torpedoes' sensors were too sophisticated to fall for such a ploy. And when McCade had suggested a destroyer, Swanson-Pierce had laughed, saying the Empire couldn't spare warships to chase after torpedoes which might or might not be there.

Van Doren spoke as if he'd read McCade's mind. "With all due respect, boss, you shouldn't worry so much." He patted the bulkhead next to him. "She's sound as an Imperial credit, not to mention that I've checked her personally, and when the time comes she'll show 'em a thing or two!" It was a long speech for the big marine. He leaned back, eyes bright under bushy brows, lips curved in a smile which held little humor. McCade smiled and nodded, wishing he shared the marine's confidence.

A few hours later McCade was reclining in the pilot's seat wearing full armor. Laurie occupied the copilot's position beside him, her face hidden by her visor. He wondered what she was thinking. Did she feel she should be sitting in the pilot's position? It had been a long time since he had taken a ship into combat. But damn it, *Pegasus* was his ship. He wouldn't always have Laurie to lean on. At least that's what he was telling himself.

Behind and slightly above them, Van Doren sat enclosed in a gun blister. Without sufficient crew to fully man the ship's secondary armament, most of it had been slaved to his position. Of course if there was an ambush, most of the battle would be fought by the ship's computer using the main armament. No human eye and brain could track tiny targets traveling at thousands of miles an hour. Not unless they got very close. Then the secondary armament would be their last chance.

"Do you think it'll work?" Laurie asked, her voice unnaturally casual.

"Sure I do," McCade lied.

After all, it could work, he thought. They had programmed the ship's computer to overshoot the nav beacon slightly. If there were torpedoes waiting, hopefully they'd be aimed at the next exit area immediately around the beacon. It would take the torpedoes a moment to detect *Pegasus* outside that area, recompute attack trajectories, and launch. That moment would be their edge.

McCade's eyes were locked on the main control monitor as the final seconds ticked away. At its center the nav beacon was represented by a white light. It appeared and disappeared as it jumped in and out of hyperspace. Then there was the second of disorientation and nausea he always felt during a hyperspace shift, followed by subtle changes in the viewscreens as the computer switched from simulated to actual images.

Now they were in normal space . . . and for a moment . . . so was the nav beacon. Close by, a yellow light blinked, probably *Leviathan*'s powercontrol module. Around it appeared a globe of red dots. Each represented a torpedo. Just inside the perimeter of the globe, almost touching a red dot, was a green light symbolizing *Pegasus*. Their plan hadn't worked. They were practically sitting on a torpedo. The torpedo vanished in a flash of intense white light before McCade could utter a sound. Van Doren's battle cry was still ringing in his ears when it was replaced by a calm but unfamiliar female voice.

"This ship is under attack. Please prepare for high-stress evasive action. The bar and all recreational facilities are closed."

McCade would have laughed, but a crushing weight was suddenly added to his chest. *Pegasus* accelerated and began to execute a series of intricate evasive maneuvers. Through blurred vision he saw the remaining red dots reorient themselves and begin inexorably to close on *Pegasus*. McCade felt a slight jolt as the ship launched torpedoes of its own. To his satisfaction he watched two red dots disappear in explosions so bright the ship's sensors were forced to dampen down or bum out. But a third red dot was closing fast.

"Enemy target now leaving primary defensive zone sector four-eight.

Engage with secondaries," the calm computer voice said. "Due to immediate defensive energy requirements, there will be no hot water for showers until two standard hours after termination of engagement."

"I've got it," McCade said as he struggled to clear his vision and concentrate.

As his hand closed around the control grip for the bow energy cannon, he heard a double "Roger" from Laurie and Van Doren. The control worked much like the stick in an atmosphere flier. As he squeezed it, a target monitor came to life in front of him. When he rotated the handle to the right the target grid moved right on the screen. McCade lined up on the growing red dot. His thumb pressed the button at the top of the handle and pulses of blue light raced out to meet the torpedo. The powerful defensive screens of the *Pegasus* flared to the edge of burnout and then held. As McCade's eyes returned to the main control monitor, he counted five red dots still hurtling toward them. Apparently either *Pegasus* or Van Doren had nailed two more. But it wasn't enough. One or more torpedoes would almost certainly get through.

"Prepare for emergency damage control," the pleasant voice said. "Due to this vessel's current tactical situation, it seems advisable that both passengers and crew seek alternate transportation as soon as possible." McCade gritted his teeth and promised himself that if he survived, the computer wouldn't. Now he knew why the ship's previous owner had restricted the computer's use of voice simulation.

"Sam! There's a chance. Hit it now!" Laurie pointed at the bright red cover located in the very center of the control console.

McCade understood immediately. Without hesitation he flipped up the cover and hit the switch it protected. This time the disorientation and nausea of the hyperspace shift was a welcome relief. The moment the shift was complete, he hit the computer override switch again, felt his stomach lurch, and watched as the screen adjusted back to normal space. Their forward motion had carried them away from the nav beacon. The light created by the five torpedoes' mutual annihilation was just starting to fade behind them. McCade felt a muscle in his left cheek begin to twitch as he thought about the odds against surviving both the torpedoes and two random hyperspace shifts.

Laurie had removed her helmet. Sweat matted her dark hair. Her face was frozen in a silly grin. "We made it," she said.

"Thanks to you," he answered simply. Her eyes registered pleasure at the compliment. Suddenly he felt old. It'd been a long time since he'd been a hot young Interceptor pilot. He should've thought of a hyperspace shift himself.

"We're a good team, that's all," Laurie said. "Isn't that right, Amos?"

"Damned right," the big man answered, lowering his bulk from the gun blister. "I told ya she wouldn't let us down, didn't I, boss?"

"The bar is now open," the computer said.

McCade laughed. "You were right, Amos, she's a great ship."

A few minutes later they had swung around and were positioned near *Leviathan*'s power-control module. It looked like an oversized tin can. A few random cargo pods were still connected to it where the explosive fittings had failed to detonate. To all appearances it was deserted. Repeated attempts to make radio contact brought no reply.

"Well," McCade said grimly, "it looks like we're gonna have to do it the hard way."

Laurie looked concerned. "I don't think that's a good idea, Sam. They might have rigged her to blow the moment someone goes aboard."

"Right, boss," Van Doren added. "Why not get some swabbies up here and let them check her out. They've got the gear for this sorta thing. Or, better yet, let's just put a torp in 'er."

"Both your suggestions are tempting, Amos," McCade replied with a smile. "But the first would take too long, and the second would leave us with a lot of unanswered questions, not to mention some unhappy owners. No, I'm gonna have to board her."

"We're going to board her!" Laurie said.

"Right, boss," Van Doren added, eyes gleaming with anticipation. McCade sighed, and shook his head in mock exasperation.

Half an hour later McCade swung open the hatch to *Leviathan*'s lock.

He paused for a moment, giving thanks that nothing had blown up, and then entered.

Back aboard *Pegasus,* Van Doren sat stoically in his gun blister, eyes searching, finger on the trigger. Below him Laurie fumed at the ship's controls. Neither was happy. But in McCade's judgment anything else would be stupid. If there was trouble it wouldn't help if they all got killed. This way they could come to his rescue if required. Besides, it was a one-person job. Or at least that's what he'd told Laurie. Deep down, a part of him wondered if he was grandstanding. Trying to make up for his failure to think of the hyperspace shift. Pushing those thoughts aside, he opened the inner hatch. What he saw was not pretty. Three bodies lay sprawled in a jumbled pile before him.

The first thing he noticed was that none of them were wearing armor. So the module had been pressurized when they'd come aboard. He checked for atmosphere and then opened his visor. A quick and unpleasant inspection revealed that none of the bodies were those of Bridger or Votava. There were two men and a woman. All three were dressed in coveralls bearing the logo of the Meteor Tug Company. They'd all been shot at close range with a small caliber slug gun. As far as he could tell they'd been unarmed. They hadn't been killed, they'd been executed. The coldness of it turned his stomach. Bridger was no longer a rational being. Any sympathy McCade had ever felt for the two fugitives was replaced by a hard knot of burning anger that settled in his stomach and wouldn't go away.

McCade allowed himself to fall back into a fold-down seat. He couldn't take his eyes off the bodies. Why? It didn't make sense. He tried to imagine how it had happened. The tug routinely coming alongside. The crew wondering aloud about the missing cargo pods. The slight hiss of escaping pressure as the locks made contact and then opened. A murmur of conversation as the crew entered, expecting to find an empty module. Instead, what? A confrontation? Probably. Followed by three cold-blooded killings. There was no doubt about who had done it. Then what? Bridger and Votava had used the tug to place the torpedoes and then headed for Weller's World. A planetary tug couldn't take them much farther anyway.

McCade fastened his armor, found a cigar butt, and lit it. The smoke helped to disguise the fetid air. His thoughts drifted back to the cockpit of his Interceptor. The image of a pirate ship sharp and clear in the old-fashioned weapon sight, his thumb on the firing stud, and two voices fighting to command him. The first a woman's voice, a pirate, pleading with him to spare her ship, swearing she had only women and children aboard. The second voice was Bridger's, hoarse from hours of shouted commands, ordering him over and over again to fire.

The cigar butt burned his fingers. He dropped it and crushed it under his boot. He began to search the tiny cabin. Bridger and Votava had lived in the tiny space for almost two months. At some point the overloaded recycler had broken down and trash had started to pile up on the deck. Discarded clothing, rotting food and other less identifiable debris were all mixed together into an unpleasant history of their confinement.

As McCade sorted through it in random fashion, he began to notice scraps of writing. Sometimes it was on common note paper, but more often than not it was on other things, the margins of pages torn out of operational manuals, on the backs of napkins, disposable plates—literally anything. For the most part the writing was incoherent, and as far as Mc-Cade could tell, meaningless. The more passages he found the more they seemed to him to be the ravings of a lunatic. McCade was familiar with Bridger's handwriting, having seen it on his own commission as a lieutenant and his final court martial, as well as several more recent documents. It was Bridger's handwriting all right. But the mind controlling it was far from normal. Bridger was either physically ill or in the process of losing his mind.

McCade paused to read the scribbling in the margin of a sheet bearing the title, "CARGO MODULE SURVIVAL KIT INVENTORY N4689." Carefully written into the margin on the left-hand side was "Inventory. Inventory. Inventory. I'll show them inventory! Marvelous inventory! Glorious inventory! Inventory sufficient to wipe out once and for all the devil's servants. Inventory too long on the shelf. Inventory I shall use to cleanse the heavens!"

It didn't make any sense, and yet it did. McCade was reminded of the metal plate. Once again he felt sure Bridger had cracked the secret hidden there. And in doing so he'd obtained weapons of some kind. "Inventory sufficient to wipe out once and for all the devil's servants," he'd said. That sounded pretty lethal. Of course if the man was operating on about half power, then he could be hallucinating too. He searched for another fifteen minutes. He found lots of additional scribbles, but nothing that made sense. Finally he gave up.

When he called *Pegasus* on his suit radio Laurie's anxious voice made him feel guilty for not calling earlier. He explained the situation, sealed his suit and started for the lock. Then something caught his eye. Bending over he picked up a handful of photographs from the litter on the deck. They'd been partially obscured by an outflung arm. Holding the pictures under an overhead light, he quickly scanned them. All were human. Outside of that he couldn't find any special commonality. Men, women, young, old, civilian, military . . . there were all kinds of people. Why would Bridger and Votava have what seemed like a random assortment of photos aboard?

Getting down on his hands and knees he searched the deck for any he might have missed. Then he noticed a corner of something sticking out of a clenched fist. Gritting his teeth he pried open the cold, stiff fingers. He removed a crumpled photograph and smoothed it out. To his surprise Laurie's familiar brown eyes stared back at him. A chill ran down his spine. What in space was her photo doing here clutched in a dead man's hand? Was he trying to communicate something? If so, what? Laurie certainly hadn't been present when he died. It didn't make sense. But then these days, what did?

He stared at the picture for a long time. Finally he stood and tucked it away. He'd decided not to show it to her right away. For some reason he couldn't quite put his finger on, he felt guilty about that decision. He sealed his suit and entered the lock. Moments later he stepped out into the starry void.

F1VE

Even though it was more than a klick away, he could make out every detail of the sprawling complex through the powerful lens. The scope was a military model mounted on a tripod. Just one of the "extras" he'd conned Laurie out of back on Earth. Not that it'd done them much good so far. McCade leaned back for a moment to rest his eyes.

They'd been watching the Il Ronn legation for two days now. So far there'd been no sign of Bridger or Votava. In fact there'd been no signs of life at all. If it hadn't been for the comings and goings of the occasional hover limo, he would have concluded that the place was deserted. Considering the on-again, off-again state of hostilities between the human and Il Ronn empires, he was surprised the aliens were even allowed to have legations on human worlds. But it seemed both sides allowed the other a limited diplomatic presence on certain worlds. If nothing else, it made mutual spying more convenient and comfortable.

That was part of what he'd learned at Naval Headquarters shortly after landing on Weller's World. To McCade's surprise, Naval Headquarters was located in a slightly dilapidated dome bordering the spaceport. Usually the Imperial Government went in for more imposing edifices. But even here the inside was brightly painted and efficient. After a short wait in a pleasant reception area, they had been shown into the commanding officer's spartan office. The officer who rose to greet them was a lieutenant. He introduced himself as John Paul Jones. Named after the ancient naval hero,

McCade supposed. The fact that such a junior officer was in command showed McCade how thin the navy was stretched along the frontier.

But even if the lieutenant was short on rank, he still managed to be intimidating. His skin was a shiny black. Intelligence gleamed in his dark eyes. He carried himself gun barrel straight, with a belligerent thrust to his chin as though daring someone to hit it. He was in a position of considerable power out here, and he knew it.

Laurie identified herself and briefly explained their mission. She also identified the fugitives, but didn't indicate why they were being sought. Jones didn't ask. Like every other officer along the frontier, he'd received instructions to watch for Bridger and Votava. If he had questions about why, he kept them to himself.

He dealt with their situation quickly and efficiently. A team was sent up to sort out the mess aboard the remains of the *Leviathan,* and a search was simultaneously launched for the tug. It didn't take his people long to find it. Since Bridger and Votava hadn't dared land at the spaceport, or bring something as large as the tug itself down through the atmosphere for a landing in the wilds, they'd left it in orbit. The tug's lifeboat was missing.

"Chances are they brought it down somewhere in the back country," Lieutenant Jones said. "The farms out there are hundreds of klicks apart and the chances of being seen are just about nil. Then it'd just be a matter of walking and hitchhiking into a town. Logansport's the biggest."

They did their best to pump Jones about local conditions. But outside of giving them some very basic information about the planet and the Il Ronn legation, he was not very communicative. He had barely enough personnel and resources to cope with his regular duties and wanted no part of whatever these two were up to. So they thanked him and followed the directions on the map he'd provided. The Il Ronn legation was located just outside Logansport. They figured that to make contact with the Il Ronn, Bridger would have to go there sooner or later. It was thin, but they didn't have anything better to go on.

So they had put the legation under surveillance, but so far they hadn't seen much. The Il Ronn didn't enjoy the planet's climate and stayed cloistered within their bio-conditioned complex most of the time.

For the hundredth time that day McCade swept the powerful lens over the whitewashed building. All windows were still barred and shuttered. Plus there were other more effective but less visible security measures in effect. Van Doren had attempted a recon the night before. He'd never seen so many sensors. He'd been able to get within a hundred feet of the complex but no farther without risking almost certain discovery. The Il Ronn certainly liked their privacy. And for all he knew, Bridger and Votava might already be in there, having been whisked in right under his nose in a privacy-screened limo.

It was frustrating, and he hoped Laurie was having better luck. He hadn't seen her since the day before. She'd suggested that he and Van Doren man the surveillance post while she tried to contact the local intelligence network. McCade had agreed. They could use all the help they could get. In the meantime, McCade and Van Doren were each doing fourteen hours on and fourteen off. The days on Weller's World were a little longer than Terra's. It wasn't that bad, as stakeouts go. During his years as a bounty hunter McCade had been through much worse.

In fact, after weeks on the ship, it felt good to be dirtside again. A cool breeze relieved the afternoon heat and rustled the slightly bluish foliage that formed a protective canopy overhead. Weller's World was actually quite pleasant. Blessed with broad temperate zones above and below its equator, it was basically an agricultural planet. Rural enterprises of all sorts flourished. Genetically modified Terran crops and animals had been crossed with native flora and fauna to produce hybrids. Over time, some of the hybrids had proved to be quite valuable. Especially those that could be used in the manufacture of pharmaceuticals. The export of hybrid agricultural products provided farmers with cash crops. They spent the money on the machinery required on their labor poor world. Since the machinery was manufactured on planets nearer the Empire's center, Weller's World also made a good market. Gradually the planet had become something of a local trade center too. Being located at the far end of the Empire's trade routes has numerous disadvantages . . . but it has some good points too. For one thing the settlers on the frontier worlds in that sector had started bringing their exportable goods to market on Weller's World. Better prices were available deeper into the Empire, but first you had to get there. At the very least, getting there would cost more. Plus there was the ever-present danger of running into pirates. No, it was better to keep the trip as short as possible. Besides, the people on Weller's World were a rough and ready bunch among whom the frontiersmen felt more comfortable.

So every day one or two beaten up old ships, pre-Empire, some of them, would lower themselves wearily onto the scarred surface of the spaceport. From their dank holds a wild assortment of strange and exotic goods issued forth to be sold at daily auction. With a show of reluctance well-dressed local merchants bought goods for a pittance, which they'd later sell for a small fortune farther into the Empire. But the profit didn't end there. The frontiersmen were eager to spend their credits on electronics, tools, chemicals, vehicles, weapons, and more. Such things meant the difference between life and death on their planets. And before they left there'd usually be one night on the town, a wild, uproarious night, to be remembered and exaggerated later. A night of profit for a legion of saloon keepers, drug dealers, and prostitutes. Yes, the merchants of Weller's World were doing very well. Plus there were whispers of darker transactions. Of mysterious ships landing in the bush. Of cargos sold, only to reappear in the market a few days later. There was little doubt that some local merchants had strong ties to the pirates. Very profitable ties at that.

There was a rustling behind him and McCade turned, slug gun half out of its holster, to see Van Doren worming his way into the small clearing.

"It's just me, boss," Van Doren said in a stage whisper.

"Sounded like a whole brigade," McCade said, grinning.

"You're just jealous of my manly proportions," the marine replied, rising to his full height within the protective screen of vegetation. "Anything new?"

"Nothing," McCade answered, indicating the legation. "But I figure we should see some action soon."

"I sure hope so," Van Doren said. "'Cause sittin' here all night ain't my idea of a good time."

McCade yawned. "Speaking of which I'm heading back to town for some shut-eye. Have a good one."

McCade returned the marine's wave and crawled out through the bluish foliage to the nearby farm road. Hidden in the bushes where Van Doren had left it was an old-fashioned electro-cycle. He wheeled it up onto the reddish dirt road, climbed aboard and whirred off toward Logansport.

He awoke panting. His heart was racing. The room felt hot and muggy. His sweat had soaked the sheet under him. The dream had seemed so real. He'd been running through the streets of Logansport. Somewhere ahead of him was Bridger. Behind him a torpedo followed. The closer he got to Bridger, the closer the torpedo got to him. From somewhere up ahead, Bridger's insane laughter floated back to him. It grew louder and louder until it filled the streets, and the people on the sidewalks began to laugh too.

There was a slight noise from the right. He froze—straining to see and hear. His right hand crept by inches toward the butt of the needle gun under his pillow. The cool metal felt reassuring in his hand. There was the scrape of a shoe on the rough wood flooring. A figure moved slowly into the path of the moonlight streaming in through his window. Both moons were full tonight. The face that moved into their combined light was Laurie's. He watched, mesmerized, as she slowly and deliberately brought a handweapon up and aimed it at his chest.

McCade's hand flashed forward. He emptied the needle gun's magazine into her chest. She made a strangled sound and collapsed to the floor. McCade rolled out of bed, hitting a chair, which went over with a crash. Scrambling to his feet he snatched the slug gun from the dresser and aimed it into the pool of darkness where she'd fallen. Then he reached over and hit the lights.

A seething pool of greenish protoplasm met his eyes. There was no sign of Laurie beyond pieces of her clothing, which were mixed in with the strange green substance. The door banged open and Laurie burst in, a small sleeve gun in her hand. She aimed it at the mess on the floor. "I heard a noise! What is it?" she asked, nose wrinkled in distaste.

McCade regarded her with a raised eyebrow. "Believe it or not . . . it looked exactly like you until a moment ago. No offense," he added dryly.

"What's it doing here?" Laurie asked.

McCade shrugged. "Beats me. . . . I woke up as you—I mean it—was about to equip me with a second navel." He nudged the fallen gun with his toe.

"You are both cretins of the first order," a hoarse rasping voice said. It came from the pool of matter on the floor. It had changed. Now McCade saw that a small, ovoid shape had resolved itself from the surrounding protoplasm. It spoke through a small round aperture in its glistening surface. "You've killed me," the voice said pitifully. "Even now I'm dying a slow, painful death. How sad. How degrading to die at the hands of bipedal tool users."

McCade and Laurie glanced at each other in amazement. "Better you than me, friend," McCade replied calmly. "What the hell are you anyway?"

The ovoid seemed to shudder and convulse slightly. Its outline blurred, and for a fraction of a second McCade saw his own face. Then the ovoid reverted to its former appearance, though slightly smaller, as if the effort had somehow diminished it.

"A Treel," Laurie said.

"Finally, a glimmer of primitive intelligence," the hoarse voice said. "You see before you a sight few are privileged to witness. A Treel in the full magnificence of his natural state. Even though I am mortally wounded, notice the incredible beauty of my body."

"I'll admit I've never seen anything like it," McCade said. "Who sent you? Why did you try to kill me?"

For a moment he thought the Treel wasn't going to respond. Then it shivered, blurred, and he found himself looking at Cadet Squadron Leader Votava.

As the alien jerked, evidently suffering another convulsion, Votava faded into green protoplasm. Suddenly lots of things made sense. He'd heard of

Treels, but never seen one before. Few had. Treels spent most of their time looking like something else. That's how they managed to survive.

Their native planet swarmed with deadly life forms. Treels could imitate them all, from a rough likeness right down to the last biological detail if they wished to. That could include internal organs, voice print, fingerprints, the whole ball of wax. But evidently McCade's darts had wounded this one so badly it couldn't sustain an impersonation for more than a few moments.

"We are the only perfect race . . . for in us the great Yareel saw fit to demonstrate the unity of all life." With that the alien began an eerie chant in his own tongue.

A host of thoughts crowded each other, fighting for dominance in McCade's mind. A Treel. As he'd just seen, a Treel could impersonate any living thing which didn't exceed its own mass. But the Treel had to model its impersonations on something. The photos he'd found aboard the *Leviathan*. Photos the Treel had used to perfect his imitations. He remembered the photo of Laurie he'd found clutched in the dead man's hand. So the man had tried to identify his killer. But it hadn't been Laurie. She'd been aboard *Pegasus* with him. No, for some reason the Treel had chosen to look like Laurie when the tug's crew came aboard. Why? So they wouldn't recognize Votava from the fax sheets Naval Intelligence had sent out. It made sense. How long had the Treel posed as Votava, McCade wondered. Days? Months? Years? Yes, years probably. He remembered the discrepancy between the psych profiles before she left Mars, and after she entered the Academy. Somewhere between Mars and Terra the Treel had murdered the real Votava and taken her place. Then in the role of Votava, the Treel could have gone to work on Bridger. Feeding his anger and hate. And then when he'd learned the secret of the metal plate, urged him to use his new knowledge. Anger buried McCade's other emotions. A cold-blooded killer that could take on the appearance of anyone it chose. The perfect assassin. Suddenly another piece of the puzzle dropped into place.

Turning to Laurie, McCade said, "Now we know how the bomb was placed on that autocart." And why I found your picture aboard the *Leviathan,* he thought to himself. "It was no sweat for the Treel to place the bomb while impersonating someone who belonged in the building, someone like you." Laurie looked puzzled for a moment, and then nodded her head in understanding.

"That's right, Sam," the Treel said in a perfect imitation of Laurie's voice. "You aren't as stupid as you look."

"Why?" Laurie said. "Why have you done these things?"

The Treel made a hoarse coughing sound. A distorted likeness of Votava's face came and went. The Treel rasped, "My native planet lies just inside the Il Ronn Empire."

"They threatened you?" Laurie asked. The Treel's protoplasm convulsed into a shaky likeness of a stern-looking Il Ronn before again collapsing into a shapeless mass. A dry racking cough issued forth and for a fleeting moment McCade felt sorry for the strange being.

"Yes, primate, you speak truly," the Treel croaked. "While great of intelligence and beautiful to look upon, my race is few in number. Were it otherwise, we too would rule a great empire! But that is not the destiny Yareel granted us. We seldom mate, and then only on our native world. The Il Ronn have threatened to destroy our planet if we fail to serve them. The inevitable result would be the extinction of my race."

"I'm sorry," Laurie said. "We oppose the Il Ronn. Perhaps we could help."

"You're too late," came the hoarse reply. "Soon the man you call Bridger will lead the Il Ronn to the War World and then, invincible, they shall prevail throughout the galaxy."

"Bridger . . . where is he?" Laurie asked urgently, cutting McCade off.

She was answered by a hoarse sobbing which McCade supposed might be laughter. "It worked twice! We used the same trick twice!" The Treel chortled.

"You mean he's here? Right here in the hotel?" McCade asked.

The alien's laughter turned to hoarse coughing. "Yes . . . here. Like me he lies ill unto death. But soon they will come and take him. They will extract the information they require. Then woe unto man." Once again the eerie chant began.

McCade opened his mouth to ask what the War World is, exactly, but never got the chance. Instead Laurie turned, aimed her needle gun and fired. He felt the sting as the dart went into his thigh. A wave of nausea rolled over him. Drugs . . . she'd used drugs. He felt betrayed. He searched for sorrow in her eyes as he sank into dark oblivion, but found none.

He surfaced briefly at times before again sinking back into unconsciousness. During those moments he gathered distant impressions. First of being carried by rough hands and then of being thrown into some kind of vehicle, followed by a long jolting ride. Later he thought he remembered a snatch of conversation.

"I say let's waste 'im, I don't fancy cartin' 'im all over town."

"No, damn it. She said ta put him in parkin' orbit for a while . . . gently like. Ya mark me, lad, she'll put ya ta the local an' I mean smart like. . . ."

Somehow listening was more effort than McCade could bear, and he slipped back into the restful darkness.

He awoke with a splitting headache. The simple action of turning his head sent a lance of pain through his neck. His left thigh hurt too, where the dart had penetrated muscle and then dissolved. He was lying on a cold stone floor. High on the wall across from him a dim street light cast its feeble glow through a barred window. Other prisoners surrounded him. Some lay on the floor, as he did. Others slept in makeshift beds. In a far corner a man quietly wept. The smell of vomit and urine was overpowering. Water dripped steadily from the ceiling and fell a drop at a time into the puddle beside his head.

With tremendous effort he tried to sit up. He was rewarded with an explosion of pain forcing him back against the cold damp floor. He lay there a long time, thinking. Obviously Laurie worked for someone besides Naval Intelligence, and had for a long time. The question was who? The Il Ronn? No, that didn't make sense. The Treel disguised as Votava had acted as their agent. So who was left? The pirates, that's who.

Suddenly the assassins made sense. They'd bothered him from the start. Bridger and Votava—strike that—the Treel hadn't sent them. They'd used mercenaries. No, someone else sent the assassins. Someone who knew the naval base and could help them get in. Someone who could tell them where McCade would be and when. Someone like Laurie. But why? He might never learn Laurie's personal motives, but those of her employers were obvious. The pirates had found out somehow about Bridger's break-through.

He remembered his computer research into Bridger's activities and his conclusion that Bridger had broken the secret of his "Directory." In spite of the computer's assurances that no one else had asked for the same information, obviously they had. Laurie must have done the same research and had reached the same conclusions. At that point either she or her superiors decided that the last thing they wanted was for McCade to catch Bridger and turn him and his secret over to Naval Intelligence. They wanted Bridger and the knowledge locked away in his head just as the Il Ronn obviously did. So, Laurie hired assassins to kill McCade, while her fellow pirates no doubt launched an intensive effort to find Bridger themselves.

But the assassins failed. So Laurie decided to use him instead of killing him. Let him lead her to Bridger. And that's exactly what he'd done. Suddenly he wanted to get his hands on her, to hurt her, to punish her for his own stupid vulnerability. And yet he knew that given the chance he still wouldn't do any of those things.

So far things hadn't gone well. McCade smiled grimly to himself in the darkness. But the Treel had added one small scrap of information to his limited hoard. What had he said? Something about Bridger leading the Il Ronn to the "War World." The name was certainly ominous, and bore some rather obvious possibilities.

Had Bridger's "Directory" somehow given him the location of an entire world? One developed by the Builders and dedicated to war? If so, and if the weapons on such a world were still intact, the implications could be enormous. There was little doubt that the Builders had possessed a science and technology superior to anything yet developed by either humans or Il

Ronn. Logically therefore the weapons developed by such a race would be truly awesome. Whoever found them first might well have the means to control all of explored space. Whatever it was, the Treel had learned of it, probably as a result of Bridger's demented ravings, and had by now communicated that knowledge to the Il Ronn.

The whole thing scared the hell out of him. If such power existed, who should control it? The human empire? The Il Ronn empire? The pirates? The more he thought about it, the less he liked any of the possibilities. Gradually the light from the window grew brighter, and his fellow prisoners began to stir. He managed to sit up.

"Got a light?" came a voice from behind him.

Automatically his hand went to his lighter and to his surprise it was there.

As though reading his mind the voice said, "If it ain't lethal, they let ya keep it."

Turning, McCade confronted a bear of a man who dwarfed the rickety chair on which he sat. McCade lit the man's cigar, and then searched his pockets for one of his own.

"Here, sport, try one o' mine," the man said, offering McCade an expensive, imported cigar still sealed in its own metal tube.

"Thanks," McCade said, looking the man over as he unsealed the cigar and carefully rotated it over the flame from his lighter. The man had a head of unruly black hair, with a beard to match. His eyes were small and bright, tucked deeply into creased flesh. His teeth flashed white when he smiled, something he did a lot. He was dressed frontier style. A dark woolen shirt was covered by a leather vest. His pants were made of a black synthetic that looked very tough. He wore lace-up boots. McCade noticed an empty knife sheath sticking out of the right one.

McCade inhaled and blew out a rich stream of smoke. "You have good taste in cigars."

The big man's laughter boomed through the cell. "Friend, I have good taste in everything. Ships, women, wine, food, and cigars, in that order. And believe me, I've had my share o' the last four lately. After all, it's gotta last me another year."

"You're from off-planet?" McCade asked.

"Sport, do I look like I belong on this dirt ball? Hell no I don't. I'm from Alice," the other man said proudly. "That's halfway out ta the Il Ronn Empire. Hit dirt here three days ago with a load o' rare isotopes. Was I ever glad to get rid o' that stuff. Hotter than an asteroid miner's dreams, it was. How about you, sport? What brings ya ta the anal orifice o' the galaxy?"

"Nothing much," McCade replied vaguely. "Just trying to turn an honest credit."

The other man nodded sagely and winked one of his tiny eyes knowingly.

"Sam McCade." He stuck out his right hand and watched it disappear into the other man's massive grip.

"Glad ta meet ya, sport. My mother named me Fredrico Jose Romero. But friends just call me Rico."

"Well, Rico," McCade said, "maybe you could tell me where the hell I am?"

"Welcome ta the Longansport municipal drunk tank, Sam ol' friend. Ya don't remember being picked up?"

McCade shook his head. He remembered the needle gun in Laurie's hand and the sting as the dart entered his flesh. By now she had Bridger and was long gone.

"Well I'll bet those spaceheads remember picking me up." Rico rubbed a huge fist with a look of satisfaction in his beady eyes.

McCade nodded agreeably. "How do we get out of here, Rico? I've got things to do and people to see."

"No sweat, friend. . . . In a few minutes they'll open up this toilet and let us out."

"No trial or anything?" McCade asked.

"Nah," Rico replied, dropping his cigar butt into the puddle next to McCade. It sizzled and went out. "That'd be bad for business. Not only would it slow the manly art o' drinkin' . . . it'd mean more taxes ta run the court. An if there's anything the local merchants don't like, it's more taxes." Rico's words were punctuated by the clanging of metal as a large section of bars was slid back by two men in police uniforms.

"All right . . . hit the bricks," the shorter of the two said. "This ain't no friggin' hotel."

Singly and in small groups, the men stood, collected their weapons from the jailers, and shuffled out through the gate. McCade noticed that the blade Rico slipped into his boot sheath was double-edged and over a foot long. Together McCade and Rico followed the others out through a maze of dank hallways and into a sun-filled street. McCade squinted as he glanced around to get his bearings.

"How about breakfast on me, Rico," McCade suggested, rummaging through his pockets and finding some crumpled local currency.

"That'd be fine, Sam ol' friend," Rico answered. "It seems I'm temporarily broke."

They flagged down a public ground car. McCade punched his hotel's name into the vehicle's computer and the ancient conveyance lurched into motion. Fifteen minutes later they entered the hotel's lobby and were greeted by an anxious Amos Van Doren.

"Boss! Nobody relieved me, so I got worried and came lookin'. . . . Couldn't find you or Laurie neither. Hotel says she checked out but you didn't, so I figured I'd wait. You okay?"

McCade assured Van Doren he was and suggested that Rico start breakfast without them. The big man nodded amiably and smiled as he ambled off in the direction of the hotel's restaurant. McCade headed for his room with Van Doren in tow; on the way, he related the events of the night before. The marine's reaction to Laurie's affiliation surprised him.

"Somethun' 'bout her always bothered me, boss. Couldn't put my finger on it. Always seemed like a cat waitin' on a mouse, know what I mean?"

McCade didn't. And that bothered him. Laurie seen through Van Doren's eyes sounded like a different person from the woman he'd known. One she'd never let him see. Or one he'd been blind to. It made very little difference.

As McCade opened the door, he saw the room was neat and tidy. There was no sign of the Treel. Not even a stain to mark where the alien had been. Laurie must have disposed of him somehow. With pirate help no doubt.

So by now Laurie had located Bridger and lifted off-planet. Soon the pirates would interrogate Bridger, and, regardless of resistance, they would succeed. Of course Bridger was ill. Very ill, according to the Treel. Sufficiently ill to delay interrogation? McCade hoped so. He needed time. He had to find out where the pirates had taken Bridger. And that wouldn't be easy. They had lots of worlds to pick from. Meanwhile the Il Ronn were no doubt looking for Bridger too. It should be an interesting race.

Thoughtfully he strapped on his gun belt. It, along with his other gear, had been left untouched.

Together he and Van Doren headed for the lobby. McCade paused by a bank of public com units. "How about *Pegasus?*" he asked. The marine looked embarrassed. McCade realized Van Doren hadn't thought to check on the ship. "That's okay, Amos. . . . Join Rico for breakfast. You'll like him. I'll call the spaceport."

A few minutes later McCade joined the other two in the restaurant. He wasn't happy, and it showed.

"Problems, old sport?" Rico asked around a mouthful of food.

McCade nodded. "It seems our ship lifted without us." Inside he was seething. Laurie had not only snatched Bridger out from under his nose, she'd also used his ship to lift him off-planet.

If Rico was curious, he didn't show it, but blood suffused Van Doren's face, and the eyes beneath his bushy brows grew hard and bright.

"I'm sorry, boss."

"Don't be," McCade said. "There wasn't any way you could've known."

"Maybe I could help," Rico said, chewing thoughtfully. "If ya have credits fer a charter, that is . . . and providin' it don't take too long."

They haggled back and forth while McCade waited for his food. A process Rico clearly enjoyed. Finally they shook on a fee which McCade thought surprisingly low. So low it made him suspicious. In fact, he began to wonder if Rico wasn't just too good to be true. If so, it could work to their advantage. As things stood, he'd lost Bridger and didn't have the faintest idea of where to start looking. Maybe Rico would provide a lead.

So they talked and joked, finally finishing breakfast about an hour later. Rico headed for his ship while McCade and Van Doren went to check out of their hotel. Adding insult to injury, Laurie had stiffed him with her bill as well. Fortunately he'd insisted on a thick wad of expense money before they'd lifted from Terra. It was still in his luggage where he'd left it. As they headed for the spaceport, McCade briefed Van Doren on his suspicions regarding Rico, and they agreed on a plan. The big man met them as they approached his ship.

"There she is," Rico said proudly. "The *Lady Alice.* Ain't she somethun'?"

McCade had never seen a more decrepit-looking ship. She was a pre-Empire freighter. Her hull was pitted and scarred by a thousand re-entries. One of her landing jacks was leaking black hydraulic fluid, and she had a list to port.

"Yeah," McCade replied dryly. "They don't make 'em like that anymore."

But Rico was oblivious to such sarcasm. As they climbed aboard, McCade began to understand why. On closer inspection he saw that, contrary to outward appearances, the *Lady Alice* was in perfect shape. Outmoded systems had been replaced with new. The ship's interior was spotless, and glistened with fresh paint. As they passed a weapons blister, McCade noticed the brand new energy cannon mounted in it. For some reason, Rico wanted the *Lady Alice* to look like she was on her last leg. Interesting, McCade thought, I wonder why?

SIX

Rico invited McCade and Van Doren to strap into the crew positions just aft of the pilot's seat. He offered no explanation for the ship's lack of a crew. Not that a crew was absolutely necessary, of course.

Thirty minutes later they had cleared the atmosphere and were in deep space. Rico unbuckled himself and swiveled his chair around to face them. He had a friendly grin on his face and a very unfriendly-looking stun gun in his huge right hand. His grin slipped into a frown, however, as he looked down the barrels of the slug guns held by both McCade and Van Doren.

"Uh-oh . . ." Rico said. "I've got a feelin' you're ahead o' me, sport. Would ya believe I was just kiddin'? No? I was afraid o' that." He dropped the stun gun.

McCade couldn't help laughing. The man's incredible effrontery was somehow disarming.

"No hard feelings, Rico. . . . But why?"

Rico shrugged. His smile disappeared. "Figure it out for yourself. I don't have nothin' ta say."

"Maybe I could change his mind, boss," Van Doren growled.

"Somehow I doubt it, but thanks anyway, Amos," McCade replied. Turning to Rico, he said, "I've got a hunch you didn't just happen to be in the drunk tank when I was. You arranged to be there." He paused and regarded the other man thoughtfully. "The frontier worlds have been organizing, haven't they? And somehow you got wind of this Bridger thing and dealt yourselves in."

Rico's face remained impassive, but McCade would have sworn he saw a flash of confirmation deep in the other man's eyes.

"Okay," McCade said. "I'll take a last try. You were taking us somewhere. Somebody wants to ask us some questions. Well, what if I told you that's fine with me? In fact, that I want to go?"

And why not, McCade thought. I don't know where they took Bridger . . . but I'll bet you've got a pretty good idea.

Rico looked thoughtful for a moment and then nodded. "That's right, ol' friend . . . but we ain't goin' there while you're pointin' them slug throwers my way."

McCade slid his gun into its holster and motioned for Van Doren to do likewise. The marine hesitated for a moment, glancing back and forth between McCade and Rico. Finally he holstered his weapon, but with obvious reluctance.

In spite of himself McCade's hand strayed toward his own gun as Rico bent over to retrieve his. A broad grin creased Rico's face as he tucked the stunner away into a shoulder holster.

"Don't worry. No more surprises. Shake?"

Rico offered McCade a hairy paw. McCade accepted. But when Rico and Van Doren shook hands, he noticed that eyes locked and shoulders tensed. Muscles bunched and writhed in massive forearms. After a moment both men sat down, apparently satisfied. When they looked his way, McCade was blowing smoke rings toward the overhead, evidently oblivious to the whole thing.

It was a three-day trip to Alice. Most of it was spent in normal space, with only a short hyperspace jump in the middle. At first McCade spent his time trying to pump Rico for information. He soon found that was a waste of time. The other man steadfastly refused to answer questions, saying, "That's not for me to say. Them that's waitin' is all great talkers. Me, I'm more a doer."

So McCade quit trying, but Rico's silence tended to confirm his theories. For one thing it suggested a strong centralized organization, rather than a loose collection of individuals acting on their own. And organization implied specialization and discipline. Both hallmarks of government. Something the frontier worlds were not supposed to have. Either petition the Emperor for admission to the Empire or forget it. That was the law. McCade wondered if Swanson-Pierce knew about Laurie's defection, or that the frontier worlds were organizing. Somehow he doubted it. There seemed to be a great deal that Naval Intelligence wasn't aware of.

If Rico was close-mouthed about his people and their aims, he was just the opposite on the subject of Alice. McCade had never met anyone so in love with a planet. And from Rico's description he couldn't figure out why. Evidently a good portion of the planet's surface was in the last stages of an ice age. Giant glaciers dominated both poles and stretched icy fingers north and south. A narrow temperate zone girdled the equator.

Naturally the first settlers built their homes in the temperate zone. But they quickly realized their mistake. The area just above and below the equator was volcanically active. Two enormous continental plates met there. As they collided, mountains were upthrust, lava flowed, and frequent seismic activity destroyed surface structures as quickly as they could be built. So the settlers retreated south and settled where the glaciers met the temperate zone. This area had its hazards too, primarily the incredible cold, but it was still preferable to the volcanic region. According to Rico, the land had a wild, frozen beauty. What's more, it was rich in minerals and there was plenty of it. A man could carve a future out of land like that— limited only by his own courage and imagination. Fusion power plants, land crawlers, energy weapons, and automedics might come in handy too, McCade thought to himself.

In spite of Rico's endless anecdotes about the planet's frigid surface, McCade wasn't ready for the cold that embraced them as they left the ship. It searched out the tiny gaps in their clothing and entered, driven by the relentless wind. It cut through the parka Rico lent him and chilled him to the bone. Rico himself seemed unaffected, smiling through a beard quickly frosted with ice. Not as amazing as it seemed since the big man was wearing a powered heatsuit.

To his relief they scrambled quickly into a heated crawler, which jerked into motion, toward the distant hills. Looking out through scratched plastic, McCade watched with surprise as the *Lady Alice* sank slowly into the ground. Then he realized the ship had landed on an elevator, which was lowering it into an underground hangar.

Seeing his interest, Rico said, "Winter storms. Cold enough ta freeze the balls off a icecat. Sixty kilometer winds. Other possibilities too," he added vaguely. "Summer now so no sweat."

Terrific. Sweat's gonna be the least of my problems, McCade thought. He looked at Van Doren, and they both shook their heads in amazement. As they drew away from the spaceport, McCade began to notice carefully camouflaged weapons emplacements. Without exception they were aimed at the sky. He didn't like the implications. Then he began to see blackened craters, burned out domes and wrecked crawlers. Smoke still poured out of what had obviously been some kind of tracking station.

He turned to question Rico, but the big man was in whispered conversation with the driver, a handsome woman in her late forties. When he leaned back, Rico's face was black with anger. McCade started to ask him what had happened, but then thought better of it. So they rode on in silence. McCade and Van Doren watched the passage of frozen scenery, while Rico sat slumped, deep within his own thoughts.

After what seemed like an hour, but was probably less, the crawler approached a snow-covered hill. It looked no different from twenty others they'd passed, but just when it seemed certain that they would crash into the hillside, an armored door as white as the snow around it slid aside, revealing a lighted tunnel. As the crawler entered, the door slid closed behind them. The noise of their passage bounced off the walls, then, without warning, the tunnel opened up into a large chamber.

McCade saw rows of parked crawlers, power sleds and snowmobiles. They looked like they'd seen hard use. In one corner mechanics swarmed over an armed crawler that evidently had been hit by an energy weapon. He couldn't tell if they were repairing it or stripping it for parts. In either case they were obviously in a hurry.

Moments later they pulled up to a loading dock. As they stepped out,

McCade and Van Doren found themselves looking into the business ends of four weapons held by some very steady hands.

"Put 'em away, ya bozos!" Rico said, stepping between the four men and McCade. "Can't ya see they're comin' peaceable? Sides which they could probably eat ya for breakfast." As the men sheepishly holstered their weapons, Rico turned to McCade. "Sorry 'bout that. How's they ta know ya'd come quiet?"

"It's okay, Rico," McCade said, glancing at Van Doren. The big marine looked doubtful, but dropped his hand from the butt of his slug gun.

"These spaceheads'll take ya ta your quarters, if'n they don't get lost along the way," Rico said with a derisive snort. "After ya've had a chance ta clean up I s'pose the bigwigs'll talk your ear off. See ya later!" With a jaunty wave, the big man lumbered off.

With two ahead and two behind, McCade and Van Doren followed the guards through a maze of corridors. Some were nicely finished and others still showed signs of recent construction. Eventually they were shown into adjoining cubicles. They were clean, but spartan. McCade lay down on the hard mattress, planning to think.

It seemed only moments later when an insistent knocking woke him. Glancing at his wrist term he saw that over five hours had passed. As he swung his feet onto the floor, the door opened and a man stepped in. He was tall and slender, dressed in frontier fashion. His movements were smooth and quick. The bones in his face were prominent but well-formed, granting him predatory good looks. His eyes were like cold chips of black stone through which McCade could see nothing. McCade didn't like him . . . and somehow knew the feeling was mutual.

"The Council wishes to see you," the man said. His expression made it clear that attendance wasn't optional.

"Good," McCade replied. "And I'd like to see them. Just give me a moment to clean up." McCade started for the tiny bathroom.

Suddenly the man was in his way. He's damn fast, McCade noted to himself.

"The Council wants to see you *now*," the man said. Before McCade could reply, he heard the unmistakable metallic sound of a slug gun going to full cock. Looking toward the sound he saw Van Doren aiming his massive handgun at the man's head. "Maybe you'd like to meet your *maker—now*," the marine said calmly.

The man paled and tensed his body. For a moment McCade thought he might challenge Van Doren's reflexes. Then, with a visible effort, the man forced himself to back down. He's no coward, McCade thought. There was implacable hatred in the eyes staring back at him.

"It's okay, Amos," McCade said, forcing a smile. "I'm sorry. I'm afraid Amos takes his duties as my bodyguard too seriously."

The other man nodded his head in a short, jerky motion, turned on his heel, and left the room, slamming the door behind him.

"You should've let me blow his head off, boss. That one'll be trouble later . . . you mark my words," Van Doren said.

"You're probably right, Amos," McCade said wearily. "But I'm afraid the Council might become annoyed if we blew their envoy's head off. I do appreciate your desire to be efficient however." Van Doren shrugged his shoulders and returned to his cubicle.

A few minutes later McCade entered the hall freshly showered and shaved. He felt better because of it, plus it wouldn't hurt to make a good impression on the Council. Whoever they were. Van Doren was right behind him.

The tall man was waiting impatiently. "You come with me," he said, pointing to McCade, "and you stay," indicating Van Doren. McCade noticed that the man had strapped on a gun of his own. His right hand hovered over its well-worn grip.

Van Doren's hand was inches from the butt of his own gun when McCade said, "Let it be, Amos. They've got all the cards right now, so let's play it their way." He tossed the marine a mock salute as he followed the tall man down the hall.

It was a short journey. A few minutes later they were ushered past a heavily guarded door and into a large circular room. It was dominated by a semicircular table of some highly polished native wood. Behind it sat four people. For some reason he wasn't surprised to see that Rico was one of them. The big man nodded in his direction and winked one of his tiny eyes.

Then McCade's attention was drawn to the woman on Rico's right. She was beautiful. Or had been. A terrible white scar slashed across her softly rounded face from high on the left side of her forehead down across her right cheek. Nonetheless, it was her large hazel eyes that dominated her face. They regarded McCade with cold curiosity.

"Welcome, Citizen McCade," she said. "Rico has told us a great deal about you. Please allow me to introduce the rest of us. On my far right is Professor Wendel. He heads our scientific team."

The professor was an elderly man who wore his thick white hair in a neat ponytail behind his head. His bright blue eyes twinkled as he inclined his head toward McCade in greeting.

"On my immediate right is Col. Frank Larkin," the woman continued. "The colonel is in charge of our armed forces."

McCade judged Larkin to be in his middle fifties, but he could have been older. His head was shaved in the tradition of the elite Imperial Star Guard—the special marine brigade responsible for the personal safety of the Emperor. His hard eyes inspected McCade as though on parade, and his nod granted nothing more than recognition.

"And of course you've met Rico, our Master at Arms," she said, "and Vern Premo, our comptroller." She indicated the tall man who now lounged against one wall. He was staring past McCade toward the woman with open avarice in his eyes.

"I'm Sara Bridger," she said coldly. "Chief Political Officer for the Council. I understand that you want to kill my father."

Confusion filled McCade's thoughts and emotions. It couldn't be. Sara Bridger had been captured by pirates and was probably dead by now. Yet he knew it was true. Without the scar she would be the same woman he'd admired aboard the old *Imperial*. Older but still beautiful. The tiny lines around her eyes and mouth added character, while taking nothing from her beauty. A beauty transcending even the scar.

"Well?" she said, unconsciously tracing the scar with a fingertip.

"I have no desire to kill your father," McCade replied evenly. "However, he is a fugitive from Imperial justice."

"You speak of 'Imperial justice.' Where is it?" she asked bitterly. "Why does the navy allow the pirates and the Il Ronn to slaughter our people? Where was Imperial justice when the pirates came yesterday, raping and burning? Last night we buried fourteen of our friends. Some were only children. Their only crime was trying to defend their homes. Was that just?"

Her eyes burned with hatred and her cheeks were flushed, serving to emphasize the whiteness of the scar. McCade realized she was close to exhaustion.

"I'm sorry," he said simply.

With visible effort she brought herself under control. "What crimes has my father committed?" she asked, steel lying just under the soft surface of her words.

"Desertion . . . and possibly other crimes I'm not free to divulge," McCade answered.

"You'll tell her whatever she wants to know!" The angry voice was Premo's. No longer lounging against the wall, he was standing, his body rigid with anger as he clenched and unclenched his fists at his side.

"That'll be enough o' that," Rico said levelly, "or would ya care ta take ol' Rico on?" For the first time McCade saw caution in Premo's eyes.

Sara Bridger broke the uncomfortable silence that followed. "Rico's right, McCade." She aimed a critical glance at Premo.

"You'll not be forced to speak." Her expression hardened. "But you must understand that, until Rico's arrival a few hours ago, I thought my father was living happily on Terra. Now I learn he's being hunted like an animal throughout the Empire. Hunted by men like you. Men who kill for money!" Disgust and revulsion played across her features.

McCade felt his hands start to shake as he remembered the marines who'd died and the bodies he'd found aboard the *Leviathan*. The muscle in his left cheek twitched uncontrollably as he spoke. "Your father has already murdered innocent people. It's quite likely he intends to murder more. If I have to kill him to stop that, I will. And you're right, I'm doing it for money. But you know what? In your father's case, I'd do it for free."

The blood drained from Sara Bridger's face, leaving it as white as the scar that bisected it. Hatred burned in her beautiful eyes. Without a word she rose and left the room.

"For that you'll die!" Premo spit the words out one at a time. McCade spun toward him, his hand over his gun and the promise of eternity in his wintry gray eyes.

Somewhere a klaxon went off. Everyone froze as a calm male voice came over the PA system. "This is a class three attack, including light armor and infantry. All active and reserve personnel report to your units immediately. All noncombatants report to your class three duty stations."

Everyone bolted for the nearest door. Premo's look promised another meeting as he turned on his heel and marched out.

When McCade turned back, the other Council members had already left, with the exception of Rico. He was lighting a cigar while regarding McCade with a raised eyebrow.

"Seems like you don't make friends too easy, ol' sport," he said, rising from his chair. "Wanna come with me'n take your antisocial tendencies out on some pirates? Sounds like they're at it again. Two attacks in two days is a little much. It's gettin' outta hand." Without looking to see if McCade followed, he turned and went out the rear door the other Council members had used.

McCade had to stretch to match the other man's gigantic strides. "What's Premo's problem anyway?"

Rico shrugged. "Who knows? Premo's Premo. I know it's hard ta believe . . . but in some ways he ain't bad. Jus' keep in mind that when it comes ta Sara, he's crazier'n a Tobarian Zerk monkey."

"I've got a feeling he's going to remind me," McCade said dryly.

"Here we are," Rico said as they turned a corner. Rico led McCade into a lift tube. Moments later they emerged into a smaller version of the chamber he'd seen before. This one had only four crawlers in it, and there was room for two more. As they got closer McCade noticed all four were armed. They hadn't been designed for combat, so they didn't have turrets. That meant the energy cannon mounted toward the front of each vehicle could only be aimed forward. A large caliber slug thrower had been installed in a blister at the rear of each crawler to deal with threats from behind. A smaller caliber automatic weapon was mounted in a blister on top of the massive machine.

"Had six o' these ta start with . . . but the pirates pared my section down ta four in the last six months," Rico said as they approached the lead crawler. He inspected its tracks and patted the machine's scarred flanks lovingly as they walked around it.

Up close the crawler towered over the two men. Intended to withstand the rigors of planetary exploration, the crawlers had been built to take lots of punishment. So with the addition of some extra armor plating and weapons blisters they made respectable heavy tanks. Just how respectable McCade was about to find out.

As they rounded the front end of the crawler, McCade saw a slim figure in overalls and a helmet straighten from inspecting a huge bogey wheel and turn to toss Rico an informal salute. "Unit Two ready for action, sir," she said. "Chuck and Sparks are aboard."

"Thanks, Paula," Rico answered as he scrambled up the rungs leading to the top hatch. "Meet Sam McCade. . . . Is Yamana still sick?"

Paula nodded toward McCade and replied dryly, "He only broke his leg last week, Rico."

"Well, ya can't 'spect me ta remember everything, damn it," Rico said, pausing at the top. "Sam here'll take Yama's place in the tail position. . . . That okay?"

McCade indicated it was. A few minutes later with help from Paula, he had strapped himself into the tailgunner's position and the crawler got under way. His weapon was an electrically driven, multibarreled slug thrower. A descendant of the ancient Gatling gun. Each of the six barrels fired hundreds of armor-piercing shells a second. It could be elevated for aircraft or depressed for surface action. McCade wondered which to expect.

Cold white light flooded his blister as the crawler emerged from its camouflaged hiding place and rumbled out across ice and rock. He watched as the other three crawlers spread out to take up positions on either side of Rico's unit. A dispassionate voice broke the steady static on his earphones. "Command to section Charlie Four . . . we have six unidentified armored units approaching your sector . . . range one klick . . . bearing one-two-oh. Have fun."

"Roger," Rico replied. "Let's go get 'em, Charlie Four."

The crawler's speed increased with a commensurate increase in the amount of vibration. McCade felt like it would shake his teeth out. He noted that, as usual, the muscle in his left cheek had begun to twitch, and it felt as though someone had poured cold lead into his stomach. He wished he was manning the energy cannon so he could see where they were going . . . and what was coming. Not knowing was the worst part. But Rico had quite understandably put him in the least critical position. A voice he'd never heard before broke radio silence with, "Unit three has visual contact with four unknowns, range approximately 750 meters bearing one-two-oh. Request permission to fire primary."

"Negative," Rico answered. "Hold fire. Units four and six confirm sighting."

For what seemed like an eternity there was only static on McCade's headset. Then, "Unit six confirms." And a moment later, "Unit four confirms . . . enemy has opened fire."

"Commence evasive action . . . and fire!" Rico shouted. McCade felt the entire crawler jerk in sympathy with the recoil of their primary armament. For at least the tenth time he wished he could see what was going on. Instead he had an unobstructed view of where they'd been. For what seemed like hours McCade listened to shouted commands punctuated by shouts of victory and groans of defeat. He was thrown from side to side during violent evasive maneuvers and jolted up and down as the crawler hurled itself across gullies in the ice and rock. Meanwhile he tried to build a picture of the battle in his mind.

The initial charge against the six pirate units netted Rico's smaller section two kills at the cost of unit four. Now the four remaining enemy units were locked in individual duels with what remained of Rico's section. Co-ordinated group action was impossible in the broken terrain. McCade's thoughts were interrupted as Rico shouted into the intercom, "Look out, Sam! That bastard's tryin' ta get behind us!"

McCade was thrown to the right as Rico put the crawler into a tight turn. If they could turn fast enough they'd be able to match the pirate unit and prevent it from getting behind them. But their adversary had the advantage and used it.

McCade watched the huge black shape fill his sight. He forced himself to hold back until it filled his sight from edge to edge. Then he pulled the triggers on the twin grips and heard an eerie whine as his gun opened up. He watched his tracer arc up and then down to meet the oncoming enemy crawler.

His stomach muscles tensed as the other unit returned his fire. The pirate unit's tracer probed and searched, trying to complete a deadly connection between the two crawlers. The blue pulses of their energy cannon wove in and out of the white tracer, forming an intricate pattern of color and movement. Then the crawler lurched under him, and he knew they'd been hit hard. Their speed dropped and McCade realized the engine noise had too. Evidently they'd lost an engine.

His fears were confirmed when Rico said, "We just took a round in the starboard engine. Prepare ta bail out."

McCade gritted his teeth and continued to hold the triggers down. Now that his own crawler had slowed it was easier to hit the enemy. Now Rico's top blister gunner had joined him in his efforts to hit the pirate's tracks. Suddenly the enemy unit slowed. They knew Rico's primary armament could only aim forward. So they planned to sit and pour it on while Rico's remaining engine slowly turned the crawler to meet them. Then using their superior speed, they'd get around behind Rico again and it would start over. Things don't look good, McCade thought grimly. Then he noticed the tendril of smoke coming from the inside of the enemy unit's track. He concentrated his fire on that spot and was rewarded with even more smoke. Then flames replaced the smoke and the other crawler stopped moving. Rico completed his turn at that moment and McCade lost sight of the enemy. He felt the recoil of Rico's energy cannon and heard the muffled sound of an explosion. They'd won.

But instead of victory yells, there was silence on the intercom. Then McCade realized he hadn't heard any radio transmission from the other units in Rico's section for some time. He was about to ask what was going on when he felt a hand on his shoulder. He looked up to see Paula holding a finger to her lips and motioning for him to follow. McCade released his harness. After some contortions he managed to turn in the cramped space of the blister and follow Paula through the narrow accessway into the crawler's main cabin.

Rico greeted him with a whispered hello and a friendly pat on the back that nearly drove him to the deck. Two other men nodded their greetings. One sat at the crawler's controls. He didn't look old enough to drink yet, much less drive a crawler into battle. He had a friendly grin, and the name Chuck was scrawled in gold thread across the left breast of his bright green jacket. A middle-aged com tech sat in front of a bank of com units and detectors. He wore a set of earphones on his balding head. After a cheerful wave he turned back to his screens.

"Nice job back there, ol' sport," Rico whispered as he motioned for McCade to join him behind Sparks.

"I had some help," McCade replied, pointing up toward the top turret.

"Yeah, Paula ain't bad. . . . Here, take a look at this," Rico whispered.

McCade joined Rico in looking over the com tech's shoulder. A battle map appeared on the screen in front of them. On it were four blinking green lights. It appeared all the units except Rico's had been knocked out. Then Rico pointed at a steady red light almost on the edge of the screen. It was rapidly moving away from the battlefield. One of the enemy units was escaping.

"Okay, Chuck," Rico whispered. "Let's go. Take 'er nice 'n' easy."

To McCade's surprise he felt both engines start up. Rico smiled knowingly. "It's just amazin' how them engines come 'n' go like that."

The crawler lurched into motion. Once they were moving, the ride smoothed out. McCade watched as obstacles appeared and disappeared on the forward viewscreen. Just when he thought the crawler could go no farther, Chuck would deftly steer them around the problem. Turning back to the battle map, McCade saw that a steady green light now pursued the red.

"I don't get it, Rico," McCade whispered. "He's still in range. Why don't we open up on him? And why am I whispering?"

"First, 'cause we wanna follow him. . . . And second, 'cause we don't know how good the spacehead's audio sensors are."

"He isn't likely to hear us talking over the engines, Rico."

"That's where you're wrong, ol' friend. Least I hope ya are. Like I tol' ya before, we used ta have six units, but they've been wearin' us down. They always work it the same way. A ship lands, off-loads armor and infantry, they hit and run, then it's up and away. Ta stop 'em ya gotta nail their ship. So on Weller's World I bought me some shielding. Blocks noise and heat. After we landed, the crew worked like a gang o' Celite stevedores ta install it. Only had enough for the engines though. Twenty feet out we're as quiet as an icecat's shadow, and as cold as his rear end."

An enormous grin bisected Rico's hairy face, and his tiny eyes twinkled with merriment. "Imagine the look on those bozos' mugs when we blow their ship out from under 'em."

Then McCade understood. Rico was planning to follow the pirate crawler back to its mother ship. Then with the pirate vessel sitting vulnerable on the ground, they would stand a chance of beating down its screens and destroying it. It was a good plan and obviously one the man had worked on for some time. However, McCade saw room for one added refinement, and, if it worked, they'd end up with a usable ship instead of a wreck.

The two men held a whispered conference. Rico was quick to adopt McCade's suggestion and quickly passed appropriate orders to his crew. After that there was nothing to do but wait. Time seemed to crawl by.

Outside, an endless parade of broken rock, ice, and stunted vegetation crossed the viewscreen in monotonous succession. After what seemed like an eternity, they topped a rise and paused, hidden among upthrust spires of rock. Ahead the pirate crawler picked its way down the slope through the accumulated scree toward the valley below.

"He's talking to the ship on a sealed beam," the com tech whispered. Rico nodded.

Below, the pirate ship dominated the valley. To McCade's eyes its long, lean shape seemed pleasantly symmetrical against the jumble of ice and rock strewn around it. A ring of hastily erected earthworks surrounded the ship. But now the weapons pits stood vacant. All personnel had been pulled back in preparation for lift-off. Now they waited for the single crawler steadily creeping across the valley floor.

McCade turned to see Paula sitting at the controls of the energy cannon. Rico and the other crew members had already evacuated the crawler, leaving Paula and McCade to complete the plan. In McCade's view that was only fair, since it was his plan and entailed additional risk. Paula refused to go, pointing out that the plan called for precision shooting, and adding that she was the best shot on the crew. No one had disputed her claim.

McCade watched as a cargo hatch was slowly retracted into the pirates' hull, leaving a large rectangular opening for their crawler to pass through. A ramp was extruded from the area just below the hatch, and as it touched the ground the crawler began to move up it. As it did so Paula squeezed the trigger. Light blue pulses of energy leapt across the intervening space to smash into the crawler and the open cargo bay. Just as McCade had hoped, both the crawler and the ship had been forced to shut down their defensive screens long enough for the vehicle to embark. The unprotected crawler was quickly reduced to a pool of molten metal. Even though the ship's hull was made of sterner stuff, it too had begun to glow. The plan had worked. The pirate couldn't close the cargo hatch with the crawler in the way, so they couldn't lift ship.

McCade tapped Paula on the shoulder. She nodded and slipped out of her seat. Two steps later she dropped through the emergency escape hatch and disappeared. McCade hit the transmit switch, sending a prerecorded high-speed burst of code racing for Council Headquarters. Then he too dived for the escape hatch.

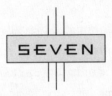

SEVEN

McCade and Paula were crouched under the crawler, huddled between massive treads, when the first missile hit. There was an ear-splitting roar and the ground shook convulsively as waves of intense heat rolled over them. But the crawler's tremendous bulk and defensive screens sheltered them from the worst of it. Paula bent over, clutching her head with both hands. McCade grabbed her arm, and they crawled toward the rear where a rectangle of daylight was visible between the huge tracks.

McCade waited for a moment, and then used a pause in the missile barrage to crawl out and run for the nearest pile of jumbled rock. He half-guided, half-dragged Paula behind him, leading her around the clumps of burning vegetation. Just as they dived into the shelter of the rocks, more missiles arrived, hitting the crawler and completely obliterating it. McCade gave thanks they weren't using nukes. However nukes would have destroyed their ship as well.

"Nice of ya to drop in," Rico said, rounding a large boulder. "But I'm gonna miss 'er," the big man said, gazing sadly at the burning remnants. "She was a good ol' girl. Plus ya wouldn't believe how many forms I'm gonna have ta fill out. The Council's real good at inventin' new forms." He grinned broadly.

Five shots rang out in quick succession. Rico nodded in the direction of the sound. "That'll be Chuck 'n' Sparks keepin' their heads down for us. Chuck's a real artist with a huntin' rifle. They won't be clearin' that wreckage for some time."

"You okay, Paula?" McCade asked. She looked a little better and smiled wanly as she struggled to her feet. McCade put out a hand to stop her, but Rico shook his head. Paula paused for a moment and then disappeared in the direction of the sporadic rifle fire.

"Paula's married to Chuck," Rico said in explanation as he settled himself on a flat piece of rock.

McCade nodded as he accepted one of the other man's expensive cigars. "How soon can we expect some help, Rico?"

The big man examined the chronometer strapped to a hairy wrist. "Well assumin' ya triggered that call for help on your way out . . ." He looked questioningly in McCade's direction and receiving a nod, continued. "Then we oughta have air cover any time now. . . and maybe ground support a half hour later."

McCade savored the cigar smoke as he blew it out into the cold, crisp air. Even in the shelter provided by the rocks the cold wind found them and seeped through McCade's parka to chill his skin.

"No offense, Rico," McCade said, "but this world is no paradise. What are the pirates after anyway?"

Rico shrugged his large shoulders. "Beats me, Sam ol' friend. Course we've always had a coupla raids a year. After refined metals mostly. But lately they've been hittin' us a couple times a week. Now suddenly it's one a day." He shook his head in amazement. "Funny part is they don't seem to be after the usual stuff. Course they take it if they find it . . . but it's like they're lookin' for somethun else."

"How long has this been going on?" McCade asked.

"Last coupla months maybe," Rico answered around his cigar.

McCade considered the other man's answer. The more he thought about it, the more he doubted it was coincidence. The pirate attacks had increased about the same time Bridger had gone over the hill.

Suddenly there was excited shouting from Paula and Chuck, followed by a roar and a sonic boom. Both men leaped to their feet and ran toward the valley wall. A breathless Paula intercepted them.

"They launched a boat from the far side of the ship!"

McCade swore to himself as Rico cursed out loud in a dozen tongues. Of course. A ship that size carried at least two lifeboats in case of emergencies or for use as shuttles. One on the port side and one to starboard. They'd picked the one on the far side to avoid detection by Chuck, Paula and Sparks. Launching a boat from a grounded ship called for consummate skill, lots of guts, and a large measure of desperation, but they'd done it. Damn! He should have thought of it. Now he'd lost his chance to ask the pirates a few questions.

There was a rolling thunder of sound as a flight of three atmospheric fighters swept over to circle the valley. "That's the flyboys. . . . Day late 'n' a credit short like always," Rico said, shading his eyes against the glare as he looked up at the specks circling overhead. "Well there's still a chance. By now Larkin's got a couple ships on patrol just outside the atmosphere."

Not much later a large freight copter arrived and disgorged some troops. McCade noticed there wasn't a uniform among them, but they were obviously well trained and disciplined. Colonel Larkin's influence no doubt. From their smoke-stained clothes and bandages he could see they had already been in action.

Before long Rico's crew was aboard the giant aircraft and on their way back to Council Headquarters. McCade sat slumped in thought, gazing at the frozen terrain passing below without really seeing it. At some point during the flight he fell asleep. When he awoke the copter was touching down.

Rico had to shout to be heard over the sound of the engines. "Looks like the battle's over, sport. The pilot says the all-clear was sounded about ten minutes ago. There was one other ship besides the one we got. It lifted 'n' got clean away. Guess it's time ta pick up the pieces again."

McCade was hungry. Rico directed him toward the cafeteria. It was packed with a swirling mob of people. Many had taken part in the fighting and wore bandages to prove it. Nevertheless they engaged in a lot of good-natured kidding. With a shouted greeting, Van Doren's grinning face suddenly separated itself from the crowd. After wading through the line, they shared a table together.

With considerable prodding McCade learned that the marine was now something of a local hero. It seemed that while most of the Council's forces were drawn off into a series of small skirmishes, the pirates launched a surprise attack against the admin complex. The Council had relied mainly on the complex's camouflage to protect it. As a result the pirates had cut their way through the mostly unarmed clerical staff with ease. Until they ran into Van Doren, that is. Aware that a battle was raging somewhere, but unable to find either it or McCade, the marine was searching for the action when it found him. After launching a one-man counterattack, he managed to rally enough clerks and security guards to hold the main corridor until help arrived. As a result the pirates failed to penetrate the core of the complex.

Van Doren made it sound like a stroll through the park. But the awed looks and frequent congratulations of the other diners testified to the marine's accomplishment. In fact, McCade mused a few hours later as he sat waiting in an empty conference room, if it hadn't been for Van Doren, they wouldn't have had anyone to interrogate. He'd managed to take the day's only prisoner.

Larkin's planetary defense forces had vaporized the lifeboat as it left the atmosphere, although the second ship had escaped. So Rico's disdain for the "flyboys" had not been entirely deserved. Meanwhile the other pirates who'd survived had escaped into the wilds. If you could call that "escape." In any case, McCade felt frustrated. He seemed to be getting nowhere fast. In order to find Bridger, he'd have to get off-planet. He had a plan for that. But once in space, what then?

McCade turned to his right as a door there slid open. One by one the Council filed in. Wendel and Larkin nodded politely in his direction. McCade noticed Larkin's uniform was ripped and soiled. His right arm was in a sling. Evidently the ex-marine believed in leading his troops instead of following them as so many Imperial officers liked to do. Rico tossed him a jaunty salute as he entered, in contrast to Premo's look of barely disguised hatred. When Sara Bridger entered the room, she appeared even more exhausted than before. To McCade's surprise, she favored him with a formal smile as the room lights dimmed.

A bank of screens came to life in front of them. Each provided a different view of a bare, cell-like room dominated by a tubular hospital bed. On its gleaming surface a naked man lay spread-eagled, his powerful arms and legs restrained by leather straps. They'd shaved his head and body hair. McCade noticed the bony ridge bisecting the man's skull from front to back. It hinted at Tillarian blood. The Tillarians were a proud, some said egotistical, race who banned all those of mixed blood from the home system. Which probably accounted for this man's presence among the pirates.

Wires and tubes ran in and out of his body like multicolored parasites feeding off a corpse. It certainly beat torture, but McCade still felt sorry for the man. An efficient-looking female technician stood nearby, monitoring a bank of complicated controls. When she spoke McCade noticed that her speech had a husky, rhythmic, almost hypnotic quality. She asked a series of simple, nonthreatening questions. Name, date of birth, and so on. But the pirate met each question with a nonsensical string of words and numbers. Apparently he'd been memblocked. The question was how deep? Superficial blocks could be broken by an expert. Deeper ones could be broken too—but the process was usually fatal.

With consummate skill the technician probed, searching gently for a way around the block. She chose her questions with care, occasionally pausing to make minute adjustments to the flow of chemicals and drugs into the pirate's body. It took more than two hours before she found a way around the block and began to receive coherent answers. By that time she'd convinced the pirate that his mission was over, and he was being debriefed by his commanding officer.

McCade added another cigar butt to the growing collection at his feet as the man related a good deal of boring detail which preceded the attack on Alice. Finally the pirate's narrative reached the part McCade had been waiting for.

"The assault began according to the plan outlined by our shop steward. Using diversionary skirmishes for cover, my foreman led us into the administrative complex. Initially we encountered light resistance. Then in corridor five, we ran into trouble. Suddenly we ran into an organized defense and accurate sniper fire. Evidently the dirties were able to rush elite security forces into the area."

McCade smiled at this description of Van Doren and his file clerks.

"So after suffering heavy casualties, we were forced to withdraw," the pirate concluded.

"And you did the right thing," the technician said soothingly. "Now, what were the objectives of your mission?"

For a moment McCade thought the pirate would balk. The question wouldn't normally be asked during a debriefing, and for a moment the man's face registered doubt. Then the technician lightly touched her controls and the pirate's features gradually relaxed.

"Our first objective," he said in a singsong voice, "was to capture Council member Bridger."

McCade looked at Sara, but her expression was lost in the dark. Premo leaned over to whisper something in her ear, to which she nodded.

"Objective two was to capture or kill any other Council members present. Objective three was to retrieve any intelligence that might be available. Objective four was to damage and destroy as much of the administration complex as possible."

The pirate's words confirmed McCade's suspicions. The recent increase in pirate attacks was somehow connected to Bridger's disappearance. Why else would they place such importance on capturing his daughter? His mind raced as the interrogation continued. By the time it was over the technician would have skillfully extracted information on everything from the quality of pirate rations to the strength of their fleet. It was interesting stuff, but more than McCade needed to know.

The Council obviously felt the same way. The room lights came up and the Council members began to talk excitedly among themselves. The bank of screens faded to black and disappeared into the wall. Then the Council swiveled their chairs around to face McCade. Sara Bridger spoke first.

"McCade, I'm sorry about the way I acted the last time we met. I'm afraid I was tired and more than a little upset." Her hand strayed to the thin white line across her cheek. "You see, the news about my father came as quite a shock. In any case your bravery and that of your friend is strong testimony on a planet where deeds still speak louder than words." With that she frowned and paused before going on. "Which isn't to say I approve of either your profession or your methods," she added sternly.

"Understood," McCade replied levelly, catching a glimpse of her capacities as a politician. He admired the way in which she had apologized and then neatly regained the upper hand.

"Now," she said evenly, "perhaps we could pick up where we left off. The Council hopes that whatever you can tell us, combined with what we just heard, may shed some light on our present situation."

McCade had already considered the alternatives and decided in favor of complete honesty. Quickly and concisely he outlined the events leading up to his arrival on Alice. He left nothing important out, briefly touching on the Battle of Hell, his subsequent court martial, and how this had led Swanson-Pierce to try and use him. McCade saw Sara Bridger's already pale face grow even whiter at his mention of the Battle of Hell. Premo was furious. He started to rise, but her hand reached out to restrain him. With obvious reluctance, he fell back into his seat.

"Go on, McCade," she said, forcing a smile.

So he did, explaining how Bridger had evidently managed to decode his Directory, which in turn had apparently provided him with the location of the War World. McCade thought he detected a flash of pride in Sara Bridger's eyes at the mention of her father's accomplishment. But it was quickly gone in the buzz of conversation that followed as the Council members speculated about the War World and its potential impact on the citizens of Alice.

After a few moments of this, Sara asked for their attention. "Quiet, please. I'm sure we all agree that this War World is cause for concern. But let's hear the rest of Mr. McCade's comments." She nodded in his direction.

She was calm and attentive during the balance of his narrative, even laughing when he described his meeting with Rico. By the time he was finished, he'd glossed over her father's relationship with the Treel in its guise as Cadet Votava, but in all other respects he'd been entirely honest.

The room fell silent for a moment. Then Colonel Larkin said, "So the Empire allows the pirates to exist as the price for peace. A price to be paid by us. I'd suspected as much but never had the guts to face it." He shook his head sadly, remembering all the good men who had died fighting token battles with the pirates.

"Not for much longer, it would seem," Professor Wendel interjected. "If the pirates pry the location of the War World out of your father, Sara, we won't be around very long thereafter."

"Not that we're gonna be that much better off if the Il Ronn or the Empire gets to him first," Rico added with a characteristic grin.

"*If* McCade's telling the truth," Premo concluded sourly.

Almost imperceptibly everyone turned toward Sara Bridger. Her eyes burned brightly in the whiteness of her face. Her hands were clenched talons in her lap. "It must be stopped," she said, her voice almost a whisper. Her face was haunted and desperate as she turned to McCade. "We must find him and stop this before they can use him. Even if it means killing him."

"No!" Premo spoke with such violence that spittle flew from his lips as he leaped to his feet. "I won't have it! He's lying! Can't you see that, Sara? He's trying to get you off Alice for some plan of his own. . . ." Suddenly one clawlike hand dived for the gun at his side.

As if by magic McCade's slug gun seemed to materialize in his hand. But before he could squeeze the trigger there was a loud cracking sound and Premo crumpled to the floor, his weapon falling from nerveless fingers. For a moment longer, life lingered in his eyes as he looked reproachfully up at Sara Bridger. Tears streamed down her cheeks and a wisp of smoke curled from the barrel of the small wrist gun in her hand. Then Premo was gone. Her eyes were still on his body when she said, "Tell the Council what we'll need, McCade . . . and they'll give it to you. Now if you'll all excuse me . . ." With a strangled sob she ran from the room.

McCade felt confused as he watched her go, wishing he could comfort her, but afraid to try. He took a step forward, but stopped when he realized that to follow her he'd have to step over Premo's body. He looked up to find all their eyes directed his way.

"Well, ol' sport," Rico said, "like the lady said, what'll ya need?"

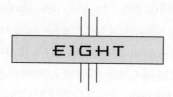

EIGHT

Five rotations later he was free of Alice but still trapped by a lack of information. Nonetheless they'd settled on a plan of action that might lead them to Bridger. It might also get them killed. His seat vibrated for a moment as the drive cut out for a fraction of a second before cutting back in. The pirate ship had seen hard use without much maintenance. It had taken the better part of four rotations to repair damage to the cargo hatch, remove the charred remains of the pirate crawler, and bury the pirates who'd been left behind when the crammed lifeboat had lifted off. They'd chosen to fight it out with Larkin's troops rather than surrender. McCade suspected they would have found little mercy in the hands of the hard-eyed colonists anyway.

To make matters more complicated, there wasn't any way to tell when the ship had last been surveyed. That information, along with the ship's log, inventory, crew list, and anything else stored in the memory of the vessel's computer had been bulk-erased by the escaping crew. They'd left a tidy little bomb behind as a token of their esteem as well. Fortunately Larkin's forces had found and disarmed it. Anyway it all added up to a lift-off in a ship held together by habit and prayer. There just wasn't enough time to do anything more.

McCade rubbed his eyes. They felt tired and dry. His body demanded sleep, but his mind wanted one more look. Once more he ducked under the hood of the lounge's small holo player and tried to focus on the planet that swam before his tired eyes. Its dull surface reflected little light. It looked like a lifeless hulk, a dark place, a purposeless rock on an endless path through space.

But McCade knew from the sketchy information gleaned from the central data banks on Alice that it hadn't always been so. When discovered by a far-ranging survey ship, clear back in Confederation times, there had been life on the planet. It hadn't been particularly attractive life, but it was life nonetheless. Dense jungle had wrapped most of the planet in a steamy embrace. Giant mountains had thrust their lofty peaks to the edge of space itself, and everywhere streams and rivers had fed lakes and seas filled with life-bearing primordial soup. A planet not unlike Terra in its early stages. But all that was gone now. Replaced by millions of square miles of featureless black rock. Confederation engineers had scoured the planet's surface clean with hell bombs. In spite of their efforts tiny microscopic organisms would doubtless start the long climb once again, but it would be thousands of years before their efforts became visible.

McCade turned the magnification up to max. The planet's surface leaped up to reveal more detail. Right on the border between day and night, slightly north of the equator, a fortress could be seen. It was huge, covering more than a hundred square miles. Originally it had been constructed as a forward base from which the Confederation could defend itself against an Il Ronn invasion. It was as close to impregnable as man could make it. Energy for their weapons flowed from the planet's core. The surface was sterilized to deny invaders even the questionable hospitality of the jungle. In fact anything which might have conceivably served an enemy was gone. Mountains, rivers, seas, vegetation—everything.

The years passed and the Il Ronn never came. Instead the Confederacy destroyed itself and the Empire was born. And then the fortress *was* put to use. Staffed with Imperial marines, it made a good prison for those who refused to accept the Empire.

Thousands of prisoners disappeared into the sprawling complex. They rechristened the planet "The Rock" after a famous prison on old Earth. There the prisoners waited to die. They had little other choice. Like its ancient predecessor, the Rock offered little chance of escape. No one could survive long on the planet's sterile surface, and nothing larger than a supply shuttle was ever allowed to touch down.

As for taking over the complex itself, why bother? Rings of orbiting weapons platforms circled the globe and covered the surface of its four moons. Originally part of the planet's defenses, it had been a simple matter to aim them at the Rock itself instead of space. However, doing so had turned out to be a mistake. One which few of the marines manning the weapons lived to regret.

At first the attack seemed like one last glorious but suicidal gesture on the part of a ragtag rebel fleet. Badly mauled by Admiral Keaton in the Battle of Hell, they'd split up hiding among the frontier worlds, eventually coming back together at prearranged times and places. They knew the war was lost, and that knowledge drove them to one last desperate act, an attempt to free their imprisoned comrades. But much to their own surprise the rebel fleet met with an easy victory. The Imperial marines fought valiantly, but they weren't prepared for an attack from space, and they were grossly outnumbered. Within hours a half-million cheering prisoners stood on the barren black plains surrounding the prison.

It didn't take their leaders long to realize there was no place to go. They had insufficient ships to lift all the prisoners off the Rock, in any case they lacked a destination. Elements of Keaton's fleet waited should they head toward the Empire, and in the other direction lay the Il Ronn, whose raiders were already making themselves felt. So once again the Rock's weapons were turned around and aimed toward space. What had been their prison became their home.

But they couldn't sit back and relax. The supplies on hand wouldn't last forever. The planet's surface wouldn't grow crops for a thousand years, even with terraforming . . . and without plant life even the atmosphere required maintenance. So food and supplies would have to come from somewhere else.

What remained of the rebel fleet began to raid commerce along the frontier to obtain food and supplies. Those they raided called them "pirates." Disliking the term "pirates," they called themselves "The Brotherhood," although in truth the Brotherhood was more like an executive council made up of representatives from occupational organizations.

Then one day the Il Ronn attacked with unimaginable savagery. For two rotations the battle raged. The Il Ronn unleashed missiles and bombs of incredible power. But the Rock's former inmates defended their home with courage and determination until finally the Il Ronn learned what Admiral Keaton had known all along. Without a civilian population to worry about, without industry to defend, a well-fortified planet can be held against any fleet. What was left of the Il Ronn armada limped off to lick its wounds.

Meanwhile one of the many small scout ships which Keaton referred to as his "eyes and ears," raced for fleet headquarters with its report of the Il Ronn defeat. Not long thereafter Admiral Keaton was shown into the Emperor's garden. The aging but still vigorous emperor lounged in the comfort of his stim bath. The two men talked for many hours. Keaton argued persuasively in favor of using the pirates as a first line of defense against the Il Ronn. The older man resisted at first, asking questions and pointing out potential consequences. But in the end the Emperor nodded his leonine head and it was agreed. It was one of his last major decisions. A few months later he was dead, and his son had assumed the throne.

McCade pulled his head out from under the privacy hood and fumbled for a cigar. Finding one, he lit it and leaned back to watch smoke swirl up toward the nearest intake vent. Getting on to the Rock, finding Bridger if he was there, and getting off alive wasn't going to be easy. Nevertheless it had to be done. Where else would Laurie have taken Bridger?

It didn't show up on the dated holo he'd been looking at but, according to the pirate prisoner, the Rock was even stronger now than it had been before. Since taking over, the pirates had expanded and improved the original structure, adding not only more comfortable quarters and recreational facilities, but more defenses as well. Chief among those were unmanned computer-controlled weapons platforms located about one light out from the Rock in every direction. Every pirate ship had an individual code printed into the atomic structure of its frame. As ships approached the weapons platforms, the code was automatically checked. If correct, the ship was allowed to pass. If not it was immediately blasted out of existence.

That's why McCade had chosen to use the pirate ship in spite of its questionable condition. Hopefully the code printed somewhere in its frame was still operational. If so they would pass the weapons platforms unmolested. If not they would die a quick death.

Wearily, he stood and made his way out of the small lounge, through the narrow corridor, and up to the control room. To his surprise Sara Bridger sat slumped in front of the huge command screen. On it, nearby stars and systems followed their stately paths as they had for billions of years. It was the first time she had left the privacy of her cabin since they'd lifted off Alice.

"It's beautiful, isn't it?" she said without looking around.

"Yes, it is," McCade answered, dropping into the seat next to her.

She swiveled around to face him, a tentative smile touching her lips. "Hello, Sam."

McCade felt something tighten in his chest when she said his name. Coming from her it seemed special somehow. A peace offering and an intimacy rolled into one. "Hello yourself," McCade replied with a smile. "How're you feeling?"

"Much better, thanks. I think it was the sleep I needed most. It seems like weeks since I've slept eight hours in a row. When the pirates weren't actually attacking, we were repairing the damage they'd done on the last raid and getting ready for the next one."

McCade nodded sympathetically. "Strangely enough, it seems you're what they were after." As quickly as the words left his mouth he regretted them. The light in her eyes dimmed as she turned back to the screen.

"Yes," she said. "Now that I know about the War World, it's obvious the pirates hoped to capture me for use as a hostage against Father's cooperation." She sighed. "I wonder how they knew I was alive and living on Alice."

"I imagine you have at least one pirate spy on Alice, if not more," McCade answered. "Nothing else makes much sense."

"Yes," she replied. "I imagine you're right."

She stared at the screen in silence and McCade couldn't think of anything to say. So they sat together in what eventually became a companionable silence. When she finally spoke, her voice had a hollow quality, as if coming from far away.

"Sam, tell me about the Battle of Hell."

"There really isn't much to tell."

"You told the Council that my father court-martialed you. . . . Why? I . . . I'd like to know, for personal reasons."

McCade was silent for a moment as the memories came flooding back across ten long years. With them came the hate and resentment that he had fought to control, but never quite conquered. Then he said, "Your father had me court-martialed for disobeying a direct order."

She turned her chair back toward him, her eyes locking with his as she said, "I think I know what that order was . . . but I'd appreciate your telling me."

So he did. Again he saw the pirate ship in the cross hairs of his sight as his thumb rested lightly on the firing stud. Again he heard the woman's pleading voice as she said, "Please, in the name of whatever gods you worship, I implore you, don't fire! My ship is unarmed. I have only women, children and old men aboard. . . . Please listen to me!"

Then the second voice, hoarse and commanding: "Fire, Lieutenant! That's an order! She's lying. Fire, damn you!"

Again he felt his thumb lift off the firing stud and watched as the pirate ship slid out of sight along his starboard side. Then the flare of the explosion in his rear screen as the pirate vessel was hit by one of the Imperial's main batteries at extreme range. Then the enemy ship was gone as its desperate captain took it into an uncalculated hyperspace jump.

For a moment Sara was silent. Then she said, "It happened exactly as you described it." Seeing his look of surprise, she said, "That's right. . . . My mother and I were aboard that pirate ship. We'd been put aboard shortly after they took the *Mars*. In fact I got this"—Her hand fluttered up to touch the scar—"fighting them at the main entry port along with the crew. And in a way I suppose it saved me from a 'fate worse than death.'" She smiled wryly. "They decided that even with surgery I'd never be pretty enough for the slave market. So they put me aboard a ship loaded with wealthy hostages. I guess they hoped to eventually ransom us, or if things went badly, use us as bargaining chips.

"Anyway, when our ship was caught by the *Imperial,* our captain piped the radio transmissions over the intercom. I think she knew what was coming and didn't want us to blame her. I'll never forget the look on my mother's face as she heard my father's voice commanding you to fire."

Tears ran down her cheeks.

"He wasn't a bad man," McCade said quietly. "He just couldn't deal with losing both of you. It drove him a little crazy."

"Thank you for that," she replied with a grateful smile. "Coming from you it means a lot. And you're right, he wasn't a bad man when I knew him. But whatever the reasons, he's become one. What he did during the Battle of Hell was wrong. And so was what he did to you afterward. And then to aid the Il Ronn against humans—worse than that, to give them the War World—there's no excuse for that." She paused. Though tears ran freely down her cheeks, her voice was calm and cold. "So if we find him, and I can't do it myself, promise me you'll kill him. It would be the greatest favor you could do for the man he once was."

McCade started to speak, but she shook her head. "Promise me," she insisted.

Reluctantly McCade nodded his agreement. There was no point in telling her that he would have done so in any case, assuming of course that Bridger wouldn't come with them.

She was silent for a moment, her eyes searching his as though looking for something important. "As you said, we escaped by taking a jump into hyperspace and then back out."

McCade put up a hand to stop her, but she shook her head and continued to speak.

"The ship was badly damaged. One of the two life rafts was destroyed. Those who could crowded into the remaining raft. Some of the wounded volunteered to stay behind. The captain insisted on staying with them." She shook her head in amazement. "It was funny really. That pirate captain would have cheerfully transported us all into slavery. But she wouldn't leave any of us on a crippled ship, Shortly after we got away, the ship blew up. We ran out of food rather quickly. There were so many of us packed into the little raft. At first we thought ourselves lucky to have plenty of air and water. Most people can last for quite a while without food. Then we learned the truth. For most of us, air and water would only prolong the suffering. We were way outside normal shipping lanes and the chances of being found were almost nil."

"The babies died first. And then the elderly. I think mother died inside as she listened to Father scream his insane orders. With her spirit gone, her body followed soon after. One by one I struggled to get their bodies into the raft's tiny lock . . . and into space . . . until eventually there were only three of us, a girl of about twelve and an old man. We tried to cheer each other up, we sang songs, and the old man told us about his life as a prospector. But eventually we ran out of things to say and retreated within ourselves. Privately I cursed the strength that kept me alive. Finally I felt myself sinking into welcomed darkness with a feeling of joyous release, certain my turn had finally come. But it wasn't to be. Instead I awoke, looking into Premo's face. He was a passenger aboard the ship that heard the raft's emergency beacon and picked us up.

"She was a tramp freighter. It seemed as though we stopped at every other asteroid to drop off supplies for some miner or lonely scientist. So Premo and I had lots of time to talk. He actually did most of the talking, while I listened. It was good actually. . . . I needed time to think.

"Like many of those who end up on frontier planets, Premo was a misfit . . . and on the run from something. I never asked what, and he never said. But he was brilliant in his own way . . . very knowledgeable about business and finance. As you saw, he was also a jealous and sometimes stupid man . . . in love with me in spite of this"—she indicated her face— "even though he knew I didn't feel the same way.

"But underneath all that, Premo was a dreamer, a man who saw the frontier worlds as an opportunity to start over, and avoid the mistakes of the past. He told me about Alice. About how it had just been opened and how beautiful it would be. What could be accomplished there and why it was important. Well, I must have listened, because when we arrived I got off and never looked back."

"You never thought about going home?" McCade asked.

"Oh at first I did. But every time I thought about it, I imagined coming face to face with my father. What would I say? Tell him he'd murdered my mother along with hundreds of other people? No. It seemed pointless. Eventually I came to think of him as dead. And it worked—until you came along." She sighed. "You saved my life that day, Sam, and I'll always admire you for what you did, but maybe it would have been better if you'd followed my father's orders. If you had, I wouldn't have Premo's blood on my hands." She held her hands up and turned them over as if actually seeing blood on them. She stood and then shuddered before half walking and half running from the room.

McCade also stood, intending to follow, to tell her how glad he was that he'd saved her life, but stopped as the intercom buzzed.

"Weapons platform comin' up, boss. . . . We oughta know if we're gonna pass inspection any minute now." Van Doren's voice was cheerful. McCade wondered if the big marine was really unaffected by the possibility of death, or just couldn't imagine that it could happen to him.

"I'll be right there," McCade said over his shoulder as he stepped out of the control room and slid down the ladder to the level below.

Van Doren sat before the computer's master keyboard. As McCade approached, the marine touched a sequence of keys with surprisingly nimble fingers and then sat back to watch the screen.

"Any moment now we'll get the incoming pulse. It should register clear as a bell on our sensors. If the code's still working the pulse will read it. If not it's taps. . . ."

"Thanks, Amos. It's always nice to know I can count on you for a cheerful word in times of crisis."

Van Doren grinned in response, his eyes peering at the screen from beneath bushy brows. The seconds ticked away with maddening slowness. There was a noise behind him and McCade turned to see Sara enter. "I thought I should be here for the big moment," she said with a wan smile. Somehow it seemed natural to put his arm around her.

When the pulse came a moment later it seemed anticlimactic.

"Brotherhood Vessel 4690 *Zebra* cleared for planetfall" flashed on the screen and then faded away.

McCade let his breath out slowly, only then realizing he'd been holding it in. The arm he'd put around Sara suddenly felt awkward and out of place. He allowed it to fall and moved to Van Doren's side as he said, "Let's see if Rico's still with us."

Van Doren punched a couple of keys and a screen came to life above him. It was adjusted to maximum magnification. At its farthest edge a green light blinked on and off. Rico was still there, shadowing them in the *Lady Alice.* Before long he'd have to stop and lie doggo. Otherwise the weapons platforms would blast him. If challenged he would claim a mechanical failure which would soon be repaired. The neglected appearance of his ship would support his story. Rico would wait for six rotations. If they hadn't made it off the Rock by then, he'd rejoin the Council and together they'd figure out what to do next. The unspoken understanding was that McCade, Sara, and Van Doren would be presumed dead.

"All right," McCade said, "it's time for phase two. Activate all the screens, Amos, and crank the sensors up to max. We'll see who else is in the neighborhood."

The marine pressed a series of keys. One by one the entire bank of screens in front of him came to life. Now they could see all the ships in their vicinity out to the range of their detectors.

There was a lot of activity. Which would be good for Rico, McCade mused. Hopefully he'd be able to lose himself in all the comings and goings. Screen by screen McCade eyed the possibilities. Pirate ships of all shapes and sizes swarmed around the planet like bees around a hive. Their radio traffic poured from the speaker over McCade's head. For the most part it was open and unscrambled, with only occasional bursts of code—an indication of how secure they feel, McCade thought. From the snatches of conversation, he began to build an interesting montage of activity.

Some of the ships were damaged from distant encounters with the Il Ronn. Others had been victorious and were making planetfall loaded with loot. Then there were the outward bound ships, hungry and on the prowl. Those they wanted to avoid at all costs. There were other ships too. Possessors of special one-time passes which enabled them to pass the weapons platforms untouched, but which had to be reactivated in order for them to leave. They were the smugglers, for the most part. Traders in stolen and illicit goods. Disliked by everyone, even the pirates, but used by all. They made their dark living buying loot the pirates didn't need or want, and then selling it on frontier worlds at below market prices, sometimes to those from whom it had been stolen to begin with.

And McCade knew that among the merchandise they bought and sold were sentient beings. Thinking and feeling creatures like Sara and her mother, snatched from merchant vessels or native planets to live out short lives on some jungle plantation or deep in a mine. But those were the lucky ones. There were special customers for beautiful young women. Customers with desires so dark and twisted no sane woman would willingly comply with them. McCade shivered involuntarily, forcing his mind back to the ships which filled the screens.

It took money to buy the kind of ships the smugglers needed. McCade knew that all too often it was supplied by the so-called legitimate merchants on planets like Weller's World. All without interference from the Imperial Navy. Just another payment on the price of peace. In any case, McCade thought grimly, very soon one of the smugglers would be out of business. They'd known from the start it would be suicide to try and land the pirate ship. By now it was overdue and probably listed as missing in action. If it suddenly showed up, there'd be pirates swarming all over it in seconds. No, it would be much better to arrive in the guise of smugglers.

"Let's pick a small one," Sara said, scanning the screen.

"That's for sure!" McCade replied fervently. Even with the element of surprise operating in their favor, they'd be hard-pressed to take on a crew of five or six.

"How 'bout this one, boss?" Van Doren indicated his choice with an electronic arrow.

"Looks like a small freighter," Sara said approvingly.

"Okay. Let's take a look," McCade said as he headed for the control room. As he dropped into the pilot's position he saw the two ready lights for the port and starboard weapons blisters pop on one after the other. Van Doren and Sara were in their places.

Gingerly he took control of the ship away from the computer. He'd had very little time with her controls and didn't know all her quirks yet. He locked onto the blinking light still marked with an arrow and sent the ship toward it in a long graceful curve. Carefully he examined nearby traffic, looking for anything suspicious. But as far as he could tell, nobody was interested in their activities. As they closed with their target, it became apparent that the two ships would meet in a relatively empty area. That suited McCade just fine.

"This one looks like a keeper," McCade said into the intercom. "I'm about to say hello, so stand by. . . ."

With that he opened the standard ship to ship channel, audio only, and hailed the other vessel. "This is Brotherhood Patrol Ship 4690 *Zebra*. Heave to and prepare to be boarded."

The reply lit up the com screen to his right. The freighter's captain sent both sound and pix. His face was narrow and his skin bore an unhealthy pallor. A forced smile revealed rows of uneven yellow teeth through which his voice issued forth as a servile whine. A tiny gold disc hung at his throat. "Of course, of course. Always happy to oblige the Brotherhood. Is Your Excellency looking for anything in particular? I have an excellent bottle of Terran whiskey aboard," he added slyly.

"Just a routine inspection," McCade replied with what he hoped was the right mixture of boredom and authority. "Can't be too careful you know. Come to think of it, I am a bit parched. . . . I'll be over shortly."

The weasellike face nodded knowingly. "It'll be a pleasure to serve Your Excellency." With that the com screen faded to black.

McCade wiped the light sheen of perspiration from his forehead and heaved a sigh of relief. It had worked. The two ships were now in visual contact. The freighter was half the size of the pirate vessel. To McCade's surprise it was relatively new and appeared to be well maintained. A measure of the profits to be made, McCade thought sourly. "Contact in about two minutes," McCade said into the intercom. "Stand by."

When the ships were a few hundred feet apart, McCade triggered the tractor beams, which locked the two vessels together. Through a series of gentle adjustments, he brought the two ships together with an almost imperceptible bump. They were touching lock to lock.

McCade ran through a mental check list as he stood and glanced around the control room. Everything seemed in order. He touched the key placing all major systems on stand-by, and headed for the lock where Sara and Van Doren were waiting. They had already pressurized the space between the two locks. McCade checked his slug gun, and the stunner hidden up his right sleeve in a spring-loaded holster. The other two smiled their readiness. McCade nodded and activated the inner hatch. With a sigh the lock cycled open, and as they stepped through he felt the familiar tug from the muscle in his left cheek.

As they entered the other ship, they were greeted by a Finthian Bird Man. He seemed to be molting. Large patches of his golden feathers were missing, revealing sections of greenish skin. His saucerlike eyes regarded them gravely.

"Welcome aboard the *Far Trader*, gentlepersons." His beaklike nose rose and fell as he spoke, his voice emanating from the translator at his throat. "Captain Fagan will receive you in the lounge if you'll step this way?"

Together they followed him through a maze of corridors and up a ladder to the next deck. Along the way they kept a sharp lookout for other crew members. They saw only one. A fragile-looking woman with gray wispy hair busily tending a hydroponics tank. As they passed Sara shot her in the back with a stun gun. The woman hardly made a sound as she crumpled to the deck. Sara never even broke stride. McCade shook his head in amazement as he followed the oblivious Finthian down another short passageway.

Moments later they entered the ship's lounge where they were greeted by the sallow Captain Fagan. Seated next to him was a three hundred pound sauroid whose smile, if that is what it was, revealed an enormous array of wicked-looking teeth.

"Welcome aboard our humble ship, Excellencies. This is my first officer, Mr. Slith. How may we serve you?"

"By keeping the amount of time we have to spend on this tub to a minimum," McCade replied arrogantly. "So let's get on with it. I'll need a print-out of your cargo manifest and a crew list. Oh yeah, and a fax of your log for the last seventy-two standard hours too."

"Immediately, Your Excellency," Captain Fagan sniveled as he punched McCade's requests into the keyboard at his side. Seconds later a printer began to whir as a sheet of plastic emerged from a slot.

Sara walked over and ripped off the sheet. She handed it to McCade with such a show of deference that he struggled not to laugh. With what he hoped was an arrogant sneer, McCade accepted the print-out and skimmed over it. Counting the captain, he saw that the *Far Trader* carried a crew of five. Sara had accounted for one on the way in, there were three present in the lounge, so there was another loose somewhere on the ship, a Cellite with the unlikely name of Sunshine.

McCade motioned to Amos and the big marine stepped to his side. "Check this out," he said, pointing to the Cellite's name on the crew list.

"Right away, boss," Amos said, and disappeared into the corridor.

Captain Fagan's features seemed to tighten. So you have something to hide, McCade thought. Not too surprising really.

"Is there a problem, Excellency? I assure you if there is, it was purely accidental. In all my years of trading with the Brotherhood I've never . . ."

"Stow it," McCade said. "It's just routine. Say, didn't you mention some Terran whiskey?"

"I did, Your Excellency," Fagan gurgled happily, reaching for the bottle at his elbow.

McCade flexed the muscles in his forearm and felt the spring-loaded holster deliver the small stunner into his hand. He brought it up and shot Fagan between the eyes. The little captain crashed to the deck, taking the bottle of whiskey and some glasses with him. McCade heard the thump of another body hitting the deck behind him and knew without looking that Sara had taken care of the Finthian Bird Man.

McCade swung left until the giant sauroid filled the sight. He pulled the trigger and waited for the alien to slump to the deck. Instead the giant creature stood with surprising ease and smiled, although on second thought McCade felt sure it wasn't a smile. He pulled the trigger again, as did Sara, who was also aiming her stunner at the scaled first officer.

"Uh-oh," McCade said. "I think he's got some kind of natural shielding against stunners."

"Brilliant," Sara said through gritted teeth, the knuckles of her right hand white where her fingers gripped the stun gun.

A strange electronic squawking sound came from the sauroid and for the first time McCade noticed the small box strapped to the alien's throat about where the human larynx is.

"Prepare to die, interloper!"

With that the huge creature produced a power knife and launched it-self straight at McCade.

NINE

McCade jumped back. As he did, Sara threw herself between him and the charging alien. The sauroid batted her aside without apparent effort. She crashed into a bulkhead and then fell to the deck. The huge creature kept on coming, but Sara had slowed it just enough to give McCade a chance. He drew the slug gun and fired twice. The heavy slugs hit Slith square in the chest and the impact rocked him backward. However, to McCade's astonishment, the alien recovered and charged again, roaring his rage through the translator—although it really didn't require translation.

The slugs hadn't penetrated the sauroid's armored skin, but they'd made him a bit more cautious. As he neared McCade, the *Far Trader*'s first officer slowed and began to circle. McCade was very conscious of the power knife which hummed in Slith's scaled hand. He knew it wasn't a knife in the conventional sense. Oh, it could cut all right! In fact its sealed energy beam could cut through durasteel as though it was warm butter. With amazing speed McCade's massive opponent lashed out. He heard the knife sizzle past his left ear as he desperately back-pedaled to get out of the way. McCade swore under his breath. He'd watched the alien's eyes, expecting them to telegraph the next move, and they hadn't. So he switched his attention to the knife, which wove back and forth in an almost hypnotic pattern.

McCade moved left, and then right, catching Slith off balance and placing Fagan's unconscious body between them. He felt the edge of the table pressing him from behind. He had nowhere to go. He had to get the knife. He knew that. He'd hunted fugitives of all races. They almost always armed themselves with weapons effective against their own kind. It was a natural tendency. McCade had done it himself in choosing the slug gun. So he had to get the knife.

Slith lunged toward him again. McCade was ready and leaped aside. The power knife made a buzzing sound as it sliced through the table top a fraction of a second later.

Then came the break McCade was waiting for. The sauroid put a huge foot on the whiskey bottle and it rolled out from under him. That plus his forward momentum brought him down. As the alien's right hand hit the floor McCade jumped on it with both feet. The knife popped free. Grabbing for it, McCade turned too late. He felt his feet go out from under him as his opponent hit them with the sweep of one powerful arm. As he hit the deck McCade saw that Slith had regained his feet and was already diving toward him. Instinctively he threw up his hands in a puny attempt to fend off the three hundred pounds of armored flesh falling toward him.

The knife was still clutched in his right hand. It sizzled as it slid smoothly into the Sauroid's chest. Then the alien's incredible weight hit him, forcing the air from his chest in one explosive breath. Blackness tried to drag him under. Desperately he tried to suck in air and push the dead weight off at the same time. Finally the scaled body rolled off. For a moment he just lay there, chest heaving as he gratefully sucked in air and waited for the darkness to clear from his sight. He staggered to his feet just as Van Doren burst through the hatch, slug gun in hand.

"Jeez, boss . . . you're always having fun while I'm gone."

"Yeah, well, the next lizard we run into is all yours, Amos."

Across the lounge, Sara stood and dusted herself off.

"You okay?" McCade asked.

"A little shaky," she answered slowly. "I'll bet I feel better than he does though." She indicated the dead alien.

"Thanks," McCade said. "What you did took a lot of guts."

She accepted the compliment without comment, but she looked pleased. "Now what?" she asked.

"Now we off-load the captain and his stalwart crew to the other ship," McCade said. "Amos, how'd it go with Sunshine?"

"Sleeping like a baby, boss."

"Okay, let's get to work."

It took the better part of an hour to get *Far Trader*'s crew through the lock and safely tucked into bunks aboard the other ship. It took all three of them, plus a power pallet from the cargo hold to move Slith. Without ceremony he went out an ejection port into eternal orbit around the Rock.

Then they were ready. McCade sent a coded radio command, and the pirate ship took off for Alice. Its manual controls were locked off and would remain so until the proper code was entered by Colonel Larkin on Alice. If the ship hung together long enough to get there.

As McCade nosed the *Far Trader* down toward the Rock, he blew cigar smoke at the com screen and waited for the inevitable challenge. He didn't have long to wait. The com screen swirled to life with the likeness of an attractive but bored-looking young woman.

"Vessel, registration number and code please."

McCade's blood ran cold. The first two questions were easy—but the third was a real lulu. Evidently Fagan had been provided with a verbal code as well as the one-time-only electronic pass recorded into the ship's hull. As he gave the ship's name and registration number, his mind raced. Would Fagan have provided the code or the pirates? If the pirates had he might as well forget it. There were billions of possibilities. But Fagan might have been asked to provide the code. And he seemed like a simple sort who'd go for something uncomplicated, something he couldn't forget. His eyes desperately ransacked the control room, searching for anything that might provide a clue. *Far Trader*'s control room was almost military in its spartan orderliness. There was no sign of the personal bric-a-brac common to most control rooms he'd seen. Then his eyes came to rest on the stylized likeness of Sol mounted high above the controls almost on the overhead.

Suddenly he remembered the tiny golden disc Fagan had worn around his neck. He was a member of the Solarian Church. Evidently a devout one.

The face on the screen no longer appeared bored. Now it was tense, with formerly soft lips pulled into a tight smile. "*Far Trader,* this is your final warning. State your code or be fired on."

"From Ra flows life," McCade said, intoning the traditional Solarian greeting. To his enormous relief, the tension drained from the woman's face, leaving only annoyance.

"Next time don't screw around so long," she said sternly. "Put it down on the light side outer ring of port twelve. Await an escort and ground transportation on grounding. Welcome to the Rock." With that the com screen snapped abruptly to black.

McCade forced his muscles to relax and reached up to wipe away the sweat that coated his forehead.

"I'll never know how you pulled that off," Sara said in amazement over the intercom.

"It was either dumb luck or Ra really is with us," McCade said, looking up at the golden disc.

Four standard hours later they sat on the ground awaiting the promised escort and transportation. Everything he'd seen in braking orbit and descent had reinforced the Rock's reputation for impregnability. They'd managed to get on the Rock, but as it was for so many others before them, the problem would be getting off again.

McCade used the time while they waited to look around. On one side black rock stretched away to the horizon. On the other, ships stood in orderly rows like a crop waiting to be harvested. As he swept the powerful lens over the forest of ships, McCade was amazed by the sheer scale of what he saw. There were all kinds: freighters, converted military ships, alien craft of all shapes and sizes, plus some small and very expensive-looking speedsters.

They were surrounded by bustling activity. Crawlers came and went, snaking between the ships with trains of loaded power pallets bobbing along behind. Cranes lifted mysterious crates in and out of dark holds. Vendors moved to and fro, hawking everything from food to spare parts. Aliens from a hundred worlds made a swirl of color against the drab rock as they hurried about on their various errands.

At regular intervals black towers stood, their broad bases forcing traffic to ebb and flow around them. At the top of each hundred-foot structure a bulbous turret bristled with antennas and weapons. Behind one-way armored glass, McCade imagined pirate sentries carefully monitoring the activity below.

He turned away from the scope and buzzed Van Doren on the intercom. "Amos, in our role as smugglers, it occurs to me we should know what we're smuggling. Take a look in the hold, and let me know what you find. I'll be surprised if it's the ten thousand eternafiber blankets mentioned on the cargo manifest."

"Right, boss... Back in a jiffy."

Turning back to the scope, McCade swept it over the spaceport again. This time he scanned the ships a mile or two away. Suddenly he swore out loud and jerked the scope back a bit. He wasn't mistaken. There she sat just as pretty as the day he'd first seen her. *Pegasus.* For a moment he just sat there, tracing her lines and running his eyes over her for signs of damage. There weren't any.

Thoughtfully, he turned away from the scope, rummaged through his pockets for a cigar butt, and then lit it with short angry puffs. So Laurie made it home. Therefore Bridger was here too. At least they were in the right place. Bridger had apparently been sick when they took him off Weller's World. Too sick to talk? Sick enough to die? There was no easy way to find out. So they'd do it the hard way.

Sara's head appeared in the control room hatch. "I think we've got company, Sam."

He nodded as a soft tone announced someone at the main entry port. A glance at the main security monitor revealed a man accompanied by an autoguard. The man was smiling and had the look of a prosperous, middle-aged business executive. His one-piece suit was expensive and beautifully cut.

By contrast, his companion was a masterpiece of forbidding intimidation. For psychological reasons its creators had granted it a vaguely human appearance. If something six and a half feet tall with a ball turret for a head and energy weapons for arms could be called human. By making it slightly larger than most men, and ugly to boot, the machine's designers had ensured that those who could be scared off, would be. But for those who were not so easily impressed, the autoguard possessed a more than adequate ability to defend itself. Capable of taking on and defeating a section of Imperial marines, such machines were incredibly expensive. However they were also impossible to bribe or blackmail, which accounted for their popularity among the Empire's rich and powerful.

Violence is definitely out, McCade thought as the entry port cycled open. As he stepped out, the visitor introduced himself.

"Joseph Sipila, Longshoreman's Union, at your service, gentlebeing," the pirate said, grinning broadly, "and welcome to the Rock." His handshake was warm and firm. McCade found himself liking the man against his own better judgment.

Glancing at his wrist term Sipila said, "Captain Fagan perhaps?"

Inwardly McCade heaved a sigh of relief. There had been the chance that Sipila and Fagan were old friends or something. McCade had a story ready just in case, but was glad he wouldn't have to use it.

McCade nodded eagerly, adopting something of Fagan's servile manner. "Yes, Excellency, my crew and I are at your disposal."

"Disposal? Fido here handles my disposals, don't you, Fido?" the other man said cheerfully. With that he laughed uproariously and slapped the autoguard on the back.

"Quite so, I'm sure," McCade said, forcing a chuckle of appreciation.

"Well, enough of that," Sipila said. "We can't stand here jawing all day long. . . . No profit in that, is there, Fagan? Goodness no. Now let's see what you've got for us. . . ."

"Here's the sample you asked for, boss," Van Doren said smoothly, appearing as if by magic at McCade's elbow and placing an electronic component of some sort in his hands. Wordlessly McCade handed it over to Sipila, who accepted it with obvious pleasure.

"A guidance module for the Dragon air to ground missile! Good work, Fagan. These are on the Brotherhood's priority list. Should bring a nice price in the market. Anything else? No? All right then, have your crew offload onto those power pallets over there, and a crawler will be along to tow 'em for you. You can ride to market in the crawler or call for a limo and an escort."

"I'm sure the crawler will be fine, Excellency," McCade whined. "There's no need to bother anyone else on our account."

"Fine then. I'll be off. Don't do anything I wouldn't do!" Grinning and slapping McCade's back, Sipila took his hulking companion and disappeared in the direction of another ship.

McCade felt the tension drain out of his muscles as he turned to the other two and in his best Faganlike manner said, "Well you heard him! Turn to! We haven't got all day." It was best to assume everything they said and did outside the ship was being monitored by the men high above in the black towers.

In spite of *Far Trader*'s automatic cargo-handling equipment, it took time and sweat to pull the six tons of electronic components out of her hold and load them aboard the waiting pallets. When they'd finished, all three went back aboard to freshen up and talk privately. McCade took a long, satisfying pull at the whiskey and soda in his hand, mentally toasting Slith as he did so. The whiskey was from the very same bottle the unfortunate first officer had tripped on.

"So what'll we do when we get the stuff to market?" Sara asked, taking a sip of the drink in her hand.

McCade shrugged. "Beats me. Play it by ear, I guess. But I can tell you this much, we came to the right place."

Briefly he told them about spotting *Pegasus*. Then all three were silent for a moment. Van Doren's expression was sour as he thought about Laurie's theft of *Pegasus* and his failure to prevent it. Sara took nervous little sips of her drink as she imagined coming face to face with her father. And McCade felt his cheek begin to twitch as he thought about the odds against ever getting off the planet.

So when the crawler arrived, all three were relieved to be doing something. As it moved smoothly into motion, McCade glanced out the rear window to see the power pallets bob and sway in their wake. Each floated easily on its cushion of air in spite of the load heaped on it. The driver was a taciturn man of vaguely oriental descent. His most eloquent phrases were grunts of various tonalities. The identaplaque above his head identified him as one Marvin Wong, a teamster in good standing.

The view that flowed by was fascinating. The Rock wasn't all weapons and grim fortifications. Pleasant-looking housing complexes came and went in a series of domes, along with elaborate recreational facilities. Here and there scrubby-looking trees struggled to survive in the imported soil. Children played around them as adults looked on approvingly, smiling and talking among themselves. On the surface it made a cheerful and innocent scene, but somehow McCade found it disturbing. None of it had been earned. It had been taken. Taken from planets like Alice and people like Sara. While these children laughed and played, others on Alice cried over shallow graves carved out of the permafrost with hand blasters. He looked over at Sara, but her eyes remained locked on the back of the driver's head.

Before long the crawler entered a huge dome. It was by far the largest structure McCade had ever seen. Larger than even the Imperial Coliseum, which covered what had once been the city of Detroit. There was an open space at its center dominated by a graceful column soaring hundreds of feet into the air. McCade sensed what whoever occupied the top of that column dominated the activity within the entire structure. Around the perimeter of the dome, broad terraces gently climbed toward the roof. The uppermost levels were sufficiently high that people could be seen flitting between them in air scooters.

Moments later, with a grunt of farewell, the driver discharged them in front of a lift tube. He handed McCade a rectangle of highly polished metal, and then without further ado, engaged the crawler's drive and headed toward a tunnel leading underground.

As they stepped into the lift tube, McCade examined the metal card. He'd never seen anything like it. He supposed it was similar to a universal credit card. But unlike a credit card, its surface was absolutely smooth. Therefore it seemed likely that whatever information it contained was recorded in its molecular structure, similar to the system the pirates used to identify their ships. McCade's thoughts were interrupted as the platform stopped on its own. Somewhere a computer monitored all arrivals and delivered them to whatever level happened to be the least crowded at the moment.

As they stepped out, McCade was again struck by the sheer size of everything. Ahead the broad terrace swept off into the distance. Beings of all races moved across its surface. He noticed they tended to stand, sit, or squat in small clumps around gray, boxlike structures. Among them moved the swaggering members of the Brotherhood's planetary police organization. Something about the way everyone hurried to get out of their way made it clear they were not public servants.

Occasionally someone failed to see them coming, or was too slow in moving out of the way, and received a careless shove or touch of the nerve stick to hurry them along. McCade made a mental note to stay as far away from them as possible.

Toward the outer edge of the terráce, an endless row of shops sold food, clothing, and recreation to the milling multitude. The variety required to satisfy the needs of so many races boggled the mind. They give you money for your goods and a place to spend it, McCade thought with grim amusement.

As they approached one of the gray, boxlike structures, McCade saw it was a combination computer terminal and com unit, not unlike those used in large maximarkets on Terra. A woman could be seen on the com screen, but there wasn't any audio. Then McCade noticed the earphones, which could be adjusted to fit a wide range of auditory organs. He picked up a set and put them on. As he did so the woman vanished and was replaced by a menu of possible races. He touched the word "Human" and watched as the woman faded back in, speaking perfect Standard. McCade knew that if he'd touched "Finthian," he'd be listening to the warbling voice of a Finthian hen.

He listened as the current transaction came to a close. One of the thousands of anonymous merchants surrounding him had just purchased five hundred all-terrain vehicles taken in a raid on a frontier world called Lucky Strike. Now he'd sell them to some other frontier planet desperate for manufactured goods. McCade glanced up at Sara. She had donned a headset and her furious expression made her feelings clear.

He slid the metal rectangle into the slot provided for that purpose. A list of those ahead of him in line flashed on the screen, along with an estimated waiting time. He decided there was plenty of time to get something to eat.

The restaurant Sara chose turned out to be excellent. Instead of the typical autochef, it employed actual cooks who clearly knew their business. After a series of exquisite courses, McCade sipped a final cup of real Terran coffee while Van Doren polished his plate with a piece of roll. During the meal Sara had entertained them with a number of fictional but hilarious accounts of her love life for the benefit of electronic eavesdroppers. At least McCade hoped they were fictional.

Glancing at his wrist term he saw it was almost time for their transaction. They paid the exorbitant bill by sliding the shiny metal card into the restaurant's cashcomp. Somewhere, much to McCade's enjoyment, a computer debited Fagan's account accordingly. Then they returned to the market.

"Next, gentlebeings, is lot 76940-A. Ten thousand guidance control modules for the Dragon air to ground missile. Since this lot is on the Brotherhood's priority list, open bidding is suspended. The Brotherhood offers the owner five thousand credits per module."

A tidy five million credits! McCade was amazed. No wonder merchants of every race flocked here.

"Accept or deny," the man droned.

McCade pushed the "accept" button. He wondered what would've happened if he'd pushed "deny." He had a feeling it wouldn't be altogether pleasant.

"Transaction complete," the man announced.

The metallic card popped out of the console. McCade removed his earphones and picked it up. He held a fortune in his hand. They could buy another cargo, load it on the *Far Trader* and lift. It's what Fagan would do. But I'm not Fagan, he thought, meeting Sara's gaze, and besides, maybe there're things worth more.

Her eyes widened and her face paled until her scar almost disappeared. McCade whirled to find himself staring down the tubes of a dozen blasters held by men in full armor. They stood in a semicircle with Laurie at its center. For the second time he searched her eyes for sorrow and found none.

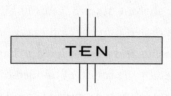

T E N

After being disarmed, they were herded through a maze of hallways, corridors, tunnels, and lift tubes that always headed down. The farther they went, the fewer people they encountered. Those they did pass ignored them. McCade decided prisoners must be a fairly common sight on the Rock. He remembered stories he'd heard about pirate prisoners winding up as slaves and shuddered.

Meanwhile the hallways and corridors through which they passed had grown darker and shabbier. Eventually lift tubes gave way to endless stairs leading down. McCade noticed it was getting warmer and more humid. Even the walls were sweating. Soon water dripped, gurgled, and slid off every surface, turning his clothes to wet rags which clung to his skin and rubbed it raw. What he had first noticed as a vibration in the soles of his boots had become recognizable as the throbbing beat of heavy machinery located somewhere nearby.

He glanced over his shoulder to see how the others were doing and got a hard shove for his trouble. A soaked Van Doren and Sara were right behind him, but there was no sign of Laurie.

The stairs finally ended in a dark area of indeterminate size. McCade decided it was probably large, since their footsteps echoed as if off distant walls. Widely spaced pools of light marked a path through the dark. Somebody rammed something hard between his shoulder blades to hurry him along. On the edge of his vision, light and dark met in gloomy twilight and he could just barely make out endless rows of old-fashioned bars. Then he realized this section dated back to the time when the entire complex had been a prison. Since then they had quite naturally renovated the upper levels first, leaving the deepest areas for detention cells and heavy equipment.

The floor suddenly shelved upward, causing him to stumble and almost fall. Strong hands pulled him back up and roughly shoved him on. Then they rounded a corner and were ordered to halt. Dark forms moved to his right, accompanied by the squeal of unoiled hinges. He was unceremoniously propelled forward. Metal clanged behind him. He turned to see the bulky shadows move off into the dark.

Not far away machinery beat out a massive rhythm that made his head hurt. He thought he heard the sound of two more cell doors closing, but they were too far off for him to be sure. He tried yelling, but there was no reply. If Sara and Amos were anywhere nearby, they evidently couldn't hear him over the machinery.

Strangely enough, other than weapons, they hadn't taken his personal possessions. If his lighter had been a miniature blaster, they would have been sorry. Unfortunately, it was only a lighter. He used it to examine his cell. Except for a plastic bench set against one wall, and some pathetic grafitti left by previous tenants, the cell was bare. McCade lit a cigar and sat down on the bench. He flinched as his back came into contact with the damp wall, and then decided to ignore it. He tried to think meaningful thoughts, but they refused to come. Eventually he lay down on the bench and drifted into an uneasy sleep.

He awoke to the clang of metal as his cell door was opened.

"If you'd be kind enough to step this way?"

He was surprised by his jailer's civil tone. As he stood to go, he realized that his back hurt from sleeping on the hard bench. He stepped out of the cell and a grav light suddenly came to life. It sat bobbing in the slight air current above and behind the jailer's head.

"I'll give you a moment to get used to the light," the jailer continued in a congenial manner.

As the light gradually increased, McCade suddenly recognized the smooth countenance of Marvin Wong, the formerly taciturn driver who'd brought them in from the spaceport. So they knew the moment we landed, McCade thought to himself. He made a note to himself to find out how.

Aloud he said, "Your vocabulary has certainly improved since we last met."

Wong smiled his agreement. "Yes, Captain Fagan, or should I say Citizen McCade? All is not always what it seems. Now if you would please follow me." Wong turned and set off without even checking to see if McCade was following along behind.

For his part McCade saw little advantage in doing anything else. He had little doubt that others waited in the darkness should he try to run. Besides, things had taken an interesting turn. Wong set a brisk pace. The grav light bobbed along between them, its ghostly glow casting enormous shadows as they moved. Empty cells were visible on both sides, but McCade saw no sign of Sara or Amos. Maybe they had already been taken wherever he was headed.

They were moving upward. At first the floor sloped. Then they climbed what seemed like endless flights of metal stairs, finally emerging into a corridor replete with normal lighting and carpet. The air flowing from a nearby vent was dry and warm, but McCade's skin was still chilled under his damp clothes.

As they marched down the corridor McCade noticed doors which interrupted its length at regular intervals. After passing quite a few, they stopped in front of one. It looked like all the rest to McCade.

Wong rapped on it three times before turning to McCade. "Go on in . . . they're waiting for you." With that he turned and headed up the hall with the now darkened grav light following faithfully along behind.

McCade watched him go with detached amusement. Why were they so relaxed now, when earlier they'd felt it necessary to throw him into a cell right out of the Dark Ages? Maybe they were trying to soften him up. Well, he decided, there's only one way to find out.

He plastered a confident grin on his face and palmed the door. It slid aside to admit him. The room was brightly lit and dominated by a long conference table. An inscrutable black man dressed in dazzling white was seated at the head of it. His eyes were hooded like a hawk's and utterly devoid of emotion. On his left sat a wizened humanoid who looked like a gnome, and on his right was Laurie, a quizzical smile touching her lips.

"Please be seated, Citizen McCade." The black man had a deep, melodious voice, which added to his presence.

"Don't mind if I do," McCade said, as he plopped into the nearest chair and immediately swung his filthy boots up onto the polished surface of the conference table. "Much more comfortable than some of your other furniture," McCade ventured, patting his pockets for a cigar.

The black man watched him with patient amusement as McCade located a half-smoked butt and lit it. As soon as it was going, the black man spoke again. "My name is Brother Mungo. On my left is Brother Urbus, and I believe you know Sister Lowe."

"I once thought I did," McCade said, inclining his head in Laurie's direction.

"Your feelings concerning Sister Lowe's execution of her duties do not concern me, Citizen McCade," Mungo said dispassionately. "Although it may interest you to know this conversation wouldn't be taking place if it were not for her intercession. Brother Urbus and I favored feeding your mass to the main reactor—a couple of microseconds of power is, after all, better than nothing . . . which is what I think you're worth. However Sister Lowe pointed out how the Emperor's minions forced you to do their bidding, and that you've been useful, albeit unknowingly so. With that in mind, we've decided to be lenient." Mungo smiled tolerantly.

"What? No hot irons, no deep probes?" McCade asked with a raised eyebrow.

"Whatever for?" Mungo said gently. "It's painfully obvious that we know more about Bridger's discovery than you do. Oh, I suppose we could wring a few pitiful details about Alice out of you, or Miss Bridger for that matter, but what's the point? Soon we will command the War World and the pathetic defenses of Alice will no longer be of interest. In fact, as it turns out we really don't need Miss Bridger either. Too bad we wasted all that effort trying to capture her." He shrugged. "That's the way it goes."

McCade fought the mixture of anger and despair that threatened to overwhelm him. Mungo's manner was insulting. Even worse was the fact that everything he said was true. McCade didn't know anything they didn't. They held all the cards. McCade blew a stream of smoke toward his boots and produced what he hoped was a nonchalant smile.

"You're quite right, of course. Can't win 'em all, I always say. By the way, just as a point of professional interest, how did you locate us so quickly?"

"Thanks to Sister Lowe, that was easy," Mungo answered with obvious relish. "She hid a tracer in the handle of your sidearm before you left Terra."

McCade's mind flashed back to her arrival on *Pegasus* to see his duffel bag flying from Laurie's hand to land in his lap. He remembered pulling the slug gun out and noticing it had been cleaned and oiled—and bugged, he thought bitterly. The moment they had landed, the tiny tracer had triggered an audible alarm and lit up a visual display somewhere. From then on Laurie had known exactly where they were every moment. How they must have laughed while he carried out his transparent impersonation of Captain Fagan!

"Enough of this silliness," Urbus said in a high, piping voice. "As Brother Mungo indicated, McCade, we see little point in your continued existence. However in deference to Sister Lowe, we're inclined to release you if you'll promise to get off the Rock and disappear. As Captain Fagan, I believe you'll have adequate funds at your disposal and a good ship. That is the bargain you made with Keaton, is it not? We'll even throw in your brutish companion for good measure." Unseen hands opened a side door and shoved Van Doren into the room. His hands were bound. In spite of that, he moved toward Mungo, but stopped when he saw McCade.

"Well?" The frown of impatience almost disappeared into the gnome's already wrinkled face.

To his own surprise McCade found himself seriously considering the little humanoid's proposal. He had everything to gain and nothing to lose. Five million credits plus a good ship would make a very good start indeed.

Actually better than what Keaton had offered. Just as quickly he rejected the notion, wryly noting that Swanson-Pierce and Keaton had chosen their tool well. Whether it was the importance of stopping Bridger and the War World, the years of conditioning at the Academy, concern for Sara, or just his own stubborn personality, he didn't know. But somehow it seemed important to finish what he'd started.

Stalling for time, McCade said, "And Sara Bridger?"

Before either man could reply, the door burst open to admit Marvin Wong. His normally unlined features were creased with worry as he hurried over to Mungo and Urbus. Leaning over, he whispered urgently in their ears. Then at the sound of distant shots and confused shouting, he whirled and ran for the door. McCade turned to watch him go. He turned back to find himself staring straight into Mungo's glittering eyes. "Sorry, McCade. All bets are off. It seems we're taking a sudden trip, and you're excess baggage."

With that he produced a small blaster and aimed it at McCade. There were two loud reports as both Mungo and Urbus slumped sideways out of their chairs.

"Well, now the fecal matter's hit the fan for sure," Laurie said matter of factly as she withdrew the still smoking slug gun from under the table. She stood and leaned over to pluck the blaster from Mungo's nerveless fingers. Tossing it to McCade, she said, "We'd better haul our fannies outta here before somebody comes along and blows them off." Then she was out the door and running down the corridor.

McCade looked at Van Doren and shrugged. He didn't trust her, but there weren't a whole lot of options. Van Doren held out his bound hands. A second later the blaster had burned through the plastic restraints and some of the skin on the marine's wrists. He didn't seem to notice. Together they bolted after Laurie.

The fighting was getting closer. The loud ripping sound of automatic slug throwers and the sizzle of energy weapons were punctuated by shouted commands and screams of agony. McCade and Van Doren caught up with Laurie where another corridor intersected theirs. She peered cautiously around the corner for a moment before snapping off a couple of shots at an unseen adversary.

"Where are we going?" McCade shouted over the noise of the conflict.

"You came to find Bridger, didn't you?" she yelled in reply without looking back. Just then a man wearing a red arm band backed around the corner firing short bursts from an automatic slug thrower. Laurie pulled him down beside her and said something in his ear, to which he nodded in agreement.

Turning to McCade and Van Doren, Laurie said, "Get ready. When I go, stay right behind me. And for God's sake, don't blast anyone wearing a red band."

McCade and Van Doren nodded in agreement. A moment later the man with the auto slug thrower stepped out from the protection of the corner and opened up. Laurie jumped up and ran across the intersection with McCade and Van Doren right on her heels. As they ran McCade heard a cry from behind as the slug thrower fell suddenly silent. He was already turning when Laurie's hand reached back to jerk him forward. Without hesitation she led them down corridors, up stairs and through a maintenance tunnel before coming to a halt and motioning them to silence.

As she carefully peeked around a corner, Van Doren retrieved an energy weapon from a tangle of bodies almost blocking the hall. Three wore uniforms with the words "Planetary Police" woven into the dark fabric. Lying dead a few feet away was a young woman, a girl really, a red band around her head and a snarl of defiance twisting once pretty lips. An empty slug thrower lay inches from her fingertips.

McCade turned in response to Laurie's touch. "There's two of them, Sam. They're guarding Bridger's room. Chances are his daughter's in there too. I don't see any way to take them except head on."

McCade risked a quick peek. What he saw confirmed Laurie's report. "I'll take the one on the left, you get the one on the right, okay?"

"Okay . . . but be careful."

McCade nodded and checked Mungo's blaster, making sure the safety was off and the charge indicator showed full. Looking up to meet Laurie's eyes, he winked. She winked back. Wordlessly they tensed, and then jumped into the open, instinctively spreading out. Both landed in the combat stance the Academy had drilled into them, feet apart, weapons raised with both hands. Laurie's guard was looking the wrong way and died without seeing who shot him. McCade's man was not only looking the right way, he was damn fast. His first shot blew air into McCade's left ear. His second went into the ceiling, as half his chest disappeared, and he toppled over backward to skid a few feet on the slick floor. Seconds later they were across the hall and through the door of a small anteroom which had evidently been used by the guards. Plates of half-eaten food, ash trays full of cigarette butts, and cheap skin mags littered every surface.

"There could be more in there," Laurie said, indicating the door to Bridger's room.

"Right," McCade replied. "Amos . . . cover the hall. . . . Okay, let's open it very slowly." Raising the blaster, he aimed it at the center of the door.

Laurie picked up a plastic chair and used it to slowly push the door open. Without warning a hand suddenly grabbed the chair and jerked on it, pulling Laurie through the door and into the room. Denied a target McCade rushed through the door to find that Laurie's assailant had her down with a hypodermic needle touching her jugular vein.

"Freeze or I'll drain her dry!"

McCade laughed and lowered the blaster. "That won't be necessary, Sara. She's one of us—at least for the moment."

Sara stood and tossed the needle into a corner. She extended a hand to Laurie and helped pull her up. "You might knock next time," she said with a crooked smile.

"Laurie, meet Sara," McCade said, looking around. Against the far wall he saw a hospital bed, almost hidden by a jungle of tubes and wires.

"Charmed, I'm sure," Laurie said, rubbing her neck reflectively where the needle had pricked her skin.

"You two will have to get acquainted later," McCade said, striding over to the bed. "Right now we've got a few problems . . . like how to get Bridger out of here." Looking down, he hardly recognized the gaunt old man who lay there with eyes closed. His chest barely moved with each shallow breath. McCade waited for the rush of hatred and felt cheated somehow when it didn't come.

"He's dying of Millette's disease," Sara said, moving to McCade's side. "They brought me here hoping I could make him talk."

Millette's disease. A rare form of blood infection first contracted by Lt. Jim Millette a hundred years earlier during an unauthorized landing on a survey planet. Unaware that he was infected, the young scout spread it to a number of planets before the first symptoms showed up. Scientists throughout the human empire had been working on a cure ever since . . . without much luck. So each standard year a few people died. Soon, it seemed, Bridger would be one of them. It certainly explained why Bridger had grown increasingly irrational, McCade thought. One of the effects of Millette's disease was a gradual deterioration of brain tissue.

"He wasn't rational enough to tell them what they wanted to know," Sara said softly. "So they brain pumped him."

It took McCade a moment to absorb the implications of what she had said. Brain pumping was illegal even in the secret interrogation chambers deep beneath Naval Intelligence Headquarters on Terra. But where knowledge exists, there are always those who will exploit it for a price. And for the completely unscrupulous, the temptation was irresistible . . . the complete transference of another's memory and knowledge, a form of theft often more profitable than any other type of crime. However the process was not without risk. From what McCade had heard, the donor usually died from neural trauma and the recipient was quite often rendered insane. It takes an unusually strong individual to deal with the complete memories, loves, hates, likes, and dislikes of another person superimposed on their own. It was said the second set of memories eventually faded, but few recipients remained rational long enough to describe how it felt.

"They made me watch while they did it," Sara said hollowly. "He recognized me, Sam. . . . I know he did. He saw me and smiled. Then this man made them begin."

"Mungo?" Laurie interjected tersely from across the bed.

Sara nodded and McCade felt her shudder. He put an arm around her. "Mungo was the recipient?"

Again she nodded and tears ran down her cheeks.

No wonder they were willing to turn me loose, McCade thought. They weren't bluffing. They really did have all the information they needed. All safely tucked away in Mungo's head. His estimation of Mungo went up a bit. Having all of Bridger's thoughts and memories in your head wouldn't be any picnic.

His thoughts were interrupted by shouted commands and the answering sound of Van Doren's energy weapon. Outside, two security men were stupid enough to turn a corner without looking first. The rest of their squad didn't make the same mistake. Firing from every scrap of cover they could find, they turned the anteroom into an inferno.

Slamming the door behind him, Amos said, "Time to go, boss. . . . Seems they won't take no for an answer." He aimed his weapon at the opposite wall.

McCade felt the blaster being jerked from his hand and turned to see Sara bum a hole through her father's head. Laurie screamed, "No!"—but jumped forward too late.

"Even he deserved that much," Sara said, handing the blaster back to McCade.

"Damn, you little fool!" Laurie said. "Now we'll have to do it the hard way."

"Let's go!" The voice was Van Doren's. Laurie was gone in a flash. McCade turned and pulled Sara after him. Van Doren had already followed Laurie through the glowing hole he'd created in the hollow plastic wall. McCade and Sara were right behind. Laurie led them through a maze of corridors and rooms, sometimes using existing doors and sometimes calling on Van Doren to make new ones. Before long, McCade was completely lost. So when Van Doren burned his way through another wall and they emerged into a conference room, he didn't recognize it at first. Then he saw Mungo and Urbus still sprawled where they'd fallen.

"This should be the last place they'll look for a few minutes," Laurie said. "Here, let me borrow that for a moment." She indicated McCade's blaster.

McCade made eye contact with Van Doren, who nodded. Curious, Mc-Cade handed Laurie the blaster. She took it, adjusted the beam to fine, turned and neatly sliced Mungo's head off. McCade stood stunned as Laurie bent over to pick up the head by one ear with all the nonchalance of a grocer handling a choice melon. The beam had cauterized the severed neck.

"What the hell?" McCade asked in amazement.

"If we freeze this quickly enough," Laurie replied matter of factly, "it may still be possible to retrieve what we need to know."

"Why you bitch!" Sara shouted, shaking with rage. "If I hadn't shot my father through the head, you would have done the same thing to him!"

"And why not?" Laurie replied calmly.

"That's enough," McCade said. "We don't have time for this. But before we go any farther, I'd like to know who's who. Let's start with the guys in the uniforms. The ones that keep shooting at us. Who are they?"

Laurie shrugged. "They're planetary police. Supposedly they work for the Brotherhood, reporting to Mungo, who was Chief of Security. Over time Mungo corrupted many of them. The one who calls himself Wong is a good example. Anyway they were acting on Mungo's orders."

"Not the Brotherhood's?"

Laurie shook her head. "As far as I know, the full Council doesn't know about the War World. As you no doubt realize by now, I was placed in Naval Intelligence as a sleeper years ago. But when Bridger disappeared, and I figured out why, Mungo was the first to know. He took Urbus in as a partner, and they planned to use the War World for their own purposes."

"And the others?" McCade asked. "The ones with the red arm bands?"

"They're members of the Committee for Democratic Reform," she replied. "They want to overthrow the Brotherhood in favor of a democracy."

"And you're a member?"

Laurie nodded. "The founder actually. I thought it would be a good idea to have some troops of my own. . . . As you've seen, I was right."

The unvarnished cynicism of it appalled and surprised McCade. This woman seemed so different from the one he'd met in Swanson-Pierce's office.

"Then why are you helping us now?" Sara asked.

"Good question," McCade added, "but you'd better hurry the answer. It sounds like they're getting closer."

Laurie shrugged. "I didn't think Mungo planned to take me with him. So I killed him before he could kill me. Plus I figure if we give them what they want, the Empire will go easy on me. Who knows? Maybe Swanson-Pierce'll give me my old job back."

"You make me sick," Sara said.

McCade watched as the blaster in Laurie's hand began to come up in Sara's direction. But before it had traveled more than an inch Van Doren hit her with a massive, openhanded blow that sent her reeling sideways as the blaster flew one way and Mungo's head another. As he helped her up, Van Doren relieved her of the small slug gun. Having retrieved the blaster McCade aimed it casually in Laurie's direction.

"There are some more questions I'd like to ask you," McCade said, "but this hardly seems like the time or the place. Pick up that head you're so fond of, and show us a safe way out of here. And by the way, if anything goes wrong, I'm gonna make sure you're the first to go."

Van Doren grinned his agreement as he stripped off his jacket and handed it to her. Laurie quickly wrapped Mungo's head in it and moved toward the opposite wall.

"I won't give you any trouble," she said. "I've got as much reason to want off this crud ball as you do." She palmed the wall.

With a slight hiss of equalizing air pressures, a panel slid aside to reveal a narrow flight of stairs leading down. As she stepped through, McCade was close behind. As they started down the steps, McCade noticed the same dampness they'd experienced coming down from the surface. From the look of it, the passageway hadn't been used for a long time. The ancient lum lights embedded in the walls cast barely enough light to show the way.

Behind him Van Doren and Sara followed, their boots clattering on the metal stairs. As they continued to descend, McCade noticed intermittent vibrations strong enough to set up a sympathetic hum in the handrail.

Ahead of him, Laurie turned a corner. As he followed he saw that the tunnel opened up into a small bay which reeked of mold and decay. The pools of stagnant water and piles of unidentifiable debris made a marked contrast to the sleek bullet shape of the empty transcar sitting beside the platform. Beyond it a short stretch of gleaming monorail reached out to join the main line which passed by outside.

Again McCade felt the vibration he'd noticed earlier. It was stronger this time. A second later a transcar flashed by with a whoosh of displaced air. It was doing more than a hundred miles an hour. Not bad for a back way out, McCade reflected. Mungo had left nothing to chance.

The transcar had been designed only for two, so the four of them were a tight fit. But after some struggle, and some profanity from Van Doren, they were all in. Laurie touched a destination on the map display and the transcar slid smoothly into motion.

Moments later they had joined the main line and now began to accelerate. Outside, the tunnel walls moved by with increasing speed until finally they became a blur. What seemed like only moments later the transcar began to slow, finally coming to a stop in a large terminal filled to overflowing with milling travelers.

One by one they struggled out of the car. As soon as they were all clear, the transcar moved away from the platform, picked up speed, and then disappeared into a tunnel.

As far as McCade could tell, they weren't under surveillance of any kind. People swirled around them, all seemingly intent on their own errands. After considerable twisting and turning through the crowd, they arrived at a turnstile. McCade slid the metal card into the appropriate slot until all had passed. Moments later they were aboard another sleek transcar and accelerating away from the station.

Laurie sat across from McCade, her features calm and composed, providing no hint that the untidy bundle on her lap contained a man's head. She seemed different somehow, but perhaps that other Laurie had never really existed outside his hopes and desires.

Both Sara and Van Doren stared out the windows at the tunnel walls and the occasional stations that they raced by. Together the four of them formed an island of silence in the sea of chattering passengers.

When the transcar slowed to a stop they followed Laurie off. Moments later they were packed into a crowded lift tube, heading for the surface. When the platform came to a stop, doors slid aside.

McCade instantly recognized the shiny black surface of the spaceport, the guard towers and the hundreds of ships which pointed up toward the night sky. As their fellow passengers streamed off in every direction, they started off toward the guard tower nearest to the *Far Trader*. They had gone only a couple of feet when suddenly a circle of glaring white light snapped into existence, pinning them against the black rock. Then came a voice that rolled like thunder and reverberated off the ranks of ships. It belonged to Marvin Wong. McCade should have been surprised, but somehow wasn't. Hadn't Wong said that all is not always what it seems? Anyway, the fact that the Brotherhood had been on to Mungo through a double agent wasn't too surprising either. McCade suddenly realized that the Brotherhood had simply allowed Mungo to do all the work for them. And if it hadn't been for Laurie's intervention, it would have worked.

"McCade . . . McCade . . . McCade . . ." Wong's voice echoed off the surrounding ships. "Stand where you are or die . . . die . . . die . . . You are under arrest by order of . . ."

McCade didn't wait around to hear the rest. Instead he aimed a quick blaster bolt toward the top of the nearest guard tower, hoping to momentarily ruin the sentry's night vision. But as he dived out of the circle of light, he realized they could probably use infrared sighting devices. Of course, with so many heat sources around in the form of people and ships, infrared would cut both ways.

Rolling up out of the somersault, McCade found time to wonder how they had been tracked. Mungo's men had taken the bugged slug gun from him, so it wasn't that. Then he knew. He reached into his pocket and pulled out the metal credit card. It twinkled with reflected light as he threw it as far as he could. As it landed, an energy beam leaped down from the tower to obliterate it. The others had formed up beside him.

Yelling to be heard over the confused shouting and an alarm klaxon, he said. "Let's add to the confusion!"

By way of demonstration, he snapped random shots at nearby ships and rolled away. The shots were quickly returned, with interest, by crew members of those vessels. They had no idea who was firing on them or why, but they weren't about to just sit there and take it.

The others quickly followed his example and within seconds a number of lively firefights developed between neighboring ships. Confused and frightened for the safety of their vessels, some captains opened fire on nearby guard towers with heavy ship's weapons, quickly reducing them to red-hot scrap metal. Other towers immediately retaliated, their energy weapons cutting down entire rows of ships like scythes harvesting wheat. Under the cover of the resulting total confusion, the four raced toward the *Far Trader*, only to see it vanish in a blinding explosion as a neighboring vessel began to fire randomly in every direction.

"*Pegasus,*" Laurie shouted. "She's over there!"

They all veered to follow Laurie, dodging between ships and ground vehicles, using what cover they could, and occasionally shooting back when fired on. As he ran McCade felt the ground begin to tremble under his feet. Ship after ship was lifting on emergency power to escape the destruction now raging from one end of the spaceport to the other. They gave the remaining ships between them and *Pegasus* a wide berth to avoid being accidentally killed by someone's launch. Paranoid even at the best of times, both smugglers and pirates were giving free rein to their imaginations, and it was every being for itself.

Panting heavily Laurie reached *Pegasus* and palmed the main entry port. One after another they tumbled into the lock and waited impatiently for the inner hatch to cycle open. As they scrambled through, McCade yelled, "Prepare for emergency lift at full boost. Activate all weapons systems and strap in!"

He ran for the control room, palming the control lock as he slid into the command chair. He noted with satisfaction that Laurie hadn't bothered to de-authorize him. As bank after bank of indicators came to life, he routinely scanned each. Everything looked good. As his fingers danced nimbly among the controls, the outside viewscreens came to life. He felt Laurie slide into the position beside him. Her presence reminded him of how things had been before planetfall on Weller's World. The memory both pleased and annoyed him.

"All systems operational," Laurie said with calm professionalism.

"Prepare for emergency lift," McCade replied. "Lift." With that he turned the large red knob over his head one rotation to the right and pushed it in.

The ship shuddered violently as her engines built thrust. McCade had one last second to survey the madness that had consumed the spaceport. Everywhere energy weapons and slug throwers spewed death and destruction. It couldn't happen to a nicer group of folks, McCade thought wryly. Then the ship's defensive screens flared as they took a direct hit. A fraction of a second later, *Pegasus* blasted off under full emergency power. McCade blacked out momentarily.

As they cleared atmosphere, his vision cleared and he felt the terrible weight come off his chest. Flicking the rear screens on, he saw pinpoints of light as more ships followed him into space. Whether they were following or just trying to escape, he couldn't tell. Switching the forward screens to high mag he was momentarily blinded by the explosion as a nuclear torpedo hit one of the fleeing vessels. At first he couldn't understand why, but as his vision returned he saw all too clearly. Most of the escaping ships had lifted without the one-way pass necessary to get by the weapons platforms which still guarded the approaches to the Rock. The platforms were doing a very efficient job.

As they got closer, McCade watched in fascination as ship after ship was snuffed out of existence, like so many moths attracted to an open flame. Then it suddenly stopped.

A group of ships formed a temporary alliance and together they attacked one of the platforms. Some of the ships were destroyed in the process, but by virtue of sheer massed firepower, they won. As the weapons platform flashed incandescent, the alliance broke and the survivors fled through the gap they'd created and headed for safer regions. Every other ship within one light realized what had happened and headed in that direction to take advantage of the newly created escape route. *Pegasus* was no exception.

"Uh-oh. Looks like we got company, boss. And I don't remember sending out any invitations." Van Doren had again chosen the top blister as his battle station.

Sara had ensconced herself in the rear weapons turret. Her voice came over the intercom loud and clear. "He's right, Sam. There's two of them closing fast. I don't think they're friendlies. Pirate destroyers by the looks of them."

McCade confirmed her guess by switching on the rear screens and boosting them to high mag. It didn't look good. Options and strategies flashed through his mind in quick succession. He tapped a request into the ship's computer asking for advice. The reply was immediate and to the point, delivered by the now-familiar voice.

"Surrender immediately. The pursuing vessels have overwhelmingly superior firepower and speed. They will destroy *Pegasus* approximately 10.5 seconds after initial engagement."

"Good. I was afraid we might be in trouble," McCade said. He met Laurie's concerned gaze with what he hoped was a nonchalant smile.

"Stand by for sudden deceleration followed by enemy action," McCade said. "Five from now. Five, four, three, two, one." With a quick flick of the wrist, he cut the power by half and felt himself thrown forward against his harness.

The two pirate ships seemed to surge forward as if by magic, splitting to position themselves on each side, placing *Pegasus* in a cross fire. McCade forced himself to wait, hoping they would interpret the sudden cut in speed as a sign of cooperation. Evidently they did, because as they drew abreast of *Pegasus* they didn't open fire. Of course it could be just an effort to capture someone alive. Or some *thing* dead, he corrected himself, thinking of Mungo's head now resting on the top shelf of the galley refrigeration unit.

Finally both ships were level with *Pegasus*. "Fire!" McCade yelled into the intercom as all the weapons that could be brought to bear fired in unison. Both destroyers were suddenly bathed in fire. Neither was in any danger. Their defensive screens were much more powerful than anything *Pegasus* could hope to equal. So when they fired in reply, they did so with the care and precision of someone who is invulnerable.

And stupid. For as they opened fire, McCade punched full emergency power again, bringing the already hot tubes to the very edge of burnout, and setting off a host of alarm buzzers and flashing lights. But McCade was deaf to the ship's protests as he watched the rear screens with the fascination born of extreme fear.

Without *Pegasus* between them to shoot at, the destroyers were suddenly shooting at each other. And before human hands and tongues could intervene, the battle computer on each vessel used part of a second to reevaluate the source of the incoming fire, the strength of the opposing defensive screens, and initiate appropriate countermeasures. A second later one destroyer vanished in a brilliant explosion and the other suddenly slowed and then stopped, apparently the victim of a damaged propulsion system.

With a groan of relief, McCade slumped back in his chair, cutting the emergency power as he did so. As the cacophony of warning buzzers and klaxons slowly died away, the computer's dulcet tones flooded the intercom. McCade would have sworn there was an edge of criticism under the apparently neutral words.

"Recent damage to this ship and its operating systems, due to actions taken under manual override, necessitate docking at a class C or better maintenance facility within the next one hundred hours of operation. The bar is open."

Sara and Van Doren's laughter echoed his own as he punched in a course for Alice, handed over control to the ship's computer, and headed for the lounge, where he intended to order a double, no a triple, Scotch. He didn't see Laurie cancel the course for Alice and enter a new set of coordinates into the computer, or hear as she selected a certain ship-to-ship radio frequency and made contact with the massive battleship some distance away.

Instead he was seated in the lounge, watching as Sara carefully applied a salve and bandages to Van Doren's burned wrists, while the marine pretended it didn't hurt. Moments later Laurie joined them. Then, when everyone had settled down to their favorite refreshments, McCade proposed a toast.

"To a successful mission and safe arrival on Alice!"

Each smiled, raised a glass, and took a sip.

ELEVEN

Hours had passed since their escape from the Rock, and McCade was feeling rather pleased with himself. Bridger had been stopped, *Pegasus* was his, and there was every reason to expect a bonus. He glanced at Sara, who was engaged in friendly conversation with Van Doren, and took another sip of his third drink. Yes, things were definitely looking up.

His thoughts were interrupted by the computer's soft chime. Laurie beat him to it and reached out to tap a few keys. The screen across from McCade came to life. Displayed on it was the likeness of a ship, along with the technical specifications pertaining to it. McCade didn't need the specs to know what it was. There's no mistaking an Il Ronnian ship of the line. A fraction of a second later, its incredibly powerful tractor beams leapt across thousands of miles of space to look on to *Pegasus*. The computer confirmed tractor beam lock-up as the Il Ronnian vessel began to reel them in like a fish on a line. McCade turned and was heading for the control room when Sara's voice stopped him.

"Sam, look!"

He spun around to see Sara pointing at Laurie. It seemed as though her face was slipping. Her beautiful features had become elastic somehow and seemed to flow and ripple in an impossible way. Suddenly she appeared to collapse and then dissolve into a pool of shivering protoplasm. The Treel! But it had died on Weller's World! Except it obviously hadn't . . . because here it was in the repulsive flesh!

"Give me the word and I'll blow her . . . I mean it . . . to mush, boss!" Van Doren growled, aiming his blaster at the Treel. Sara sat perfectly still, looking back and forth between the Treel and McCade in amazement.

"I don't think that'll be necessary, Amos," McCade replied calmly. "It appears our friend here already *is* mush."

"Jape as you will, rigid ones," the Treel replied, switching now to its own hoarse voice. "For seldom is true beauty understood by those un-blessed by the great Yareel.

"However," the Treel added pragmatically, "notice who is in possession of this small but effective blaster." With that a pseudopod emerged from the alien's liquid presence, grasping a shiny new weapon only recently taken from the ship's small arms locker.

McCade gestured for Van Doren to lower his weapon. "Don't bother, Amos. I don't think your blaster's up to the job anyway. On Weller's World, I put enough needles in it to kill six humans."

"You speak the truth, primate," the Treel replied smugly. "Since my race is perfect, we are impossible to kill, however on Weller's World it suited my purpose to let it seem otherwise."

McCade didn't believe Treels were impossible to kill. He just hadn't fig-ured out how to do it yet.

He lit a cigar and said, "So what's up?" He followed the question with a stream of blue smoke.

"I would have thought that obvious . . . even to you," the Treel replied. "We must deliver Mungo's head to the Il Ronn. In a few minutes they'll take us aboard, where they will extract what they wish to know from Mungo's brain. At that point my job will be over. Excuse me while I inform them of the situation here."

With that the Treel extruded another pseudopod which promptly transfigured itself into a perfect likeness of Laurie's hand—right down to her fingerprints, McCade imagined. Nimble fingers entered a series of numbers and letters, which were no doubt part of a prearranged code.

Watching the alien's confident movements, McCade silently cursed himself for the worst kind of fool. It had finally dawned on him that Laurie, the real Laurie, the one who had both saved and betrayed him, was dead—and had been since Weller's World.

Carefully he searched his emotions, trying to find either sorrow or satisfaction. Both seemed justified. But neither emerged to dominate the other. Yet the Treel was running up quite a butcher's bill. A bill that would have to be paid one day. First there had been Cadet Votava, then the crew of the tug, Laurie, and God knows how many others who had died supporting the Committee for Democratic Reform.

"So you killed her," McCade said flatly. His voice calm, even conversational. But his eyes were cold and bleak. Looking at them, Sara suddenly understood the part of his life she'd never seen. The professional killer stalking his prey.

"Yes, I'm afraid so," the Treel replied calmly. Now that the message had been sent, the alien seemed relaxed and almost gregarious. "No sooner had she rendered you unconscious with her traitorous dart than she turned on me. Injured though I was, my marvelous body was still able to momentarily assume the form of a Linthian Rath snake, with predictably fatal results. It seems, like most of you rigid ones, she was duplicitous in the extreme, appearing to work for the Imperial Government, but actually in the employ of the pirates." The alien's gelatinous body undulated for a moment as though to aid its thought process. "I will admit, however, that while assuming her form I learned that she was quite loyal to the Brotherhood's full Council. I doubt that Brother Mungo could have corrupted her as he did me."

"And then?" McCade asked.

The Treel sloshed back and forth a little in what might have been a shrug. "Events conspired to frustrate my noble plans. Laurie's henchmen soon arrived, evidently to help neutralize you, a task she had already carried out with admirable efficiency, and I was barely able to hide her body before assuming her identity. The situation forced me to reveal Bridger's location in the hotel. He was comatose and badly in need of medical attention. The rest should be obvious even to one of your limited mental acuity.

"In my role as Laurie, I had to accompany Bridger to the Rock and wait there for an opportunity to, ah, serve my employer. Fortunately Bridger's illness delayed their attempt to gain access to his mind. For a while it looked as though I would fail. Bridger grew increasingly less coherent and finally they brain pumped him. Fortunately you blundered in, presenting me with an opportunity to obtain the desired information and to escape as well."

McCade did his best to shrug nonchalantly. "So just for the record . . . what is the War World like?"

"Who knows, rigid one," the Treel replied conversationally. "Bridger never did tell me . . . that is, Votava . . . anything you couldn't surmise from the name alone. It is evidently a world having to do with war. More than that I couldn't say. And for that matter I don't think Bridger could either, for all of his raving. All he knew for sure was that it exists. And where. Soon the Il Ronn will retrieve that knowledge from Mungo's frozen brain tissue, and I shall be free of the entire matter. A freedom I shall relish, by the way."

With that the strange being seemed to withdraw into itself. Only the unwavering blaster suggested its continuing attention.

As they neared the Il Ronnian vessel, it grew in their screens to blot out nearby constellations with its complex tracery of hull, weapons platforms, power modules, and other less identifiable parts. A lighted rectangle appeared in the black metal hull as a hatch slid aside to admit them. Inside the enormous hanger bay, *Pegasus* came to rest next to a row of one-man interceptors. The human ship was only slightly larger than the alien fighters.

They were searched and then escorted, without ceremony, through a maze of passageways and corridors. Their guard consisted of a heavily armed squad of tall, thin Il Ronnian troopers. Their uniforms identified them as members of the Sand Sept, an elite fighting force roughly analogous to the Imperial Marines, and just as famous for their valor.

As they walked, McCade began to sweat. The temperature within the ship was uncomfortably high. It served to remind McCade that the Il Ronn had evolved on a desert planet. Which of course explained their preference for hot, dry worlds.

Finally they arrived on what was clearly the ship's command level. The ten or fifteen Il Ronn present didn't even glance up from their glowing control panels and monitors as the humans were led through and ushered into a side compartment.

As the prisoners entered, McCade experienced a brief moment of disorientation. As quickly as it came, it was gone, and he found himself standing on extremely fine white sand which shifted under his feet. The sand was tinged here and there with streaks of red, and it reached out to meet a violet sky. The sun beating down on his shoulders was incredibly hot. McCade looked at his two companions and shrugged. There was no one else in sight.

The Treel had been escorted off under separate guard shortly after they'd left the ship. Instinctively it had assumed the guise of an Il Ronn. McCade was amused at the obvious discomfort of the Il Ronnian troopers who had marched it off, with Mungo's cold-packed head tucked securely under one arm.

To their right, the air seemed to buzz and shimmer. A huge Il Ronn seemed to appear from nowhere, although McCade realized the alien was actually entering via the same hatch they had used. The sensurround was that realistic. Suddenly he realized he'd have a hard time finding his way out of the compartment without help. The alien paused for a moment as if inspecting them. Its eyes were lost in the black shadow cast by the prominent superorbital ridge above them. McCade was struck by the resemblance between the giant alien and ancient pictures he'd seen of a mythical being known as the "Devil."

He stood on long, spindly legs which ended in broad, cloven hoofs. McCade noticed these hoofs seemed to float on top of the fine white sand rather than sinking into it as his boots tended to do. The Il Ronn's leathery skin was hairless, and even had a reddish hue. It seemed to blend with the red streak in the sand behind it. Long, pointed ears lay flat against his head, and to complete the devillike image, the Il Ronn had a long tail ending in a triangular appendage. At the moment, this appendage hovered over the alien's head, providing shade from the blistering sun.

McCade knew he wasn't the first to notice the resemblance between Il Ronn physiognomy and the traditional Judeo-Christian image of evil personified. In fact some scholars thought that the aliens' devillike appearance might account in part for the almost instant enmity which sprang into existence shortly after the first recorded contact between human and Il Ronn. They suggested that after thousands of years of exposure to an evil image closely resembling the Il Ronn, humans could not view them objectively. This was a favorite argument among those opposing war with the Il Ronn.

Other scholars disagreed, suggesting that early depictions of the devil were not imaginary, but real, and were based on early visits to Earth by Il Ronnian explorers. This theory couldn't be simply laughed off, since there was ample evidence that the Il Ronn had developed a star drive thousands of years before Man. However, being a more deliberate and cautious race than Man, their empire expanded slowly, allowing humans to eventually catch up. Proponents of this last theory went on to point out the brutal tactics still employed by Il Ronn scouts when contacting less advanced indigenous races. They maintained that if the Il Ronn did establish and maintain a temporary colony on Earth, their dealings with humans might have earned them a well-deserved reputation for evil, which they eventually came to symbolize.

So in their view, the hostility between the two races was natural, and based as much on history as on current events. This particular argument was favored by those who felt all-out war with the Il Ronn was inevitable. As far as McCade knew, the Il Ronn themselves had never commented on either theory.

He noticed that unlike many traditional images of Satan, the Il Ronn in front of him had no horns. But he more than made up for this biological oversight when he opened a lipless mouth to reveal a wealth of deadly-looking teeth. His voice was surprisingly melodious.

"Greetings. I am called Reez. Commander Reez of Star Sept Four. I apologize for receiving you here in the comfort of my own environment. But that is the privilege of the victor, is it not?

"I'll assume your silence implies acquiescence," he continued after a moment. "I would like to thank you for delivering such important information into our hands . . . even if it *was* only through your incompetence. I assure you we will use it to speed the inevitable end of your pathetic empire."

McCade was really sweating now—small rivers of perspiration running off his body. Reez evidently understood the significance of that.

"I see you find the heat of our native environment uncomfortable. However I fear even greater discomfort may await you in the slave markets of Lakor. I'm told that conditions there are quite rigorous. Pleasant though, when compared to your subsequent existence on some mine world." He paused to study Sara in a calculating way.

"You, my dear, are another matter. I suspect they'll find other uses for you. Ugly by conventional human standards, it's true . . . but on Lakor there is a market for everything, even ugliness. I'm sure someone would find your disfigurement exciting. How wonderfully twisted, don't you agree?"

The scar across Sara's face was white against her flushed skin. Both Mc-Cade and Van Doren were already in motion when a hand flamer materialized in the Il Ronn's three-fingered hand. They jerked to a halt. Reez shook his head in pretended amazement.

"My what an emotional race! You have already served me well, although unintentionally, and as a reward I offer you the opportunity to continue in that service. Who knows? After the fall of your empire, we will need cooperative human administrators. Such a role could be yours. So the choice is between comfortable service to me . . . and the slave markets of Lakor. Which will it be?"

To his surprise McCade found himself giving the alien's proposal serious consideration. After all, it wasn't his fault Laurie had turned out to be a double agent and everything had gone to hell. But two things kept getting in the way. First, he felt sure that if he agreed to serve the Il Ronn, he'd be forced to act against the Empire. True, he had no reason to love the Empire, but he did care about his own kind. Second, he couldn't help remembering the Treel. Life as a servant to the Il Ronn didn't seem all that attractive. In fact it just amounted to a choice between one kind of slavery and another.

Reez stood waiting, contempt and arrogance surrounding him like a cloak. McCade tried to look into the alien's eyes, but found only darkness. Mixed feelings of revulsion and fear made his pulse pound, and he found it took all his strength to speak.

"I can't speak for my companions," McCade said, "but personally I'd prefer the slave market of Lakor to your company any day."

With that he spat into the sand between the alien's hoofs and thereby sealed his fate. His action was a wanton waste of water and to a people for whom water had religious significance, it was a deadly insult. It implied that the commander's father should have showered his sperm on the desert, rather than use it to fertilize his egg-mother.

For a long moment, Commander Reez stood perfectly still . . . and Mc-Cade was afraid he'd gone too far. He'd known that the same action by another Il Ronn would have provoked a death duel. But he'd allowed both his fear and courage to control him long enough to hit back the only way he could.

When Reez spoke, his voice was as cold as death. "So be it." He turned to Sara and Van Doren. As one they spat into the sand before him.

The Il Ronnian officer regained his composure with effort, but his voice was like the icy distance of space itself. "I will not grant you the swift death you obviously seek. Instead, you will die slowly, as befits your kind, working, as animals should, for the profit of their betters. A fate for which your entire race is woefully overdue."

The air buzzed and shimmered as the alien departed. Seconds later their guards appeared, and this time they were far from gentle. Commander Reez had evidently made his displeasure known.

They were shoved, kicked, and pushed back through the labyrinth of tubes and passageways before being literally thrown into some kind of detention cell. A superficial examination of the cell revealed that no effort had been spared to make it both primitive and uncomfortable. For an Il Ronn that is. The cell had been cooled to a temperature which felt just about right to McCade. Gone too was the intensely bright lighting favored by the aliens. The dimmer, warmer light was quite a relief to human eyes.

Nonetheless the cell was still far from comfortable. There was no furniture, no sign of sanitary facilities, and no source of the Il Ronnian's precious water.

Glancing around the bare, seamless walls, McCade searched for some signs of the sensors, which he knew to be there. He couldn't see them, but that wasn't surprising. Knowing that all conversation would be monitored, by unspoken agreement all three remained silent. If Van Doren was worried, there was no sign of it in his cheerful thumbs up. Sara managed a smile and a conspiratorial wink. McCade smiled back and closed his eyes. Suddenly he was very tired. He resisted the impulse only briefly before, realizing there was nothing he could do, he let himself drift off to sleep.

He awoke to find the other two already up. A quick inventory revealed that he was sore, hungry and scared. Then the acceleration began. They were smashed down against the metal floor with tremendous force. That lasted for a few seconds, which seemed like hours. Then without warning the acceleration and gravity disappeared. Shortly after that the cell began to tumble. Since there were no hand holds or ways to strap themselves down, they tumbled with it. They were all experienced at weightlessness and quickly adjusted to it. But not before collecting some bumps and bruises from the unpadded cell.

As he glided from one surface to another in response to the cell's tumbling movement, McCade tried to figure out what was happening. He couldn't believe the gigantic Il Ronnian warship was out of control and tumbling end-over-end through space. But if it wasn't, then they were no longer aboard. Suddenly the acceleration made sense. The cell wasn't part of the ship and never had been. It was probably a cargo module that had been modified to include breathable atmosphere. It was probably equipped with a microcomputer and some retro-tubes as well. Reez had simply swung by Lakor and unceremoniously blasted their module down toward the planet, having warned someone on the surface of some incoming merchandise.

It was quick, simple, and efficient. But it was also uncomfortable and dangerous, McCade thought as the module tumbled again, throwing him toward the opposite bulkhead. A fact which Commander Reez had no doubt considered. McCade executed a somersault and hit the bulkhead feet first, legs properly flexed, and then pushed off toward what had once been the deck.

Meanwhile Van Doren and Sara were likewise occupied. The marine demonstrated surprising grace and agility for a man his size. However his moves were nothing compared to Sara's. She had managed to transform the situation into an aerial ballet. In fact, she was apparently enjoying herself. Watching her, McCade remembered her as she'd been years before. Young, beautiful, and completely untouchable. Separated from him by an entire obstacle course of social and financial barriers. Junior officers weren't welcome in the quarters of mighty captains. Particularly those who couldn't even afford the null-G ballet lessons Sara had taken for granted. And now here they were. Trapped in a cargo module hurtling down toward some unseen world. A world on which they would all be just so much meat for sale.

Her movements were lithe and precise. Each flowed seamlessly into the next as though planned and rehearsed for months. Her face was lit with a beautiful smile which somehow made the terrible scar disappear. Watching her made him feel good. And that surprised and confused him. It scared him too . . . because it made him realize how much he would miss her if they were separated. Somehow, without his realizing it, she'd become both friend and ally without the years of association it usually took to produce either relationship.

His thoughts were interrupted by the realization that gravity had begun to return. As it did McCade felt himself gradually grow heavier and heavier. They had evidently entered Lakor's atmosphere. Unfortunately the module was still tumbling end-over-end. What had been almost a game was now deadly serious. With added weight it became much harder to avoid hitting the metal bulkheads. On top of that, McCade knew he was getting tired. He had begun to sweat. With each movement, the next grew harder to perform. He saw the other two were also having difficulty—Van Doren more than Sara.

The sensation of weight continued to increase. McCade's reactions slowed accordingly. He started to make mistakes. Each time he made a mistake he paid a price in pain. Finally both he and Van Doren lost control. They crashed into the surfaces and into each other, making it increasingly difficult for Sara to maneuver around them. Reez could not have administered a more efficient beating if he'd been there in person.

Sara fared slightly better. She watched with concern as the two men were inexorably beaten, knowing there was nothing she could do to help them. Only her training and perfect conditioning had saved her so far. But she too was beginning to tire.

McCade watched with a strange sort of dispassionate interest as the gray metal surface came up to meet him. Somehow he couldn't summon even the slightest response from his leaden arms and legs. He could do no more than note the impact as his body slammed into the bulkhead and his head bounced off hard metal. A tremendous wave of pain rolled through his body and threatened to pull him under. One more, he thought. One more should do it. Then I won't feel anything anymore. The prospect seemed wonderful.

Then the module stopped tumbling. It seemed as if Reez had known the precise moment at which they'd be unable to take anymore, and had programmed the module's tiny computer to fire the retros at just that moment. McCade knew that was impossible. Nevertheless, he cursed Reez in a dozen languages as the module slammed down through layer after layer of atmosphere, bucking and shaking as though it would come apart at any moment. Each time it shook, another wave or pain rolled through him until one finally carried him with it, down into a dark abyss.

TWELVE

McCade wasn't sure which was better—being conscious or unconscious. Both had advantages. Being conscious was good because you knew what was going on. For example, he was vaguely aware of the impact as the cargo module splashed down, presumably in a large body of water. Then he felt rough hands jerk him out of the module and throw him down into the stinking bilge of an ancient hovercraft. With a stuttering roar, they had then bounced off across the water toward an unknown destination.

At that point the delicious darkness of unconsciousness beckoned. And who was he to refuse? True, you didn't know what was going on, but that had its good points too. For one thing, you didn't feel it when a short squat Lakorian kicked you in the ribs a couple of times just for the fun of it.

Unfortunately, toward the end of the ride, McCade came to and found he had to stay that way. Waves of filthy bilge water kept slapping him in the face. Cautiously he looked around, moving only his eyes. No point in letting them know he was awake. Directly in front of him he saw two Lakorian ankles. Each was as big around as his thigh. They seemed to end in broad, webbed feet, but he wasn't sure, since the swirling bilge water allowed only glimpses of them.

Beyond the Lakorian who was serving as helmsman, McCade could see Sara. She was tied hand and foot. Suddenly he realized he couldn't feel his own arms and legs. Sure enough they were tied too—very tightly. His circulation had evidently been cut off for some time. Just then the Lakorian helmsman stepped forward slightly, allowing McCade to see Sara more clearly. She seemed to be watching some activity behind him. He couldn't tell what it was. More Lakorians probably.

After a moment she glanced his way. A look of concern clouded her features. He caught her eye and did his best to smile. It hurt. After a look of relieved surprise, she nodded in reply. Allowing his head to move naturally with the movement of the hovercraft, he managed to look farther to the right. He could just barely make out Van Doren's boots. As McCade watched, they moved as the marine tried to find a more comfortable position. His legs were tightly tied at the ankles. At least we're alive, McCade thought grimly. But for how long?

Hours passed before they made landfall. If you can call a swamp "land," McCade thought sourly. The hovercraft stopped at the top of a mud ramp. Two stumpy Lakorians hoisted McCade and Sara over their shoulders, climbed out of the hovercraft, and then sloshed across an open space ankle deep in mud. It took two of them to lift and carry Van Doren. Head down over a Lakorian shoulder, McCade couldn't see much of their surroundings. It seemed like mostly mud and lush green tropical foliage. It started to rain.

Unfortunately the rain seemed to have no effect whatsoever on the rancid body odor of the Lakorian carrying him. In fact, if anything, it seemed to make it worse. McCade noticed from his vantage point only inches away from the alien's skin that it was exuding an oily substance. Whatever the substance was, it was making the water run off the creature's greenish skin, and it smelled terrible.

With casual violence the Lakorian threw McCade into the back of a huge trailer. He hit the floor and slid on the layer of filth which covered it, before hitting a number of other occupants. They snarled and screeched and grunted their objections in a variety of tongues. One large, bearlike being cuffed him back in the direction of the door, where he collided with Van Doren on the way down. The heavy metal door slammed shut as the vehicle jerked into spasmodic motion.

McCade rolled up against Sara. After considerable fumbling, they managed to untie each other. Then while Sara was working on Van Doren's bonds, McCade stumbled to his feet. His arms and legs ached with returning circulation and bruises. Trying for balance, McCade swayed over to the open bars, which provided warm, fetid air, dim, dappled light, and barely managed to hold up a shabby roof. It was raining harder now, and the water made a drumming sound as it pounded down on the metal over their heads.

Peering out between the bars, McCade saw they were being towed by a large tractor type vehicle with an enclosed cab. It was equipped with huge balloon tires that seemed designed to float the vehicle when necessary. Looking at the passing terrain, McCade got the feeling it would be necessary quite often in fact.

The landscape was an unending procession of lakes, pools, rivers, and puddles, separated by islands of lush plant life. About half the vegetation was green, the rest was black and rotting. Immense tree trunks reached up through the tangled growth toward the sun. Vines and parasitic plants draped themselves around the huge trees, adding to the verdant maze.

Here and there animal life was visible too. Large, bovine creatures on six legs browsed on huge piles of weeds they pulled from the bottom of shallow lakes. Above them small, spindly figures skittered and screeched at the passage of tractor and trailer. Once some unseen marine presence threw a casual tentacle into the trailer as if reaching for an hors d'oeuvre. However, after the bearlike alien grabbed it and bit off a four-foot length of rubbery flesh, the remaining stump was withdrawn with considerable haste. The bear spit out a mouthful of tentacle with an expression of distaste and returned to its taciturn silence.

For the first time McCade really looked at his fellow prisoners. Evidently the slave markets of Lakor didn't play favorites, because they were definitely a mixed lot. Besides the bearlike creature, there were a couple of bedraggled Finthians, their plummage covered with muck, a single Cellite, eyestalks drooping dejectedly, and a complete Seph grouping. McCade remembered having read somewhere that the Seph were trisexual. It took a grouping of three to reproduce. They were huddled together in a furry mass that occupied one corner.

"An unlikely group, aren't we," Sara said, her smile almost obscured by the dirt on her face. In spite of the dirt, he found her smile appealing and bent over to kiss her. Her lips were soft and met his with a pleasant pressure which he returned, with interest.

"Excuse me, boss . . . but I think you better see this," Van Doren said.

"It better be good," McCade said, smiling at Sara before turning to the bars.

"Good it probably ain't," Van Doren replied sourly, spitting through the bars. "Not on this pus ball. You gotta wonder why anyone comes here. And what's more, why are those folks out there runnin' around in the rain?" He pointed out through the bars.

At first McCade couldn't see a thing. Then after allowing his eyes to adjust, he began to detect shadowy figures moving swiftly through the foliage. They seemed to be carrying long, thin objects. They could have been sticks. They could also be weapons. The three of them continued to watch the shadowy forms for some time. Even on foot and moving through dense undergrowth, the unknown figures seemed to have no difficulty keeping up with the slow-moving vehicle. Sometimes they would disappear. But a few minutes later they would be back, moving through the rain like ghosts.

If the Lakorians in the tractor's cab were aware of the watchers, they gave no sign. Both tractor and trailer continued their ungainly progress through the rain forest, lurching from one pond to the next. Gradually night began to fall. As dusk deepened into the blackness of night, the tractor driver flicked on powerful floodlights to push back the dark. Meanwhile a variety of nocturnal animal and plant life had switched on luminescent lights of their own. The net effect hurt McCade's eyes. The watchers could no longer be seen, but somehow he knew they were still there. Watching and waiting.

After a while McCade, lying beside Sara on the filthy floor, fell into a fitful sleep. It seemed perfectly natural to put one arm around her, and she snuggled up to his chest. She too fell asleep, stirring only occasionally and waking him from his confused dreams. Then all hell broke loose.

An aerial flare went off, lighting up the entire area. Somewhere an automatic projectile weapon began to stutter, and tracers arced in toward the cab. Instinctively all the prisoners hit the deck. But none of the fire seemed directed toward the trailer. Energy beams flicked out from the tractor to rake the underbrush. In spite of the rain, the vegetation immediately caught fire as though doused with liquid fuel. Evidently some of the plants exuded an extremely volatile sap. At times McCade thought he saw figures darting back and forth behind the flames. As far as he could tell, the incoming fire wasn't making much of an impression on the tractor. It had evidently been armored against just such attacks. He also noticed that the watchers continued to direct all their fire against the tractor and not the trailer. Whether this was calculated to spare the prisoners, or simply in recognition of their impotence, he couldn't tell. But he couldn't help feeling that any enemies of the Lakorians were friends of his.

A hidden speaker somewhere in the trailer squawked to life. This was followed by some kind of speech in a language McCade didn't know. No sooner had it ended than it started over in Standard. "We are under attack by criminal elements. Do not be frightened. You will not be harmed. Remain calm. The perpetrators of this unlawful attack will soon be destroyed."

As soon as it was over it began again. This time it sounded like the warbling speech of the Finthians.

It was obviously prerecorded, and McCade found that interesting. For one thing it meant that such attacks were probably very common. Why else would they prepare an announcement? It also implied some kind of organized resistance to the present planetary government. By whom? he wondered. For what reason? There weren't any obvious answers. Meanwhile the battle raged on. Neither side seemed to be making much of a dent in the other. The tractor continued to lumber forward, pulling the trailer along behind. However the watchers seemed able to keep pace without apparent difficulty, and both sides continued a desultory exchange of fire.

Finally, as if bored with the whole affair, the Lakorians opened up with an automatic flechette gun. Heretofore they hadn't used it, probably due to the extremely expensive ammunition it consumed. It sprayed thousands of explosive flechettes per second into the undergrowth. The countless tiny explosions combined to create a continuous roaring that sounded like a giant beast gone mad. Incoming fire dwindled to almost nothing right away. Whether the attackers had been decimated by the flechette gun, or had simply withdrawn when it opened up, McCade couldn't tell.

For a while they waited, expecting the attack to begin anew. But it didn't. One by one they dropped off again into exhausted sleep. Even the occasional roar of night feeders, disturbed by the passage of tractor and trailer, failed to wake them.

It was daylight when McCade opened his eyes. The rain had stopped, allowing occasional shafts of sunlight to penetrate the forest canopy and splash through the bars onto the huddled prisoners. Outside, a light mist ebbed and flowed along the contours of the ground.

Before long they began to pass occasional dwellings. Without exception, they were built on pilings, and were therefore immune to the comings and goings of the water below them. Most were circular and had domed roofs. The roofs were hinged in some fashion, allowing certain sections to be folded open. Quite a few were exercising that option, apparently to take advantage of the sun.

Gradually the tractor and trailer bounced and jolted onto increasingly busy thoroughfares, and it wasn't long before they entered a good-sized town. McCade noticed that even clearly commercial buildings never exceeded three or four stories. The water-soaked ground probably wouldn't support more weight than that, he thought. Of course, it could be a shortage of appropriate technology too. He remembered reading that buildings higher than three stories weren't common on Terra either, until after the invention of the elevator. Everywhere he looked he saw a strange juxtaposition of current technology and primitive culture. As far as McCade could tell there were no public utilities as such. If a homeowner wanted power, they could buy their own small fusion plant, otherwise forget it. That seemed to suggest a weak or nonexistent central government. Maybe the slave traders were in control. That would explain a lot.

All-terrain vehicles were popular, though. It was a rare dwelling that didn't boast a late-model vehicle sitting out front, often right next to the rotting wooden boat it had replaced. By the same token, the streets seemed more accidental than planned. It seemed as if they had been superimposed over and around an extensive canal system. The canals had evidently fallen into disuse. They were choked with water weed, and were apparently regarded as nuisances by Lakorian drivers. Equipped as they were with all-terrain vehicles, *they* tended to regard any ground not actually occupied by a house or tree as part of the road.

McCade wondered what would happen to the Lakorian economy if the slave trade suddenly disappeared. Most of the off-world income would disappear along with it. All-terrain vehicles would run out of imported fuel and be left to rust by owners who couldn't afford to import it privately. And, McCade thought to himself, a lot of folks would suddenly start repairing their boats.

The tractor-trailer twisted and turned endlessly through narrow and often obstructed streets before finally jerking to a halt in front of a raw-looking stockade. "Uh-oh, boss," Van Doren said. "This looks like home sweet home."

"Home maybe," Sara replied, holding her nose, "but sweet it isn't."

McCade silently agreed. An unbelievable stench surrounded the stockade. The reason was obvious. An open ditch followed the perimeter of the wall, creating an informal moat. The moat was filled to overflowing with rain water and the sewage generated by thousands of slaves, past and present. The stockade itself had been constructed using the time-honored system of digging a trench, standing logs upright shoulder to shoulder, and then filling in around the bottom with dirt. As the tractor drew near, a gate made of rude-looking planks swung open to admit it and then squealed closed as the vehicles lumbered clear.

The tractor ground to a halt in the large open space dominating the center of the stockade. The passage of vehicles and thousands of feet had turned the dirt there to mud. In the exact center of the open space stood a wooden platform. Its surface had been worn smooth by constant use and bore ominous-looking stains. A striped awning had been rigged over it to keep off the rain, granting it a sort of false gaiety. McCade didn't need a tour guide to explain the platform's purpose. It was empty now, but would be in use as soon as the slave auctions began. Beyond the platform was a swirling mass of flesh, feather and scale—citizens of a hundred worlds—talking, laughing, bickering, and fighting. Passing the time as they waited for the next round of buying and selling to begin.

For the first time since landing, McCade began to feel afraid. Up to now he'd assured himself that some sort of chance to escape would present itself and he'd be ready. But it hadn't and now it looked as though it never would. There was a screech of rusty metal as a Lakorian guard opened the gate on their trailer. With a series of grunts, kicks, and unintelligible commands, he forced them out. They stood in a bedraggled huddle ankle deep in the muck of the compound. McCade tried to get his bearings and spot weak points in the stockade. He hadn't found any when the sorting began.

Three stumpy Lakorian guards waded into their midst and started pushing and shoving. With expertise born of much practice, they roughly grouped their prisoners according to race. No sooner had that been accomplished than they stepped in and began sorting by sex. As a squat guard grabbed Sara and jerked her away, McCade jumped on its back and tried for a choke hold. He might just as well have tried to choke an oak tree. A second guard peeled him off without much effort and smashed him down into the muck with a single blow from some sort of cudgel. McCade picked himself up just in time to see Sara disappear into one of the low slave pens which lined the inside of the stockade wall. His head buzzed from the blow, and his stomach knotted up in fear and anger. He had tensed for a hopeless run toward the slave pens when he felt a firm grip on his arm.

It was Van Doren. "Whoa, boss. Not now. We'll get our chance later."

At first McCade was ready to throw Van Doren's hand off and go anyway. But after a second he calmed down enough to realize the marine was right. There wasn't any point to it. Even if he outran the closest guards, he couldn't outrun the energy weapons he'd seen mounted at regular intervals along the top of the stockade.

He nodded and felt Van Doren's hand fall away. The Lakorian guards were leading one of the Finthians, evidently a hen, away toward the pens. They had also taken one of the three Sephs. Evidently one qualified as a female and the other two as males. The two males were obviously distraught and uttered pitiful squealing noises. The single Cellite meanwhile stood in dejected misery. Next to him the bearlike alien remained impassive. McCade could detect no sign of fear or dejection in the shaggy brute's stance. He noted with interest that large brown eyes, black nose, and large rounded ears were taking everything in. It stood at least seven feet tall and probably weighed three hundred pounds. A powerful friend indeed if some kind of alliance could be forged.

Then it was their turn. The remaining Finthian, along with the two Sephs and the dispirited Cellite, were herded off in one direction, while McCade, Van Doren and the bear were taken in another. After sloshing across the compound, they were shoved into a pen, and an iron door slammed closed behind them.

It was dim inside the pen, lit only by one old chem strip and what little sunlight managed to find its way in through cracks and holes. The dirt floor was relatively dry and slanted toward a ditch at the back of the cell, thereby encouraging runoff. The ditch contained a sluggish flow of water, and judging from the smell, served as part of the open sewer system.

A few informal kicks quickly testified to the soundness of Lakorian construction techniques. So much for knocking the wall down. McCade found a spigot, from which he managed to coax a trickle of water. After slaking their thirst and scraping off what dirt they could, McCade and Van Doren plopped down and leaned against a wall.

"I don't suppose either one of you fellow homosaps has a dope stick secreted about your persons?" The voice was a rumbling basso and originated from their shaggy cell mate. The most surprising thing was that he spoke perfect, unaccented Terran.

"Sorry," McCade replied, patting his pockets. "Don't use 'em much. I might have a partly smoked cigar though."

"Any port in a storm, my granddaddy always said," the big creature replied as McCade handed him a half-smoked cigar.

Having found a shorter butt for himself, McCade lit up and leaned over to light the other's as well. Van Doren watched the ritual suspiciously as though sure their furry companion was up to no good. When both had their cigars drawing satisfactorily, the bear said conversationally, "You know, we're in a lot of trouble."

"Really?" McCade asked with a raised eyebrow. "You mean this isn't the Lunar Hilton?"

"Go ahead . . . kid around," the other said, gesturing with his cigar. "But don't blame me when you're sweating your ass off in some mine."

"I won't," McCade said with a smile. "But while we're on the subject of you, who are you anyway? Did I understand you to say 'fellow homosaps' earlier? No offense, but most humans come with a lot less hair."

"No offense taken," the bear said calmly. "I'm aware of my hirsuteness. But that's what you've got to expect if you're an Iceworld Variant. By the way, the name's Phil. Sorry about the little love tap I gave you in the trailer. It was just a reflex action."

McCade had heard of Variants but never met one. That wasn't too surprising since he knew they were damned expensive. Variants started out as normal humans. But after extensive biosculpting, something doctors on Terra specialized in, they ended up suited to one particular and usually exotic environment. In Phil's case, he'd been sculpted for work on the Iceworlds. Considering that Alice fell three classifications short of Iceworld status, McCade shuddered to imagine what such worlds were like.

"How come you didn't tell us this in the trailer?" Van Doren growled.

"I was waiting to see what kind of folks you were," Phil replied amiably. "Frankly I don't always choose to associate with fellow homosaps. But when you jumped that guard in the compound, I knew you were my kind of folks."

"This must be a little tropical for you, isn't it?" McCade asked.

Phil nodded in agreement as he blew a long column of smoke into the humid air. "Frankly it's hotter than an Il Ronnian steam bath."

"Somehow they knew you were human, because they put you in here with us," McCade mused.

"Hey, boss," Van Doren said. "If he's a human Variant, then he's probably augmented too." The marine continued to regard Phil with suspicion.

"Good point. Phil?" McCade said evenly. "How about it?"

"Sure," Phil replied with the wave of a hairy paw. "I'm augmented. All the usual stuff. Back-up infrared vision, amplified muscle response, razor-sharp, durasteel claws, the whole ball of wax. Doesn't do me much good against energy weapons though."

"Nonetheless," McCade said, "it can't hurt. How did you wind up here anyway, Phil?"

Phil shrugged eloquently. "I'm a research biologist indentured to United Biomed. Me and Mac. He was my partner. Anyway, we were outbound to our station on Frio IV with a load of supplies. That's when the pirate jumped us." Phil took a long, final drag from the cigar before stubbing it out.

"We didn't stand a chance," he said soberly. "When they came aboard they gunned Mac just for the hell of it. Called him a freak." Phil shook his huge head, and his lips peeled back to bare the durasteel teeth that ran the length of his short snout. "God help 'em if I ever catch 'em," he said through a growl.

McCade nodded his understanding. "Tough break, Phil. . . . Pretty much the same as what happened to us." He waved his cigar butt vaguely.

"Yeah, sure," Phil said as one round ear twitched. He obviously didn't believe a word of it.

All three were silent for a while. McCade found he couldn't stop thinking about Sara. He tried to force thoughts of her out of his mind so that he could think, plan, find some means of escape. But it didn't work.

Time passed and when the door to their cell finally screeched open, McCade found himself face-to-face with Brother Mungo.

THIRTEEN

The door clanged shut. McCade stared at Mungo with disbelief. It couldn't be. He'd seen Laurie slice Mungo's head off. He'd seen her carry it around. And later he'd seen the Treel deliver it to the Il Ronn. Nonetheless Mungo sat across from him, head firmly seated on his shoulders, eyes on the dirt floor.

"Boss . . ." Van Doren broke the silence.

"Yeah, I know, Amos," McCade answered wearily. "It's our old friend the Treel again. Well, what brings Your Supreme Softness to our humble abode? Slumming?"

Mungo's hooded eyes came up to meet his. McCade forced himself to remember that it wasn't really Mungo. It wasn't even the Treel impersonating Mungo. The sadness in those eyes was the Treel's. Speaking with Mungo's deep, melodious voice, the Treel made no attempt to hide his identity.

"As usual, you jest, rigid one. Nonetheless I shall answer your question. The great Yareel has seen fit to frown upon me. A great sadness is upon me. My suffering is beyond all knowing. I am not here of my own free will."

"Wait a minute. This guy's a Treel?" Phil interrupted.

McCade nodded.

"No kidding!" Phil exclaimed. "I remember coming across them in exobiology . . . but a real one. Damn! They're really rare."

"This one isn't," McCade replied. "Every time we turn around we trip over him."

"Why's he wearing the chemlock?" Phil asked.

"Chemlock?" McCade looked, but didn't see anything unusual about Mungo's appearance.

"Yeah," Phil insisted. "Right there behind his left ear. See it. The little black box."

McCade moved closer to take advantage of what little light there was. The Treel ignored him. It was almost invisible against Mungo's black skin, but sure enough, there was a small container tucked behind the man's left ear.

"That's a chemlock," Phil explained. "It's feeding tiny amounts of chemicals into his bloodstream. If you try to take it out . . . boom! A charge goes off and so does his head. Somebody thought it up as a way to medicate psychopaths while allowing them back into society. Never seemed to catch on though. . . . People didn't like having them around. Afraid they'd blow up without warning, I guess."

"Let's see if it really works, boss," Van Doren said cheerfully.

"Why, Amos! I'm ashamed of you. It wouldn't be fair for Mungo to lose his head twice in a row, now would it?" McCade said sternly.

"As usual, I will ignore your jibes, rigid ones. Essentially you are correct. The little container dispenses chemicals which affect my metabolism and prevent me from changing appearance. A small gift from Sept Commander Reez. He thought forcing me to appear human on a permanent basis was quite amusing." The Treel shrugged. "It's all I deserved for trusting a rigid one."

"So why the falling out?" McCade asked, settling down again by Van Doren.

The Treel paused for a moment as though gathering its thoughts. There was pain in its eyes. "You were taken away. It was hot and uncomfortable in my native form, so I assumed the guise of an Il Ronnian officer. I was escorted to the ship's recreational area and told to wait while they took Mungo's brain to a lab for pumping.

"After a while, I grew bored and decided to take a look around. There was a library just off the lounge. The auto-attendant ignored me, so I entered, hoping for a glimpse of my native planet. I selected the appropriate survey tape and plugged it into a holo player."

Watching Mungo's eyes, McCade saw the Treel's pain turn to despair.

"I turned it on. I looked, and looked again. There was nothing. Where my planet had once circled the 'Light of Yareel,' there was only the blackness of space."

The Treel looked at each of them in turn, his eyes searching their faces. Making sure they understood the significance of what he'd said. Looking for something. Compassion? Understanding? McCade couldn't tell.

"They destroyed it a year ago while I attended your Academy as Cadet Votava. They blew it up. My world, shattered into a new asteroid belt. Shattered too was the future of my race." With that his eyes fell, and he began to chant in his native tongue. The chant had an eerie quality that sent a shiver up McCade's spine. It was filled with sadness and loneliness.

In spite of Cadet Votava, Laurie and all the others the Treel had killed, McCade felt sorry for the strange alien. In a way the Treel was as much a victim as those he'd killed. After a few minutes, the chanting stopped, to be replaced by an uncomfortable silence. McCade broke it with a single word.

"Why?"

The Treel looked up through Mungo's pain-filled eyes. "I asked their computer that very question. The answer was to quell a rebellion against Il Ronnian authority. As I explained to you once before, the Il Ronn have long held our planet hostage against the good behavior of agents like myself."

A look of pride suffused Mungo's face. "But apparently my brethren at home were not as easily intimidated as I. They rose up and fought as only Treel can. Imagine fighting a race which can endlessly shift forms. One moment vicious carnivore, the next your commanding officer, and then perhaps yourself. We have never been a large race, but nonetheless the Il Ronn lost every battle. Remember that they also had to fight the endless variety of dangerous life forms that populated my planet. In the end, they had to destroy the planet or lose face. Something they cannot stand. So now I and a few like me are all that's left."

Even Van Doren seemed touched. His voice was gentle as he said, "And they caught you?"

The Treel nodded Mungo's head. "I don't know how long I sat there staring at the print-out. It must have been a long time. When I looked up, Reez was standing in front of me with a sneer on his face." The Treel sighed.

"They paralyzed me. . . . Yes," he waved a hand in McCade's direction, "it can be done if you know what to use. Some rather pointless negotiations ensued, during which Reez attempted to secure my continued services. I refused, of course. I have some self-respect. Then I was forced to assume this form. The chemlock was inserted to make sure I would remain this way. I was then sent down in a shuttle. Actually it was your ship if I'm not mistaken," the Treel said, nodding toward McCade. "And here I am. Selling me into slavery as a human amused Commander Reez greatly."

"The bastard," Van Doren said, imagining what he'd do to the Il Ronnian officer if he had the chance.

"You know," Phil said thoughtfully, "if I had some lab facilities, I think I could disarm and remove that chemlock."

"An interesting offer," McCade replied. "However I'm not sure it would be a good idea. Our friend here tends to be a little undependable given too much freedom. Besides, I like the way he looks, don't you, Amos?"

Van Doren grunted in the affirmative.

"I have a feeling my fellow homosaps are being less than forthright," Phil said gently as he examined a gleaming durasteel claw. "Perhaps you should tell me how all this began."

McCade thought about it for a moment and concluded there was little point in keeping Phil in the dark. Plus there was always the possibility that he might help. So he briefly outlined the events leading up to their present predicament.

When he was finished, Phil gave a low whistle. "So now the Il Ronn know where the War World is and you don't."

"True, I'm afraid," McCade confessed.

Suddenly the Treel sat up and spoke. "Yes, rigid ones, suddenly I understand. The great Yareel has truly blessed me! I shall be the instrument of his revenge! I shall bring down destruction upon the Il Ronn! And you shall be my allies. Together we will destroy the infidel!"

The three humans looked at each other in amazement. From the depths of despair, the Treel had somehow been transformed into a religious zealot, and an arrogant one at that. McCade's thoughts were interrupted by the rasp of unoiled metal as someone unlatched the door to their cell.

A huge Lakorian foot kicked it open. "Out," was all its owner said.

They obeyed; there seemed no advantage in doing anything else. One by one they emerged from the dim cell to stand blinking in the Lakorian daylight.

"Move."

The order was accompanied by a powerful shove from behind, and McCade found himself propelled toward the wooden platform which dominated the center of the compound. Now it was surrounded by a milling crowd of shouting, gesticulating buyers. The slave auction had begun.

McCade was surprised. For some reason he had expected more time to pass between their arrival and subsequent sale. He felt he should have developed some sort of plan. A means to escape. Something. But for the life of him he couldn't imagine what. As they moved toward the platform, he searched for some sign of Sara. There wasn't any and his spirits sank even lower. The crowd parted to let them through. Around him McCade heard snatches of conversation. He could understand most of it since it was in standard, which functioned as a sort of universal trading language. As the humans made their way through the crowd, their merits were enthusiastically debated.

"Look at the big one, Forn. . . . If we were careful with him, he might last a whole year."

"Mebbe, mebbe, but how 'bout the furry one. . . . I say he'd do right well."

"Get serious, Forn. He'd be fine on an iceworld, but he wouldn't last a week on Lava."

"Up."

Another shove boosted McCade up the first two steps. As he gained the top he saw what might have been a Cellite being escorted off the other end of the platform. He couldn't be sure.

They were lined up without ceremony and told to strip. As McCade complied, he noted with interest that the auctioneer was an android. A General Electric Model Twenty, if he wasn't mistaken. Its makers had granted it a vaguely human appearance, though without much attention to detail. Some of its metal parts had begun to rust in the humid climate of Lakor, and it had taken some heavy-duty dents. However, in spite of the cosmetic flaws, the droid proved to be a skilled auctioneer. Evidently it had its own built-in amplifier, because when it spoke its voice boomed out across the compound with sufficient volume that even the most distant buyer could hear with ease.

"Gentlebeings . . . your attention, please. Before you is lot three on your print-out. Four human males, all in good health, all capable of running simple machinery. I direct your attention to item four. You will notice this item is an Iceworld Variant and a skilled biologist. You may wish to consider him for specialized activity. As usual we will take bids for the entire lot first. If we have no acceptable bids for the lot, we will then auction off each item separately. Bidding for lot three can now begin."

Bidding began at four thousand credits offered by a nasty-looking human dressed in worn body armor and using a nerve lash for a swagger stick. He was immediately outbid by a female Zord who, having no vocal apparatus, signaled her bids in universal sign language by use of her tentacles. Then the bidding grew hot and heavy, moving too quickly for McCade to track. The price had reached sixteen thousand credits when suddenly a booming voice cut through the cacophony as though it wasn't there.

"Twenty thousand credits, sport, and let's have done with it!"

With sudden hope, McCade searched the crowd and sure enough, standing like an island in the sea of bodies, was Rico. An enormous grin split his bearded face and tiny eyes twinkled merrily.

"Not that they're worth even half that," he added, laughing uproariously.

There were no further bids. "Sold to the human for twenty thousand credits," the android said. "Pay the slave master and collect your property."

McCade barely managed to snatch up his clothes before a Lakorian guard shoved him toward the other end of the platform with a grunted, "Off."

He was still struggling into them when a massive slap on the back threatened to drop him into the mud. "Good to see ya, ol' sport! Course I wasn't plannin' on seein' all of ya like that!" Once again the big man broke into gales of laughter.

McCade grinned and shook Rico's hand. "Go ahead, Rico, have your fun, I was never so glad to see something so ugly in my whole life! I thought we'd lost you back at the Rock!"

Just then Van Doren arrived. He and Rico proceeded to dance around each other, trading blows. When they stopped to shake hands, there was a moment of silence as muscles knotted and sweat broke out on their foreheads.

"Are they always like this?" Phil inquired as they watched the two men straining to best each other.

McCade nodded. "Worse, if anything. Maybe you'd like to join in." He looked Phil up and down. "I suspect you could take them both."

The huge Variant shook his head. "No thanks, given a choice I'm more the cerebral type."

With grunts of expelled air, Rico and Van Doren broke off their contest. Their happy grins indicated another draw.

"Well now that you've got that out of your systems, maybe we can get on with other things," McCade said in mock annoyance.

"What was that, slave?" Rico asked with a grin. "I paid good money to take this? Come to think of it, how am I gonna explain the twenty thousand credits to the Council? They're already complainin' about my expense account."

McCade laughed and then said worriedly, "Speaking of the Council, Sara is around here somewhere, and we've got to buy her out too."

Rico's expression darkened to one of concern. "'Fraid I've got some bad news for ya. Sara's gone. She was sold a few hours ago . . . before I got here . . . and the buyer's long gone, with her in tow."

"Damn!" McCade exclaimed in frustration. "Off-planet?"

Rico shook his shaggy head. "Nope. They headed for the interior." He gestured toward the jungle, which crowded one end of the stockade.

"The guy who bought her is some kind of Lakorian nobleman. Calls himself 'King,' but I understand there's some who dispute that."

"Well what are we waiting for?" McCade asked grimly. "Let's go see the King."

Rico didn't move. He just smiled bemusedly and raised an eyebrow. "No offense, but what happened to the War World? Last time I heard it was top priority. If it's really as important as ya said, Sara'd want us ta deal with that first."

"And it is important, Rico," McCade said sheepishly. "I guess where Sara is concerned I've developed tunnel vision. Besides, for the moment we've hit a dead end where finding the War World is concerned."

Rico grinned ear to ear. "So it's like that, is it. . . . Well I'm glad to hear it. Just remember, ya treat her right or you'll answer ta Rico!" The big man slapped McCade on the back. "So what're we waitin' for? Let's go see the King!"

As they walked toward the gate, the other three fell in behind.

"By the way, who're those two?" Rico asked, gesturing over his shoulder with a thumb. "The only reason I bought 'em was ta keep it simple. Somebody might have run up the bidding on you or Amos. What're we gonna do with the hairy one?"

"Hell, Rico," McCade replied with a grin, "he isn't that much hairier than you are!" As they walked McCade filled the other man in on Phil's background and Mungo's true identity.

When McCade had finished, Rico glanced in the direction of the Treel and said, "That one'll bear watching. I don't like the look in his eye."

McCade nodded in agreement.

As they passed through the gate, Van Doren and Phil offered the Lakorian guards a parting gesture older than universal sign language. They were stoically ignored.

"Now what about you, Rico?" McCade asked. "How in the world did you manage to end up here at the perfect moment?"

"Well . . . first off, it wasn't perfect. If it had been, we wouldn't be goin' after Sara. Anyway it wasn't all that hard. I waited off the Rock just like we agreed. Had a coupla tense moments with a pirate destroyer but managed ta convince 'em I was relining a bare spot in the port tube. Then all hell broke loose, and I wasted a lot of time picking you outta the mess. Finally I managed ta pick up the minibeacon Sara was wearin," Rico said.

"Wait a minute," McCade interrupted. "What minibeacon? I don't remember any minibeacon."

Rico looked embarrassed. "Well ol' sport, Professor Wendel's people worked it up. It's specially shielded and undetectable. She's wearing it right under the skin near her left shoulder blade. Seemed like a good time to try it out." Rico shrugged and grinned. "Let's just say they wanted some insurance.

"Anyhow I sorted ya outta the herd usin' the beacon. I saw ya waste those two pirates—nice piece o' work by the way—and busted my buns tryin' ta catch up. Just as I was gettin' close, the biggest Il Ronnian ship I've ever seen came outta hyperspace and locked on ta ya." Rico gestured eloquently. "After that I just followed ya here. Fortunately there's lotsa slavers comin' and goin' so nobody asked me any questions. Then I lost some time sellin' *Lady Alice* or I woulda been here sooner."

"You sold *Alice* . . ."

"'Fraid so. They wouldn't let me buy ya with my good looks, ya know."

"I'm sorry, Rico. I know what the *Lady* meant to you. I'll make it up to you somehow."

"Not to worry. Feast your eyes on my new transport. Handsome, ain't she?"

McCade stopped in amazement. The vehicle to which Rico referred so proudly was a monument to the determination of durasteel molecules to remain in close proximity to each other. Its dents had dents. It was leaking fuel and lubricant from a dozen points. Entire treads were missing from the giant tracks. Rust had eaten deeply into its huge hull. And it *was* huge. It stood at least fifty feet high and twice that in length. The front end consisted of a circular energy projector the diameter of the vehicle itself. The center of the projector was hollow for some distance back, eventually narrowing down to a hole about five feet across. In operating, the energy projector could cut a circular hole through solid rock. Then the loosened material could be funneled back to be pulverized and superheated. After treatment with various additives, the liquid soil and rock would then be spun out behind the machine to form a perfect tunnel. If ore was located, the shaft thus created could be used to mine it.

"I bought her used," Rico said proudly.

"Thank God," McCade muttered, inspecting the vehicle's scarred plating. "I'd hate to ride in anything that looked that bad new."

McCade's comments were lost on Rico. He had already started to extoll the vehicle's virtues. "They brought 'er dirtside ta do a mineralogical survey. Guess they hoped they'd find somethin' worth minin', but no such luck. Guess that's why slavin's so important here'bouts. Anyway everything ya could possibly want's built right in. Food, supplies, sleepin' quarters, even showers. She's got 'em all. Plus a few surprises. Come on."

A control box of some kind suddenly appeared in Rico's hand. He pressed a button and a door slid aside. Then a set of pneumatic stairs unfolded with a hiss of escaping air to touch the mud. McCade and the others followed Rico aboard.

The vehicle's interior was in marked contrast to its exterior. Everything showed signs of wear, but appeared to be well maintained, and was reasonably clean. Originally designed for a crew of ten, it provided more than enough space for their small group. Besides the creature comforts, the vehicle boasted considerable armament, including auto-slug throwers, energy weapons, and a single battery of multipurpose missiles.

"Nice, Rico," McCade said, peering into the sighting scope of an energy weapon. "But is all this necessary?"

"'Fraid so, ol' sport," Rico said, handing McCade one of his imported cigars. "There ain't no public transportation where we're goin'. The King likes it that way. Plus I hear there's some real nasty critters waitin' out there. Not to mention the King, who ain't likely to welcome us with open arms."

McCade nodded agreement as he remembered the trip to the stockade. The armament would probably come in handy.

"How about air travel though?"

Rico shook his head as he blew out a stream of blue smoke. "Nice thought, but the King don't allow no atmospheric stuff . . . 'cept his o' course. Sorry, but that's how it is."

"Thanks, Rico," McCade said. "You've done a fantastic job. How soon can we get under way?"

"Right now. Just give me a few minutes to crank 'er up."

While Rico ran through an operations list, McCade wandered back to check on the rest of the group. Van Doren had made himself busy checking out various weapons systems, the Treel sat lost in meditation, and Phil was halfway through an enormous sandwich in the galley. McCade realized it had been a long time since his last meal. He plopped down at the mess table and began building himself a sandwich.

"Rico's up forward, cranking her up, Phil," McCade said. "We're going after Sara Bridger. Frankly we could use your help, but you don't owe us anything. If you'd like to bailout, now's the time to do it. Rico's probably got enough credits to get you off-planet. How about it?"

Phil chewed a gigantic mouthful of sandwich thoughtfully for a moment before speaking. "Well I've been thinking, Sam. Like I told you, my partner's dead and chances are the company thinks I'm dead too. Why tell 'em otherwise? I've got another seven years to run on my indenture, assuming of course I survive that long. Well, maybe I could spend those seven years my way. From what you said, Rico's planet would be just right for a Variant like myself. So if they'd take me I'd like to sign up."

"United Biomed's loss would seem to be Alice's gain," McCade replied cheerfully. "I can't speak for Alice, but Rico sits on the Council. Let's ask him."

A few minutes later Rico was pumping the paw of Alice's newest citizen by executive decree. "If those bozos from Biomed ever show up on Alice, we'll arrest 'em for something and ship 'em out. By the way," Rico said, looking the big Variant up and down, "remind me ta talk with you 'bout a reserve commission in the militia."

As the huge vehicle's engines thundered into life, McCade entered a small stim shower. He was a free man again, and he wanted to look like one.

FOURTEEN

Big fat raindrops splattered against the windshield and made a drumming sound on the roof of the giant crawler as it fought its way through thick undergrowth. A steady wind bent the vegetation toward them, adding considerably to the strain on the howling engines. Inside the cab it was warm and dry, but far from comfortable. Every few seconds the violent motion of the machine threatened to throw McCade out of his seat. His shoulders were already sore from countless encounters with the harness holding him in place. In the driver's seat next to him, Rico frowned in concentration. They had tried the autopilot but found it couldn't deal with the irregular terrain. And deal they must to reach the glowing green dot representing Sara's minibeacon some two hundred miles ahead. At least she was still alive.

Rico's tiny eyes flitted from one instrument to the next while his large, hairy hands played over the controls with surprising dexterity. So far Rico's skill had taken them over sixty-degree slopes of loose rock, through a labyrinth of giant trees, and on one occasion, across a lake, underwater, an activity which didn't bother the machine, but scared the hell out of Mc-Cade.

In spite of all that, McCade felt better. He had slept for twelve hours, eaten an enormous breakfast, and then donned a one-piece black coverall which Rico assured him also functioned as light body armor. Welcome too was the new slug gun resting low on his right thigh, and the plentiful supply of cigars which filled the breast pockets of his jump suit. Rico had thought of everything.

As the crawler lurched along, McCade tried to plan for what lay ahead. It wasn't easy. For one thing they knew very little about what they might face. What Rico had been able to learn was a jumbled amalgamation of fact and fiction. The challenge lay in figuring out which was which. Sara's beacon had remained stationary for more than twenty hours, suggesting that she had arrived somewhere. Presumably King Zorta's castle. Nobody knew for sure because, with the exception of Zorta's most trusted advisors, those who went to the castle never came back. In fact it was rumored that the King's desire for privacy was so strong that those employed to build the castle were buried under it.

Without doubt, the King had good reasons to protect himself. For one thing there was a considerable number of other Lakorian nobles who felt that killing the former King didn't necessarily entitle you to his throne. They did, however, feel that it was a good place to start. As a result there had been numerous, though so far unsuccessful, attempts on Zorta's life.

Also counting against him, in McCade's estimation, the King had systematically encouraged the population to turn from their traditional pursuits of farming, fishing, and light manufacture to an economy dominated by the slave trade. At first the population enjoyed the foreign exchange thus generated, but gradually their enjoyment began to wane as rumors began to circulate—rumors about slave raids on remote Lakorian villages. Then too, taxes had begun to rise dramatically. As a result, tax evasion had become a popular hobby. To counter this trend Zorta introduced a policy of not only executing tax evaders, but their families as well. As a result of these and similar policies, the King's popularity was decidedly limited. Nonetheless, due to an effective army and air force, he continued to rule. And it seemed would continue to do so indefinitely.

All they really knew was that Sara was probably being held in the King's castle. McCade forced his thoughts away from any consideration of why she had been taken there or what might happen to her. He forced himself to concentrate on how to get her out. In spite of the machine's violent motion, he found himself drifting into a light sleep, during which he imagined an endless procession of fantastic schemes by which the castle walls could be breached. Unfortunately something always seemed to go wrong at the last moment. His reverie came to an abrupt halt, along with the crawler itself.

"Damn! I'm afraid we've got trouble, ol' sport," Rico said, releasing his harness and sliding out of his seat. "'Cordin' ta the diagnostics, we've got some kinda problem with the port engine. Not too surprisin' considerin' the kinda country we've been going through. Anyway I'm goin' below for a look-see. Stay here and keep an eye on those sensors. Keep in mind that without the port engine we ain't got enough juice ta power the defensive screens."

On that cheerful note he was gone.

McCade flicked the detectors from low to high intensity. The driving rain rendered the high mag video cameras useless beyond a few yards. The metal detectors showed trace elements in the soil and surrounding vegetation, as did the radiation screens. Infrared indicated a variety of life forms in the area. They ranged in size from very large to very small. As far as McCade could tell, there were about the same number they'd been seeing all along. He sat back, lit a new cigar and kicked his feet up. As he smoked, he scanned the monitors occasionally, watching for changes.

The intercom chimed and Rico's voice boomed forth. "It appears we lost a bearing. Looks like a three-hour job. Say, send Amos down ta help, would ya? I need someone with more brawn than brains!"

At that point Van Doren broke in with, "The truth is he hasn't got a clue on how to change a bearing! Guess I'll go down and save his ass like always."

McCade laughed as the intercom went dead. Glancing up at the monitors he thought at first glance that they all looked the same. Then something about the infrared monitor made him take another look. Then he realized that the number of red blobs on the screen had doubled. Not only that, they were slowly moving to surround the crawler.

His eyes stayed glued to the infrared monitor as he reached for the intercom button.

"Phil . . . I think we've got company. I'm not sure *what* they are, but they're a lot of them, and they're slowly surrounding us. I'm delegating control of both waist turrets to 'local.' I suggest you pick one and stand-by. And while you're at it see if old Softie will come out of meditation long enough to kill a few infidels. If there's trouble we could use him in the other turret."

Phil's voice came back, calmly efficient. "You've got it, Sam. . . . We'll be on line in a minute."

As he watched the red blobs continue to surround them, McCade noticed that even more were slowly drifting into the screen's range. One by one he activated the crawler's weapons systems until all the indicators glowed green. All the while, the blobs continued their encirclement. Was it random movement of a herd of animals that just happened to be feeding in the area? Or were they guided by some intelligence? There was no way to tell. And until full power was restored, there wasn't much they could do. If the red blobs were hostile, limping at them on one engine wouldn't help much.

Conditions remained static for more than an hour. The gradual gathering of red blobs had peaked at about two hundred. Occasionally smaller groups of four or five would break away and disappear off screen. However their absence was balanced out as other small groupings and individuals drifted in.

McCade stubbed out his latest cigar and sipped a little cold coffee, trying to wash the raw taste out of his mouth. His left cheek twitched, and his eyes hurt from staring at the monitors. He leaned back in his seat, consciously forcing his muscles to relax. Looking up he noticed with interest that the rain seemed to be slacking off. As a result the high mag video cameras had begun to clear. Without warning the rain stopped completely and McCade found himself looking at a scene of barbaric splendor.

His first impression was of vibrant shimmering color which ebbed and flowed with the movement of animals and riders. The huge, six-legged reptillian animals wore trappings of bright blue. Each carried three Lakorian riders decked out in bright orange with dark brown trim. The lead rider of each animal carried a wicked-looking lance from which a long, green pennant flew. Behind him his two companions were armed with efficient-looking energy weapons of a design unfamiliar to McCade. And behind them, each mount carried a large set of saddle bags, filled no doubt with food for the riders and power paks for the weapons. It was an impressive and intimidating sight which, McCade reflected, was probably the whole idea.

The intercom chimed, followed by Phil's awed voice. "Holy Sol, would you look at that! What do you think, Sam . . . friend or foe?"

"Beats me, Phil," McCade replied. "But let's stay ready for anything."

It was hard to guess the intentions of the Lakorians because of the constant movement. Evidently their reptillian mounts didn't like to stand still. However the riders were obviously experienced and, while their animals remained in motion, they themselves managed to stay in the same position relative to all the other mounts.

As the warm sunshine came into contact with the wet earth, a ground fog began to form, making it seem as though the Lakorians were floating. As McCade watched, a single animal separated itself from the rest and began to move toward the crawler. Unlike the other mounts, this particular animal carried a single rider. The lance he bore carried a flag on which some complicated device had been embroidered. McCade also noticed a long whip antenna extending up from the back of the saddle to sway in the light breeze. Whoever he was he had a powerful radio at his disposal and that implied friends somewhere. Something to keep in mind.

A hundred yards from the crawler the reptillian mount stopped momentarily as its rider dismounted. The Lakorian planted his lance in the ground with something of a flourish and then assumed a position closely resembling parade rest. His animal began to pace back and forth behind him.

As McCade released his harness he hit the intercom once more. "Rico, Amos, you've been tracking all this?"

"Yeah, boss. . . . We've been watching with one eye. Looks like a convention of pleasure dome pimps to me."

"Thank God you chose the marines and not the diplomatic corps," McCade said, getting up. "How long till full power?"

"Well, ol' sport," Rico answered, "we've been takin' a few short cuts, but even so it's gonna be another hour for sure."

"Okay," McCade replied. "It appears their leader's ready for a little talk, so I'm going outside."

"Wonder why he don't just call us on that radio," Amos wondered out loud.

"No way to tell, Amos," McCade said. "But I suspect there's some kind of ritual or formality involved."

"Or maybe they just want to waste you," Phil said suspiciously. "You're gonna be awfully exposed out there."

"True," McCade replied, checking the load in his slug gun. "But chances are he just wants to talk. If so there's the possibility of getting some help. Frankly, gentlemen, from what I've seen so far, I think we need it,"

"In that case, talk his arm off," Phil replied with a chuckle. "We'll cover you. Won't we, Softie?"

The Treel's voice sounded distant and bored over the intercom. "Of course. Let's get on with it."

"Grab your pocket-com on your way out," Phil said. "We might as well listen in."

McCade agreed and stopped long enough to pick up one of the small devices, activate it, and slip it into his breast pocket. As the hatch opened and the stairs unfolded to touch the ground, McCade took a deep breath of the fresh clean air. In a few hours the smell of rotting vegetation would once again dominate, but for the moment the rain had washed everything clean. His boots sank into the soft, spongy ground as he walked. Each one made a sucking sound as he pulled it free, and each grew heavier with accumulated mud the farther he went. Ahead the Lakorian still stood where McCade had last seen him. He waited patiently for McCade to approach while the giant steed paced back and forth behind him. As McCade got closer he saw that the Lakorian was handsome, by the standards of his race. He had a high forehead, two wide-set, intelligent eyes, broad cheekbones, a short, rounded snout having three nostrils, and a wide thick-lipped mouth. He was slender by Lakorian standards too, though still heavier than any human, and he stood a good foot shorter than McCade. McCade stopped a respectful distance from the Lakorian and, unsure of proper etiquette, bowed formally, a widely accepted sign of courteous greeting.

The Lakorian responded in kind. When he spoke it was in the High Standard favored by the Empire's nobility. His accent was atrocious. "Who have I the honor to address, and be you noble or vassal? I am Baron Lif."

Glancing down at his plain black jump suit and then up at the Baron's bright ceremonial garb, he understood the Lakorian's confusion. "My apologies, Baron, for not greeting you in more suitable garb, but I'm afraid my companions and I have foresworn normal dress due to a period of religious pennance. I am Sam McCade, Knight of the Round Table and trusted defender of King Arthur's court." He prayed Lif did not share his boyhood fascination with ancient legend. Especially Earth legend. He'd purposely chosen a rank below Lif's, having found through past dealings with aristocracy that this was less threatening, and placed them in a more amenable frame of mind.

The Baron nodded understandingly. "I too weary of the priesthood's restrictions, good Knight. I sometimes wonder if they have aught to do but think up new ones!"

McCade laughed appreciatively at the nobleman's joke and waited to see what direction the conversation would take next.

With the formalities taken care of, the Baron seemed disposed to get down to business. "I wish to bid you welcome to my poor barony and its meager resources. As you can see I ventured out this morning for a hunt, accompanied only by my personal bodyguard. I could not help but notice that your crawler seems somewhat incapacitated. How may I and my men be of help?"

McCade wasn't fooled for a moment. He was well aware that in spite of the Baron's polite phraseology, Lif had just informed him that he was trespassing, that the troops present were only part of the force at his disposal, that they knew the crawler was undergoing repairs, that the Baron therefore had the upper hand, and that McCade had better produce a good explanation of his activities and very quickly indeed.

Operating partly from intuition, and partly from shrewd guesswork, McCade assumed a slightly conspiratorial demeanor. "Well Baron, I appreciate your kindness. As it happens my men will soon have the crawler repaired, and we'll be able to resume our journey. I hope we haven't inconvenienced your hunt."

"Not at all," Lif said with a negligent wave of the hand. "Where are you bound? This is not easy country. Perhaps I could offer you a guide?"

A spy is more like it, McCade thought as he smiled his thanks, but I have no intention of letting you off that easy. "Once again the Baron is too kind. But to answer your question, my mission is one of the utmost delicacy. Involved is a lady of noble birth who now finds herself in compromising circumstances. Now I must beg the Baron's indulgence, for I have said too much."

"Not so, good Knight! Though we be of different races, surely we are bound by the common threads of nobility. Your difficulties are mine. I insist that you allow me to help," Baron Lif said earnestly.

McCade shook his head doubtfully. "I dare not impose further on your good graces, Baron. And in all truth the matter may be better left unspoken of, lest I unknowingly compromise one or both of us. After all I am a stranger in a strange land and know not what alliances and conventions I might unintentionally violate."

With considerable satisfaction, McCade saw from Lif's expression that the Lakorian nobleman was deeply and completely hooked.

"I assure you, noble Knight, that whatever you say shall remain a secret between us and shall not be the cause of offense on my part. Pray tell me more of this matter, that I might assist."

Haltingly at first, as though unsure of himself and searching for words, McCade spun a tale made of both fact and fiction. The way he told it, Sara was the irresponsible daughter of a doting King Arthur. Ignoring her father's urgings, once too often she had taken off in her speedster, alone, unescorted, to visit her married sister on the fourth planet of their system. En route she had been chased and captured by pirates, who sold her into slavery. McCade and his men had managed to track her down by following the shielded signal broadcast by a minibeacon each member of the royal family wore. Now they were following that signal to her location, the castle of a certain King Zorta, whoever he might be. There McCade hoped to buy her freedom and restore her to the arms of her loving father. As McCade completed his tale, he watched Baron Lif's eyes light up as the significance of the beacon sank in. No doubt about it, the Baron bought the story hook, line and sinker. Nonetheless the Lakorian nobleman was nobody's fool and hid his interest well.

Lif shook his head sadly. "Yes, a sad tale indeed. The young ones never listen. I fear it is a condition common to all races. But don't give up hope, my friend. I feel certain that the gods ordained our meeting, for I see common ground upon which we might meet and aid each other."

"Nothing would please me more," McCade answered enthusiastically. "In all truth I have worried greatly about our ability to make our way through the wilderness to King Zorta's castle. The plant and animal life on your planet are so . . . er . . . vigorous."

The Baron laughed, a deep and genuine guffawing sound that made his mount shy away. "Sir Knight, your tact does you credit. We shall get along well, you and I. But enough of this. Our plans should be completed over a good meal, with Vak to wash it down."

As McCade began to protest, Lif held up a gauntleted hand. "No, I won't hear of it. My hunting lodge is nearby. As soon as your machine is repaired, we shall escort you there."

Much as a jailer escorts a prisoners, McCade thought. The Baron rattled off a radio frequency on which McCade could contact him, vaulted into the saddle, and sent his steed galloping off.

McCade heaved a sigh of relief, turned, and made his way back to the crawler. Once safely inside he was greeted by hoots of laughter over the intercom.

"Boss, you could sell vacuum to asteroid miners," Van Doren chuckled.

"Yeah, ya sucked 'im in real good," Rico agreed. "Only now that ya got 'im, what're ya goin' ta do with him?"

"Finish reeling him in, of course," McCade responded. "And then put him to work."

A few hours later the crawler followed the leading elements of Lif's bodyguard out of the thick vegetation and into a large clearing. A sprawling wooden building dominated the clearing's center. It was quite large, and seemed even bigger because it had been built on ten-foot pilings. As Rico guided the crawler up to the lodge, Lif's household troops began to picket their mounts under the structure, between the massive pilings.

Over McCade's head a speaker crackled into life. "Welcome to Tree-home. As soon as the demands of your machine are satisfied, Sir Knight, please join me for dinner. Your squires are welcome also."

McCade left the Treel to watch the crawler, and Phil to watch the Treel. He was also concerned about Phil's reception within the lodge. There was no way to predict Lif's reaction to the Variant.

Together, McCade, Rico, and Amos picked their way through the mud to the lodge under the watchful gaze of a small honor guard. With the emphasis on "guard," McCade thought with amusement. Together they mounted a flight of stairs leading up to intricately carved double doors where they were met by a uniformed major domo. The Baron certainly likes to do things with style, McCade reflected as they were shown into a large hall with vaulted ceilings. A log fire blazed at the far end of the huge room, its flickering light dancing across tapestry-hung walls. However the room's even temperature hinted at central heating. It seemed a comfortable marriage of old and new.

As they approached, Baron Lif rose to greet them. He had been seated at a long table of highly polished wood.

"Welcome! Please be seated here at my right hand, good Knight. Welcome, gentlebeings. Sit wherever you like." Lif clapped his enormous hands. "Bring food! Vak for my guests!"

During the polite conversation preceeding dinner, McCade tried, without success, to get comfortable in the oversized chair. Then a seemingly endless procession of food and drink began. All was native Lakorian fare in which meat and vegetables played equal parts, often in the form of stews and casseroles. Most of it was quite good, although a couple of dishes were hardly to McCade's taste . . . particularly the white grubs served live with hot sauce.

Throughout the meal their Lakorian-sized mugs were never empty of the alcoholic Vak. It packed a real whallop, and it was soon clear the Baron intended to drink them under the table. He would have succeeded, too, if the humans hadn't anticipated such a move and taken inhibitors prior to dinner. But, in spite of that precaution, McCade's head was buzzing by the time the dishes had been cleared away and serious conversation began.

Baron Lif opened the negotiations politely. "Earlier, my friend, you indicated some concern about your ability to carry out your mission, given the natural impediments native to my planet."

"Absolutely true, Baron," McCade said somberly, slurring his words ever so slightly. "I'm afraid that even with the crawler we may not make it, or if we do, it may be too late."

"Too late?" the Baron asked with open curiosity.

"Yes," McCade answered sadly. "The Princess has been conditioned to commit suicide rather than suffer the indignity of slavery. Of course it would break the King's heart. But there's no helping it. Can't have a princess as a hostage or a slave. On top of that, without the beacon we won't even be able to find her body and give it a decent burial." McCade belched, excused himself, and swayed slightly in his chair.

"Quite, quite," Lif said, nodding in agreement. "You say if she dies the beacon is extinguished also?" he asked sharply.

"It's powered by her nervous system," McCade explained blandly, waving a hand and almost knocking over a full mug of Vak.

"Yes . . . I see," the Baron replied thoughtfully. "It would appear we must act quickly."

Now you're getting the idea, McCade thought, trying to suppress the buzzing in his ears.

The Baron regarded McCade with a shrewd look. "Perhaps, my friend, we can serve each other, and in so doing accomplish much. I am going to confide something in you and your men, which if it were known, could mean my death." Lif paused dramatically, looking at each man in turn.

Both Rico and Van Doren struggled to look both serious and impressed. But since both were more than a little drunk, neither was very convincing. Fortunately the Baron was no expert on the nuances of human facial expressions and appeared satisfied.

"Your secret is safe with us," McCade said reassuringly, barely managing to disguise an enormous belch as a cough.

"I and certain other Lakorian nobles have long sought to overthrow the King," Lif said importantly, glancing around as though the King himself might be lurking behind a tapestry.

"No!"

"Surely you jest!"

"Really? Well . . . I'm sure you must have compelling reasons."

Each of the humans sought to outdo the others with expressions of incredulity.

Apparently satisfied with the impact of his revelation, Baron Lif proceeded to document in boring detail the many transgressions and crimes for which the King should be made to pay. McCade noted with amusement that mistreatment of the commoners and slavery were not on Lif's list of complaints.

Finally having reached the end of his lengthy indictment, the nobleman said, "Now pay close attention, gentlemen, for this is where our interests meet. For years my friends and I have been unable to topple this tyrant king because we couldn't find him. The location of his castle is a closely held secret. We've tried everything to find it. Our spies never return. Atmospheric craft are shot down. In short all our attempts have been frustrated."

"Why not just assassinate him and have done with it?" Van Doren asked respectfully. "Surely he appears in public occasionally."

Lif nodded. "Believe me it's been tried, good Squire. More than once.

But Zorta's bodyguard has always proved effective. And we must not only crush the man, but we must also seize his base of power."

And his money, McCade thought cynically as he took another sip of Vak.

The Baron leaned back as a satisfied smile touched his lips. "But finally the King has made a fatal mistake. He bought a poor innocent girl as a slave. Unknown to him, the girl is a princess. And hidden in her body is a beacon. A beacon which can be tracked."

Lif paused, allowing the silence to add significance to his words.

"And tracked it is. Tracked by a loyal knight bent on rescuing this fair maiden. Tracked too by the knight's loyal friend and ally, Baron Lif. Tracked to the very doorstep of the King's castle, soon to be pulled down around his very ears!"

With a roar of approval, McCade, Rico, and Van Doren banged their mugs on the table and then lifted them to drink the Baron's health.

FIFTEEN

Each time the crawler lurched, McCade thought he was going to die. He had the worst hangover he'd ever experienced. Sitting next to him, Rico was cheerful enough as he conned the huge machine over, around, and through the frequent obstacles. Outside somewhere Baron Lif rode with his troops. And if his constant chatter on the radio was any guide, the Lakorian noble was in fine fettle. McCade consoled himself by reflecting on their excellent progress. With Lif's scouts ranging far ahead and warning them of the worst hazards, their speed had picked up considerably. Meanwhile the green dot still glowed steadily on the nav screen. But it was close now and with each passing hour it grew slightly larger. McCade wondered if he'd live to get there . . . or if it really mattered. He massaged his throbbing temples and yawned. Elaborately informing Rico that a nap was in order, he headed for a bunk, unaware of Rico's knowing smile or his unsympathetic chuckle.

A full rotation later, McCade felt better. In fact he felt very much better. Not only had he fully recovered from the residual effects of too much Vak, but he found they were at least halfway to their destination. Outside the crawler, a downpour obscured the video cameras as usual, but the infrared sensors showed another kind of progress as well.

Thousands of red blobs now moved along in company with the crawler. Included were not only Baron Lif's troops, but those of many other nobles as well. Hardly an hour passed without a baron, count or duke joining their informal army. Although Lif was outranked by more than half the nobility present he had still managed to retain overall control through his special relationship with the humans, and his own political skill. Not an easy feat since many present had more experience in fighting against Zorta. McCade remembered vividly the night attack on the slave tractor. No doubt about it, there were some very tough folks out there.

Nonetheless by tactfully referring to himself as "Military Coordinator," the Baron had nudged, maneuvered, wheedled, and cajoled the disparate forces into a semblance of military order. McCade couldn't help but admire Lif's organizational skill.

Rico just shook his head and said, "He'd fit right in on the Council, ol' sport. Likes ta talk, that one does."

By evening of the second day, Lif had suggested a halt to rest the troops and prepare for battle. The other nobles quickly agreed, most being unused to a full day in the saddle. They also agreed to a council of war, each seeing it as an opportunity to express his valuable opinions on strategy . . . and to get rip-roaring drunk.

As darkness fell, the nobles made their way to a large tent which had been erected near the crawler. McCade went too, with Van Doren at his side. Lif had suggested that, religious vows allowing, they dress formally. He wanted them to make an impression on the assembled nobility and McCade promised to do his best. So as McCade and Van Doren entered the tent, the huge marine was dressed in full black body armor, and was wearing every kind of weapon they could strap on him. A helmet with a mirrored visor completed the effect. He hovered by McCade's shoulder . . . the very image of death incarnate.

Lacking any uniform or other ceremonial garb, McCade had chosen stark simplicity. From the supplies he'd put aboard the crawler, Rico produced a new set of gray leathers in McCade's size. These, combined with shiny knee-high boots, produced a military aspect. Phil had contributed a pin in the shape of a sunburst, which he normally used to fasten his kilt. It now shone brightly on McCade's chest, either a medal or a badge of rank, whichever the observer chose to make it. Trying his best to appear both aloof and confident, McCade took his place next to Baron Lif at the circular table, which almost filled the tent's interior. The table had been his own idea, solving as it did the endless problems of rank and precedence created by such a gathering. It had amused him to borrow yet another aspect of King Arthur's legendary court.

Once all the nobles were present, and the obligatory ceremonial toasts had been drunk, Baron Lif called the meeting to order.

"Thank you for your attendance, noble friends. We are gathered on the eve of a great victory. For years the tyrant Zorta has escaped his just reward, and now he shall have it. Death!"

A resounding cheer went up, interspersed with, "Hear! Hear!" Once the cheering and applause had died down, Lif stood and turned toward McCade.

"With us tonight is a great warrior from a distant kingdom. His is a mission which would credit any knight, the rescue of a fair maiden."

There was another cheer and more applause, which Lif waved into silence.

"Through his efforts, we now stand at the threshold of victory. Friends, I ask you to honor Sir Sam McCade."

With a roar of approval the Lakorians stood and drank McCade's health. As they sat down they looked expectantly in McCade's direction.

McCade stood, and allowed his eyes to roam the circumference of the table while the silence built. Then when every eye was upon him he spoke. "My Lords, I greet you in the name of my liege, King Arthur. Though he dwells on a distant world, I assure you his heart and hopes are with us tonight. Though we are of different races, nobleblood flows through all our veins, and will soon merge and mingle to bathe the soil of your beautiful planet. Soon we will fight and perhaps die, side by side." Here McCade paused and allowed a smile to touch his lips. "But friends, it comforts me to know that if I fall and take that final march toward either heaven or hell, I shall do so in the very best of company!"

The applause was deafening and lasted for three or four minutes. When it finally died away, Baron Lif stood and said, "Well said, my friend. Now let us discuss our plan of attack."

For two hours Lif allowed the debate to ebb and flow. Proposals, strategies, and plans of all kinds were raised, discussed, and rejected by those favoring their own approaches. Throughout all of it Lif listened attentively, maintaining an uncharacteristic silence.

Meanwhile McCade had begun to wonder if Rico had dozed off or something. He was just about to send Van Doren to find out when he heard a tremendous commotion outside the tent. Shouted commands were heard, along with the screech of reptillian mounts and the clash of loose gear. All eyes were on the tent flap as it was suddenly thrown aside. With perfect timing Rico strode through the entrance with a squad of Lif's elite scouts following behind. He was dressed exactly like Van Doren and in company with the colorful Lakorians made quite a sight. Looking neither right nor left, he marched to where McCade and Lif sat. Bending down between them he whispered in their ears.

"Looked pretty impressive, didn't we, Baron? How're ya doin', sport. . . . Hope everything's goin' good. Well that oughta do it. . . . See ya later." With that Rico snapped to attention, delivered a salute worthy of the Imperial Honor Guard, did an about-face, and marched out of the tent with the scouts following behind.

His features now etched in lines of concern, Baron Lif slowly stood to address the gathering. Rico's performance had accomplished its purpose. The debate had ended and the audience had been delivered back into Baron Lif's hands.

"Friends, critical information has just come to my attention. As you know we are within a half day's march of Zorta's castle. Therefore it seemed prudent to send out scouts to locate and probe his defenses. As you have just witnessed, a squad of my elite rangers under the command of Sir Sam's squire have just returned. The intelligence they have gathered on their daring mission behind Zorta's lines is astounding."

Lif couldn't resist letting them sit and stew for a moment before taking them off the hook. "Penetrating the very heart of the area indicated by the beacon's signal, they found nothing. Ground defenses and troops . . . yes.

Hundreds in fact. But where Zorta's castle should stand, where the beacon says it does stand, there is nothing."

Expressions of confusion and consternation filled the tent as everyone tried to talk at once. McCade shifted uncomfortably in his oversize chair, wishing Lif would get on with it. From the start he'd understood the value of some drama, and the necessity of some verbal sleight-of-hand, but the Baron was overdoing it.

Twelve hours before, Van Doren and two of Lif's scouts had penetrated the King's defenses in broad daylight. The big marine had found it surprisingly easy to do. In fact Amos could tell that the defenders were completely unaware of the approaching army. Having never been challenged here, Zorta's forces were more than a little sloppy. Once behind the King's lines, Van Doren had expected to run into a castle, complete with battlements, flags, weapons emplacements, the whole ball of wax. Instead he found nothing. Zero. Zilch.

Suspecting more than met the eye, Van Doren had set up and used a small but sophisticated detector pak he'd brought with him. The truth practically jumped out at him. Or up at him, as the case might be . . . since every reading on the detector indicated he was standing on top of an immense underground complex.

Van Doren and the scouts slipped back through the lines to notify McCade. McCade informed Lif, and together they had planned the evening's charade. McCade's thoughts were interrupted as Lif delivered the punch line.

"Finally, my friends, our brave lads have laid bare Zorta's secret. For years our spies and secret aircraft have searched for his castle without success. Now we know why. The beacon does not lie. Zorta's castle is before us. But not above ground as we have always assumed! No. The cowardly cur has made his home underground like the lowly animal he is. Let's bury him in it!"

When the predictable reaction had died down, the nobles were ready to listen to the plan that Lif and McCade had carefully constructed. Heaving a sigh of relief, McCade pulled out a cigar and added another source of pollution to the already foul air.

The next day dawned brightly clear. There wasn't a cloud in the sky and nothing could have been worse. They had counted on the usual downpour to cover their attack. Fighting in rain and mud was no problem for the Lakorian troops and their mounts. They were used to it. In fact they preferred it. The more superstitious of them saw the sunny day as a bad omen, causing Baron Lif to become concerned about morale. However they all agreed the attack should go on as planned. If not they would soon be discovered and annihilated by Zorta's air force. Besides, their rather unorthodox plan of attack should offer some protection.

So Rico and McCade sat, side by side, waiting for the signal to attack. Lif and Van Doren had just finished a final strategy meeting. Bit by bit, Lif had come to seek more and more advice from the marine, who was after all an expert at ground warfare.

Now Lif was with his troops attending to a few last-minute details. Van Doren was manning the crawler's missile battery, while the Treel and Phil were strapped into the waist turrets. McCade would control the bow weapons and Rico would have his hands full operating the crawler.

The speaker over McCade's head crackled to life as Baron Lif gave the uncharacteristically short order: "Go." Rico revved the crawler's powerful engines, shifted into gear, and they lurched into motion.

They traveled as they had before, turning and twisting over and around the many obstacles. For a long time there was only radio silence. Then the forward elements of Lif's force came into contact with Zorta's outer defenses. At first the King's unprepared troops fell back in total confusion. Before long however they rallied and began to put up stiff resistance. Then by prior arrangement Lif's troops backed off slightly, keeping Zorta's soldiers engaged, but minimizing casualties.

Meanwhile Lif was flooding the airwaves with bogus radio traffic that seemed to confirm a stalled assault.

Rico and McCade looked at each other and smiled.

"Well, let's give it a try, Rico."

The other man grinned, eyes twinkling. Stubby fingers stabbed a series of buttons, resulting in a loud, whining sound. The sound, plus an indicator light, were the only signs the energy projector had come into use. But McCade knew that a cone of force was being projected in front of them, and that anything it touched would be cut, pulverized, melted, and spun out behind them. That's how it's designed to work, and it had better work if they were to succeed.

Rico pulled a lever and the crawler's nose dropped. As it did, the cutting beam made contact with the wet ground. A tremendous cloud of steam rose to hide the crawler from Lif's amazed troops. The huge machine began to vibrate as earth and rock were cut and pulverized to feed its mechanical maw. Gradually the vibration grew more and more intense until McCade wondered if the crawler would come apart. Beads of sweat formed on Rico's brow until they got large enough to run down his face and glisten in his beard. His bright little eyes saw only the controls before him as he fought the big machine.

Moments later they were underground. As McCade watched, the forward and side video cameras went black behind armored hatches, leaving only the stern monitor. On it McCade saw a short tunnel with glowing red walls slanting up to a bright blue sky. They were on their way to Zorta's underground refuge. McCade knew that as soon as the tunnel cooled sufficiently, a horde of Lakorian troops would enter and follow the crawler downward until it breached the walls of the underground complex. Then things would really get interesting.

But until then, success or failure rested on Rico's brawny shoulders and on the machine he fought to control. Designed for short, exploratory tunnels, the crawler was being pushed to its limits. There wasn't a thing McCade could do but hang on and pray. Pray that the plan worked, and pray that if it did Sara would still be alive when they got there. As the crawler ground its way down, the sensors began to go crazy. From all indications there was a major heat source, a high concentration of radioactivity, and massive amounts of metal, all up ahead.

Then somewhere deep in the guts of the crawler something broke with a resounding clang. Fear struck the pit of McCade's stomach. His left cheek twitched uncontrollably as he looked at Rico.

Through gritted teeth Rico said, "Port engine again . . . just couldn't take it. Same bearing."

"Can we keep going?" McCade asked as a terrible groaning noise began.

"For a while," Rico said, fighting to correct a sudden skew to the left, "until she bums up. Then we walk. Or should I say dig?" Rico grinned before turning back to his controls.

McCade fought to control the combination of fear, impatience, and frustration he felt. He knew Rico was doing all that could be done. Still it was hard to just sit. Glancing up at the sensors he saw that they were much closer. "Just a little bit farther," he chanted under his breath. "Just a little bit farther."

The stern monitor showed a much longer tunnel now, with only a small circle of daylight still showing at the far end. As McCade watched, dark shapes began to obstruct the light as Lakorian troops began to pour in behind them. Then they were gone . . . obscured by clouds of steam as they sprayed water on hot spots. Pretty soon all the troops would be committed. Then, if the crawler broke down, Zorta would be able to trap Lif's entire force by putting a single section at the tunnel's entrance. They'd roll a few charges down the passageway, and that would be the end of it. For months Zorta would think about the army that buried itself, and laugh.

Forcing such thoughts aside, McCade resumed his chant. "Come on, baby . . . just a little bit farther."

Acrid smoke began to seep into the control room from the engine compartment. The grinding noise was now punctuated by a regular thump, and the overall vibration had grown much worse. Next to him Rico was bathed in sweat. His eyes were locked on the sensors and his lips moved in silent prayer. They were close. Very close. Then as though in answer to their prayers they were through. The front end of the crawler dropped twenty feet with a sickening crunch that left McCade's stomach somewhere on the overhead. All the external video cams came back on, along with a host of warning buzzers and trouble lights.

McCade hit the quick release on his harness as he checked the monitors. They had broken through the durocrete walls into some kind of warehouse. Stacks of crates stretched off into the distance in orderly rows. As far as McCade could tell there wasn't anybody around at the moment. He had a feeling that this wouldn't last long.

Hitting the intercom he said, "Amos, Phil, grab Softie and let's bail out. Do your best to set up some kind of a defensive perimeter until we get some troops out of the tunnel."

"Right, boss," Van Doren's voice came back. "Tell Rico this is the worst parking job I've ever seen."

Rico grinned as he picked up an energy weapon and backpack from behind his seat. "Typical back seat driver. Ya just can't please everybody, ol' sport."

McCade laughed with relief as he grabbed his knapsack and auto-slug thrower. "Well, let's ruin Zorta's day!"

Moments later they were outside the crawler, spreading out to take up defensive positions. Behind them the crawler loomed like a beached whale. Its bow was smashed into the warehouse floor and its stern still rested in the tunnel some thirty feet up. There would just barely be room for the Lakorian troops to squeeze by the crawler and out the tunnel. While the others set up interlocking fields of fire, McCade climbed onto some of the crates.

They had been lucky to break into an unpopulated area of the complex. But they were going to need some transportation soon. Once the leading elements of the troops left the tunnel, they would have to move quickly, before Zorta could organize his forces and respond. Otherwise they would be bottled up in the warehouse area and might never break out. From the top of the crates McCade had an excellent view of the surrounding area. It took only a moment to spot a wheeled vehicle hooked to a train of power pallets loaded with cargo. Quickly scrambling down he started to work his way through the stacks of material and toward the vehicle. Then he heard a shouted Lakorian command and the sizzle of an energy weapon. The battle had begun.

Peering around a corner McCade spotted Zorta's troops. Only a half section or so, thank God. They had taken cover behind some duct work and were under fire from Rico and the others.

Turning his attention back to the vehicle, he took a deep breath, got set, and dashed across the open space between the crates and the small tractor. He knew he was in full view of the Lakorians and expected to feel the impact of a hit any second. He reached the vehicle and ducked around to the other side, surprised they hadn't spotted him, but damned glad.

In the driver's seat he found himself facing strange controls. Fortunately the answer was absurdly simple. In place of an ignition code there was a simple "on-off" switch. Flicking the switch to "on," he tapped the accelerator experimentally and then the brake. They worked perfectly.

Glancing over his shoulder he saw that two Lakorians were down and the others weren't looking his way. No time like the present, he decided, and put his foot to the floor. It was wasted effort. The little electric motor wasn't geared for fast getaways and was woefully underpowered to boot. Very gradually the little tractor eased into motion with its loaded train of power pallets following dutifully along behind.

McCade turned the handle bars and felt the vehicle's sluggish response as it headed sedately across the open floor toward the distant protection of the crates. From his left he heard a Lakorian shout and knew he'd been spotted. Gritting his teeth and gripping the handle bars until his knuckles turned white, he continued to hold the accelerator to the floor as the tractor gradually built up speed.

The flash of an energy beam cut across in front of him, leaving a black line on the durocrete floor. Swerving left and right he did his best to ruin their aim, but there was an impact as the rearmost power pallet was cut in two. Deprived of power, the front half of the pallet fell to the floor and was dragged along with a terrible screeching sound. It cut the tractor's speed in half. His eyes desperately searched the controls until he found a pictograph of the train. He touched the last car in line and then the button with the universal "disconnect" symbol on it. To his tremendous relief he felt the surge of speed as the wreckage fell away. Seconds later he was safely hidden behind some crates and weaving in and out toward the wrecked crawler.

Rounding a final stack of boxes, he saw the leading elements of Lif's troops making their way out of the tunnel and down to the warehouse floor. Swinging in front of them, he saw the Baron and waved. Lif immediately understood the need for transportation and ordered his troops to jump aboard.

Rico, Van Doren, Phil, and the Treel hopped aboard too as McCade headed the tractor up a wide ramp. Glancing in his rear view mirror he saw that Rico and Van Doren had the troops hard at work taking cargo from the center of each pallet and throwing it overboard, thereby creating a hollow space in which they could take cover. It wouldn't protect them from energy weapons, but it would provide some defense against slug throwers. The ramp continued to lead upward in a gentle curve. McCade kept expecting to run into an organized defense, but they didn't. Later he would learn that Zorta had placed most of his available troops on the upper levels of his complex, assuming Lif would try to break in from above. When they tunneled in from below, the King should have moved his troops down to meet the invaders. Unfortunately for him, Zorta refused to believe the early reports of a subterranean breakthrough, and by the time he did, it was much too late.

However not all of Zorta's troops were on the upper levels. Some were engaged in routine chores on the lower levels, and some were off duty. These were more than sufficient to cause the invaders problems and quickly did so. Listening to the garbled reports of an underground invasion that flooded his belt radio, one corporal used his head. Quickly drafting every private in sight, he used them to erect a barricade across the main ramp leading up from the lower levels. At his direction the troops used anything that was handy, including office furniture, packing crates, and a wealth of odds and ends.

As soon as it came into sight, the tractor came under fire. The corporal had placed his men well, and they knew their business. All McCade could do was keep going. If they left the protection of the train there was no cover at all. If he tried to turn around, he'd expose the length of the train to raking fire. He gritted his teeth and ducked, as did Baron Lif. A second later an energy beam sliced through the tractor's cab about head high, leaving behind the smell of hot metal and burned plastic.

Meanwhile, led by Van Doren and the others, Lif's troops opened an ineffectual fire on the barricade. Their efforts were hampered by the tractor and pallets in front of them, and their aim wasn't improved any when McCade began to swerve from side to side in an attempt at evasive action.

However Rico did manage to intimidate Zorta's troops with an automatic grenade launcher he'd picked up somewhere. As he targeted a line of explosions across the top of the barricade, the defenders were forced down and back.

The Treel did his part as well, yelling "Die, Infidel," as he systematically picked off enemy troopers.

McCade held the tractor's accelerator to the floor, but as before he found he couldn't make any real speed. The tractor took its own sweet time to cover the remaining yards and finally crash into the barricade.

McCade squeezed between a huge packing crate and a filing cabinet only to find himself the target of a wicked, foot-long bayonet in the fist of a charging Lakorian regular. McCade's slug gun bucked three times, stitching big black holes across the soldier's chest and spraying gore out behind him. The alien's inertia carried him past to crash into the barricade before sliding to the floor.

Around him similar encounters were taking place as McCade jumped on top of a desk. "Take prisoners! We need prisoners!" he shouted.

His reward for exposing himself was a searing line of pain across the top of his shoulder. He spun around, searching for the source and found it. The slug gun roared twice and the impact of the huge slugs blew one side of the Lakorian's head off before spinning him around like a top.

Then, as quickly as it had begun, the battle was over.

"Over here, boss!" Van Doren shouted. "We've got a live one!"

McCade arrived to find there were four live ones. And as luck would have it, one of them was the same corporal who had ordered the defense.

"So far he's not talking, boss," Van Doren said crossly. "Shall I knock him around a little?"

"First allow me to test my powers of persuasion, good Squire." Baron Lif smoothly inserted himself between Van Doren and the corporal. "We have a saying. The wise man trades words before blows." With that he began talking to the soldier in low, urgent tones.

As the Baron interrogated the corporal, a second contingent of his troops arrived from the tunnel and formed up to advance upon command.

At a gesture from Lif, McCade moved over to join him. To McCade's surprise the corporal was smiling as he ripped Zorta's insignia from his own uniform. His three remaining subordinants were doing likewise.

"I would like to introduce you to Staff Sergeant Poka, good Knight. The sergeant and his men have decided to ally themselves with the side of freedom and justice."

And the side that's winning, McCade thought. "Welcome aboard, Sergeant," McCade said. "You and your men put up a valiant defense."

Poka inclined his head respectfully. "Thank you, sire. How may my men and I serve you?"

"First as guides, I suspect," Lif answered, looking at McCade for confirmation. "I assume that was why you called for prisoners, my friend."

"Exactly, my lord," McCade bowed slightly. "I suggest you and your men strike out for Zorta's quarters under the sergeant's guidance. Once Zorta is in your hands, his troops will cave in rather quickly, I think. Meanwhile, if one of the sergeant's men could be spared, we will search for the Princess."

"Of course, good Knight, it shall be as you say." The Baron regarded McCade silently for a moment before speaking again. "You and your men have forged links of friendship not easily broken, my friend."

Lif was saying good-bye. Somehow he knew McCade didn't intend to be around for the victory celebration—or defeat—whichever might occur. As he gripped the Baron's hand, McCade saw genuine regret in the Lakorian's eyes. To his own surprise he realized he too felt regret. Lif was a crafty bastard, but a good bastard all the same.

Sergeant Poka detailed a Private Ven as McCade's guide. Ven was undersized, by Lakorian standards, and had a shifty look about him. McCade had a hunch their new guide would be about as dependable as a Linthian Rath snake during the mating season. With that in mind, he called Phil over.

"Phil, I'd like you to meet Private Ven. He's going to take us to the slave quarters, aren't you, Ven?"

The Lakorian nodded eagerly, eyes shifting nervously back and forth between the human and the Variant.

"Make sure that nothing happens to Ven, Phil," said McCade meaningfully.

"Gotcha, Sam," Phil replied with a grin that revealed rows of durasteel teeth. "Ven and I are going to be real close friends, aren't we, Ven?"

The Lakorian didn't reply, seemingly unable to tear his eyes away from those gleaming teeth.

Lif's troops meanwhile had begun their advance up the ramp in search of King Zorta.

After a short huddle with Ven, Phil said, "According to my good buddy here, the slave quarters are directly above us. Evidently the lower levels of the complex are considered the least desirable. We broke in on the lowest or utility level. Above us are the slave quarters, kitchens and mess hall. The troops are quartered on the level above that, and then comes a floor dedicated to Zorta's private quarters and guest suites. The very topmost level is all for defense and features an air strip and a small spaceport."

He looked at McCade with a raised eyebrow. McCade nodded his understanding. It was something they had to think about. With the tractor gone and their crawler out of action, they needed a way out. If they could find Sara and then reach the top level, maybe they could steal a plane. Time would tell.

"All right, let's get moving," McCade said, reloading his slug gun. He'd lost the auto-slug thrower somewhere, but decided not to look for it.

Using an electronic key, Ven opened one of the hatches spaced at regular intervals along the ramp's wall. Once open, the hatch revealed a vertical ladder, evidently provided for maintenance purposes. Without hesitation Ven started climbing upward and Phil followed. McCade was next. As he climbed, he found the spacing of the rungs more suited to shorter Lakorian legs than his own. Below him Rico, Van Doren, and the Treel followed. Cold air blew down against his face. Evidently the shaft also served as part of the air conditioning system. By the time they reached the next landing, McCade was out of breath and damned cold to boot. With Phil and Ven, he waited on the landing, catching his breath as Rico, Van Doren, and the Treel climbed up to join them.

Ven opened another hatch and peeked out. A moment later he slipped through the opening, motioning to the rest to follow. They emerged into a side corridor which was, for the moment, empty. As they followed Ven down the hallway, McCade could hear the distant sounds of an alarm gong and fighting. Lif's forces had evidently made contact with Zorta's troops.

"Stop!"

The order came from behind them and was answered with a bolt from Van Doren's energy weapon. A soldier wearing half a cook's outfit and half a uniform crumpled to the floor, his weapon falling from dead fingers. They were off and running after that. Ven led them from one corridor to the next with remarkable speed. Of course the fact that Phil was right behind him probably helped.

As they ran they traded occasional shots with barely glimpsed troops who also seemed to be running somewhere. But they managed to avoid prolonged firefights. Until Ven whipped around one corner too many without looking first. They rounded the corner and ran full tilt into a whole section of Lakorian troops. Fortunately the soldiers were facing the other way with their weapons trained on a large steel door. In a flash McCade guessed why. The slaves were taking advantage of Lif's attack and were trying to escape. The searing white light of the energy beam cutting its way around the lock from the other side confirmed his guess.

Unfortunately Ven's inertia proved to be so great he was unable to stop and crashed full speed into the rearmost trooper, who took several others down with him as he fell. Taking advantage of the confusion thus created, McCade and the others hit the deck and opened fire. Caught between hostile fire and a steel door, it didn't take the noncoms long to decide that discretion was indeed the better part of valor and try for a hasty retreat down a side corridor. Their orderly withdrawal was turned into a rout when Rico brought his grenade launcher into play.

Approaching the steel door, McCade felt a wave of heat and smelled a mixture of smoke and Lakorian body odor. He noticed that the cutting beam had almost circled the lock. He stepped back and went to kneel beside Ven's body. At McCade's touch the Lakorian's eyes flew open and flitted about, shrewdly evaluating the situation. Satisfied the danger had past, Ven quickly regained his feet, evidently untouched, and confirming McCade's estimate of the Lakorian's potential for duplicity.

"Well, sire," Ven said blandly as he dusted himself off, "I guess we showed them!"

With a loud clang, a six-inch thick circular slab of metal hit the floor. Slowly, against the resistance of its normal mechanical system, the huge door was rolled aside to reveal a mob of angry slaves. They were waving weapons of all kinds, from chair legs to captured energy weapons. As the door slid out of the way, they charged, and then jerked to a sudden halt at a sign from their helmeted leader.

The leader took two paces forward before lifting the helmet's visor. "Well, Sam," Sara said, "what took you so long?"

SIXTEEN

Then she was in his arms, covering his face with kisses, laughing and crying at the same time. She filled not only his arms, but his heart and mind as well. For the first time in years, he felt really happy, and he didn't want to let go of either Sara or the feeling.

Nonetheless Rico managed to get his attention with a none too discreet cough. "Turn 'er loose there, sport, and give someone else a shot. Always hoggin' all the pretty women."

"Rico!" With a shout of glee Sara was lifted and spun around like a little girl. Laughing, she said, "Put me down, Rico! This is no way for Council members to act. It's not dignified."

"Not dignified, huh," Rico said as he put her on her feet. "How about that outfit. Since when did Council members go around wearin' nothin' but two scraps o' cloth and a helmet?"

Looking down, Sara blushed. McCade saw that Rico was right. Sara had made her escape in a wispy two-piece costume that left very little to the imagination.

"Well I like it," McCade said.

Sara made a face and turned to Van Doren. "Well Amos, at least you're always nice to me." Standing on tiptoe she kissed him on the cheek. Much to McCade's amusement, the big marine turned bright red with embarrassment and didn't say a word.

Then Sara caught sight of Mungo and stepped back, bringing up her energy weapon.

Moving quickly to her side McCade said, "No Sara, it's not Mungo. It's the Treel again. For the moment, he's on our side. Believe me it's a long story."

"The rigid one speaks truly," the Treel said. "We are fellow warriors in the service of the great Yareel! Death to the infidels!"

"Like I said, it's a long story," McCade said, seeing her amazement.

"And time is what we don't have, Sam," Phil interjected. "Those troopers will probably be back with friends for company."

"I'm sorry," McCade said. "Sara, meet Phil. By the way, he's now one of your constituents."

If Sara was surprised by Phil's appearance, she gave no sign of it.

"I'm pleased to meet you, Phil," she said. McCade watched in astonishment as the big Variant bowed gracefully to gently kiss her hand. "The pleasure is all mine, beautiful lady."

Turning to McCade, Sara said, "Is he always like this?"

"No, thank God," McCade replied with a smile. "He hasn't tried to kiss any of us. Anyway he's right about getting out of here. Say good-bye to your friends over there, and let's get going."

"Good-bye?" she said. "I can't just leave them here. They followed me. What if some of Zorta's troops come back? They wouldn't have a chance. No," she said firmly, "they'll just have to come along." Her face was set and determined. McCade had seen that expression before and knew trying to change her mind would be a waste of time.

For their part, the slaves stood patiently awaiting Sara's orders. There were about thirty of them representing perhaps a dozen races. As far as McCade could tell, they were all females, which made sense. No doubt Zorta kept his male and female slaves separated.

"All right," he said. "Tell them to follow us. Ven, what's the fastest and safest way to reach the air strip?"

After a moment's hesitation, the Lakorian replied, "There is a way, sire. It won't be comfortable, but I believe it will be safe."

As he followed Ven down the corridor, McCade had complete confidence in the alien's choice. After all, his greenish hide was on the line too. They turned into a hallway lined with metal carts.

"These are food and laundry carts, Sire," Ven explained. "They are sent from one level to another in these vertical conveyor shafts."

By way of demonstration he lifted a sliding door to reveal a shaft only slightly larger than the carts. Inset in the wall of the shaft were endless belts mounting metal arms climbing up and out of sight in eternal progression. Grabbing a nearby cart, Ven shoved it through the open door and into the shaft. It was smoothly engaged by the next set of rising metal arms and lifted out of sight.

Turning back to McCade, Yen said, "Your opinion, sire?"

"You were right, Sergeant. It isn't going to be comfortable, but it looks like a good idea."

McCade would have sworn Ven looked pleased in a sly sort of way.

Quickly they organized the rest. McCade, Phil, Sara, and Ven would go first, then the slaves, followed by Rico, Van Doren, and the Treel. Ven opened a small access panel and set the controls for the uppermost level.

Climbing onto the top of the cart, McCade felt awkward and damned silly as Ven pushed it into the shaft. Rico's huge grin confirmed his suspicions. The metal arms engaged the cart with a slight jerk, and he started smoothly upward. It wasn't too bad for him, but it would be a tight fit for Rico and Phil. As the cart moved upward and past the next two levels, McCade heard the sounds of battle, but they were faint and some distance away. But as the cart approached the next level, the one which housed Zorta himself, the sounds grew louder. Much louder. Craning his neck to look up, McCade saw why.

The next access door up was open. Light, smoke, and noise flooded through to fill the shaft. Pulling his slug gun, McCade inched around to face the door. Seconds later, as his cart drew level with the open door, McCade had an excellent view of the battle raging in the corridor outside. Almost in front of the door a brightly garbed Lakorian officer wrestled with two of Zorta's bodyguards. It took McCade a second to realize the officer was Lif, and another to shoot one of his adversaries in the leg. Then they were gone as the cart carried him up and away.

Bracing himself McCade got ready for the next and last level. As the cart reached it, automatic machinery opened the door, ejecting both Mc-

Cade and the cart. Together they rolled out of the shaft and into a milling mass of Zorta's troops. Surprise was all that saved him. The slug gun roared five times and five troopers fell. Leaping off the cart he landed in a forward roll. Behind him the cart was melted to slag as a dozen energy weapons were brought to bear on it.

McCade pulled the trigger three more times and two more died. Now it was his turn. His gun was empty and there was nowhere to run. Then he was blind-sided by a huge noncom wielding a wrench. He went down hard and stayed down. He was conscious, but just barely, and no matter how he tried, his body just wouldn't get up. Nonetheless he could watch what went on in a distant sort of way. Just as the troopers began to move his way with every intention of finishing him off, Phil emerged from the shaft.

He didn't have the advantage of surprise, and as it turned out he didn't need it. Had Zorta's troops nailed Phil as he emerged from the shaft, they would have won. Instead part of their attention was still on McCade and their first shots went wild. They didn't get a second chance. McCade had never seen anything like it. Phil had gone into full augmentation.

Implants fed chemicals into his brain, nervous system, and muscles. His response time was amplified. His strength doubled and then tripled. His movements became a blur of continuous motion. Without hesitation, Phil moved in among the Lakorian troops. His motions became dancelike as he whirled, leaped, and executed the intricate movements of death. Around him Zorta's soldiers died by the dozen, cut down not only by Phil's weapons, teeth and claws, but by their own comrades as they fired in panic trying to hit the augmented Variant.

Sara and Ven emerged from the shaft, adding their fire to Phil's efforts. As the shaft ejected the slaves, they fell to the floor and took advantage of the shelter the carts provided. By the time Rico, Van Doren, and the Treel arrived, the fight was over. The few remaining soldiers had fled, leaving behind a scene of unbelievable carnage.

As Van Doren helped McCade to his feet, Rico surveyed the damage and said, "Wait till ol' Larkin gets a load o' this one! Phil's a one-man army!" Shaking his head with amazement, Rico went over to help the shaggy Variant patch up the wounded.

The motion involved in standing up had sent waves of pain pounding through McCade's head. Reaching up to touch its source, his fingers encountered a growing goose egg and came away red with his own blood. He obeyed Van Doren's command to sit down on a piece of broken cart, and Sara's gentle hands cleaned and closed the cut, using the contents of his own first aid kit. She also cleaned and disinfected the shallow wound across his shoulders. The disinfectant stung. Finally she hit him in the arm with a styrette. Moments later he felt the drug spreading through his system, pushing back the pain.

Sara nodded knowingly. "It feels good now, Sam, but you're going to pay the price later on, when it wears off."

"Thanks," he said, allowing her to help him up. "With any luck at all we'll be well clear of here by then."

He reloaded the slug gun while glancing around. They were standing in the middle of a large aircraft maintenance area. Aircraft in various stages of repair were parked in a series of bays filled with tools and test equipment. Beyond them other aircraft were visible, in a line stretching off into the distance. Hopefully some of those would be operational.

"All right," McCade yelled. "Let's go." With that he started jogging toward the distant planes. Surprisingly he felt no pain, just a feeling of elation, which he knew was too good to be true. As he cleared the maintenance area, the view opened up to reveal something just beyond the farthest planes. Something familiar but impossible. His heart leaped and he broke into a full run, afraid his eyes had deceived him. They hadn't. *Pegasus* sat on a small pad, wisps of vapor curling up and around her warm tubes, a patch of blue sky visible overhead where a section of roof had been slid back. Then he noticed the ground crew. They were lounging around, apparently waiting for something or someone. Zorta. It had to be. He'd left himself a back door in the form of *Pegasus*. McCade ran even faster. Maybe he could slam that door, get his ship back, and clear the planet all at the same time. A cry went up behind him as the others saw his intention and raced across the hangar toward the slender shape of the spacecraft.

"Spread out!" Van Doren shouted. "Spread out or you'll be cut down with a single beam!" Slowly they separated into a line abreast as they continued their charge.

On his right, Sara uttered a most unladylike war cry as her long white legs carried her toward the enemy. The scar across her face was a white slash and in her brief costume she looked like an avenging goddess of war. To McCade's left Phil loped along in huge, ground-eating strides, his rows of gleaming teeth making the weapon in his hands seem redundant.

McCade felt happy, even joyous, and completely without fear. A part of his mind told him to be careful, that the drugs were affecting his judgment. Another part of his mind replied, "Who cares?" Then they were within range. Energy beams rippled and flashed incandescent while slug throwers boomed out a staccato challenge. Two of the charging slaves fell, hit by an automatic weapon. Farther down the line another was burned in half by an energy beam, her severed legs still moving, pumping, until her lower torso toppled and fell.

Whether it was the returned fire, or the sight of the oncoming and apparently suicidal mob, McCade couldn't tell, but abruptly the ground crew folded and ran, leaving behind three or four unfortunate comrades.

Yelling to get Van Doren's attention, McCade said, "Throw a perimeter around her, Amos. I'm going aboard to check her out!"

"Right, boss!" Van Doren acknowledged with a wave of his hand.

As McCade headed toward the ship, the marine was already barking commands to the ex-slaves, all of whom were now armed with weapons taken from Zorta's troops.

As McCade entered the ship, Sara was right behind him. The first thing he noticed was the smell. The ship reeked of Lakorian body odor. The next thing he noticed was dozens of boxes of clothing and supplies Zorta had put aboard just in case. They filled the tiny cabins and spilled out into the main corridor. The King certainly didn't travel light. The lounge contained more than just luggage. It had been transformed into a throne room, complete with a gilded, Lakorian-sized acceleration couch. Above it, Zorta had mounted a full-sized 3-D likeness of himself. Like most official portraits, it looked anything but natural. Zorta stood in a stylized pose, noble head lifted, eyes apparently focused on something not quite visible to mere mortals. McCade decided the King was definitely on the homely side, as Lakorians go.

Turning to Sara he said, "It appears Zorta has no intention of staying to share his well-deserved defeat with his loving subjects. I don't think that's very sporting, do you?"

"You're absolutely right, Sam. They just don't make Kings like they used to. I think we should help him meet his royal obligations, don't you? Of course Commander Reez will be disappointed . . . but that's life!"

"Disappointed?" McCade asked, suddenly serious. "Why will Reez be disappointed? For that matter, why is he still around? I assumed he would be on the War World by now, raising the Il Ronnian flag or something?"

Sara shook her head. "So did I. But while I was waiting for my turn to entertain some of Zorta's human guests"—She made an expression of distaste—"I kept my eyes and ears open. The grapevine around here is incredible. Since slaves never leave alive, everyone talks freely in front of them. Anyway it didn't take long to find out that Reez had been in and out of here for a long time. In fact he and Zorta have a deal. In return for various kinds of technology, Zorta agreed to loan Reez some troops. That's how Zorta wound up with *Pegasus*. Reez gave it to him as a present to seal the agreement."

McCade's heart went out to her as her face reflected briefly the fear and uncertainty she had felt, though there was no hint of either in her voice or words.

As though reading his mind she said, "I'm okay, Sam . . . thanks to you and the others."

"What I can't figure out is why," McCade said thoughtfully. "Reez has troops of his own."

Sara nodded. "Yes, but not enough to hold the War World if it comes to a fight. All he's got is the contingent aboard his ship. He's way too far from home to use a combeam, and he's afraid to go there for more troops because the Empire might discover the War World while he's gone. After all, he knows if we're looking, then there's probably plenty of others looking too. So he plans to land Lakorian troops to hold the War World until he can bring in more Il Ronnians. Plus if there's a fight, it's Lakorians who will die." She paused for a moment and then continued. "I think that's the real factor." Her lips curled derisively. "Because it reduces the potential magnitude of Reez's failure should things to wrong. He's acting on his own, after all . . . something Il Ronnians aren't noted for . . . and the defeat of his troops in an unauthorized conflict could end his career."

McCade frowned thoughtfully. He knew Sara was right. As far as the Empire's social scientists could learn, the Il Ronn operated from consensus, a fact which many felt had allowed the human empire to grow at a faster rate, thus making it possible for them to catch up with the more advanced Il Ronn. By nature humans were much more independent and willing to take risks.

"Zorta was going to meet Reez?" he asked.

Sara smiled. "Reez tricked him into heading up the expedition to the War World. They are to meet in orbit today. Zorta's troops lifted off yesterday."

That would account for Lif's relatively easy victory, McCade mused, for there was little doubt in his mind that Lif was winning. With a large contingent of Zorta's troops up in orbit, they had encountered lighter resistance . . . and that had made the difference.

McCade's eyes were drawn once more to Zorta's portrait. Suddenly he had an idea. It was beautiful! He started laughing and grabbed Sara, picking her up and planting a kiss on her lips. Looking up at him with curious eyes, she laughed too, and asked, "What are we laughing about?"

"That would be telling." He chortled. "Go get Phil and Softie. Tell them we've got an idea they'll like."

She made a face at him, but left as he started rummaging through Zorta's luggage. Before long he had assembled an outfit quite similar to the one the Lakorian king had worn for his official portrait. Picking up the rest of the luggage in the room, he crammed it into a storage compartment and managed to close the hatch.

Sara arrived with a curious Phil and indifferent Treel in tow.

"What's up, Sam?" Phil asked, looking around the lounge, his eyes coming to rest on the golden throne. "Kind of gaudy, isn't it, Sam? Frankly I thought you'd have better taste."

"It's Zorta's taste, not mine, I assure you," McCade laughed. Quickly he filled the Variant and alien in on what Sara had found out.

"So," he concluded, "since Reez is expecting Zorta this morning, I thought we should oblige." He looked up at the portrait and then over to the Treel. "If you get my drift."

Phil burst out laughing, along with Sara.

The Treel looked thoughtful for a moment and then said, "Actually not a bad plan, rigid one. In the guise of Zorta I could gain entry to the Il Ronnian ship, and then devise the means to eradicate those who offend the eyes of Yareel." His eyes took on a dreamy, wishful look. "Unfortunately, however, I am limited to my present form by the device implanted behind my ear." He reached up to touch it.

"That's where Phil comes in, I hope," McCade replied. "How about it, Phil? You said you might be able to remove the chemlock."

"Yeah, with the proper facilities, I said," the Variant answered, glancing around. "And frankly this isn't what I had in mind. How good is the sick bay on this space-going bordello anyway?"

"Now you watch your mouth," McCade grinned appreciatively. "With the exception of the throne, this is my bordello you're talking about, and my sick bay is pretty good."

"Okay, let's have a look," Phil replied. "Just remember two things. First I've got to disarm the chemlock's explosive device. If I screw it up you won't be able to find enough of me or Softie to say prayers over, plus you won't be going anywhere in what's left of this ship. Secondly we're gonna have to work fast. In an hour or two at the most, I'm gonna fall apart for a while. It's the price I pay for using full augmentation. It really bums up energy and afterward I come down hard. So if we're gonna do it, we'd better hurry up."

McCade nodded his agreement, wishing they could delay the operation and do it in space. But with Phil about to crash, and the need to show

Zorta to the Il Ronn after lift-off, there didn't seem to be much choice. So he led them to the galley. Through clever design the galley was easily converted to a small but efficient surgical suite. Phil pronounced it adequate and hurried to prepare the Treel. Over McCade's objections, Sara insisted on acting as Phil's assistant.

"It's got to be done, Sam, and I'm the best one to do it." Her mouth was set in a hard, determined line. "Besides," she added, "if the real Zorta shows up, they're going to need you outside."

Accepting the inevitable, McCade went back through the main entry port to confer with Van Doren and Rico.

The two humans had organized the former slaves into a respectable defensive zone around the ship. Lighting a cigar with careful movements, McCade could feel the medication starting to lose its effect. Like Phil, before long he wasn't going to be worth much.

"How 'bout the ship's guns, ol' sport?" Rico asked after McCade had explained his plan. "If Zorta shows up with some of his troops we may need somethin' a little heavier than pop guns."

McCade agreed, and it wasn't long before he was glad he had provided weapons all around. They heard the engines first.

The roaring noise was magnified by the walls of the hangar. The noise was soon followed by a flying column of armored vehicles which were headed directly for the spacecraft. As soon as they came into range, Rico opened up with the ship's guns, immediately blowing two of the ground cars to bits.

Their advantage didn't last long. Someone in Zorta's command had some brains and knew how to use them. Maybe even Zorta himself. In any case the vehicles picked up speed and quickly closed, with *Pegasus,* sweeping around the ship to encircle it before screeching to a halt. When they stopped they were so close to Van Doren's defenses that Rico couldn't fire without hitting the defenders as well as the enemy.

Piling out and using their vehicles for cover, Zorta's troops opened fire. McCade noticed they were careful not to hit *Pegasus.* Zorta clearly didn't want to lose his way out. Van Doren took advantage of this fact by deploying his forces so that the ship was directly behind most of them, thereby increasing the odds of Zorta's troops hitting the spacecraft. As a result the column of incoming fire dropped off dramatically. Zorta's soldiers were ordered to take careful aim before each shot.

Not so constrained, McCade and Van Doren urged the former slaves to pour it on. They did so without hesitation. Knowing Zorta was out there somewhere, each hoped it would be her energy bolt or slug that cut him down.

McCade chose his targets with methodical care. Aim, squeeze off two shots, and then aim again. After nine shots reload. He felt a touch on his shoulder and turned to find Sara crouched by his side. There were tiny lines around her eyes, hinting at the strain she'd been under.

"Phil's done, Sam. You've got to see it to believe it. He did an incredible job."

McCade bent low, using what cover there was, and followed her to the main entry port. Once inside they made their way to the lounge. As he entered McCade found himself face to face with a perfect likeness of King Zorta. Even though he'd seen the Treel's abilities demonstrated before, it was still astonishing. The Treel was sitting right below the Lakorian king's portrait and the likeness was exact. Phil had collapsed in the throne and was snoring softly.

"We're working on his speech," Sara said, indicating the Treel. "We found some recordings in his luggage of various speeches Zorta's given and our friend here will pattern on those."

"I assure you, rigid ones, given my enormous intellectual capacity, it will be child's play. Then I shall storm the very heart of the infidel stronghold!" the Treel said fervently in what McCade assumed was Zorta's voice.

"Good idea," McCade replied dryly. "However there's one little chore we'd like you to do first."

"You have been fair, rigid one," the Treel intoned gravely. "Ask me not to spare the infidels. All else within my power shall be yours."

"I'll not ask you to spare them," McCade said with equal seriousness. "Only to delay slightly that moment when the great Yareel shall cleanse them from this existence."

"Granted, rigid one," the Treel said. "Continue."

Turning to Sara, McCade said, "Tell Van Doren and Rico to pull back into the ship. We're about to lift."

When she made no move to go he said, "The slaves too, of course. In fact they are an important part of the plan."

Sara smiled and disappeared into the corridor.

"Now," McCade continued, turning back to the Treel. "Here's the plan. We'll send three or four of the Lakorian slaves along with you, ostensibly as part of your harem. They'll be of considerable assistance when push comes to shove." And they'll have instructions to kill you if you make one wrong move, he thought to himself. Each would be equipped with an overdose of the substance obtained from the chemlock Phil had removed.

The Treel nodded.

"Once you're aboard Reez's ship, just sit back and relax," McCade continued. "Reez will head for the War World to off-load you and your troops. We'll follow. Once there, we'll have the coordinates."

"And then, rigid one? What would you have me do then?" the Treel asked.

McCade shrugged. "I guess that's up to you. But I suggest you insist on taking personal command of your troops. Reez will agree. I doubt he wants Zorta along when he goes home to collect his 'attaboys.' Once he's gone we'll whistle up some Imperial assistance, they'll return Zorta's troops to Lakor, and you'll probably be knighted. End of story."

"That sounds most satisfactory," the Treel replied, much to McCade's surprise. "It's a good plan, rigid one. I am sure it will work."

So am I, McCade thought as he found a half-smoked cigar and lit it. Then why am I so damned worried? he wondered.

SEVENTEEN

McCade watched the main entry port monitor as the last former slave dashed aboard and Van Doren closed the hatch behind her. Outside, a hail of slugs hammered the hull as energy beams probed and searched for a way in. Zorta had changed tactics. Seeing they were about to lift, he no longer cared if his troops hit the ship, and they were doing so with a vengeance.

McCade wasn't too worried, since the hand weapons they were using wouldn't even scratch the ship's paint job. Of course there was always the possibility of cumulative damage or of Zorta bringing up heavier weapons. With that in mind he opened the intercom and said, "Okay, let's hose 'em down, Rico. Try to move them back out of the blast area while you're at it. Otherwise they'll get cooked as we lift off."

"Nothin' to it, ol' sport." Rico sounded cheerful as he opened up with the ship's guns.

As the spacecraft's heavy weapons traversed the area, Zorta and his troops quickly pulled back. Once they were out of the way, Rico did his best not to hit them. Lif's troops would be along soon to mop them up. McCade smiled to himself as he imagined the meeting between the Baron and his former king. It would have been a pleasure to see.

"Sam! Look!"

Beside him Sara pointed at the bow screen which moments before had shown only sky. Now the blue rectangle was growing steadily smaller as powerful motors worked to close the camouflaged roof. Zorta hadn't given up. Within minutes they would be trapped under the roof and unable to lift off.

McCade's voice boomed throughout the ship as he shouted, "Stand by for emergency lift!" Turning to Sara he said grimly, "Let's hope everybody's strapped in. This is going to be rough."

Quickly running through the pre-flight checks, he noticed that Zorta's techs had given the ship a complete overhaul. How considerate, he thought as he reached up, grabbed the red knob, turned it to the right, and pushed. The ship shook as the engines built thrust, spewing flame and heat out in all directions. The vehicles left behind by Zorta and his troops exploded from the heat, throwing out a curtain of red hot shrapnel that clattered against the hull.

Straining against the acceleration, McCade released the ship's defenses from manual to automatic as a familiar female voice flooded the control room. "This ship is under attack by an unknown number of atmospheric craft. Please stand by for high-speed evasive action and high G forces. Due to the time elapsed under manual control, it is impossible to guarantee your safety. Although defensive missiles have been launched, this computer and the ship's manufacturer disclaim all responsibility for any subsequent damages to this spacecraft, its passengers, or contents, consistent with Article 47, subsection eight, paragraph three of Imperial Insurance Regulations."

McCade watched as the atmospheric fighters were snuffed out one after another. They were no match for the heavier armament of the spacecraft. They tumbled out of the sky in ones and twos, leaving dark smears of smoke against the blue sky to mark where they went down. As the ship's computer added even more acceleration, McCade felt himself pushed down into a wall of pain. The medication had completely worn off and his head felt as though it might explode. As the pain smashed into him, McCade searched for and found the welcoming darkness.

When he awoke it was to the realization that the pain was gone. Cautiously he moved this way and that, searching for the pain, and couldn't find it. With that in mind it seemed worthwhile opening his eyes. To his surprise

McCade found himself stretched out on his bunk in the master stateroom. They must have moved him down from the control room after he'd passed out. Concern flooded his mind. The fighters . . . and Reez in orbit above them. What was going on?

With an effort he managed to sit up and swing his feet over the side of the berth. With the exception of a narrow path, pieces of Zorta's luggage still covered the deck. Using the bulkheads and boxes for support, he made his way into the lounge and collapsed into a seat. He still felt a bit weak. Sara and Van Doren were there and looked up with surprise.

"Hey, boss, what are you doing up and around?" Van Doren asked with obvious concern.

"Trying to kill himself, that's what," Sara said, moving over to sit next to him.

"You two worry too much," McCade replied, patting his pockets for a cigar. "I laugh at pain. I'm bulletproof and will live a million years. What happened to the fighters anyway?"

"Long gone," Sara replied. "A few seconds after you passed out, we cleared the atmosphere."

"And now we're on our way to the War World, we hope," Van Doren added sourly. "Although you couldn't prove it by me. Reez is probably sucking us into some kind of trap." His big fingers tapped out a nervous rhythm on the seat beside him,

Sara shrugged. "Anything's possible, I guess. But personally I doubt it. I think Reez bought the whole thing. And why not? It all went just like he expected it to. We met him in orbit, instead of one of us, he saw Ven on the com screen, we matched velocities and locks, King Zorta went aboard with slaves, assured Reez that his troops were winning on the ground, and made one request."

"Which was?" McCade asked.

"That his yacht not be taken aboard," Sara replied. "Zorta insisted that his crew be allowed to follow on their own as a training exercise. At least that's what he was supposed to say." She shrugged. "It must have worked, because here we are."

"Yeah," Van Doren said. "Here we are, wherever that is."

"O ye of little faith," Rico said, squeezing his bulk into the crowded lounge. "Good ta see ya up and around. How ya feelin'?"

"Great," McCade lied with a smile.

"Well that's good," Rico replied, "'cause I got a feelin' things are about to get interestin' again. We just had a com call from some Il Ronnian sub-sept commander. He fed the computer coordinates for a hyperspace shift. Told Ven it's comin' up in about ten minutes." With a wave of a hairy hand he disappeared in the direction of the control room.

Rico was at least partly right. About ten minutes later McCade felt the slight nausea and momentary confusion characteristic of a hyperspace shift. But he was wrong about things getting interesting. Instead they got very boring. Two standard days passed without anything further happening to break the monotony. That, plus the fact that *Pegasus* was severely overcrowded, quickly began to wear on them.

Besides McCade, Sara, Van Doren, Rico, and Phil, the little ship was also carrying Ven and about fifteen former slaves. Each dealt with the boredom and overcrowding in his or her own way. McCade slept and ate the first day away. Rico prowled the ship searching for routine maintenance chores to do. Van Doren exercised the ship's weapons, offering classes in gunnery. Some of the former slaves took him up on it. Meanwhile Phil just spent his time asleep, waking only briefly for meals and a little conversation before dozing off again.

At first Sara stayed busy organizing shifts for meals, sleep, and exercise. But before long, things pretty well ran themselves. So for something to do she began an inventory of Zorta's considerable luggage. Although the Treel had taken a few changes of clothing along to the Il Ronnian battleship, he'd chosen to leave most of Zorta's belongings behind. Among them Sara discovered a suitcase full of computer tapes on Lakorian governmental affairs. She began scanning them, and before long was immersed in the endless detail of planetary affairs.

Toward the end of the second day, McCade felt both better and worse at the same time. Physically he was much better. The combination of rest and medical treatment had done wonders. But emotionally he was tense and edgy, wishing desperately for something to do and unable to find it. Everyone else had found something to keep them occupied and had somehow disappeared inside it. For a while he tried reading, then holo games, and finally took to prowling the ship in search of somebody to talk to. But nobody wanted to talk. So, in deference to the already overloaded air scrubbers, he was sitting in the lounge chewing on an unlit cigar and fuming when Rico's voice came over the intercom.

"Well, folks, Ven just heard from our pointy-tailed friends, and you'll be glad ta know we're comin' outta hyperspace in a few minutes . . . unless o' course you'd like to extend this luxury cruise."

Rico didn't need the intercom to hear the jeers and howls of outrage that followed. Grinning, he poked the intercom button again and said, "Sam, ol' sport, I think we could use ya here in the control room."

Happy to have something to do, McCade made his way to the control room. "What's up?"

"I ain't sure. But from the way they phrased it, I think Reez is plannin' ta cut it real close. First they told Ven ta prepare for a shift and fed us the coordinates. But here's the interestin' part. They also specified the orbit they want us to park in."

"So maybe we're going to come out right on top of the War World," McCade mused. "Reez is probably in a hurry to dump Zorta's troops and then run for reinforcements."

"Seems like it," Rico said, his tiny eyes twinkling. "And all we gotta do is sit back and wish him bon voyage."

"That's right," McCade replied with a grin. That's right, *I hope*, he thought to himself. For some reason he couldn't shake the feeling that it wouldn't be quite that simple. A few minutes later and they emerged from the hyperspace shift.

McCade watched with intense curiosity as the screen cleared. Where the computer had projected the War World as a featureless globe, lacking sufficient data to do anything else, the real thing now hung before them.

It was smaller than most planets yet larger than most moons. The scattered clouds covering it testified to an atmosphere. Bodies of blue water were visible, but, unlike anything he had seen before, they were strangely geometrical, each forming a perfect circle of uniform size. There was green vegetation too. But it also had an unnatural appearance. It covered the worldlet in alternating squares, making it look like a checkered ball. The areas not covered by either water or vegetation were metallic gray. The gray squares displayed various textures, suggesting surface structures of some kind, but with one exception were too far away to identify. The exception was clearly visible due to its vast size. It was a spaceport. A huge spaceport, large enough to ground a fleet. And right in the middle of it McCade saw something that shouldn't have been there. Frowning in disbelief he punched the forward screens to high mag and then sat back in his seat as it became apparent that he'd been right. There she sat, looking foreign among the gantries and support equipment left by the long-dead race. An Imperial destroyer.

"What the hell?" McCade said in amazement. "How did they get here?"

"That ain't all, ol' sport," Rico said, pointing a stubby finger at the second screen. "Take a look at that."

As he spoke another ship emerged from behind the far side of the globe and orbited into full view. There was no mistaking her lines. An Imperial Class A Freighter. As they watched, a shuttle detached itself from the huge ship and started down toward the surface. Whether it departed in reaction to the arrival of the Il Ronnian battleship, or was simply unaware of it, McCade couldn't tell. It didn't get far. The little ship exploded and literally disappeared as the Il Ronnian warship opened fire.

"They didn't have a chance! That bastard!" McCade pounded his fist on the arm of his chair. As he spoke the freighter herself came under fire. Her defensive screens came up and flared through all the colors of the rainbow as the incoming fire grew more intense. Though the freighter had no offensive armament to speak of, it did have plenty of defensive capability and lots of power. Most of that power was now going to the defensive screens and, for the moment, they were holding. But McCade knew that in the long run the Il Ronnian battlewagon would beat the screens down and win.

He glanced at the first screen just in time to see a missile hit the grounded destroyer. It still seemed mostly intact, but now had a noticeable list to starboard. There wouldn't be much help from that quarter.

"I guess it's up to us," McCade said grimly as he reached for his harness and began to strap himself in. "Rico, tell 'em to stand by for combat and evasive action." As he reached over to activate the ship's weapons systems, he felt an iron grip on his wrist.

"Whoa ol' sport . . . not so fast," Rico said, his eyes serious. "This play-pretty ain't no match for a ship o' the line."

"Goddamnit, Rico, let go," McCade said, trying to pull his arm loose from the other man's viselike grip. "You saw what they did to the poor bastards in that shuttle. Maybe we can distract them a little, slow them down, buy a little time."

"Sure, ol' sport," Rico replied calmly, "like about thirty seconds, which is how long this little toy's gonna last. There's a better way."

For what seemed like an eternity but was only a fraction of a second, cold gray eyes locked with bright brown ones. Then McCade said, "Okay, Rico, say your piece, but make it damned quick."

Rico spoke earnestly as McCade listened. When the bearded man was through, McCade chuckled and said, "I'll probably be sorry, but that's just crazy enough to work. Let's give it a try. Rico, get Ven up here while I get ready."

A few minutes later he was wearing full armor and strapped into the harness of the sleek little Interceptor. He'd completely forgotten about it until Rico reminded him. It seemed like years since he'd asked Laurie to substitute it for the ship's boat, and been surprised when she'd agreed. Rico had stumbled across it during the hyperspace shift from Lakor. Looking for something to do, he'd decided to pull a maintenance check on the ship's lifeboat. Opening the lifeboat bay, he'd been surprised to find the deadly shape of a Navy Interceptor in place of the tubby little lifeboat he'd expected. McCade listened to the intercom channel on his headset as Rico and Ven got ready. He used the time to run through the Interceptor's preflight program. Everything checked out, just as Rico said it would.

"All right, Sam, stand by," Rico said over the intercom. "Remember, after Ven does his bit, we'll wait till the last second before givin' ya the go, so be ready, and don't waste any time."

"Yes, Mother," McCade said sweetly. He was answered with a snort of derision. Moments later the deception began as Ven called the Il Ronnian ship.

"This is Captain Ven commanding His Majesty's yacht, Lakor Avenger. Please respond." McCade almost laughed out loud at the name Zorta had bestowed on the small ship.

McCade couldn't see the video but could easily imagine the stern countenance of Commander Reez as he appeared on the com screen.

"Captain Ven, as you can see we are presently involved in an action with an Imperial Navy ship. What do you want?"

With a masterful blend of timidity and dogged determination, Ven replied: "With all due respect and my apologies for the inconvenience, sire, but His Majesty left very strict standing orders which I disobey at my peril. In the case of a naval engagement, it is His Majesty's wish to assume personal command of this ship that he might lend personal assistance to our noble allies, the Il Ronn."

McCade knew Reez wouldn't believe a word of it, and he wasn't meant to. It was exactly the kind of order the real Zorta might have left to ensure his escape from potentially dangerous circumstances.

Commander Reez allowed himself an audible snort of disbelief as he replied, "I assure you, captain, that the King is in absolutely no danger. We have already destroyed one Imperial ship, disabled a second, and the third will soon follow. However if you must, I suppose you must. Stand by."

McCade fidgeted in the small cockpit, checking his instruments for a third time.

"Uh-oh," Rico said.

"What's going on?" McCade demanded. He felt isolated. The muscle in his left cheek twitched.

"They just launched about ten of their Interceptors," Rico replied evenly, "which means we're in deep trouble."

"I'd say *they're* a bit shorthanded myself, boss," Van Doren's voice interjected. "All secondary weapons positions are closed up and ready."

"Royal yacht *Lakor Avenger*," came a different Il Ronnian voice. "Permission to come alongside granted. Please dock at lock four just aft of our port solar panels. We are standing by."

So far so good, McCade thought. The plan was working. Reez had decided to be magnanimous. And why not? He was winning and could therefore afford to humor Zorta and his staff. Besides, he still needed the King and his troops to hold the War World while he went for reinforcements. Something that no doubt seemed even more important now that the Imperial Navy had also located the War World.

"Thank you, my lord," Ven replied humbly. "We are on our way."

"Understood," the Il Ronnian snapped and was gone.

McCade felt *Pegasus* bank and begin a smooth turn to intercept the Il Ronnian ship. "Stand by . . . ," Rico said. "Hold, hold, hold . . . all right, he's let his screen down, we're inside, the screen's up behind us, hold, hold, all right go! Good luck, sport!"

With that the bay doors opened and the Interceptor was ejected into space and immediately left behind as *Pegasus* continued her arc toward the warship's lock.

McCade ignited his engine, felt it cut in, and banked down toward the bow of the Il Ronnian vessel. Suddenly a hard Il Ronnian voice flooded McCade's headset.

"Attention Royal yacht. Our sensors have detected an unauthorized launch of a power vessel now closing with our ship. It has five seconds to alter course or be destroyed."

"Uh-oh," Rico said. "Looks like they're on to ya, sport. We'll pull off as many as we can! Looks like there's five fighters comin' your way."

"Roger," McCade said grimly. "Here goes nothing!"

Below, the surface of the huge ship raced by. Like all of its kind, the Il Ronnian vessel had not been designed to pass through planetary atmospheres. Therefore no attempt had been made to streamline its hull. Vents, pipes, weapons platforms, turrets, launch tubes, and much more formed a metal maze across the surface of the ship's hull, adding to the sense of speed as he raced toward the bow.

Ahead, five dots filled his target screen, and as he watched they resolved into the form of Il Ronnian fighters. Without conscious thought, his fingers followed the deeply memprinted pattern learned years before, activating weapons systems and checking for system malfunctions. As the range closed, his hand tightened on the control stick, and his thumb was poised over the trigger of his two energy cannon. The Il Ronnian fighters fired first, and quickly regretted doing so, as their heat-seeking missiles sorted out the closest and most intense heat source around, and went for it. Unfortunately for them, the closest intense heat source was their mother ship. A series of explosions along the surface of the huge vessel marked where their missiles hit.

The Il Ronnian pilots were aghast at what they had done. In a way, their mistake was quite natural. They had been trained to fight outside the mother ship's defensive screens, where a misdirected missile could explode harmlessly against the powerful defensive fields that surrounded the vessel during battle.

While their attention was still on the destruction created by their own missiles, McCade opened fire. Two of the fighters exploded, while the third, still shocked by what he'd done, and scared by the sudden destruction of the other two, dodged into a bank of cooling fins and blew up. That left two Il Ronnian fighters still out there, and unfortunately they showed every sign of being very very good. Unlike their brethren, they had realized the potential problems missiles might cause, and like McCade, were relying on energy cannon. Fortunately they missed on the first pass. One moment they were there, growing large in his target screen, and then they flashed by and were gone.

Instinctively McCade dove his Interceptor down until it was just barely skimming over the surface of the large ship. His muscles were tight, and his eyes narrowed in concentration as he searched for and found his target. He knew he had only seconds before the two fighters, and maybe more, would be on his tail again, and this time they might not miss. It was just ahead. A raised area, just behind the bow, crowned with a thicket of sensors and other gear. In the center of the area was an open platform on which the Il Ronnians could land the skeletal maintenance craft used to perform repairs on the ship. That was where he planned to land. If he succeeded, he'd be sitting right on top of the control room, which contained the ship's computer, navigational instruments, and of course Reez himself.

"Watch out behind you, sport! There's two of them on your tail!"

Rico's warning was punctuated by bursts of blue light as the two Il Ronnian fighters tried to nail him. Doing his best to ignore them, McCade brought the little ship into line with the landing platform, waited as long as he dared, and then killed power. He'd waited too long. The Interceptor was moving too fast. He was overshooting the platform. Desperately he hit both his retros and the tractor beams. The beams were very light, but they made the difference. As the beams locked on to the larger vessel, he felt himself jerked down to meet it.

He hit with a crash and the screech of tortured metal, carving a violent path through the forest of sensors and antennas as he did so. As the noise died away, he glanced around, surprised to be alive and unhurt. The Interceptor had come to rest half on and half off the platform. Not one of his better landings, he decided, but what the hell, you can't win 'em all.

Swiveling his head, he looked up through the cracked canopy searching for signs of the two fighters. One after another they flashed by before swooping off to return and fly by once more. McCade slumped back into his seat with a satisfied grin. Not a damn thing they could do. If they shot at him they'd hit their own ship's control center too. As he chinned the transmit switch in his helmet, he noticed the cockpit pressure had fallen to zero. Evidently the Interceptor had been holed in the crash. His suit tanks were good for two hours. Hopefully that would be enough.

"Okay, Rico. I'm in position."

"Glad to hear it," Rico said with a chuckle. "For a minute there it looked like you were gonna land *in* the control room instead of *on* it."

McCade responded with a rude noise. Rico laughed, and then adopted a more serious tone as he said, "This is Fredrico Jose Romero, Council member of the Independent World Alice, and presently in command of the ship you know as the *Lakor Avenger*. I call upon Commander Reez to surrender his ship and all personnel aboard. Failure ta do so will result in the immediate destruction o' your ship. Before you reply, Commander . . . remember there's an Imperial Interceptor armed with two nuclear torpedoes sittin' over your head. The pilot is prepared ta activate a timer which will allow him time ta escape before the torpedoes completely destroy your ship. Ya have one minute to respond."

McCade waited nervously for the Il Ronnian response. He was all too aware that there was no timer which would allow him to escape before the torpedoes detonated. The only way he could use them was to program them to explode on contact, and then fire them the ten or twelve feet that separated his launch tubes from the Il Ronnian hull. He'd win, but he wouldn't be around for the victory party. He wondered if he could do it. Finally, Commander Reez broke the silence.

"This is Star Sept Commander Reez. My officers and I accept your offer of surrender, rigid ones. We will power down and await further orders. Out."

EIGHTEEN

As McCade stepped down onto the surface of the War World, it felt strange. He wasn't sure why. Everything seemed normal enough. A light breeze brushed his cheek, carrying with it the sweet scent of distant flowers. The warm dry air tasted good after the fetid atmosphere of the ship. But a pervasive silence cloaked everything. There were no birds chirping or insects buzzing, and as far as the eye could see, there was no movement, and aside from the destroyer slumped some distance away, no sign of life. He jumped at the sudden pinging noise as the ship's tubes started to cool. Feeling foolish, he turned to see the last of the slaves disembark under Phil's watchful eye and mill around looking curiously at their surroundings.

"Well, Phil, if we aren't back in an hour or so, you and the girls capture that destroyer and hold it against our safe return."

Phil laughed and waved a hairy paw in reply.

If the navy ensign was amused, he gave no sign of it. Ensign Peller was from the destroyer. They had grounded on the taciturn orders of the destroyer's captain, who sent them the chubby young officer as a guide, probably on the theory that Peller was the most expendable man aboard. After all, with a crippled ship to repair, the captain wasn't going to send anyone useful. And Peller certainly wasn't useful, at least to them. So far all of McCade's questions had been answered with "I don't have that information, sir," or, "I'm sorry, sir, I really wouldn't know."

As far as McCade could tell, the young officer's mind was as blank as his face.

"This way, sir," Peller said with carefully modulated politeness, and led them toward a distant structure.

McCade was struck again by the unreality of their surroundings. The unnatural symmetry of the landscape, the ensign's featureless face, and the timelessness that seemed to be part of the very air they breathed.

"It just ain't right, boss," Van Doren whispered from behind.

McCade understood the marine's reluctance to raise his voice. The silence was oppressive. He felt Sara's hand slip into his. As they walked hand in hand across the slick surface of the huge spaceport, they were awed by their own visions of what it had once been like. From its size, hundreds of ships must have grounded at once. The planet's name suggested huge war fleets, yet their surroundings held none of the grim oppressiveness common to the military installations they knew.

Come to think of it, where were the weapons emplacements, fortifications, and other military paraphernalia which should be all over the place? Why call it the "War World" if it had nothing to do with war? The silent gantries and clusters of support equipment lining the edge of the spaceport gave no answers.

"Where're we headed?" Rico asked with forced casualness. McCade turned and shrugged. "Your guess is as good as mine, Rico. Mr. Peller here says our presence has been requested. He didn't say by who."

If the young officer heard McCade's comment he gave no sign. Eventually they approached a massive arch of shiny red stone. Centered under the arch, a high wide door stood open in silent invitation, the darkness beyond it providing no hint of what might lie in wait, but its huge size suggesting a heavy flow of traffic. As they neared it, McCade saw it was flanked by metal plates set into the stone.

Each was covered with writing in a language he hadn't seen before. Or had he? He stopped and dredged his memory for a connection. Then it came. Bridger's plate. The one he called the "Directory." The plate in front of him and the inscriptions which covered it looked exactly like the one Bridger had found on his artifact world.

The rest of the group had followed Peller through the door and were waiting inside for McCade to catch up. As he hurried toward them, he considered the implications of what he'd just discovered. In retrospect, Bridger's discovery was truly amazing. He'd been right all along. His metal tablet *had* been a directory.

A directory to various artifact worlds, complete with coordinates. A simple road map for a long-vanished race. Driven by his hatred and deepening insanity, Bridger had picked the one that seemed to meet his need. The War World. Joining the others, McCade shook his head to Sara's silent question. He didn't want to share his thoughts with Ensign Peller. The game was not over, and he couldn't tell yet where the advantage lay.

They followed Peller down a short hall which suddenly widened into a huge chamber that once could have been a lobby. Rows of parked ground cars, tractors, and power pallets of Imperial manufacture filled most of it. McCade found that intriguing, since it suggested the navy had been in residence for some time. Long enough to need ground transportation and to have had it shipped in. He was reminded of the freighter still in orbit above.

After climbing into an open staff car, they rode in silence through the enormous corridors and halls, all of which shared the same dim, artificial light. It had a warm glow, suggesting a preference for orange or red light. Occasionally they passed giant halls filled with seats never intended to accommodate a human body. McCade noticed they were narrower than human equivalents, with higher backs and longer seats, suggesting tall, thin beings with long, spindly legs.

There were hundreds of side rooms, both large and small. From glimpses of these chambers, McCade saw that while a few were filled with unidentifiable objects, most were bare, though it appeared they hadn't always been that way. Empty pedestals, display cases, and shelves spoke of things no longer there.

The ground car turned a corner to enter a large, circular room. In it a huge, three-dimensional star map dominated all else, suspended somehow in midair, glittering as billions of miniature stars and planets wheeled through intricate paths, acting out a dance as old as time itself. While probably intended to merely reflect the natural movements of suns and planets, it managed to be much more, a work of art, a living sculpture. Circular seating surrounded it and reached up into darkness on every side.

As they climbed out of the car, their eyes were drawn to the map and its stately movements. Where had they gone, those who conceived and created this? What had happened to a race capable of such learning, architects of an entire planet, creators of such beauty?

"Beautiful, isn't it?" Swanson-Pierce said, stepping out of the shadows, into the light. His eyes too were locked on the beauty that swirled above. "I thought you'd like to see this." Tearing his eyes away from the map and turning to McCade and his people, Swanson-Pierce said, "Well, Sam, I see you've managed to indulge your weakness for dramatic violence once again."

"Lucky for you I did, Walt," McCade replied, hiding his surprise behind a cigar. "Otherwise you would have wound up as the best-dressed specimen in some Il Ronnian exobiology lab."

"I must admit we weren't expecting company, at least not so soon," the naval officer replied, strolling toward them. "But I will take this opportunity to thank both you and your companions. Hello, Section Leader Van Doren. Good to see you. Council Member Romero. You've played a critical role in all this. Thank you. And this must be none other than Sara Bridger. We were introduced many years ago, Council Member, but I doubt you remember that. I was pleased to learn of your survival."

Sara extended her hand. "Of course I remember. You've done well, Captain. I remember my father saying you were a very promising young officer."

Taking her hand, Swanson-Pierce executed a formal half-bow. "You are too kind, madam. I had great respect for your father and his death saddened me."

"Thank you," Sara said simply, "but it had to be."

"Yes," Swanson-Pierce replied. "It had to be. Come, you may find the seating none too comfortable, but it's all we have. I'm sorry I can't at the moment offer refreshments."

"Which brings us to a very interesting question," McCade said, shifting in his seat and examining a cigar with care. "How did you find out her father *was* dead? Or that she was alive for that matter?"

"Quite simply, actually," Swanson-Pierce answered. "Major Van Doren told me. Under the cover of weapons practice, he's been sending off message torps on a regular basis."

McCade swore, turning toward Van Doren. The big marine shrugged sheepishly. "Sorry, Sam. . . . For whatever it's worth, they were good reports."

Turning back to Swanson-Pierce, McCade said, "Congratulations, Walt. I should have known. I figured Laurie was your watchdog, while actually there were two."

"And a good thing too," the naval officer said, smoothing an imaginary wrinkle from his right sleeve. "Lieutenant Lowe's true loyalties were something of a surprise, and I'm sure, in retrospect, you'll agree that Major Van Doren came in handy from time to time."

"Granted," McCade replied, "But why, Walt? I mean why go through this whole charade? It's obvious you already knew where the War World was."

Swanson-Pierce was silent for a moment as he perched on the armrest of an alien chair. He looked at each one of them before he answered.

"Time, Sam. The answer is time. This 'charade' as you call it bought us some time. To understand why that's important, you must realize that, in most respects, I told you the truth from the very start." The naval officer held up his hand to still McCade's unuttered objections.

"Yes, yes, I'll admit I didn't tell you everything we knew, however; the fact remains that what I did tell you was mostly the truth. As you know by now, Captain Bridger finally managed to decode his so-called 'Directory,' and came up with a list of artifact worlds plus coordinates for each. On that list he found one called the 'War World.' We kept an eye on him, but frankly we didn't think he could manage to get away. By the time we realized our mistake, it was too late."

Swanson-Pierce looked at Sara and shrugged apologetically. "By then of course he was no longer sane. He became fixated on the War World as a weapon of vengeance. He imagined it to be a world dedicated to war, an arsenal which he could use to destroy the enemy which had robbed him of his wife, his daughter, and his career. With it he could destroy the pirates. If doing so meant giving that arsenal, plus his expertise, to the Il Ronn, then so be it, for he saw the pirates as the greater threat."

The naval officer gestured at their surroundings. "As you can see, his vision of the War World was not entirely correct."

"But not entirely wrong either," McCade said.

The other man nodded.

"It was a museum, wasn't it?" McCade asked. Swanson-Pierce smiled. "Good for you, Sam. I'm glad to see there's a cultured side to your personality. Yes, this whole planet is what we would consider a museum. A museum dedicated to war. The funny thing is, we can't figure out if it was built to glorify war, or to warn against it. The displays we found here could be interpreted either way. Which you see depends on your own attitude.

"In any case our experts say it was probably just part of a network of such planets, each dedicated to a particular subject, or area of interest, although most were probably natural, rather than artificial like this one. There's even the possibility that this entire worldlet is a converted battleship."

McCade tried to imagine a battleship the size of a small world. The very idea was mind boggling.

"So now you're stripping it of whatever knowledge and power you can." Sara's voice was icy.

"True enough," Swanson-Pierce replied calmly. "Although in truth the process is almost complete. It will be, as soon as we finish loading the freighter you were kind enough to save. And, for what it's worth, we've learned a great deal. Like most military museums, this one contained endless displays of what the curators considered to be antique weapons and other related gear. Needless to say much of it was quite new to us, and I might add, quite useful. Little items like the original design for a hyperdrive, for example." The naval officer smiled sardonically, enjoying the impact of his words.

"Hyperdrive?" McCade said in amazement. "I thought it was invented back during the civil war." He knew that in the hands of the man who would later declare himself "Emperor," it had proved the key to winning the war, and had later become the foundation of the Empire.

"As a student of naval history," Swanson-Pierce replied, "you'll remember an admiral named Finley."

McCade thought back to his Academy days. "Finley? The one they call the Father of the Navy?"

"The same," Swanson-Pierce agreed. "As it happens Finley's rise to that lofty rank was fueled more by luck than brave determination and brilliant service. It seems that as junior lieutenant, Finley commanded a small scout assigned as part of the escort for a supply convoy. The convoy and its escort were ambushed and nearly wiped out. With his two-man crew dead, and badly wounded himself, Finley tried to head for the nearest friendly planet. He never got there. Instead he stumbled onto this planet. It was pure blind luck. But luck that served the human race well."

"Served the Empire well, is more like it," Sara snorted.

Swanson-Pierce shrugged and smiled disarmingly. "I understand the way you feel. However, keep in mind that we're talking about something as fundamental to our present existence as hyperdrive. You'll recall that when Finley landed here, we didn't have one. And all the evidence suggests that the Il Ronn, who shortly thereafter made their existence known to us, did. In fact most experts agree they were substantially ahead of us in all areas of technology, at first contact."

Swanson-Pierce examined his immaculate fingernails critically, and then looked up meaningfully.

"So," he continued, "if Finley hadn't managed to patch up his ship, and limp back with the coordinates of this planet, I think it's fair to say that instead of our present standoff with the Il Ronn, we would now be their slaves, a circumstance none of us would enjoy. I might also add that it was hyperdrive, after all, which made possible the colonization of planets like Alice. So while the knowledge gained here did help establish the empire you despise, it also made possible the rather chilly freedom you relish on Alice."

Sara was silent as McCade dropped his cigar on the floor and crushed it out with his boot.

"So," McCade said, "the Empire's been systematically looting this place for years. How many of the Empire's so-called 'scientific discoveries' were really found right here?"

"Some," the naval officer replied distastefully as he watched McCade smear the remains of the cigar under his toe. "But by no means all. Although I'll admit some have been spin-offs of the artifacts found here. But, as you saw on your way in, that's pretty much over now. Oh we've got lots of stuff to study, and no doubt we'll make more discoveries, but time's running out. You asked if there's a point to all this. Well there is. By using the knowledge found here, by keeping the source of that knowledge secret, by pitting the pirates against the Il Ronn, we've managed to buy some time. Time to achieve parity with the Il Ronn."

"What about the other worlds listed on my father's Directory?" Sara asked suspiciously. "Are you looting those too?"

"Unfortunately the answer is no," Swanson-Pierce answered patiently. "We've investigated hundreds of them without finding anything like this," he said, gesturing to their surroundings. "Many of the planets listed turned out to be among those already discovered by accident. Others were new to us, but no more productive than the other artifact worlds already known. This world was evidently a fluke. Because it's artificial and self-repairing it has been able to defy the effects of time. Again, we aren't sure if it was built for this purpose, or converted from another use. In any case, we haven't found anything else like it."

Swanson-Pierce smiled. "I'd say that's more up to you, and those like you, than it is to us. Anyone who really thinks it through soon realizes the future lies with planets like yours, rather than with the fat, complacent inner worlds. Already you have secret governments and are starting to form loose interplanetary ties."

Sara started to object, but Swanson-Pierce held up a restraining hand. "Don't bother to deny it. Give our intelligence people a little credit. As I was saying, you've started to organize. Who knows what final form that organization will take? Another confederation? An Empire? Something new? It's hard to say . . . but, whatever it is, it will replace the present order."

"Has anyone notified the Emperor of all this?" McCade asked with a raised eyebrow. "He'll probably want to update his résumé."

"Oh I think his job's safe for quite a few years yet," Swanson-Pierce replied, tugging on a cuff. "As is mine. Keep in mind I'm talking about the long run. But if the Emperor were here, I think he'd agree with what I've said. He's not a stupid man. Of course there are stupid men and women, many employed by the Empire, all of whom would not agree. Those who benefit most from a system don't like to envision its destruction."

For a moment there was silence all around. McCade finally broke it. "So what about us? There's a shipload of Il Ronnian prisoners in orbit up there." He gestured toward the ceiling.

Swanson-Pierce regarded him with pretended surprise.

"Prisoners? You must be mistaken, Sam. Prisoners imply armed conflict, which in turn suggests war. And we aren't at war with the Il Ronn. If we were, we might very well lose. No, I'm afraid there's been a terrible mistake. We'll apologize, they'll apologize, we'll remove the radio control unit you put on those torpedoes, and everyone goes home happy."

"Except the crew of the shuttle they destroyed," McCade said.

"And except for the pilots of those fighters you blew out of existence," the other man countered dryly. "Plus any personnel lost when their own missiles hit. No, I think it's about even. With that in mind, Council Member Romero, perhaps you'd be so kind as to contact their commanding officer, what's his name, Reez? Explain that there's been a terrible mistake. He'll understand. I'd do it myself, but I'd rather stay in the background, if you don't mind."

Rico nodded his agreement.

"Well I guess that about wraps it up then, Walt," McCade said. "I can't say it's been a pleasure, but that's life. I assume you'll clear my title to *Pegasus?*"

The naval officer nodded. "Who knows, Sam, we might even throw in a bonus. Where do we send it?"

McCade looked at Sara. She smiled and he saw the future reflected in her eyes.

"Send it to Alice, Walt. . . . From what you said, that's where the action's going to be."

As Swanson-Pierce extended his hand, McCade saw something come and go in his eyes. Something that just might have been envy.

They left him there, hands folded behind his back, staring up at the map of a long-forgotten empire, dreaming of what had been, and what was yet to be.

On the surface again, McCade stopped and turned to face Van Doren. Try as he would, he couldn't find any anger at the other man's deception. "Thanks for everything, Amos."

The marine's huge fist tightened around his own. Amos smiled from beneath bushy brows. "Anytime, Sam. You take care out there. Save me a place. Who knows . . . I can retire in a few years, if I live that long."

"You'd better!" Sara said fiercely, hugging Van Doren's huge frame.

"That's right, sport," Rico said, coming up behind them. "We're always short o' bozos with more muscle than brains!"

As the two men gripped hands in one last trial of strength, McCade looked up toward where the Il Ronnian ship orbited high above. In a few minutes Rico would place the com call to Commander Reez. After a brief diplomatic ballet, Lif's Lakorian troops would be off-loaded onto the surface of the War World to await transportation home, and the armorers from the destroyer would go up to disarm the torpedoes which still stood guard over the Il Ronnian battleship's control room.

To the Il Ronnian's surprise, King Zorta would not be found aboard their ship. Perhaps he was killed when the missiles struck. Or maybe he attempted to reach his yacht in space armor, and being inexperienced, failed. In any case they wouldn't spend much time worrying about it now that Zorta's usefulness had come to an end.

The Lakorian troops would return home to find King Lif on the throne, the relieved populace telling of Zorta's death or imprisonment.

They might for a while tell confusing stories of an imposter who fooled everyone and then disappeared without a trace. But who would care?

That, however, wouldn't help the Il Ronnians, who might never learn that their commanding officer was really a Treel. After all he'd been through, it had taken McCade awhile to figure it out. But something about the Il Ronnian surrender had bothered him from the first. It had come too easily, too quickly, but it was more than that. Then it hit. Reez had said, "My officers and I accept your offer of surrender, rigid ones!"

Only the Treel talked like that. Somehow the strange little alien had killed Reez, gotten rid of his body, and taken his place. He knew Walt wouldn't approve . . . but so what? McCade wondered what the Treel would do. Would he destroy the ship, and himself with it? Or would he be satisfied with killing Reez, and continue to impersonate him, perhaps for years, waiting for a time and place in which to more fully avenge the extinction of his race.

There was no way to know. But over the years, McCade would often think of old Softie, and chuckle to himself.

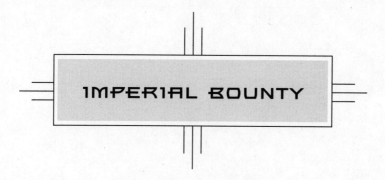

IMPERIAL BOUNTY

This one is for my father,
William Holt Dietz

McCade was hunting an icecat. Or maybe the icecat was hunting him. It wasn't clear which, but it didn't matter much, since he was in deep trouble either way. First, because he didn't know much about hunting icecats, and second, because icecats knew a lot about hunting people. Which wasn't too surprising since they'd been at it for fifty years. That's how long humans had been on the iceworld called Alice. The process of natural evolution had molded icecats into killers, and to them, humans were targets just like everything else.

Naturally the colonists had fought back, but it wasn't easy. Icecats can move with amazing speed, and never give up. Their name comes from a vague resemblance to Terran cats. Unlike Terran felines however, icecats have heat-sensitive membranes located in the center of their foreheads. Operating like infrared scanners, these membranes allow them to lock onto radiated heat, and follow it even through a raging blizzard if necessary. They also have excellent vision, good hearing, and lots of teeth. All of which explains why icecats are normally hunted by well-armed groups instead of individuals. "Not that I planned it this way," McCade said to himself.

It had all begun when a roaming icecat attacked a small herd of variant caribou about twenty miles to the south. In a matter of minutes the rampaging beast had almost wiped them out. By the time Lane Conners arrived, there were bodies everywhere. And when Conners attempted to defend a wounded animal, the icecat jumped him too. He had used his pocket com to call for help. Moments later his wife, Liz, hit the big red panic button just inside the door of their pre-fab dome and raced to his side. A general distress call went out, and as luck would have it, McCade was closest.

McCade was returning home from a series of routine law and order visits to the small mining settlements which dotted Alice when the alarm came in. It had been a long trip. But on Alice you don't ignore a distress call. Not if you want anyone to show up when it's *your* ass on the line. Amazingly enough the rancher was still conscious when the medics arrived. As they loaded him into the chopper he grabbed McCade's arm. "Get the sonovabitch for me, Sam. Otherwise he'll be back . . . and next time it might be Liz or one of the boys."

McCade saw such agony in the rancher's eyes that like a fool he agreed, ready to say anything to get Lane into the helicopter and on his way. So as the med evac chopper disappeared into the southern sky, McCade got into his aircar and took off toward the north. What looked stupid now had seemed reasonable back then. Rather than wait for help, or take the time to put together a pack, he'd decided to follow the icecat's tracks north hoping for a quick, easy kill. He should've known better. When it comes to icecats . . . there's no such thing as a quick, easy kill.

So he'd dropped his aircar into a clearing, and set out on foot, trying to get ahead of the beast and ambush it. But so far all he'd seen was ice, snow, and the low, twisted evergreens which passed for trees on Alice. "Where the hell are you anyway?" he asked in frustration, but there was no answer except the crunching sound of his own footsteps as he walked through the ice and snow. Around him the shadows grew longer and darker, creating a thousand hiding places, any of which might conceal an icecat.

As evening approached it brought with it a frigid breeze, supercooled by glaciers a hundred miles to the north, and sharp as a knife against the small area of unprotected skin at his throat. Walking cautiously he reached down to turn up the internal temperature of his heatsuit. Eventually he'd run out of power for it. Maybe he'd freeze to death while waiting for an icecat to kill him. The thought struck him as funny somehow, so why wasn't he laughing? "You're losing it, Sam old boy," he said to himself. "Pull your-self together. You've been in worse spots."

And it was true. In his days as a professional bounty hunter he'd come close to death many times. But somehow those encounters were different. He'd been in control, always the hunter, never the hunted. Here that was re-versed; the icecat was in control. It could fight or disappear, and whichever it chose, there wasn't a damn thing he could do about it.

Suddenly he stopped, his eyes riveted to the snow in front of him. The icecat was close. There was no mistaking the huge plate-sized paw prints which overlaid the cross-hatched pattern of his own boots. The sonov-abitch was following him! And had been for some time. Together they'd made a large figure eight. With a sinking feeling McCade realized how far he'd come. The aircar was miles away.

He glanced over his shoulder one more time, and started up a nearby slope, instinctively seeking higher ground. Perhaps he could find a better vantage point toward the top. Eventually his path was blocked by the sheer face of a cliff. Locating a small crevice which would protect his back, he forced his way in, and did his best to make himself comfortable.

During his climb, the already dim sun had sunk farther in the overcast sky, making it even colder. McCade reached down to turn up the gain on his heatsuit, and then thought better of it. Even on its present setting the power pak wouldn't get him through the night. He did his best to settle down and concentrate on the task at hand. "All right you flea-bitten sonov-abitch . . . I'm ready when you are . . . come and get it."

Another hour passed. He scanned the area below for the umpteenth time. Even under his visor's high mag setting, there wasn't much to see. He was about to give up when he saw something move out of the corner of his eye. Or had he? Maybe it was just a trick of evening's half light. No, there it was again, a shadow among shadows, a momentary blur only half seen.

Then he had it, a long low body, winter white giving way to summer gray, almost invisible against the volcanic rock. A strong neck supported a large triangular head, with two fan-shaped ears that twitched slightly as they sampled the evening breeze. Huge eyes moved this way and that, each independently scanning the area for any signs of danger. If they looked his way would they see him? And what about the animal's ability to sense radiated heat? Could it detect him?

McCade felt a lead weight drop into his gut as the beast's hideous head swiveled toward him and stopped. How good was his heat shielding? Maybe there was some leakage that the icecat could detect. The icecat snarled, the thin lips of its false mouth pulled back to reveal razor-sharp teeth. The sound echoed back and forth off the cliffs.

The last echo of the icecat's snarl was still dying away when the animal vanished into the shadows. McCade thought about all those teeth and shuddered. The ones he'd seen were bad enough, but he knew there were still others located in its abdomen. Icecats have two mouths. A false mouth used for breathing and killing, and a real mouth, exclusively devoted to eating. Having made a kill, icecats immediately drape themselves over the body to keep it from freezing, thus bringing their real mouths into contact with the carcass. By sliding this way and that, icecats can efficiently strip a man-sized carcass in minutes, all the while keeping their false mouths and sensory organs available for defense. It is, the biologists like to point out, a very efficient adaptation to conditions on Alice. McCade didn't doubt it, but had no desire to take part in the process himself.

Nonetheless he stood up. To hell with waiting. If he didn't move soon he'd freeze to death. So if the icecat wouldn't come to him . . . he'd go to it. He felt the muscle in his left cheek twitch as he shifted the comforting weight of the slug thrower from one arm to the other. The weapon had a rotary magazine filled with alternating hollow point slugs and shot shells. As the planet's only police officer, it was just one of the many weapons McCade carried in his aircar. Properly handled it could take out a squad of Imperial Marines. Unfortunately, he thought, icecats are tougher than marines, and probably smarter.

Carefully he eased his way out of the rocky crevice. There wasn't much cover as he moved downslope, but he used what there was, pausing every now and then behind outcroppings of rock to check his surroundings. He was almost at the bottom when he spotted the icecat making its way across the opposite slope, pausing every now and then to scan ahead for radiated heat, or sniffing the breeze for a foreign scent.

Apparently satisfied with its surroundings, the beast moved off toward a patch of bare rock, attracted perhaps by the glow of radiated heat surrounding it. A few more yards and McCade would be close enough. He flicked the weapon's safety to the off position and moved forward.

Later he wasn't sure what warned him, whether it was an almost imperceptible sound, a tiny disturbance in the air, or some sixth sense, but whatever it was caused him to step right, and saved his life.

The second icecat hit him a glancing blow as it went past, knocking him down, and jarring the weapon out of his hands. Fighting its own inertia, the big animal scrambled to turn around, while McCade clawed desperately for his sidearm. He felt the slug gun come free just as the icecat leaped. The gun roared four times before the huge body landed on him, driving all breath from his body and plunging him into suffocating darkness.

Pushing up with all his might, he fought desperately to get his breath, almost gagging on the animal's stench. In spite of his efforts the icecat's muscular body didn't give an inch. Instead it squirmed, and slid this way and that, trying to bring its real mouth into contact with his flesh. The intervening heatsuit was the only thing between him and all those teeth. In a few seconds those teeth would make contact with the wire mesh of the suit's heating elements, eat through those, and go to work on him. Wire mesh! It gave him an idea.

He pushed up as hard as he could with his left hand, and managed to slide his right down until he found the heatsuit's controls. Fingers fumbling, he accidentally turned the knob to the right, before realizing his mistake and turning it to the left. He prayed there was enough juice left in the power pak to do some good. A second later the icecat's teeth came through the suit's tough outer fabric and made contact with the inner wire mesh. As the power pak's full output hit the icecat's nervous system, the cat convulsed and jerked away.

Momentarily freed, McCade quickly rolled left, and landed on the auto-slug thrower he'd lost earlier. As he picked it up he saw the icecat was already back on its feet, shaking its head like a dazed prizefighter, and preparing to attack again. The weapon in his hands seemed to weigh a ton. With a strange sense of detachment he watched the icecat shift its weight, gather itself, and leap into the air. Meanwhile the barrel of his weapon continued its slow journey upward. Some distant part of his mind noticed the animal was bleeding profusely from six or seven bullet wounds, and wondered if anything could kill it. Finally the slug thrower completed its upward arc, and he touched the trigger. The icecat seemed to run into an invisible wall. It crumpled in midair, and for a moment it was enveloped in a pink mist, as blood and flesh sprayed out behind it. Then it landed with an audible thud, and slid the last couple of feet, until its head almost touched the barrel of his gun.

For a moment he just sat there, too shocked to move. Finally he struggled to his feet, unable to take his eyes off the icecat's huge body, shaking like a leaf. Then he heard the other icecat roar and, whirling, heard the sound of his weapon merge with his own screams. The animal was already in the air, his slugs stitching a bloody line across its chest, when his weapon clicked empty. Closing his eyes McCade waited for the inevitable impact. Instead there was just a dull thump followed by silence.

Opening his eyes, he saw the second icecat was also dead, lying only a few feet from the first. Suddenly his legs gave way and dumped him on the ground. He did his best to throw up, but failed. When the dry heaves finally stopped, he leaned back, and took a look around. It was almost completely dark. He shivered. A quick check confirmed that his suit's power pak was completely exhausted. Well, he couldn't complain about that since it had saved his life. Of course, what good was that if he froze to death?

"You're losing it again," he told himself, "cut the crap and do something useful." Shivering, he tried to think. The aircar was miles away, and he wasn't sure he could find it in the dark. So he should stay put and build a fire. With what? He knew from previous experience the low scrubby vegetation didn't burn worth a damn. Still, he had to do something. Trying to stand, he reached out to steady himself, and his hand encountered something warm. The body of the first icecat.

Of course! Given their bulk the dead icecats would take a while to freeze. Maybe even all night. That gave him an idea. It wasn't pleasant, but it might save his life.

Taking a deep breath, he drew his power knife, flicked on the blade, and went to work. Twenty back-breaking minutes later, he'd finished, and was curled up inside the icecat's warm abdominal cavity. Outside, large piles of entrails lay where he'd thrown them, steaming as they released their warmth into the cold night air, twitching as smaller nocturnal animals gathered to share the unexpected feast. Eventually larger animals would arrive, and start in on the main carcass, but by then it would be morning, and they'd be welcome to it. That was the theory anyway. By now he was so tired he didn't care if it worked or not. Sleep was all that mattered. Doing his best to ignore where he was, and the stench that went with it, McCade curled up even tighter and drifted off to sleep.

ONE

The outer layers of the icecat's body had frozen during the night. Now he was trapped. Panic began to crowd in around his thoughts, but he pushed it back, swallowing the bile which rose to fill his mouth, forcing himself to think rather than feel. Gritting his teeth, McCade slid one hand down to the cargo pocket on his right thigh, fumbled for a moment, and then retrieved the power knife. Moving carefully so he wouldn't drop it, he brought the knife up in front of him, flicked it on, and heard the reassuring hum as its sealed energy beam came to life. It sliced effortlessly through frozen flesh and bone. Moments later he was crawling out of the animal's carcass onto the snow and ice.

He stood slowly, stretching cramped muscles as he looked around. Nothing. The ship he'd heard must have landed some distance away.

Taking his helmet off, McCade strolled over to the other carcass and sat down. It was hard as rock, and somewhat ragged, since small animals had been nibbling on it during the night.

Grinning, he fumbled around inside his heatsuit for a moment, found a broken cigar, and lit the longer half with his lighter. He took a long satisfying drag. As he blew a thin streamer of smoke toward the sky, the sun suddenly broke through the clouds, and he felt its warmth touch his cheek. He smiled. It felt good to be alive.

A few moments later a familiar figure rounded an outcropping of rock and headed his way. McCade waved and the other man waved back. Rico moved easily for a big man. And he *was* big. His extra-large heatsuit bulged

over his muscles, and his enormous strides quickly ate up the distance between them.

He looked at McCade and shook his head in pretended amazement.
"Well, sport, I guess I've seen it all now." Rico's tiny eyes twinkled merrily
as he spoke. "First ya catch an icecat and rip him apart with your bare
hands. Then, just for the fun of it, ya ambush a second one and kill him
too. No offense, Sam, but at this rate we're gonna run outta icecats in a
week or so, and then what'll we do for fun?" Rico shook his head again in
mock concern.

McCade grinned as he stood up and extinguished the cigar butt under
the heel of his boot. "Very funny, Rico. Now cut the comedy, and give me a
hand. I lost a couple of slug throwers around here somewhere . . . and certain members of the Council are notoriously tight with a credit."

Rico laughed. "Tight ain't the word for it," he agreed. "Downright
stingy's more like it. But as long as your wife's headin' the Council we'll be
runnin' a tight ship. Hell, you're lucky Sara ain't countin' your ammo."

"Don't give her any ideas, Rico, or I'll be throwing rocks at icecats from
now on."

"Speakin' o' which, Sam, how the hell'd ya manage ta get into this mess
anyhow?"

While they searched for the weapons, McCade told him the whole
story. "All things considered, I was incredibly stupid," he finished.

"True," Rico said with a big grin.

McCade laughed. "Up yours, Rico."

Rico poked an icecat carcass with the toe of one boot. "All jokin' aside,
you're damn lucky to be alive, ol' sport," he said soberly. "Looks like a
mated pair. Well, come on . . . we've got places ta go an people ta see."

"Bullshit," McCade replied as they crunched through the ice and snow.
"I'm going home. First Sara's gonna chew me out for being so stupid, and
then I'm going to bed."

"Well, you're right about Sara chewing ya out, but ya ain't going ta bed,
not yet anyway," Rico answered with a grin.

"Why not?"

"You'll see," Rico said mysteriously, and steadfastly refused to say more until they reached the clearing where McCade had left his aircar. As they broke into the open space, McCade saw one whole end of the clearing had been scorched all the way down to the permafrost, and sitting in the middle of the burned area was a small ship. Not just any ship, but a captain's gig, the kind that belongs to an Imperial Cruiser. It had fast lines and a flawless paint job.

"What the hell is that doing here?" McCade demanded.

"Your old friend what's-his-name sent it. The one with two last names."

"Swanson-Pierce? You mean he's here?"

Rico nodded and pointed one index finger upward. "He's got a cruiser, a tin can, and two DEs up there, and wants ta see ya."

McCade scowled and turned toward his aircar. "Whatever he wants can wait. By now Sara's worried, and I need some sleep."

Rico shrugged. "Suit yourself, ol' sport, but Sara's up there too."

McCade sighed. Swanson-Pierce could mean only one thing, trouble. And as usual he'd managed to set up things his way. By getting Sara aboard he'd made sure McCade would come to him, plus they'd meet on his turf, and he'd set the agenda. It was all vintage Swanson-Pierce.

They were met just inside the lock by a solicitous young officer who introduced himself as Ensign Peel. He had a soft, friendly face and a firm handshake. Peel showed them into a small cabin just aft of the control room and disappeared forward to assume his duties as copilot.

As they strapped themselves into acceleration couches, McCade took a look around. Someone had lavished a great deal of attention on the ship's interior. The bulkheads and acceleration couches were covered in carefully muted fabrics and, here and there, the polished glow of ornamental brass and exotic wood caught and held his eye. The whole merged to convey a sense of restrained elegance. It all screamed—no, murmured—Swanson-Pierce.

McCade felt himself pushed down into his seat as the ship roared upward. The pilot knew her business and cleared atmosphere only a quarter rotation away from the large Imperial Cruiser orbiting Alice. McCade watched the overhead screens as they approached, and the vessel grew even larger.

She was one of the new Jupiter Class ships. Miles long, she was a tracery of gun platforms, missile tubes, laser mounts, and other less identifiable installations. She had none of the streamlined beauty common to ships designed for atmospheric use, but what she lacked in grace, she made up for in raw power. In minutes she could lay waste to all but the most heavily fortified cities. Beyond her McCade saw a glint of reflected sunlight marking the location of an escort.

Ahead a small rectangle of light appeared as a hatch slid open to admit them. As their pilot skillfully matched velocity with the larger craft and slipped into the launching bay, McCade felt like a minnow being swallowed by a whale. Inside were rows of neatly parked Interceptors, their sleek deadly shapes reminiscent of bullets waiting to be fired.

As always, four were on condition red: tubes hot, weapons armed, ready for launch. McCade knew how it felt. You were proud to slide into the cramped cockpit because Interceptor pilots were the elite. The cream of the Academy. And you were scared, not of the enemy, but of yourself. You'd rather die than screw up.

Then one day the waiting was over. Wing after wing of Interceptors blasted out to give and receive death over the planet Hell. Entire fleets maneuvered through complex computer-generated patterns probing for strength and weakness. But for you the battle was much more personal. It was you against them. Your skill, your reflexes, your ship against them.

Finally the moment came, and with it a strangely silent explosion as a pirate ship blossomed into a miniature sun. You scanned your screens searching for the next target. There it was. A large ship just ahead. You felt the groove, the almost magical connection between you and it, and knew you couldn't miss. Relying on muscle memory, and years of training, you lined it up and prepared to fire. Suddenly a voice breaks your concentration.

"Please, in the name of whatever gods you worship, I implore you, please don't fire. My ship is unarmed. I have only women, children, and old men aboard . . . please listen to me."

And listen you did. You believed her. But a second voice comes over your headset. The voice of your commanding officer, Captain Ian Bridgar, hoarse from hours of shouting orders, tense with hatred for the pirates who took his wife and daughter. "Fire, Lieutenant! That's an order! She's lying. Fire, damn you!"

But you didn't fire. Instead you watched the pirate ship slide out of sight, taking with it your career, identity, and honor. For you have disobeyed a direct order from your commanding officer, and his word is law.

McCade's thoughts were interrupted as the pilot's voice came over the intercom. "Welcome aboard *Victory*, gentlemen, Ensign Peel will act as your guide."

There was lots of traffic in the corridor as the third watch went off duty and the first came on. The two colonists attracted a good deal of attention as they walked along. Especially McCade. His blood-smeared heatsuit, two-day stubble, and hard eyes were difficult to miss.

Ignoring the stares, they followed Ensign Peel through a maze of corridors and passageways. Eventually, they moved into officer territory, passing a spacious wardroom, and arriving in front of a large open hatch. A pair of marine guards snapped to attention and presented arms. Peel saluted in reply and announced his party. "I have the honor to present Council Member Fredrico Jose Romero and Citizen Sam McCade."

Suddenly a shapely female figure in a blue one-piece ship-suit burst through the hatch and threw herself into McCade's arms. She proceeded to kiss him, hug him, and scold him all at once. "Going after an icecat all by yourself . . . you are the most hopeless man I've ever met . . . are you all right . . . is this your blood . . . how could you . . ."

McCade covered her lips with his, and marveled for the millionth time that this wonderful armful could be the daughter of the same man who'd court-martialed him. There was silence for a moment as she melted against him, before suddenly pulling away. "Oh, no, you don't, Sam McCade. You're not getting off that easy, not until you admit you were stupid."

He looked down into large hazel eyes set above a straight, determined mouth. A terrible white scar slashed down across the soft roundness of her face. She'd been aboard the liner *Mars* when it was attacked and boarded by pirates. As they burst through the main lock Sara had been there, fighting shoulder to shoulder with the ship's crew. Coolly she had aimed and fired, killing at least two, before a boarding pike had knocked her unconscious, and left her scarred for life.

In a way the disfigurement had saved her. Instead of selling her as a slave, the pirates had held her for ransom. Ironically she and her mother ended up aboard the very ship which McCade had refused to destroy during the Battle of Hell. In a desperate attempt to save her damaged vessel, the pirate captain had made a random hyperspace jump but it was too late. Knowing the drives were going to blow, the captain ordered those who could to abandon ship. Sara and her mother were among those shoved into a crowded life raft and launched into the darkness of space.

Minutes later the larger vessel exploded, leaving them alone and far from any civilized world. Being a step below a lifeboat, the raft had no drive of its own, so for weeks they drifted aimlessly in space. One by one they began to die. Her heart broken by her husband's insane ravings, Sara's mother was among the first to go. More time passed, until only Sara and two others survived. Finally rescued by a tramp freighter, Sara had made her way to Alice, and never looked back.

Then McCade had shown up, searching for her father, determined to kill him if necessary rather than allow the secret of the War World to fall into Il Ronnian hands. Mutual dislike slowly gave way to wary cooperation, friendship, and then love. So McCade saw past the scar, seeing only the love and concern in her eyes. She was still waiting. "I was stupid," he said, grinning.

Suddenly she was back in his arms, planting kisses all over his face, and fussing over his appearance. Then she leaned back and wrinkled her nose. "Great Sol, what's that odor?"

Meanwhile, the two marine guards did their best to ignore the whole thing and failed. Both were losing the battle to keep a straight face. Flushing slightly, McCade gently disentangled himself and followed her into the large cabin. It reflected the same elegant taste he'd seen inside the gig, which wasn't too surprising, since both belonged to the same man, Walter Swanson-Pierce.

As Walt moved out from behind his rosewood desk to shake hands with Rico, McCade saw the naval officer was at his perfectionistic best. Body trim and fit, uniform just so, graying hair carefully combed, calculated smile firmly in place.

Then it was McCade's turn, and as they shook, McCade noticed the thick gold stripe on the naval officer's space-black sleeve. He grinned. "So it's Rear Admiral now. Congratulations, Walt. Rear Admiral—a rank that describes you perfectly. A reward for cleaning out all the War World's little secrets, I assume."

Swanson-Pierce chose to ignore the dig. Instead, he looked McCade carefully up and down, eyes lingering here and there, as though counting each bloodstain. "Why thanks, Sam, I suppose you're right. I'm sure the successful disposition of that problem did play a part in my promotion. Nice of you to help. Meanwhile, I see you've managed to maintain your usual standard of sartorial elegance—no, that's not quite true—actually, you look even worse than usual."

Rico and Sara looked at each other and shrugged. They'd seen it all before. They'd have to wait it out. They dropped into chairs, Rico grinning in anticipation, Sara frowning in disapproval.

"So," McCade said, also dropping into a chair, and swinging his filthy boots up onto the polished surface of the officer's desk. "What brings the mighty Imperial Navy to this corner of the frontier? Slumming?"

As he moved around behind his desk Swanson-Pierce did his best to avoid seeing McCade's boots. "No," he answered evenly, "actually we're on our way somewhere else." He gestured vaguely. "I thought it would be nice to visit old friends."

McCade snorted in disbelief. "Get serious, Walt. You haven't got any friends. Nobody's got that strong a stomach." Ignoring Sara's look of disapproval, he took out a bent cigar, and talked around it as he puffed it alight. "Besides, you wouldn't go ten feet out of your way to visit your own mother."

Swanson-Pierre shook his head in mock concern. "Well, I see life on Alice has done nothing to improve your temperament, Sam. Sad, very sad. I don't know how you stand it, Sara. You deserve better. But," he said airily, "I will admit there's a matter of business I'd like to discuss."

McCade swung his feet down and stood up. "Come on, Sara. We don't need whatever this is. Nice seeing you, Walt. Don't trip on any pirates as you leave."

But to his surprise Sara remained seated. And a stubborn look had come over her face. He knew that look and groaned inwardly. "I think you should hear what he has to say, Sam," she said. "Then, if you still feel the same way, we'll leave together."

McCade knew when he was beat. He fell back into his chair, knocking a large lump of ash off his cigar. Swanson-Pierce watched in horrified fascination as it fell and then exploded against the rich carpeting. He winced as McCade automatically placed a boot over the ashes and rubbed them in.

"OK," McCade said. "So what's this all about?"

Swanson-Pierce looked up from the stained carpet and forced a smile. "Admiral Keaton and I want you to find someone for us."

McCade shook his head. "Forget it. I gave up bounty hunting."

"Even if you could prevent a war?"

"War, hell." Ten to one that was just more of Walt's bullshit. The old patriotic approach. Well, it wouldn't work this time. McCade was tired of chasing fugitives from planet to planet, tired of living the way they lived, alone and afraid. Besides, Sara didn't want him to. She detested bounty hunters. But why hadn't she objected? Because she believed whatever Walt was selling. He looked over and found her face a purposeful blank. She was trying her best not to sway him any more than she had already. Meanwhile Swanson-Pierce was grinning, aware of McCade's inner conflict, and enjoying it.

"All right," McCade said reluctantly, "I'll consider it. Who's the mark?"

Swanson-Pierce took his time, leaning back in his chair, obviously savoring the moment. "We want you to find the Emperor."

McCade's eyebrows shot up in surprise, but before he could ask the obvious questions, an emergency klaxon went off. The ship was under attack.

TWO

Six torpedoes were launched at *Victory*. Two hit, and obliterated the De-stroyer Escort which happened to be coming alongside at that particular moment. One malfunctioned, and raced off toward the warmth of the sun. Another was intercepted, and destroyed by an unusually alert Interceptor pilot. The last two hit *Victory* and blew up.

McCade and the others were thrown to the deck by the force of the ex-plosions. A host of alarms and klaxons went off. All over the ship hatches automatically slammed shut, turning the vessel into a honeycomb of air-tight compartments. The lights flickered, went off, and then came back on again. They were dimmer now since all available power had been automat-ically shunted to the defensive screens.

The com screen lit up before the naval officer could touch it. "Lt. Com-mander Muncy reporting, sir. Battle status negative. We have no targets on our screens . . . with cross-confirmation from our surviving Escorts. Initial evidence suggests a single vessel, a destroyer, or perhaps a light cruiser. It entered normal space approximately a quarter light out, fired six torpe-does, and immediately reentered hyperspace. Two hit us, two hit and de-stroyed the *Amazon*, one was intercepted, and one malfunctioned. Our remaining Escorts and Interceptors have assumed a defensive formation in case of further attack."

Standing now, McCade looked at the screen and saw there was pande-monium behind Muncy. Medics were running by with stretchers, officers were shouting orders, and a damage-control party was busy fighting a small electrical fire. But Muncy's face showed no trace of concern. Only a subtle tightness around her eyes betrayed the pressure she was under. A real pro, McCade thought to himself.

"Thank you," Swanson-Pierce replied evenly. "You may proceed with your report."

Muncy nodded. "I'm sorry to report that the bridge took a direct hit. Captain Blaine and his executive officer were killed instantly. The second officer is missing, and the third is severely wounded. I have assumed command."

"Noted and approved, Captain," Swanson-Pierce said briskly. "Extent of damage?"

"The bridge, main computer, and all primary controls were completely destroyed, sir. Ten killed, three wounded." She glanced over her shoulder and saw the damage-control party extinguishing the last of the flames. "All fires are out and the worst sections have been sealed off. Initial analysis indicates secondary computer and main peripherals are undamaged. Estimated time to sixty percent effectiveness, one hour forty minutes. We also took a torp in the galley and hydroponics section. Four killed, two wounded. We'll be on emergency rations until further notice."

By now both Sara and Rico were standing next to McCade. Neither was injured. "Speaking for Alice, our hospital and its staff are at your disposal, Captain," Sara said. "Plus any other assistance we can provide."

McCade saw gratitude in the officer's eyes. "Thank you. I'll notify medical."

"One last thing, Captain," Swanson-Pierce said, "and then I'll let you get back to your duties. Did we ID the enemy ship?"

"Negative, Admiral," Muncy answered evenly. "No positive identification. Since our hostile was in normal space for only five seconds, there wasn't much time. And what data we had on her was lost along with the main computer. However, our Escorts say her parameters provide a ninety percent match with Imperial design. As you know, both the Pirates and Il Ronn have taken a few of our ships over the last few years."

"Yes, yes," Swanson-Pierce replied vaguely. "That would account for it."

As he spoke, McCade noticed the other man had turned pale, and his knuckles were white where they gripped the edge of the com console.

"Well, thank you, Captain. You've done an excellent job under trying circumstances. Carry on, and let me know if there's anything I can do to help." Swanson-Pierce forced a smile. "At the moment, however, I imagine you can get along without an Admiral peeking over your shoulder."

Muncy grinned her agreement, but replied tactfully, "Over the next few hours I suspect I'll have lots of questions. With your permission, I'll call back then?"

"Of course," Swanson-Pierce said. Muncy nodded and the screen faded to black.

McCade lit a cigar and blew a stream of smoke toward the ceiling, where it was sucked toward the nearest vent. "Maybe you'd better take it from the top, Walt. Including that stuff about finding the Emperor. How did you manage to misplace him?"

Swanson-Pierce grinned crookedly at McCade. "Well, I'm afraid it's a bit complicated."

"Surprise, surprise," McCade said sourly.

"Actually it *was* a bit of a surprise," the other man said agreeably. "A somewhat nasty one. You see the Emperor died about a month ago."

McCade lifted an eyebrow. "It's a bit out of my line, Walt. What you need is an angel, not a bounty hunter."

Swanson-Pierce smiled patiently. "It's his successor we want you to find. We're reasonably sure the rightful heir is alive; we just don't know where. That of course is where you come in."

Rico shook his head in amazement. "I know we're pretty far out on the rim, but if the Emp croaked, even we'd hear about that."

The naval officer shook his head. "Normally you'd be right Rico . . . but in this case only a handful of people know. Until we've found the Emperor's rightful successor, it seems best to keep his death a secret. Although, I'm afraid . . ."

"Oh no," McCade groaned. "Don't tell me, let me guess. The people who just took a shot at us know, and they don't favor the rightful heir."

"I'd say give that man a cigar," Swanson-Pierce grinned, "except he's already got one."

"I knew it," McCade said. "As usual your people have screwed up, and you want us to bail you out. Well, forget it. We're sorry, but we've got enough problems of our own. If you folks want to squabble over the throne, what's it to us? The Empire has damned little say out here . . . and we prefer it that way." Out of the corner of his eye, McCade saw Sara start to speak, and then restrain herself. Damn. For some reason she was still on Walt's side.

Swanson-Pierce paused for a moment as if gathering his thoughts, and then spoke through steepled fingers. "To understand why it's important to you, and every other planet along the rim, you've got to understand the circumstances of the Emperor's death. Unfortunately the Emperor loved to hunt. It drove his staff crazy of course, but he insisted. He'd been doing it for years and from all accounts was quite good at it. His quarters were full of trophies from hundreds of planets. An uglier assortment of dead carcasses you never saw. Anyway, each year he looked forward to his annual safari. There was the thrill of the hunt, the companionship of his favorite cronies, and an escape from the pressures of office."

"Yeah," McCade added sarcastically, "it must be tough having everything you want."

Swanson-Pierce ignored the interruption and continued his narrative. "This year he decided to visit Envo IV, a primitive planet located on the far side of the Empire from here, and well known for its vicious animal life. Apparently he had his heart set on bagging an Envo Beast. From all accounts they're herbivores, but weigh a couple of tons apiece, and are extremely territorial. I understand both his bodyguard and the locals were aghast. They apparently run the damned things down with armored vehicles, and then finish them off with shoulder-launched missiles. But the Emperor wasn't having any of that."

The naval officer shook his head regretfully. "Say what you will . . . the man had guts. He insisted on going it alone . . . even against Envo Beasts."

McCade reached out to deposit some ash in an ashtray, and missed. It cascaded toward the rug. Sara gave him a dirty look which he somehow managed to avoid meeting.

"Anyway," Swanson-Pierce continued, "something went wrong. The Emperor missed his shot and was badly gored. He lived for about two days. They tried everything, but it was hopeless. Medicine is still pretty primitive on Envo. All they could do was make him comfortable and wait for him to die. Knowing his death was imminent, the Emperor sent for a courier. When the courier arrived, the Emperor ordered everyone else out of his chambers. A short time later the courier disappeared, and the Emperor was found dead. Some said the courier had killed him, and a bounty was placed on his head, fifty thousand credits dead or alive."

Swanson-Pierce looked from one to another as if checking to make sure he had their attention. "Suffice it to say this courier is a very resourceful man, and eventually made it to Terra where he delivered the Emperor's message to Admiral Keaton."

The naval officer took a moment to study the cigar he was holding, intentionally allowing the suspense to build, watching McCade from the corner of one eye. Finally, much to the Admiral's satisfaction, McCade scowled his surrender. Victorious, Swanson-Pierce returned to his narrative. "Before he died the Emperor chose his successor, and sent word of his choice to Admiral Keaton, the one man he trusted to carry out his wishes."

McCade quickly reviewed what little knowledge he had about the Emperor's family. He knew the Emperor's wife had died quite young, and if he remembered correctly, there was a son named Alexander as well as a daughter named Claudia. It seemed the son was something of a playboy, always making headlines with his outrageous behavior, eventually disappearing some time ago en route to Mars. Needless to say there'd been an intensive search at the time, but nothing was ever found. Most assumed Alexander was dead, but a few insisted he'd simply gone into hiding, and would eventually show up. Nobody, except possibly the Emperor, seemed very concerned.

Claudia, however, was another story. She'd taken her position very seriously indeed. While the sons and daughters of other high-ranking officials tried to discover new ways to have a good time, or pursued fashionable careers, she entered the Academy. At her own insistence she was shown absolutely no favoritism. So when Claudia graduated first in her class, it was due to her own ability, and not her father's influence. She was subsequently assigned to the cruiser *Defiance.* Not long thereafter, the *Defiance* had the misfortune to drop out of hyperspace almost on top of an Il Ronnian raider which was operating inside Imperial space. Even the navy couldn't ignore that.

"PRINCESS DEFEATS ALIEN HORDE" the headlines read. In truth the Defiance was twice the size of the Il Ronnian raider, and there were only thirty members of the "ALIEN HORDE." Nonetheless, the Il Ronn put up a tussle, Claudia was wounded, and the press had a field day. The net effect was even greater celebrity status for the princess. She continued to serve with distinction, and eventually left the navy with a reserve commission as a Commander, seemingly determined to follow in her father's footsteps. The navy first . . . then politics. If it was good enough for Daddy, it was good enough for her.

At first she headed a variety of commissions, represented her father at ceremonial occasions, and performed other largely symbolic functions. Gradually, however, Claudia worked her way into positions of genuine responsibility, heading up a succession of small governmental departments, until finally her father agreed to place her on the Board of Military Governors. It was a position of some power, since it was the Board's responsibility to oversee the military on the Emperor's behalf, and that included approving all promotions above the rank of commander. The Board also oversaw the navy's budget and general state of readiness. As a result, some very important people began to take Claudia seriously, and many wondered if the Emperor had already chosen her to succeed him.

McCade shrugged. "So I suppose he chose Princess Claudia."

Swanson-Pierce nodded understandingly. "A logical conclusion . . . but as it happens . . . he didn't."

"Ya mean he picked the boy instead?" Rico asked.

"Exactly," Swanson-Pierce said.

"But why?" McCade asked. "I'd always heard Prince Alexander was about as worthless as they come. Surely the Emperor knew that."

"I honestly don't know why he picked Alexander," Swanson-Pierce said with a frown. "All I can tell you is that Admiral Keaton believes the Emperor had good reasons for his choice. According to Keaton, there was a special bond of some sort between father and son, even when Alexander was at his worst. The Admiral also believes the Emperor feared what Princess Claudia might do if she assumed the throne. Unlike her father, she's a hawk, and believes war with the Il Ronn is inevitable. In her opinion we're better off fighting them now, rather than waiting and being forced to do so later, when they're even stronger."

Now McCade was beginning to see why Sara had sided with Swanson-Pierce. If Princess Claudia took over, she might destroy the delicate balance of power preventing war between the human and Il Ronn empires. For a number of reasons humans and Il Ronn were natural enemies. Strangely enough, their mutual hostility stemmed more from similarities, than differences. Both races were ardently expansionist, and as their respective empires grew in size, the once-thick band of frontier worlds separating them grew constantly thinner. As this occurred, squabbles over real estate became increasingly common. Fortunately, the Il Ronn had evolved on a hot, dry world and, in spite of a reverence for water, detested the wet worlds so loved by humans. Nonetheless both sought certain rare ores and isotopes, and would fight for any planet which contained them.

However some of the mutual dislike stemmed from other, less obvious, causes. For one thing, the two races had very different histories and cultures. The Il Ronn had been around a long time. In fact, most authorities agreed they had preceded man into space by thousands of years. Had their culture allowed the giant leaps made possible by individualism, instead of the slow but steady growth of group consensus, chances are the Il Ronn would have rolled over the human race while it was still living in caves. But they didn't. They preferred instead a deliberate expansion, in which each potential acquisition was painstakingly studied, and then carefully annexed.

Not so the humans. Once in space, their sphere of influence expanded in rapid fits and starts, sometimes accomplishing in days what the Il Ronn might have taken centuries to do. Unfortunately, the opposite was also true. Internal dissension, bickering, and laziness often destroyed human gains more quickly than they were made. The result was two large empires of roughly equal size and power, both of which were inexorably expanding toward each other.

For years, the first emperor, and then his son, had worked to forstall the almost inevitable collision. While both had worked to prepare the Empire for the possibility of war, both had also done everything they could to avoid it. Even to the point of tolerating the pirates because they helped keep the Il Ronn in check.

Nonetheless, some had always felt conflict was certain, and couldn't be avoided. Claudia was one of these. So, if she took the throne, there was a good possibility that war would follow.

And, since only the frontier worlds separated the two empires, they would be the most likely battlefield. And that accounted for Sara's interest in helping Swanson-Pierce. She was trying to protect Alice.

McCade imagined hell bombs falling, entire cities turned to black slag, millions or even billions of lives lost, and all to please a few power-mad idiots on both sides. Viewed that way, he really didn't have much choice. For better or worse, he'd have to find the idiot prince, and put him on the throne. "OK," he said, looking from Swanson-Pierce to Sara. "I get the picture. It sounds like we don't have a helluva lot of choice."

Sara smiled, a look of relief in her eyes. "I'm sorry, Sam, but it's in our self-interest."

McCade blew a long streamer of smoke toward the floor. "As usual you're right, honey . . . but I'm still waiting to hear how Walt managed to lose a prince. I take it from what you said earlier that Alexander's still missing?"

The naval officer looked embarrassed and tugged at his cuffs. "I'm afraid so." He looked up resentfully. "And say what you will, it's not easy to keep track of somebody who's not only wealthy, but a bit looney to boot."

"Even so," Rico observed thoughtfully, "it seems ta me if ya turn the whole navy loose on it ya can't lose."

At that Swanson-Pierce looked even more embarrassed. "You're quite right, Rico. I wish we could. Unfortunately that's not possible."

"Why not?" McCade and Sara asked the question almost in unison. Sara was just as curious as McCade, since her earlier conversation with Swanson-Pierce hadn't proceeded this far.

The naval officer paused as he slumped farther down in his chair. "Because," he said, "at least half the navy doesn't want Prince Alexander found."

McCade slowly shook his head back and forth, marveling at his own stupidity. "Of course. I should have known. The ship which just popped out of hyperspace and slipped us those torps wasn't captured by the pirates or Il Ronn. It was navy, wasn't it? Somebody who doesn't want Alexander on the throne."

"Claudia," Sara said to herself. "It's got to be Claudia."

Swanson-Pierce nodded reluctantly. "Evidently the Emperor believed Alexander to be alive. Nonetheless, in his message to Admiral Keaton he indicated that if Alexander can't be found within three standard months, Claudia must ascend the throne for the good of the Empire. Claudia believes Alexander is dead . . . but she's not taking any chances."

McCade gave a long, low whistle. "Claudia doesn't want her brother on the throne . . . and knows you're trying to find him and put him there. My, my, Walt. She must want you in the worst way. Can't say as I blame her, of course. God knows you're irritating! Nonetheless, sending a light cruiser after you strikes me as a bit excessive."

The other man allowed himself a bleak smile. "I admit the princess is annoyed with me, and Admiral Keaton too for that matter. However, you'll be interested to learn she's not too thrilled with you either. In fact she's already hired the Assassin's Guild to kill you." For a long time only the hiss of the air conditioning filled the room.

THREE

No matter how many planets McCade saw, there would always be something special about Terra. Even though he'd spent far more time away from Earth than on her, she still seemed like home. And many others felt the same way. In fact, for most humans, Terra would always be the emotional center of the Empire. After all, it was from her ancient surface that thousands of ships had lifted and disappeared into the blackness of space. In those days there was no hyperdrive. The colonists had crawled toward the distant stars, often taking years to make the one-way journey. Many died along the way. Sometimes entire ships, and even groups of ships, disappeared without a trace. Of course, some made it too. Their weary worn-out vessels dropping out of alien skies never to rise again. But even then the struggle was far from over. Hostile environments, poor equipment, and a lack of experience finished most colonies off within a few years. But a precious few somehow managed to beat the odds. Through good planning, or just good luck, they managed to hang on. Over time, they grew more numerous, eventually prospered, and even formed an interstellar government. A virgin planet was chosen as a capital and populated with millions of people sent to represent thousands of worlds.

But it wasn't easy. Advantage for some always meant sacrifice for others. Special interest groups battled constantly, alliances were forged and then broken, laws passed and then ignored. Finally a coalition of systems seceded from the Confederation. A terrible civil war followed.

From the ensuing chaos there emerged a single man strong enough, and smart enough, to build something from the ashes. His followers pro-claimed him Emperor.

Though many things to many people, the Emperor was above all else a master psychologist, a PR man par excellence. During the early days of his rule he sensed Terra's symbolic and emotional value, and decided to leave the bombed-out Confederation capital as it was. Rather than rebuild, he declared it a monument to peace, thereby creating a permanent reminder of his greatest victory, and restoring Earth to her former glory. It was a popular decision.

Of course, some refused his rule. Especially those who'd fought valiantly against him during the civil war. Many of them headed for the Empire's frontiers. They eventually became pirates, raiding the Empire's commerce, and plundering the frontier worlds along the rim. At first the Emperor tried to destroy them. He sent Admiral Keaton to find and wipe out the pirate fleet. Keaton found them near the planet Hell and, while soundly defeating them, didn't manage to destroy them.

Elements of the pirate fleet escaped, later attacking an Imperial prison world in an attempt to free their imprisoned comrades and, much to their own surprise, winning. Having no other place to go, they were eventually forced to make the prison their home. If you can call an impregnable fortress, surrounded by orbiting weapons platforms, "home."

Having no desire to waste ships or lives attacking the pirate headquar-ters, the Emperor decided to tolerate the pirates as long as they didn't get out of hand. A pragmatist to the end, the Emperor decided the pirates might feed off the Empire, but by god they would defend it as well. Their eternal skirmishes with the Il Ronn made for less pressure on the navy, which in turn lowered taxes, which made his wealthy supporters happy. Not long after making that decision, he died and his son took the throne. Now the son was also dead, and *his* son must follow, or the entire Empire might be lost.

McCade looked at Terra on his main viewscreen and sighed. She floated against the black backdrop of space like a blue-green jewel wrapped in cotton. He was approaching her slowly, almost reluctantly, delaying the moment when *Pegasus* entered Earth's gravitational field and was pulled down toward the surface. Once there he'd be committed, forced to begin the search for Alexander, and unable to quit once he got started. And it wouldn't be easy. Arrayed against him were Claudia, her personal retainers, and a vast number of governmental and military personnel willing to do her bidding.

According to Walt, a large number of people were betting their careers that the prince wouldn't be found. Or, he thought grimly, that if found, the prince wouldn't live long enough to take the throne.

And, if Claudia's plans for McCade were any example, they were probably right. She must have a spy on Admiral Keaton's staff, because within hours of his decision to solicit McCade's help, she'd filed with the Assassin's Guild for a level-three license on the bounty hunter. A level three would allow the assassins to kill not only McCade, but anyone else who happened to be in the way as well. It was legal, but damned expensive, and indicated how much she wanted him out of the way. And to make things even worse, he'd run up against the Guild in the past, and they were no doubt looking forward to evening the score. It was a depressing thought.

He shook his head ruefully, and Terra disappeared behind a cloud of smoke as he puffed a new cigar into life. He tapped a few keys on the control console. *Pegasus* picked up speed, and started down toward the planet below. Somewhere down there he'd find Alexander's trail. It was more than two years cold, but he'd find it. Just as he'd found so many others over the years.

Bounty hunters were a strange breed. Hated by fugitives, disliked by planetary police, and romanticized by the public, they lived a strange twilight existence between two worlds. Heroes one moment, villains the next, bounty hunters soon learned to trust no one but themselves. They lived to run up their score, both for the financial rewards involved, and for their own egos. In so doing they performed an important function.

Like every other human society the Empire generated its share of criminals, sociopaths, and perverts. While most planets had some form of police force, there was no interplanetary agency for law enforcement. Oh, it had been suggested often enough, but ultimately no one wanted to pay for it. The last thing people wanted was more taxes. Besides, the planets valued what independence they had, and weren't eager to create still another Imperial agency to start mucking around in their affairs. So, bounty hunters were just another expression of the Emperor's pragmatism. If it works, leave it alone. And it certainly worked.

Bounty hunters could access a current list of interplanetary fugitives on any public terminal. Listed were their names, aliases, histories, habitual weapons, and, most important of all, the size of the reward offered for their capture or death. Sometimes the reward was conditional, specifying a particular fugitive must be brought in alive, but that was rare. Normally dead was just fine. Having picked a particular fugitive, the bounty hunter would punch the person's name and ID number into the terminal, and request a hunting license for that particular individual. This was an important step, since capturing or killing a fugitive without a license was considered a public service, and produced nothing more than a thank you letter.

McCade grinned to himself. It had happened to *him* once. And he'd sworn it would never happen again. Which is why he'd spent a lot of time and energy convincing Swanson-Pierce to offer a little extra motivation in the form of a reward. A sort of Imperial bounty.

Public service was well and good, but there was retirement to think about and besides, there was always the chance somebody might blow his ass off. Deep down, however, he knew the idea of giving Walt something for free just plain grated on his nerves. So, one million credits seemed like a nice round number. Sara resisted at first, until McCade suggested that perhaps Swanson-Pierce should throw in a class "A" fusion reactor for Alice as well, and then she'd jumped on the bandwagon with a vengeance. A class "A" reactor would provide enough power for the planet's needs well into the future. Walt never knew what hit him. Sara quickly had him wrapped around her little finger. In fact, Walt was damned lucky to get off that easy. McCade smiled at the thought.

"You're grinnin' like a roid miner on his way out of a pleasure dome," Rico observed, dropping into the copilot's chair.

"Well, there she is, Rico," McCade replied, waving his cigar butt at the main viewscreen. Terra more than filled the screen now as McCade slipped them into a descending orbit. "Trouble."

Rico shrugged philosophically. "I dunno, ol' sport. Seems ta me we've got 'em outnumbered. Wait till they get a load o' Phil."

Suddenly a rigidly calm female voice flooded the intercom. "Alert. Alert. My scanners indicate a dangerous carnivore is aboard and about to enter the control area. I recommend immediate use of class 'A' hand weapons."

"I thought you said you'd have that damned computer fixed," Phil growled as he stepped into the control room. The voice was a deep basso and emanated from a shaggy, bearlike form which had just appeared from the ship's lounge. Phil was a human variant, biosculpted for life on ice-worlds like Alice. He was a highly trained biologist . . . although he didn't look it . . . since very few scientists are seven feet tall and weigh three hundred pounds. Clad only in a plaid kilt of his own design, Phil made an imposing figure. He had large rounded ears, a short snout, and a shiny black nose. But Phil also had other less obvious attributes. Among them were infrared vision, amplified muscle response, and razor-sharp durasteel claws. For short periods of time he could go into full augmentation making him the biological equivalent of a killing machine. Which accounted for his presence. The search for Alexander was likely to get rough, and since the other two had rescued him from the slave pens of Lakor, and paid off his indenture, he figured he owed them one.

"Sorry about the computer, Phil. I just haven't had time yet to get it fixed, but I will."

Phil sat down and lit a dope stick. "I hope so. A rude computer can turn into a dead computer real easy." He looked up at the main screen. "Well, there she is, the planet named dirt."

"Yup," McCade said, glancing over his shoulder. "Fortunately it's winter where we're going, but it's still going to be a bit warm for you."

Phil growled deep in his throat. "Maybe I'll luck out and run into a blizzard."

Pegasus bucked a little as she hit a layer of colder air, and McCade gently forced her nose back down. "Damned little chance of that, Phil. This isn't Alice, you know. Weather programmers don't go in for blizzards. It generates too many hysterical com calls. Hell, you'll be lucky if it rains."

"Yeah, I know," Phil agreed regretfully, "but a guy can hope."

No one answered, and all were silent for a moment as Terra rose to meet them. The vast blueness of the Atlantic Ocean rolled by, quickly followed by the neat symmetry of the coastal cities, and then the dark green of the interior. Eventually the huge forests gave way to the endless interlocking circles of irrigated roboculture. Wherever he looked, McCade saw a carefully maintained balance between man and nature. He knew that when they left the ship, they'd find only clean air, and pure water. Pollution and crowding were things of the past. The damage had been repaired, and where nature seemed flawed, man had put it right. So what if the forests tended to have square corners, and the mountains seemed unusually symmetrical, a clean, safe environment was well worth it. Or that was the theory anyway. In McCade's opinion the whole thing seemed too structured, too tidy. It reminded him of something Walt would put together. Besides, he knew the problems of crowding and pollution hadn't really been solved. They'd simply been exported. Heavy industry and excess population had been shipped to other less fortunate planets, in order to make way for the neat parks and beautiful cities which now graced Terra.

His thoughts were interrupted as they neared Main Port, better known to spacers as "The Glory Hole," the biggest civilian spaceport on the North American continent. It now covered the area which had once been designated as "Chicago." For hours now the ship's computer had been in communication with Imperial Ground Control. Initial identification, clearance, and navigational data had all been handled by the two computers. Now as they neared the spaceport, a series of approach parameters flashed on his com screen, and McCade's hands danced over the controls. Responsive as always, *Pegasus* wound her way through the thickening air traffic, and then lowered herself into her assigned berth.

Once the ship's engines were shut down and secured, McCade took a moment to sweep his scanners across the surrounding area. A wide assortment of ground vehicles hurried to and fro on various errands, ships lifted and landed, but no one seemed particularly interested in *Pegasus*. Good. He liked it that way, even though he knew it didn't mean much. By now, Claudia, and anyone else who cared, knew they had landed. He'd considered arriving incognito, but rejected it. In spite of Terra's defenses, McCade felt sure it could be done. But there just wasn't enough time. A really effective cover would take weeks, maybe months, to establish and use. Besides, according to Walt, there was only one person who might know where to start the search. And she was apparently one of Claudia's best friends. So why bother to arrive in secret, and then be forced to come out into the open?

Therefore, McCade had decided on the direct approach. Land, find Lady Linnea as quickly as possible, and depend on Rico and Phil to cover his back. That's why they planned to check into a hotel. Although they might be safer aboard the ship, it would be very easy to watch, and that would make it hard to slip away undetected. Hopefully the crowds and activity of a large hotel would help to cover his movements. If they were fast enough maybe they could pull it off without any trouble. "And maybe we'll run into some flying cows too," McCade muttered to himself as he strapped on his handgun, and settled its familiar weight low on his left thigh. He'd put on a new set of black leathers in honor of the occasion, and they creaked as he moved.

Rico and Phil were already in the main lock when he arrived. Both were heavily armed. Phil wore a shoulder holster with a small submachine gun nestled in it and carried an energy rifle over his shoulder. Rico wore a sidearm and cradled a grenade launcher in his arms as well. Not that anyone would notice. The societal price for legalized assassination and interstellar bounty hunters is an armed population.

They left the ship together, hopping aboard one of the articulated shuttles which wound its way from ship to ship, finally stopping at the main terminal. There they joined the throng of fellow spacers, mostly human, but well sprinkled with aliens as well. It was quite a mob. Among them were the crisply uniformed officers of a deep-space liner, a bird-like-Finthian merchant-prince, complete with entourage, a hard-looking freighter captain with two of her crew, and a somewhat shabby Zordian diplomat, his oral tentacles weaving a complicated thought into universal sign language. McCade couldn't tell if the tall woman striding along beside him understood or not. Also present, but less conspicuous, were other bounty hunters. He even recognized some of them. But whether he knew them or not, a practiced eye easily picked them out of the crowd. For one thing, they were alone. Most bounty hunters made damned poor team players. And for another, their eyes were constantly on the move, sweeping the crowd for mem-printed faces, like a beachcomber checking to see what the tides brought in.

Gradually the crowd was funneled through a series of robo booths. As McCade stepped inside, hidden scanners searched his body for signs of contagious disease, his retinal and dental patterns were cross-checked with his stated identity, his weapons were analyzed for illegal technology, and an officious-sounding computer simulation demanded to know what cargo he'd brought to Imperial Earth. McCade indicated he had no cargo to declare, agreed to obey all the laws, customs, and edicts of Imperial authority. And promised he'd have a good day—something he wasn't sure of, but hoped would come true.

Because his variant status had slowed his identity check, Phil was the last one out of the booths. First his retinal patterns and dentition were considerably different than those he'd been born with. His biosculpting had been done right there on Terra, and after a little digging, the computer had found his records. Then the computer noticed he'd been indentured to United Biomed as a biologist. He was supposed to be on Frio IV working off his debt. So, what was he doing on Terra? After some hurried consultation with United Biomed's mainframe, the computer learned his indenture had been purchased six standard months before by the government of a planet called Alice. Not long thereafter Phil's certificate of indenture had been used to light one of McCade's cigars, and there'd been one hell of a party. Phil was growling as he emerged, swearing at those who had programmed the customs booth, and threatening them with immediate dismemberment.

Once outside the terminal there was a swirl of activity as a variety of vehicles fought for a position at the curb. There were shiny new hover limos, stately sedans, and more than a few beat-up old taxis. As McCade stepped up to the curb a particularly decrepit-looking ground car of ancient lineage slipped between a limo and another taxi with only an inch to spare, and then screeched to a halt right in front of them. The driver leapt out, and ignored the outraged horns and invective of his fellow drivers, to race around and open a rear door for them.

"Taxi, sirs?" The young man's insouciant grin and obvious eagerness were hard to resist. He had light brown hair, an average sort of face, and wore a disposable gray coverall. The words "Maxi Taxi" were imprinted over a pocket crammed with pens, pencils, a comb, and a cheap pair of sunglasses. McCade normally used the less expensive autocabs, but it was Walt's money, so what the hell. He nodded and preceded the other two into the back of the car. It smelled of the disinfectant robo cleaners sprayed on everything. Given Rico's and Phil's bulk, it was a bit crowded, but not uncomfortable. Moments later the car jerked into motion and they were off.

"Where to?" the driver inquired as he smoothly inserted the ungainly vehicle into the flow of traffic, and accelerated away from the terminal.

"The Main Port Hilton," McCade replied.

"Yes, sir!" their driver said enthusiastically, and the car picked up even more speed.

Suddenly McCade felt vaguely uneasy. He couldn't put his finger on it, but there was something familiar about the taxi driver. Like most bounty hunters, McCade had trained himself to remember faces, and he was increasingly sure he'd seen the one reflected in the rearview mirror before. Surreptitiously he reached down to try the door handle. It was locked. And even if it wasn't . . . by now the car was moving too fast to jump. Glancing up at the mirror, McCade's eyes met the driver's, and the young man grinned. Only there was no humor in the man's smile. Or was it his imagination? Maybe he was just jumpy knowing the Guild was after him. The

Guild! Then he had it, but a moment too late. Just as he remembered where he'd seen the driver's face before, the car swerved into an alley and came to a screeching halt. The driver whirled and McCade found himself looking down the business end of a needle gun.

"Welcome to the Glory Hole, stupid," the driver said, all traces of boyish charm suddenly gone.

"I assume he's addressing you, Sam," Phil said calmly, measuring the distance between himself and the gun.

"Shut up, fur face," the driver grated, shifting the gun an inch toward Phil. "Go ahead and try it. I could use a fur rug for my living room."

"Relax, Phil," McCade cautioned. "I don't think our friend here plans to kill us. At least not at the moment. For one thing he's trapped us, and for another he hasn't delivered a warning. So if he takes us out . . . the Guild will be forced to hunt him down themselves." McCade was referring to the fact that while assassination was legal, certain ground rules had been established to give the intended victim a fighting chance. After all, those who made the rules knew that unless specifically exempted by the Emperor, they could become targets themselves. According to the rules, intended victims couldn't be tricked into an enclosed area, or other physical trap. Assassins were supposed to reveal identifying clothing just prior to an attempt, deliver an audible warning, and allow their intended target five seconds to react. And the Guild was committed to hunting down and killing any assassin who broke the rules. Not because they were concerned with fair play, but because if they didn't, assassination might become illegal.

The driver nodded his agreement. "That's right, shitheads. Mr. big-deal bounty hunter knows the rules. But don't push me or I might break 'em and take my chances."

Right then Rico belched, causing the needle gun to jerk his way. Rico covered his mouth in mock embarrassment. "Excuse me, ol' sport. I didn't mean ta scare ya like that."

McCade noticed the flush that started around the young man's neck and worked its way up across his face. There was hatred in the eyes which met McCade's, and he was holding the needle gun so tightly his fingers had turned white. He spoke through gritted teeth. "Real cute, asshole. But just remember you're all dead meat. Especially you, McCade. I want you to know that, think about it, sweat it through your pores, and piss it into your pants. Just remember, when they make your breakfast, I'll be in the kitchen; when you walk on the street, I'll be in the crowd, and when you go to sleep, I'll be in your dreams. And then, when I'm good and ready, I'm gonna kill you, just like you killed my brother Deke."

It all came rushing back. There were three assassins. Spread out to place McCade and his two escorts in a cross fire. He remembered how the middle one's amplified voice had echoed off the walls of the corridor. "Attention! A level-three licensed assassination will be carried out on Citizen Sam McCade five seconds from now." He remembered diving and rolling, snatching up a fallen weapon and swinging it left until the sight was filled by an assassin. A slightly older version of the driver. He remembered the incandescent holes his weapon punched through the wall before it came to bear and tore the man into pieces of bloody flesh. "Your brother did his best to kill me," McCade said flatly.

But they were wasted words. The driver was so centered on his own hate and need for revenge that he didn't even hear. "Just remember my face, shithead—cause it's the last thing you're ever gonna see." And with that the assassin opened the door and was gone.

FOUR

McCade opened the door of the speeding hover car and jumped. The ground came up fast, and slammed into his left shoulder. He rolled, crashing through the low bushes and down into the bottom of a drainage ditch. He gritted his teeth against the pain and forced himself to remain motionless. It was pitch-black and damned cold. A few seconds later a second hover car roared past showering him with blown gravel and dirt. "Talk about adding insult to injury," McCade mumbled to himself. But at least they'd fallen for it. Painfully he rolled over, made it to his knees, and then his feet. Now the second car's taillights were tiny red eyes way down the road. One, then the other, winked out as the car took a curve.

Somebody was going to spend a boring evening following Phil and Rico all over Main Port. It had been a long day, and winding up in a ditch didn't make it any better. After their taxi driver-cum-assassin deserted them, McCade had managed to crawl into the front seat, and start the car. Later they'd left it a few blocks from the hotel and walked the rest of the way.

As they checked in, McCade insisted on the hotel's best, paying in advance from the generous wad of expense money he'd wangled out of Walt. For a moment it seemed as though the hotel manager might say something about Phil, but right then the biologist smiled, revealing rows of durasteel teeth. The manager had turned pale, and assigned Phil the ambassador's suite.

While McCade's suite was smaller than Phil's, it was still big enough, including a small swimming pool, exercise room, and office. The latter boasted a com set which would have looked right at home on the bridge of a battleship. He flopped into a chair and gave the com set Lady Linnea Forbes-Smith's unlisted number. Using a soft female voice, the com set thanked him, and promised to put the call through quickly and efficiently. Lady Linnea wasn't expecting his call, but Walt felt that if the prince was alive, she might be able to provide some sort of lead. McCade had his doubts. After all, Walt also said she was Claudia's best friend. So, if she knew something, why tell him? As usual Walt probably knew more than he was saying: part of the old "only tell 'em what they need to know" routine.

After an auto receptionist, a secretary, and a personal assistant, Lady Linnea finally came on the line. Hoping for the best, McCade tackled the subject head-on and, much to his surprise, found she was eager to see him. She was also quite concerned that no one find out that he had. They agreed to meet that evening.

McCade, Rico, and Phil had used the rest of the day for rest and relaxation, leaving the hotel just about dusk. Jumping into their rented hover car, they pulled out into light traffic and headed toward the fashionable suburbs. McCade had kept an eye on the vehicles behind them, and sure enough, there was a tail. It was a sloppy job, which suggested either incompetence or arrogance. Either way, he'd have to dump them. They might be assassins, Claudia's people, or even Naval Intelligence, acting on Admiral Keaton's behalf. But Lady Linnea's instructions were quite specific. No one must know that McCade had seen her.

So they'd checked for other ground vehicles, air surveillance, and everything else they could think of. Nothing. Someone thought the single ground car was enough. They were wrong.

Ignoring his aching shoulder, McCade climbed up the low bank and slipped through the shrubbery which fronted the road. A few feet farther on, he found the eight-foot-high stone wall which encircled Lady Linnea's suburban estate. Feeling his way along, he found the narrow gate exactly where she'd said it would be. And true to her word it was unlocked.

Was it all too easy? Was there an ambush waiting on the other side of the gate? He paused in the shadows and gave his eyes a few more seconds to adjust to the half light. It was dark, but the ambient light from distant streetlights, plus the light from the mansion itself, made it possible to see. He carefully eased his handgun out of its holster, and brought it up next to his left shoulder. You never ever go through a door handgun first. Not if you want to live anyway. Conscious that the split second in the gate would be the most dangerous, McCade went through fast and low, quickly ducking around the trunk of a large tree. Nothing. He heaved a sigh of relief. Now he heard faint sounds of music and laughter coming from the direction of the mansion. Lady Linnea was holding a party.

Moving quietly, he drifted from one pool of shadow to the next, sensitive to the smallest movement or noise. He passed through concentric rings of security scanners, an empty dog run, and then a fifty-foot stretch of lighted duracrete, all without detection. The lady was as good as her word. So far anyway.

McCade made his way to a small side entry. He passed his hand over the scanner three times in quick succession. He heard quick footsteps on the other side of the door. It slid open to reveal one of the most beautiful women he'd ever seen. And except for some expertly applied makeup, she was completely naked.

Working on the assumption that women who appear at the door naked want to be looked at, McCade looked. In fact he took his time, starting with her neatly manicured feet, and moving slowly upward. She had long shapely legs, softly flaring hips, a tiny waist, full pink-nippled breasts, and a beautiful face. Her dark swept-back hair had been dusted with something that sparkled, and reflected the light as the warm air blew through it. She had big brown eyes, a small straight nose, and a full sensuous mouth.

"Would you like to make love to me?" she asked with an amused smile.

"I'd love to . . . but unfortunately I'm married," McCade replied regretfully.

"How old-fashioned of you," she replied, somehow demure in spite of her nudity.

"I'm not," McCade countered with a grin. "It's my wife who's old-fashioned."

Her laughter was warm and open. "So what *can* I do for you?" she asked with a twinkle in her eye.

"I'm here to see Lady Linnea."

She smiled as her hands came up to cup her breasts and then run down along the smooth contours of her body. "But you have seen her, Sam McCade." A mischievous glint came into her eyes. "And rejected her. Not something I'm used to." She enjoyed his discomfort for a moment longer, before taking his hand and pulling him gently inside.

The door closed noiselessly behind them as she led him down a narrow corridor. Since she had a delightful walk, McCade found himself enjoying the journey, quite oblivious to the possibility of a trap. Fortunately there was none. Instead, she led him up some stairs and down another corridor. A side door slid open at her touch and he followed her inside.

As they entered, soft lighting brightened to illuminate a comfortably furnished study. Real books lined one wall, the latest in com equipment took up another, while a third was hidden by a heavy curtain of red fabric. Lady Linnea touched a button and the fourth wall became transparent. Beyond it, thirty or forty naked men and women frolicked in an indoor swimming pool. Though many were quite elderly in chronological terms, their biosculpted bodies glowed with youthful vigor. "Don't worry," she said, "they can't see us. Nude pool parties are all the rage right now."

Reaching into a closet, she withdrew a robe made of a silky material. As she slipped it on, and cinched it around her waist, she grinned in McCade's direction. "I wouldn't want your wife to get mad at me."

"Neither would I," McCade replied, taking a seat in a richly upholstered chair. Lady Linnea sat down opposite him and regarded him seriously.

"I must warn you, Citizen McCade, that you're in great danger."

"Sam," McCade replied. "My friends call me Sam."

"All right," she agreed. "Sam. But I'm not really your friend, Sam . . . though I might like to be if things were different. But with the possible exception of Admiral Keaton, I doubt you have any friends on Terra at the moment. None that count anyway. And while I've done my best, I can't guarantee your safety, or mine for that matter. The simple fact is that Claudia doesn't want Alexander found . . . and no one wants to offend Claudia. After all, in a few months she may be an empress. So naturally everyone wants to please her."

"And you?" McCade inquired. "What do you want?" He wished he could light a cigar, but there wasn't an ashtray in sight, and for some reason the thought of lighting up here, in spite of that, never even crossed his mind.

In answer she reached out to touch a button. Powered by some hidden motor, the heavy curtain slid slowly aside to reveal a huge holo tank. It swirled into life revealing the likeness of a young man and woman standing in a garden. It took McCade only a moment to recognize the woman as a younger Linnea, and the man as Prince Alexander. It was a candid shot, taken at a moment when both people were aware only of each other. The look passing between them spoke louder than words. They were obviously in love. And, McCade realized, still were. At least Lady Linnea was. Otherwise why the curtain-covered holo tank?

As if reading his thoughts she said, "You ask what I want. The answer is simple; Alex is all I ever wanted."

"Then help me find him," McCade said, glancing from the holo to her.

There was pain in the eyes which met his. "I want to, Sam . . . but I can't do so openly. If Claudia found out, she could ruin me, and my father as well. His company depends on navy business, and as a member of the Board of Military Governors, she could make sure all the contracts go to someone else. Besides . . . she thinks of me as one of her best friends . . . and, in every way but this, I am. We grew up together, and were very close before she went off to the Academy. So, if it wasn't for Alex, I wouldn't be doing this."

"Then why ask me here? If you can't or won't help, what's the point of this?"

She sighed. "I can't help you directly, but as Walt told you, I may be able to steer you in the right direction. Did you know Walt and I are distant cousins by the way?"

"No," McCade replied thoughtfully as he looked around, "but somehow I'm not surprised. He'd be comfortable here."

"And you're not?"

"No offense," McCade said as he watched her wealthy guests throw a large ball back and forth across the pool. "But you mentioned something about steering me in the right direction."

She nodded, a half smile touching her lips. "I know where he was when he disappeared."

McCade regarded her skeptically. "According to all the papers he boarded his yacht, took off for Mars, and never arrived."

"True as far as it goes," she agreed. "But I have something to show you." She stood and stepped over to her desk where she tapped a combination into the keypad inset into its surface. There was a tiny click, and the lap drawer popped slightly open. Taking out a small box covered with gold filigree, she opened it, removed a small object, and handed it to McCade.

It was a small cube made of cheap plastic. Turning it this way and that, he saw that five sides were inscribed with an apparently random series of numbers: seven, eighteen, fifty-six, two, and eighty. The sixth side bore the letter "J" with a circle around it. He held it up to her and said, "Mean anything to you?"

She nodded. "It's the Joyo logo." Then McCade understood. Everyone had heard of Joyo's Roid, though few had been there. Originally it was just one of the many asteroids orbiting between Mars and Jupiter. Then a miner named Jerome Joyo came along searching for rare ores, hot isotopes, or anything else he could dig out and sell. But when his robo driller broke through the asteroid's crust, he found a series of large empty caverns, and not much else. Most miners would have packed up and moved on, but not Jerome Joyo. He'd paid a hefty fee for the rights to that asteroid . . . and by god it better pay for itself. So he plugged up the holes he'd made, pressurized the interior, and rented caverns out to fellow miners for use as warehouse space. A nice safe place to store extra gear, the odd shipload of ore, or a few crates of stolen merchandise. It was a unique service, and much in demand. Soon there was a constant flow of miners coming and going. This inspired Joyo to open a saloon. After all, why not take advantage of all that traffic, and turn another credit or two? And turn a credit he did. He did so well, in fact, that the saloon grew into a gambling casino, which also prospered, eventually giving birth to other entertainments, until Joyo's Roid finally evolved into a playground for the extremely rich. Although some said there was still a darker side to Joyo's business activities as well.

"That came by regular mail about three months *after* Alex dropped out of sight," she said.

"Was there a note or some other kind of message with it?" McCade inquired as he handed her the six-sided piece.

"No," she answered simply, accepting the plastic cube as though it were a religious relic. "But I knew it was from him. It was his way of letting me know he was all right. He was always sending me symbolic gifts. That's the sort of thing that makes it hard to forget him."

McCade lifted one eyebrow in a silent question.

Lady Linnea dropped back into her chair and curled her feet under her. When she spoke it was with the calm deliberation of someone who's given the subject a lot of thought. "Sam, it's important that you understand that Alex wasn't just another rich playboy. Oh, he was for a while, but that was just another in a long list of experiments. He also studied psychology for a while, then null G ballet, which somehow got him interested in unarmed combat, and that led him into a fascination with human history, and so forth. I guess you could say Alex is something of a romantic. It used to drive his father crazy. The Emperor wanted him to settle down, and prepare himself to rule. But Alex wanted to examine all the possibilities. All the things he could potentially be . . . instead of the next emperor."

"And you think he disappeared on purpose," McCade finished for her, "as part of another experiment."

She nodded eagerly. "Exactly. Before he left on that trip, he was talking about how hard it is to know yourself when everything you do ends up on the holo. I think he wanted to find out what he could do without either the advantages or disadvantages of his position."

"I see," McCade said thoughtfully. Though he didn't really. The whole thing didn't make much sense to him. While everyone else is out working their butts off trying to make money, this bozo has tons of it, and doesn't want it. Instead he wants to find out what life's like without it. Hell, it's miserable. Everyone knows that. But she obviously believed and understood Alex. They were both silent for a while.

After a moment McCade asked, "Feeling as you do, why didn't you go with him?"

Much to his surprise, she looked down at her lap, apparently ashamed. "He didn't ask me. I'm afraid he didn't trust me." She looked up, and he saw a tear trickling gently down her cheek. "And he was right. At first I didn't understand. If I'd known I would have betrayed him, thinking it was for his own good." She wiped the tear away with the sleeve of her robe. "But not anymore. I've done a lot of thinking since then. Anyway, I'm sure he'd want to know about his father's death."

McCade rose to go, impatient now that he had a lead. "Thank you, Lady Linnea. I appreciate your help."

"You'll go to Joyo's Roid?"

McCade nodded. "It's the only lead I have."

Silently she led him back to the small side entry, and out into the chill night air. The warm-air blowers came on, but she unconsciously cinched the robe more tightly anyway. She turned toward him and paused. For a moment her eyes searched his face, as though looking for some sign of what would come, and then, as if finding it, nodded to herself. "You'll find him, Sam McCade. And when you do . . . tell him I love him . . . tell him we need him."

McCade found himself nodding in agreement. She smiled, stood on her tiptoes, and kissed him on the cheek. "And tell your wife I think she's a very lucky lady." With that she was gone. The door hissed closed, and he was alone.

This time he didn't bother to dash from shadow to shadow. Instead he just strolled through the trees as though he owned the place. A few minutes later he stepped out of the bushes and onto the road. A light flashed twice from down the road, and he heard the sound of a hover car starting up.

Phil and Rico had dumped the tail and come back for him. Good, it would have been a long hike to the nearest transcar terminal. The car pulled up next to him, and the blast of warm air felt good as the door opened, and he climbed inside.

"Good ta see ya, sport. Where to?" Rico asked cheerfully.

"The hotel, Rico. And in the morning we'll get our butts off this planet while they're still intact."

"A wise decision indeed," Phil agreed soberly as he fed more power to the big turbine, and they accelerated smoothly away from Lady Linnea's estate.

F1VE

The sun was barely in the sky when they left the hotel for the spaceport. No one said anything, but all three were nervous. Why hadn't the assassins struck? Surely they wouldn't allow their prey to leave Terra unmolested? Yet nothing happened. Hands hovered near gun butts as they entered their rented hover car, eyes scanned the sparse early morning traffic as they drove toward the spaceport, and minds grew edgy waiting.

As they neared the spaceport, they heard the rolling thunder as ships lifted off, and saw distant sparks of light shoot upward toward the blackness of space. Then the green belt surrounding the spaceport came and went, followed by the outer perimeter security fence, and the outlying buildings. Still no assassins.

So as they pulled up in front of the main terminal, the muscle in McCade's left cheek had begun to twitch, and his gut felt like it was full of liquid lead. Where the hell were they? He felt like screaming, "Come on out, you bastards, and let's get it over with!" Nonetheless he did his best to hide it. Never let 'em see you sweat.

They took turns going through the customs booths. While one was processed the other two stood guard. When all three had been cleared, they left the terminal and jumped on a shuttle bus. As it neared *Pegasus*, McCade's spirits began to soar. "We made it, by God!" For some reason the assassins had left them alone, and soon they'd be safely off-planet.

Then as quickly as they'd gone up, his spirits came tumbling down. "Looks like trouble up ahead, Sam," Phil said tensely. "There's about twenty marines waiting by the ship." McCade wished he had Phil's enhanced vision. Without it the marines looked like little dots.

"Marines?" McCade wondered aloud. What the hell were marines doing here? Could they be assassins disguised as marines? No, that was expressly forbidden by law. But it didn't bode well. Marines meant the government, which in turn meant Claudia, and all things considered, he'd rather deal with the assassins. At least you could shoot at them.

As the bus began to slow, they looked at each other and shrugged. "We'll have to play it by ear, gentlemen," McCade said.

"Somebody already played with *his* ear," Rico commented, inclining his head toward the marines. Rico was referring to the marine major who stood facing the shuttle, his back ramrod straight, a leather-covered swagger stick tapping one leg. Where his left ear should have been, there was only scar tissue. His bullet-shaped head was shaved in the style of the elite Star Guard, and his features seemed made of stone. A real hard ass. McCade knew the type and didn't like them.

"Citizen Sam McCade?" The authority in the Major's voice evoked the many years McCade had spent in uniform, and he almost replied with a conditioned "Yes, sir!" Instead he took his time, looking the Major over, as though examining a strange species of alien insect under the microscope. A scarlet flush started at the Major's stiff collar and worked its way up across his face. Finally, just when it appeared the Major might explode, McCade said, "I'm Sam McCade. Nice of you to drop in. Are you here to help with the luggage?"

By now a vein throbbed in the Major's forehead, and only his iron will, wedded to thirty-two years of disciplined service, was keeping McCade alive. The Major's eyes narrowed as Phil and Rico drifted off to each side. Three targets instead of one. They'd take on twenty marines by God! If only his orders allowed, but there was no point in wishing, best to just swallow his pride and get it over with. "Citizen McCade," he said formally, "I am Major Tellor. It is my honor to convey a message from the Imperial household. You and your companions are hereby invited to attend the finals of the 3-D games as guests of her royal highness, Princess Claudia. We are your escort."

McCade eyed the front rank of marines. They had a choice. Take on the marines, or accept the so-called "invitation." And McCade didn't like orders. But taking on the marines looked like a major project. Each held his energy weapon at port arms. Within a second they could bring them up and fire. And these were not recruits. They were hand-picked veterans. The choice was really no choice at all. "Well, Major," McCade replied lightly, "this is an honor. We'd love to come. Right, men?"

"Wouldn't miss it for the world," Rico replied with mock gravity.

"Charmed, I'm sure," Phil added in a bass growl.

McCade thought he saw a flash of disappointment in the Major's eyes as he murmured an order into his wrist com. Moments later, three helicopter gunships clattered in out of the sun and blew dust in every direction as they touched down. Climbing aboard the nearest chopper, McCade knew he'd made the right decision. Even if they'd managed to take out the marines, the gunships would have arrived a few seconds later and cut them to shreds. At least they still had their weapons and therefore a chance, however small.

It took about an hour to reach the Imperial Coliseum. McCade tried to use the time constructively by imagining what Claudia might say and how he'd respond. He quickly bogged down in all the possibilities and decided to watch the scenery instead. As they approached the coliseum McCade remembered that the ancient city of Detroit had been completely leveled to make room for it. First came the miles of green fields and forest which served as a buffer between the coliseum and the surrounding suburbs. Then came the vast parking lots filled with ground cars, aircars, hover cars, and more. They sparkled and glittered in the morning sun.

Then came the coliseum itself. It had been excavated rather than built. Layer after layer of earth had been carved away to create broad terraces, each cascading downward to the next, until finally reaching the flat playing field hundreds of feet below. Each terrace had been carpeted with variant green grass so tough it could compete with the strongest synthetic carpeting. Then the terraces had been divided into sections. Patrons could choose the type of seating they preferred. There were large sections of comfortable seats, complete with built-in holo tanks, on which they could watch the action below. Or, they could lounge about in the open grassy areas, appropriate for picnics or sunbathing. Tastefully placed clumps of trees offered shade and pleased the eye. Gone was the duracrete ugliness of most arenas. The whole thing was more like a park than a coliseum. Each terrace also offered a variety of restaurants and snack bars to serve the multitude of people who packed the place. People were everywhere. Their clothing created a multicolored moving mosaic that shifted endlessly over the green grass. McCade estimated there were at least a million people in the coliseum, and room for more.

At the very center of the coliseum stood a tower as tall as the arena itself. In spite of its location, the tower's slim profile blocked very little of the playing field. It too was terraced, offered a variety of seating choices, and a number of open-air restaurants. But there was more. This was the province of the rich and powerful. Streams and waterfalls cascaded down the sides of the tower, to feed countless swimming pools, and eventually fill the moat below. Miniature villas dotted its sides, each a small mansion in itself, each the private preserve of a wealthy individual or family.

Above, the climate-controlled blue sky promised only the best of weather, and below, the miles and miles of now-empty playing surface promised moments of excitement in otherwise dull and pampered lives. As their chopper lost altitude, McCade wondered what sort of games were popular these days.

McCade put those thoughts aside. Claudia was waiting somewhere below, and he wasn't looking forward to meeting her.

The chopper landed with a gentle thump, and they were quickly herded into some sort of a lift tube. The platform dropped quickly before coming to an abrupt stop. From the tube's banged-up interior, McCade got the impression it was normally used for freight. A subtle insult by Major Tellor? Probably.

They were led off the platform, and through a bewildering maze of halls and corridors. When they finally emerged into sunlight once more, they were standing on a narrow terrace, with an incredible view of the surrounding coliseum. However, the quality of the view suddenly deteriorated as Major Tellor stepped into it. His expression was anything but pleasant. Glancing around to make sure no one was listening, he spoke in tones pitched so low, they couldn't be heard even a few feet away.

"Now, you three clowns listen, and listen good. You're about to have an audience with Princess Claudia. For some reason she insists you be allowed to keep your weapons. I recommended against it, and was overruled. I don't like to be overruled, so I'm pissed. And when I'm pissed, I like to hurt people. I'd like to hurt you. So I'm going to watch everything you do . . . and if one of you even brushes a weapon with his hand . . . he's dead meat. Maybe one of you will give me an excuse—and please, God—let it be you." The Major drove the last word home by stabbing a stiffened index finger into McCade's chest. Because McCade was wearing body armor under his clothes he didn't feel it. He looked down at the Major's finger and then up into his eyes. Slowly he smiled his most insulting smile.

"Yes, mommy, we promise to be good. Now get lost."

For a moment Phil thought McCade had pushed the Major too far. Murder blazed in his eyes. With a major effort, Tellor managed to bring his anger under control, and take a step backward. "You've been warned, scum." With that he executed a perfect about-face, and disappeared to their left. No sooner was the marine gone than a beautiful woman appeared. At first McCade couldn't quite place her. Then she smiled, and he realized it was Lady Linnea Forbes-Smith. She looked different with her clothes on.

In fact she was like another person, cold, distant, and imperial. As she introduced herself, she allowed no flicker of recognition to touch her features, and when she asked them to follow, it was more an order than a request. She led them toward the far end of the terrace, where McCade saw a single glass-topped table, and two chairs. One was already occupied by a young woman, who could be none other than Princess Claudia. He wasn't sure, because her face was shaded by a large disk of brightly colored fabric which hovered above her. He assumed it was kept there by some sort of anti-grav device.

They were still fifteen feet away from Claudia's table when Lady Linnea paused, and skillfully guided Rico and Phil into waiting chairs. Apparently the princess wanted to speak privately with McCade. Rico and Phil were more than a little relieved. Neither wanted to sit down and make polite conversation with Claudia. "Try not to do anything crude, Sam," Phil cautioned airily. "Rico and I have our reputations to consider."

"I'll keep your reputations in mind throughout," McCade promised dryly.

"The princess will see you now, Citizen McCade," Lady Linnea said tactfully.

"I think she means you should get your butt in gear," Rico suggested as he lit a cigar.

Linnea smiled in spite of herself, and said, "We shouldn't keep the princess waiting."

McCade nodded, and as he turned to go, he would've sworn he heard her whisper, "Good luck, Sam!" but couldn't be sure. As he approached Claudia's table, he was surprised to see how young she was. Thirty at the most. Somehow he'd thought of her as older than that. She had hard blue eyes, a long straight nose, thin lips, and shoulder-length blond hair. Her clothes were fashionable, but cut with almost military severity, and seemed too big for her thin body. She was playing with a silver stylus. He noticed that her nails were clipped short and blunt and her fingers were heavily stained by some sort of chemicals. Later he learned her hobby was experimental hydroponics. A little something she'd picked up in the navy.

She looked up at his approach, her eyes quickly taking him apart, and putting him back together. Having found no surprises, she smiled slowly and said, "Have a seat, Citizen McCade. You may address me as Princess, or Your Highness, whichever you choose. Based on your computer profile, I suspect you'll find 'Princess' to be more comfortable. It allows one the semblance of equality . . . and I sense that's important to you. After all, you've always had trouble dealing with authority, haven't you?"

McCade couldn't help but admire her style. In seconds she'd managed to take complete control of the situation, remind him of her powerful position, and put him on the defensive. He forced a smile as he sat down. "You're quite right, Princess. But perhaps my distaste for authority is something we have in common. For example . . . it's my understanding that your father chose your brother to rule the Empire . . . yet you're trying to take the throne. Aren't you acting against your father's wishes?"

Claudia's eyes narrowed momentarily. She wasn't accustomed to open criticism, and didn't like it. Nonetheless there was an opportunity here, and like her father she was a pragmatist, so she suppressed her anger. "You have a quick tongue," Claudia said dryly, pointing the stylus at him like a spear. "However I admire directness. It's one of the many military virtues." She paused, leaning forward slightly. "So, by all means . . . let's be direct."

As she locked her eyes with his, and focused the raw power of her iron will on him, McCade felt an almost physical impact. "You're right. I do intend to take the throne." As she spoke she jabbed the stylus into the air in front of her to emphasize her words. "First, because I'm best qualified; second, because I'm convinced my brother is dead; and third, because I want to, and there's nobody strong enough to stop me."

She leaned back as though giving McCade time to absorb what she'd said. When she continued her voice was calm, almost reflective. "Even though I believe my brother is dead, there's always the chance I'm wrong. And it's a chance I don't plan to take. That's the bad news for idiots like yourself who want my brother on the throne." She smiled humorlessly and said, "However, here's the good news. You don't have to die. In fact, I'm the reason you aren't dead already. Haven't you wondered why the assassins didn't attack? Because I ordered them not to, that's why. And I can cancel that level-three license altogether. Then you could even earn that bounty you're after. In fact," she added, leaning forward eagerly, "I'll add fifty thousand credits to whatever they've offered you."

"That's a lot to pay for *not* finding someone," McCade said evenly.

Claudia laughed. "You misunderstand me. If my brother's alive I *do* want him found. Better now than later." She paused for a moment, tapping the stylus against the palm of her left hand. "Yes, if he's alive, I want you to find him, and then I want you to kill him."

A chill ran down McCade's spine, and he sat speechless. He'd expected her to be hard, but not cold-blooded. Maybe the Emperor had known what he was doing after all. Whatever Alexander was like, he couldn't be as bad as his sister. She was waiting, so he tried to come up with a reply, but was saved by the resonant male voice which suddenly filled the coliseum. "Ladies and gentlemen, citizens of the Empire, fellow sentients of all races, welcome to the finals of Three-Dimensional Combat. Today's games are brought to you by Princess Claudia."

Right on cue, a boxy-looking robocam floated silently up and over the edge of the terrace, zoomed in on the princess, and flashed her picture to the thousands of holo tanks located throughout the arena. She smiled and waved. A roar of approval filled the coliseum. McCade was suddenly reminded of what he'd heard about the ancient Roman emperors. They too had traded games for public approval.

Then the camera was gone, and the announcer's voice flooded in over the applause. His voice had taken on a decidedly somber tone. "After months of bloody combat . . . only two of the original thirty-two teams remain. Many have died, or suffered permanent disfigurement for the sake of our entertainment. Others have fought valiantly but lost . . . and now dwell on some distant prison planet. I ask you, one and all, for a moment of silence, during which we can pay our respects to those who have fallen, or lost everything but their lives." His voice echoed away into stillness as the moment of silence began. McCade noticed Claudia was using the stylus to beat out an impatient rhythm on the edge of the table. The clicking sound seemed amplified by the surrounding silence.

Then the announcer was back, cheerful now, as he warmed up the audience for the coming events. "Now, ladies and gentlemen, fellow citizens and sentients, prepare yourselves for the unbelievable spectacle of the 3-D finals, as our skilled warrior teams take their respective positions. At the north end of the coliseum . . . it is my honor to introduce the Green Rippers!"

A tremendous cheer went up, as a forest of green lasers flashed, pulsed, and rippled across the north end of the playing field. Loud pulsating background music filled the air, its heavy bass beat throbbing and ominous, quickly building toward a climax of sound. As the climax came, so did a brilliant flash of green light, which slowly faded from McCade's retinas to reveal the Green Rippers. There were nine altogether. Each was dressed from head to toe in green. Three wore light armor and anti-grav belts which allowed them to hover in midair. Below them were three more, dressed in heavy-duty body armor suitable for fighting on the ground. They sat on three-wheeled vehicles. Rocket launchers had been mounted right in front of the drivers. The last three members of the team wore medium-weight armor and jump paks. McCade quickly realized they would make or break their teams. Their jump paks would allow them either short hops in the air, or sustained ground combat, whichever they chose. So being the most versatile players, they would be the most critical.

As the applause died down, the announcer came on once again. "And entering the south end of the coliseum—still undefeated after weeks of grueling combat—are the Red Zombies!" There was a flash and the quick crack of an explosion. Red smoke filled the south end of the stadium. An eerie whine filled the coliseum, steady at first, and then pulsating. The smoke pulsed too, glowing now as though invested with a life of its own, so that when the Zombies emerged, it seemed as though they'd stepped out of hell itself.

Once again, the crowd went wild. Only this time the cheering was even louder. Apparently the Zombies were favored to win. McCade noted with interest that Princess Claudia applauded enthusiastically with the rest as the red-suited team took up their positions. Like the Rippers, they had an air squad, a ground squad, and three jumpers. McCade noted with professional interest that the Green Rippers' weapons were anything but uniform. Apparently each warrior was free to choose whatever weapons they thought best. A glance at the Zombies confirmed his theory. They too were armed with a bewildering array of weapons, including at least one ancient battle axe.

McCade glanced at Claudia, but she seemed intent on the upcoming contest, so he turned his attention in that direction as well. A member of the Rippers' ground squad stepped forward with raised hand. The crowd quieted and, in marked contrast to her warlike image, the woman's voice had a melodious quality, hinting at a less violent past. McCade wondered what she looked like. But whatever her face might reveal was hidden by the reflective visor covering her face. When she spoke, there was pride and determination in her voice. "Ladies and gentlemen, citizens of the Empire, fellow sentients, the Green Rippers salute you. Let victory be ours!" Then she stepped back between the other two members of the ground squad and mounted her vehicle as the crowd roared its approval. McCade found himself gripping the arm of his chair so tightly his knuckles were white. He wanted her to win.

Looking at Claudia, he saw her grin savagely as the center member of the Zombies' ground squad dismounted, and took a step forward. "Ladies and gentlemen, citizens of the Empire, fellow sentients, the Zombies salute you. Let it be ours to live, and theirs to die!"

The crowd went berserk, almost drowning out the announcer as he said, "Let the games begin!"

The contest was short and brutal. These were professional killers, their skills honed to razor sharpness by months of relentless battle, interested in one thing, and one thing only, killing the members of the opposing team as quickly and efficiently as possible. And they were very good. Those who weren't had died long ago.

Both teams employed some common strategies. Because both teams had to traverse at least half the length of the field before the fight could begin, naturally the air teams came into contact first. Nonetheless, it was the ground teams which got off the first shots. As their heavy tricycles roared toward center field, both sides launched heat-seeking missiles. First blood went to the Rippers, as a Zombie bike blew up in an orange-red ball, and hurled hot shrapnel in every direction.

Meanwhile a Zombie missile homed in on some poorly shielded hot-water pipes and blew up. The initial explosion didn't kill anyone, but the resulting steam and scalding hot water badly burned those sitting nearby.

Now, as robo repair units and medics hurried to help, there were two sources of excitement for the bloodthirsty crowd.

The air teams made contact slightly north of Claudia's villa, soaring and swooping as each tried to outmaneuver the other, their terse comments flooding the PA system. The jumpers arrived second, and the ground team showed up last. Now, with all members present, a pattern began to emerge.

Rockets expended, the ground teams dismounted to fight it out toe to toe, three Rippers against the two remaining Zombies. Meanwhile, both squads of jumpers concentrated on the opposing team's air squad, trying to take them out of action as quickly as possible. Energy weapons flared, chemical weapons boomed, blades flashed, and at least one mini-missile exploded, turning a Ripper into red mist.

Suddenly a battle axe flashed, slicing through green body armor to bury itself in a Ripper. As her scream filled the air, McCade knew it was the woman who'd spoken for the green team, and felt a lump rise to block his throat. As she fell, the fortunes of the Green Rippers seemed to fall with her. Two members of their aerial squad tumbled out of the air, one after the other. Then they lost a jumper. The two remaining green jumpers did their best to assist the remaining airborne Ripper, but it was too late. Moments later, he too died, the jumpers followed, and then the remaining members of the green ground squad. The battle was over. The Zombies had won.

The crowd cheered, and the medics arrived to sort out the wounded from the dead. McCade felt empty inside, watching with sick fascination as a medic put a foot on the woman's body, and pried the bloody battle axe loose.

"So," Claudia said casually, picking up where they'd left off, "what's it going to be . . . death for you . . . or for my brother?" He noticed the excitement of the battle still colored Claudia's cheeks, and her breathing was quick and shallow.

McCade pulled out a cigar and lit it without asking permission. Once he had it going, he inhaled deeply. The smoke came out with his next words. "I'm not a hired killer."

Claudia sneered. "A fine point, I would think. Frankly, the difference between a bounty hunter and a hired killer escapes me. Nonetheless I suppose that's your final word?"

"I'm afraid so," McCade agreed calmly.

"Then good-bye, McCade." With that she stood and brought the stylus-shaped microphone up to her mouth. A robocam had appeared to hover in front of her. Thousands of Claudias filled thousands of holo tanks as the audience turned their attention to her. "Ladies and gentlemen, citizens of the Empire, and my fellow sentients, I, Princess Claudia, bring you a special treat." She paused, turning to point a quivering finger at McCade. "The legal assassination of the infamous bounty hunter, Sam McCade!"

SIX

"Holy Sol!" The announcer swore to himself as he swung his feet down off the console. This was going to be something special! He grinned in anticipation as his fingers flew over the keyboard. A hundred feet under the surface of the playing field, he was all alone in the control room, except for a variety of robotechs which kept things running. While he tended to be messy, the robotechs were relentlessly tidy, and more than made up for his sloppiness. The control area gleamed, polished surfaces reflecting the muted glow of a thousand indicator lights, cool air whispering through the ducts overhead. He sat on a raised dais, in front of a huge console, watching the thirty monitors mounted above it. Each had a different shot, and represented a different robocam. And the robocams were the least of his minions. There were also the computers and a small army of specialized robots to do his bidding. With their help he ran the enormous facility all by himself. And a boring job it was. After you've seen a few thousand combats they all start to look the same. Nonetheless, he prided himself on his ability to manipulate the crowd's emotions. He could have delegated the task of announcing to a computer, but didn't because it felt good to make the crowd roar with approval, or groan with disgust. It was in fact the only redeeming aspect of his job.

He sighed, shifted position, and ignored the hiss of pneumatics as his large power chair tried to adjust to his small frame. In spite of his deep, resonant voice, the announcer was a little man, and as unlike the warriors who battled above as night is from day. He had beady brown eyes, shoulder-length hair, and skin the color of white chalk. As usual he was dressed in a robe and sandals. By personal choice he lived under the playing field, and rarely ventured out. Years before he and society had mutually rejected each other, and neither had come to regret the decision.

Quickly scanning the monitors, he saw the robocams had dutifully responded to his commands, and positioned themselves to give him good shots of the action. He cut from the shot of Princess Claudia, to a wide shot with the Red Zombies in the foreground and the audience beyond. He knew the princess wouldn't appreciate a televised exit. She really had it in for this McCade guy. Whatever the reason, it must be something big. He might be a bit isolated, but he knew major league politics when they slapped him in the face. After all, it's not every day the princess personally fingers somebody for the assassins. Yeah, he had a special feeling about this one, and knew the audience did too. The excitement was almost palpable. He activated the wireless mike at his throat. "Come on . . . let's show the princess some appreciation!"

The roar of the crowd filled the coliseum as a squad of marines led by Major Tellor rushed in to surround Princess Claudia and escort her off the terrace. As she left, Claudia didn't even glance at the men she'd condemned to death. That was already part of the past, and her mind was on the future. Her future, the way she wanted it to be.

As the princess and her escort disappeared through durasteel doors, Major Tellor turned and shouted, "Good riddance, asshole!" Then he was gone.

No sooner had the Major spoken than a voice McCade recognized as that of the taxi-driving assassin filled the arena. "Get ready to die, McCade!"

"Doesn't anybody like you?" Phil asked calmly as he checked the action on his submachine gun, and then tucked it back into its shoulder holster.

"It's his breath," Rico interjected as he made sure the safety on his grenade launcher was in the off position. "Sam's breath would kill an Il Ronnian Sand Sept Trooper at thirty paces."

"I'm forced to disagree," Phil replied thoughtfully, sighting down the length of his energy rifle. "The truth is he's ugly. Uglier'n a swamp beast headed south. Sorry, Sam, but somebody had to tell you."

McCade's reply was forever lost, as the word "assassin" began to flash on and off across each Zombies' chest, and a cheer went up from the crowd. The formal warning had begun. Assassins must also reveal red clothing, but since the Zombies were already dressed in red, that rule had been fulfilled. It occurred to McCade that a 3-D team comprised of professional assassins was hardly fair to the other teams. But, he reflected as he checked the load on his handgun, what else is new. Now he understood why they'd been allowed to keep their weapons, so that the assassination would be completely legal.

It was the taxi driver who delivered the formal warning. "Attention! A level-three licensed assassination will be carried out on Citizen Sam McCade five seconds from now!"

The announcer cut from the tight shot of the assassin, to a tight shot of McCade. The bounty hunter exhaled a tight stream of cigar smoke, flicked the butt over the edge of the terrace, and said something to the shaggy variant on his right. Damn! If there was only some way to mic them. Oh, well, it would still be good. Of course with, let's see, eight Zombies left, the three of them probably wouldn't last long. But on the other hand, none of them looked scared, and from all appearances they knew how to handle their weapons, and that was a good sign. Maybe they had a chance after all. Holy Sol—what if they won—that would really give the crowd something to cheer about! The underdogs come from behind and all that. Attendance would soar, and bigger crowds were more fun to manipulate. The announcer began to hope.

"There's not much the ground team can do to us off the top . . . since we're up here . . . and they're down there," McCade observed. "Nonetheless, when they get into range, Rico can work them over with the grenade launcher. Phil, I'm afraid you're the only one who can deal with their aerial squad, and I'll try to keep the jumpers busy. Questions?"

"Yeah," Phil replied, "what's a nice variant like me doing in a place like this?"

"Talkin' too damn much," Rico said with a grin. "Here they come."

Naturally the aerial team arrived first. They opened fire at long range, liberally spraying the terrace with lead and coherent energy. Ducking down behind the low wall which ran the length of the terrace, McCade forced himself to wait. Rico did likewise. Neither had weapons appropriate to the situation. Phil however was another story. Resting his energy rifle on the top of the wall, he fired with scientific precision. Meanwhile, the Zombie air team twisted and turned trying to throw off his aim. And it would have worked on anyone but a variant. But Phil had gone into full augmentation, and his enhanced vision, combined with perfect coordination, cost two Zombies their lives.

He killed the first by carefully punching an energy beam through his reflective visor. The pulse of coherent energy burned a perfect hole through the man's head, while simultaneously pushing his brains ahead of it. So as the energy beam emerged from the back of his helmet a jet of blood and brains came with it. Meanwhile, his belt continued to keep his body aloft and propel it forward. Seconds later it crashed into the side of the tower and slowly cartwheeled to the ground below.

Phil's second kill was less elegant than the first, but equally effective. He aimed for the woman's chest, but as if sensing his intention, she suddenly tried for more altitude. As a result his shot hit her anti-grav belt and destroyed its power pak. She fell like a rock, and her scream followed her down to the hard surface of the playing field.

As the second member of the aerial squad died, the volume of incoming fire fell off, and McCade stuck his head up to take a look around. The jumpers were damned near on top of them. Scrambling to his feet, he realized they intended to jump over him and land on the inside of the terrace. Then with the jumpers behind, and the remaining member of the air team in front, they'd be caught in a cross fire. He jumped to the top of the wall and yelled, "Clear the terrace!"

Following his own advice, McCade leaped out and away from the terrace. As he fell toward the playing field far below, there was a sickening moment when he thought he'd misjudged the distance, but then the robocam was there, floating below him, and as he hit, he threw his arms around it and held on.

As luck would have it, the announcer had activated that particular camera just before McCade jumped from the terrace, so the whole crowd lived the moment with him. The announcer swore happily as he fought to keep the robocam from crashing. What a shot! The crowd watched as McCade struggled to obtain a one-armed grip, finally managed to do so, and then pulled his handgun. Suddenly the crowd began to cheer. Deep underground, the announcer grinned. Their sympathies had shifted.

McCade felt the robocam slowly sinking, and heard a grinding noise from inside it as the announcer pushed its drive to the edge of burnout. Then he saw that the jumpers had landed on the terrace, and one was now bouncing out toward him. But the Zombie had jumped too hard and was coming almost straight down. As he went past, McCade fired four times, and saw all four slugs hit their mark. The jumper continued on down to crash into the ground.

Meanwhile, the two remaining members of the Zombie ground team had taken up positions below McCade, and were firing upward. McCade almost lost his grip as two slugs hit him and were deflected by his body armor. Any closer and they'd have gone right through. Then he felt the robocam jerk as a slug hit it. It was sinking even faster now, and trailing gray smoke. In a few seconds he'd land right in their laps.

Suddenly there was a loud cracking sound, and a Zombie disappeared in a red-orange ball of flame. Rico had managed to scramble down to the next terrace, and bring the grenade launcher into play. But now McCade was so low the big man couldn't fire again. If he did, the flying shrapnel might kill both friend and foe.

McCade twisted around, trying to bring his gun to bear on the man below, but found he was unable to do so. He watched helplessly as the Zombie took off his helmet and threw it down. It was the taxi driver. Grinning a sadistic grin, the assassin raised a minilauncher, and took careful aim. He squeezed the trigger, and then watched with amazement as another robocam swooped in front of the tiny missile, and disappeared in a flash of light. The small explosion peppered McCade with tiny pieces of plastic and metal, but none of it penetrated his body armor.

"That's one for me, you bastards!" the announcer shouted gleefully as he banged his fist on the console. "This is my show . . . and it's gonna end my way!"

McCade let go of the robocam and jumped. His feet hit the assassin right in the chest, and threw him over backward. Falling backward himself, McCade hit the surface of the playing field hard, and had the wind knocked out of him. His mind ordered his body to get up, but nothing happened. All his effort seemed centered on sucking precious oxygen into his lungs. Not so the assassin. Shaken but not hurt, he staggered to his feet, and pulled a sidearm. McCade felt the oxygen hit his lungs and the energy flow through his body at the same time. He rolled right just as the Zombie pumped two large caliber slugs into the ground where he'd been. Coming up on one knee McCade fired three times, the first shot taking the assassin in his right knee, the second in his chest, and the last between his eyes. As he toppled and fell a tremendous cheer went up from the now-partisan crowd.

McCade looked up as he heard a string of shots from above. A jumper tumbled end over end to crash onto a distant terrace, and Rico uttered a defiant battle cry. Then McCade's heart fell as the big man's scream of victory ended in a grunt, and he crumpled to the ground. The last of the aerial assassins had nailed him from above.

With a growl of rage, Phil leaped thirty feet straight up, and wrapped the flying assassin in a bear hug. Locked together, they began to drop as Phil's additional weight overloaded the anti-grav belt. As they fell, Phil slowly closed the circle of his arms. The assassin listened helplessly as his armor started to creak and groan. Then with a sort of morbid fascination, he heard loud cracking noises as it began to break, followed by the snapping of his own bones. Mercifully he lost consciousness before he hit the playing field and Phil landed on top of him.

By the time McCade arrived, Phil was already starting to get up, the assassin's body having cushioned his fall. "Thought I'd drop in and give you a hand," the big variant growled.

The last Zombie was a jumper and he moved as though his heart wasn't in it. He jumped from a high terrace, and McCade picked him off with a single shot. After his body hit the field there was total silence for a moment, followed by wild unrestrained applause as the entire audience came to its feet. Not only had the underdog won, he'd done it in spectacular fashion, and they loved it.

McCade wasted no time basking in their applause. Rico was down. He couldn't tell if the big man was dead or wounded, but either way, that was his first priority. And his second priority would be getting the hell out of there, before Claudia could arrange another attempt on their lives. To his surprise a robocam bumped into his arm and the unmistakable voice of the announcer issued forth. "Your friend is only wounded. He'll be okay. My robots have him in an automedic right now. Is there somewhere you'd like to go?"

"The spaceport," McCade replied gratefully. "We've got a ship there."

"Gotcha," the announcer replied. "Do exactly as I say and you'll reach the spaceport without further trouble. After that, you're on your own."

McCade agreed, and soon found himself in a robo-controlled aircar along with Phil, and an unconscious Rico, whose entire right leg had disappeared inside an automedic. A cloud of brightly colored aircars flitted all around them. They were all listening to the announcer on their radios, and, urged on by his voice, they waved and cheered. Doing their best to smile cheerfully, McCade and Phil dutifully waved back. The unofficial escort was the announcer's idea, and a very effective one. Not only would the crowd make it difficult to execute an attack, they also made it stupid to launch one. With McCade and his companions riding a wave of public approval, to attack them within minutes of their victory would not only smack of poor sportsmanship, it would also amount to very stupid politics. McCade knew Claudia was a lot of things, but stupid wasn't one of them. To take and hold power she would need a good measure of public approval. She'd just lost some by taking a public position and losing. At this point a public attack could turn a minor loss into a major public relations disaster. So McCade felt fairly sure she'd control her temper and bide her time. Meanwhile, they'd get the hell off Terra and into the relative safety of space.

A few minutes later the aircar landed next to *Pegasus*. Under McCade's watchful eye, two robots transferred Rico from the aircar to the ship. Then he and Phil engaged in one last round of waving and smiling, before ducking into the main lock, and cycling the outer hatch closed. Once in the control room, McCade was amused to find that a second customs inspection had been waived, and *Pegasus* was already cleared for lift-off. Apparently Claudia was as eager to get rid of them as they were to go.

After considerable urging from Main Port ground control, the swarm of aircars backed off to a safe distance, and gave *Pegasus* enough room to lift. As she roared toward the sky, the announcer swung his feet up onto the console, and lifted a glass in salute. For the first time in many years he felt good about himself. "Good luck, McCade. We made one helluva team."

SEVEN

"More food, slaves, and while you're at it, more cigars!" Rico's voice boomed over the intercom.

"Shall I kill him, or would you like the honor?" McCade asked Phil.

Phil shook his shaggy head in amazement. "I'm a trained biologist, and I can't believe that a single man can eat that much, and be that big a pain in the ass. It isn't normal."

McCade grinned. "If you're suggesting that Rico isn't normal . . . I'll go along with that."

"I heard that!" Rico said accusingly. "Here I am, layin' wounded . . . nearly starvin' ta death . . . and my friends sit around insultin' me . . . me—the one that saved their miserable lives . . ."

McCade reached up and flipped a switch, cutting Rico off in mid-complaint. "Well, much as I'd like to hang around and shoot the breeze with you guys, it's time to get to work."

"Sure," Phil grumbled, "you take off for Joyo's Roid while I stay here with the crazed convalescent. Why don't I go while you stay?"

McCade grinned as he got to his feet. "Because I'm the bounty hunter, remember? And besides, from what I hear, it's damn hard to get off Joyo's Roid unless they decide to let you. So somebody's got to be here to save my ass if I get in trouble."

Phil sniffed loudly, only partly mollified. "Maybe, but just make sure you don't have too much fun."

"I promise," McCade replied readily, and flipped the intercom back on.

". . . not to mention the many favors I done them. By the way, did I mention cigars? How many cigars have I given you, Sam McCade? A hundred? A thousand? And you won't bring Rico a cigar? Shame on you . . ."

Phil groaned out loud, and McCade gave him a jaunty wave as he slid out of the control room. Stopping by his cabin he grabbed a box of cigars, took a fistful for himself, and then threw the rest into Rico's cabin. Grabbing his carryall he headed for the lifeboat.

It was a tubby little affair, barely large enough to hold six very friendly adults. McCade secured the tiny lock, slid behind the rudimentary controls, and strapped in. He had a choice between Emergency Launch and Normal Launch. He chose normal. As the boat's computer ran an automated pre-flight check, atmosphere was pumped out of the launching bay, and the outer doors cycled open. He felt the gentle push of a repellor beam, and the boat floated free of the larger ship. As usual, zero gravity caused McCade a momentary queasiness, but he did his best to ignore it, and it soon passed. A quick scan of the boat's control board showed all systems were go. Looking up he saw *Pegasus* and felt a momentary pride. Her long graceful shape reflected the sunlight, and he paused for a moment to admire her.

Originally a navy scout, she'd been decommissioned during a round of budget cutbacks, and purchased by a wealthy businessman. He'd converted her to a yacht. She was comfortable, fast, and very well armed. Unfortunately the businessman was accused and found guilty of drug smuggling. He went to a prison planet, and *Pegasus* was returned to the navy. Eventually she'd been given to McCade as partial payment for services rendered while searching for the War World. Yes, outside of a computer which occasionally said strange things, she was a good little ship. Confident that Phil and Rico would take care of her, he tapped a course and new identification code into the boat's computer, and settled back for the ride.

An hour later Joyo's Roid loomed large in his single viewscreen. He saw the occasional gleam of reflected light as another ship arrived or took off, but otherwise the asteroid appeared lifeless, a huge chunk of rock following its own lonely path through the solar system. Years before, Joyo had put some spin on the asteroid to create a little gravity, but not too much. That way his rich, but sometimes corpulent, guests could enjoy some of the more rigorous sexual entertainments normally off limits to them. And that, like everything else Jerome Joyo did, was calculated to put even more money in his pockets.

But regardless of whatever commercial benefits gravity might confer on Joyo's wallet, the asteroid's spin could make for a tricky landing, and McCade was just about to ask for landing instructions when his com set buzzed softly. He touched the accept key and was greeted by a face so androgynous he couldn't tell if it was male or female. He or she had long blue hair, big blue eyes, full red lips, perfect teeth, and a long straight nose. Regardless of sex, there was something exquisite about the face, something compelling, and quite exciting. His or her voice had a soft sexy quality. "Welcome to Joyo's Roid, gentle being. A thousand pleasures await you." He or she paused to run a pink tongue over red lips, and then smiled, as if aware of the thoughts running through McCade's mind.

"If this is your first visit to Joyo's Roid, please turn your ship's navigation over to our computer and answer the questions on the rest of the form."

The information requested was mostly financial in nature, addressing the crucial question of whether he could afford Joyo's pricey pleasures, or should be politely turned away.

His answers were all lies with one exception. When asked for a credit reference, he provided an account number for the Imperial Bank on Terra, registered to one Samuel Lane. Seconds later, confirmation was flashed back from Terra, and Joyo's computer practically kissed his rear end. Apparently Walt, or Naval Intelligence, had a sizable number of credits in that account. Too bad Walt hadn't provided an access code as well. He could've retired early.

Now the pitted brown surface of the asteroid was only a hundred feet away. Thanks to Joyo's computer, the boat had matched the roid's spin, but the surface was still coming up fast. McCade was starting to worry when two enormous doors slid aside to reveal a lighted tunnel. He watched as a large yacht moved majestically out of the tunnel, and slowly accelerated toward Earth.

Then his boat rocked a tiny bit, as a tractor beam locked on, and pulled it into the tunnel. It was perfectly symmetrical and lined with duracrete. Tractor-beam projectors studded the walls at regular intervals, and McCade wondered why, until dozens of colorized beams suddenly shot out to lock the ship in a matrix of energy. The tractor beams would be used to move the boat from one end of the tunnel to the other. Otherwise, vessels entering or leaving the asteroid would be forced to use their repellors. The roid's gravity might be weak, but it must still be dealt with. And dancing a ship down a long narrow tunnel on repellors takes a lot of skill, more skill than the average pilot's got, so McCade figured the expensive tractor-beam system had probably prevented lots of accidents. And accidents would cost Joyo money, not to mention bad press. The man thought of everything.

The colored tractor beams were a good example. They were normally invisible, but by colorizing them, something boring and mechanical had been transformed into a work of art. The beams were all colors of the rainbow, and as they crisscrossed each other, they created endless geometric shapes. McCade was impressed.

The com set buzzed again, and McCade was disappointed when a man in evening clothes appeared. He was thin to the point of emaciation, his voice was smooth and oily, and he wasn't half as interesting as the exotic creature who'd come on before. He had a receding hairline, bored eyes, and a professional smile. "Welcome to Joyo's Roid. I am your host Jerome Joyo. The tunnel will be pressurized in a few moments, but please don't attempt to leave your ship, it will be transported into our parking area where you can disembark in comfort. If there's anything that I or my staff can do to make your stay even more enjoyable, please don't hesitate to ask. Thank you." The screen faded to black. The head man himself. McCade wasn't impressed.

Moments later the large external doors closed, and McCade's small craft began to move forward, still carried along by the rippling tractor beams. Up ahead were another set of durasteel doors. They would open as soon as the tunnel was pressurized. Meanwhile McCade sat back to enjoy the light show.

As the boat approached, the gigantic doors slid aside to reveal a large chamber beyond. At least three or four hundred ships of all shapes and sizes were parked in neat rows. There were yachts, some large enough to carry hundreds of people, a couple of small excursion liners, and all sorts of smaller craft. McCade saw everything from tiny two-person speedsters to sturdy tugs and freighters. Apparently not all of Joyo's customers were wealthy.

As the boat moved through the doors and into the cavern, new tractor beams took over, carefully transporting the boat over the rows of neatly parked ships, and gently dropping it into a vacant slot. McCade noticed he'd been sorted by size, and dropped into a row of smaller vessels.

Once again the com set buzzed softly. This time text flooded the screen, accompanied by a computer-simulated voice. "Welcome to Joyo's Roid, Citizen Lane. There is a selection of free gifts waiting for you in the reception area compliments of Jerome Joyo himself. Please enjoy your stay, and let us know if there's anything which fails to please you."

As the text and voice faded away, McCade made a mental note to remember his new name. It wasn't much of a disguise, but it couldn't hurt. By now Claudia's people were probably burning vacuum looking for him. But it was a big empire, and assuming Lady Linnea hadn't spilled her guts, they had no reason to look for him on Joyo's Roid.

He shut down all the boat's systems, grabbed his carryall, and stepped through the tiny lock. An obliging robot had already placed a rolling set of stairs there for his convenience. As he stepped off the stairs onto the duracrete surface of the parking area, an autocar rolled up, and offered him a ride. McCade declined, preferring to walk the half mile to the reception area. It wouldn't hurt to know the layout just in case he wanted to leave in a hurry. The tunnel and lock arrangement would make a quick departure difficult; nonetheless, such precautions had paid off in the past. With that in mind he did his best to memorize the area as he walked along between the rows of parked ships. The lighter gravity put a spring in his step, and it felt good to stretch his legs.

———

Cy could barely see as he rolled the last few feet to the power outlet. For hours he'd been hiding among the parked ships, dodging both people and robots, waiting for his chance. But he couldn't wait any longer. He had to get some juice or it was all over. The tiny trickle of power remaining in his storage banks was being diverted to life support, and it wouldn't last much longer. Most of his peripherals were down, and his mains were malfunctioning, which explained why he could barely see. So he'd left his hiding place and made a run for the DC receptacle. Most of the asteroid's electrical systems ran off alternating current, and there were only three direct current outlets on the whole damned rock. That miserable bastard Joyo had sealed two of them just for the fun of it. And that left only one, a maintenance outlet which should be right ahead. And there it was, the blessed three-prong receptacle, the very center, of his collapsing universe. Summoning the last few ergs of energy left him, he extruded a power pickup, and tried to ram it home. He missed. Damn it! He could barely see through the fuzzy vid pickup. Was this the way he'd die? Unable to get it up and in? He laughed deep in the recesses of his metal body. It was a long time since he'd had to worry about getting it up. One more try. Just one more try. He'd just have to take more power from life support and hope for the best. Reaching way down to the very bottom of his being, he found a tiny bit of remaining strength, and shoved it up and out. The power pickup twitched, and then launched itself toward the receptacle. It made a perfect connection.

Cy's spirits soared as he felt the power and energy flow through his systems. Greedily he guzzled DC current, reveling in his new found strength. Suddenly his audio pickups came back on, and the first thing he heard was the sound of Rad's hoarse laughter, and that meant he was in deep trouble.

Rad was one of Joyo's drive techs. Most of the time he worked on Joyo's private fleet, but sometimes he filled in for the techs who worked on customers' ships, and today was such an occasion. "Well . . . what have we here . . . a power pirate that's what. Mr. Joyo isn't gonna like this. You know you're supposed to pay for what you get. Hey, Dag, look what I've got here!"

Cy's world was suddenly plunged into darkness as Rad pulled his power lead and picked him up. Desperately Cy dumped all systems except life support. They'd tortured him before, and there'd be pain enough without watching and hearing them do it. Hunkering down inside himself, he waited for it to begin.

"Here catch!" With that Rad launched Cy into the air like a big beach ball. As the silver globe spun toward him, Dag danced back and forth, as if unsure where it might land. A stupid grin split his fat face as he dodged this way and that.

"I've got it . . . I've got it," Dag shouted confidently, and then just as the metal sphere was about to land in his arms, he pretended to trip, allowing it to fall and hit the deck. As Cy hit the duracrete millions of tiny feedback circuits fed pain directly into his brain. The pain came in waves, in hard jagged spears, in explosions so intense he wished he were dead.

Rad laughed uproariously. "Jeez, Dag, you've gotta be more careful, you might scramble what brains Cy's got left. Now com' on and pass him back to me."

Dag grinned, and walked around and around the metal ball as if picking his shot. Then with considerable drama, he lined the ball up with Rad, drew back a huge boot, and kicked it as hard as he could. Another tidal wave of pain hit Cy's brain as he rolled across the floor toward Rad. One or two more and it would be over. The small amount of power he'd received would be exhausted and the internal systems cushioning his plastic brain pan would stop functioning. Then one final concussion would put him out of his misery. He found he was looking forward to it.

Rad blocked the rolling sphere, paused to make sure of his aim, and then put everything he had into the kick. Cy screamed, unconsciously activating his speech synthesizer, so the sound echoed off the cavern walls. Even as he screamed Cy cursed himself for his weakness, and swore he wouldn't make another sound. Then he felt himself jerked to a halt. He waited for Dag to pick him up or kick him. Nothing. Not knowing was driving him crazy. He activated a single vid pickup. Someone had placed a large boot on top of him. A tall man with black hair and hard eyes. He had a cigar clenched in his teeth and smoke dribbled out the corner of his mouth. Friend or foe? Hoping for the best, but expecting the worst, he opened an audio pickup.

The man with the hard eyes spoke first. "Hello, gentlemen . . . what's up?"

"Just havin' a little fun's all," Rad replied resentfully. "Now if you'll jus' pass me that ball I'd sure appreciate it."

The tall man nodded thoughtfully as he dropped a carryall next to Cy, and allowed his left hand to fall on the butt of his handgun. Dag looked at the man and then at Rad. He didn't like this. This guy looked like trouble. He tried to catch Rad's attention, but the drive tech's glittering eyes were locked on the stranger.

"Maybe you didn't hear me," Rad said through gritted teeth. "I said pass me that ball."

"First time I ever heard a ball scream in pain," the man replied calmly. "Now that's a real curiosity. And I like curiosities. In fact I collect 'em. So I think I'll just keep this ball for myself. I hope that meets with your approval." The man grinned, and Dag knew he didn't care if they approved or not.

For a long moment Rad considered using the wrist gun tucked up his right sleeve. Sure, Joyo'd be pissed, but this guy didn't look like any big deal, and Dag would back his story. But something held him back, a primitive sense of survival which had managed to keep him alive for thirty-two years. The way the other man waited, the way his fingers brushed that gun butt, he was different somehow. Deep down Rad knew, that in spite of the spring-loaded holster, he'd be dead before the wrist gun even slapped his palm. He shrugged his shoulders and spat onto the duracrete. "So keep it . . . who gives a shit? Come on, Dag . . . we've got work to do."

As the two men departed, McCade bent over and picked up the metal sphere. Holding Cy with one arm, he picked up his carryall with the other, and headed for the reception area. It was clearly marked with a neon sign.

"DC power . . . I need DC power soon . . . dying." The weak voice came from the metal sphere.

It was weird, but if a metal ball could scream, then talking seemed reasonable too. "OK, my friend," McCade said, "DC power it is. My treat just as soon as I check in."

Cy wanted to express his gratitude but couldn't find the energy, so he allowed himself to sink back into darkness, carefully monitoring the trickle of energy which flowed to his life support systems.

The reception area was huge, and sparkled with a thousand lights. Tiers of balconies reached up to a ceiling hewed from brownish rock. Gentle music merged with the hum of subdued conversation to create a comfortable jumble of background sound. Thick carpeting, well-padded furniture, and tasteful decorations all combined to create a feeling of restrained elegance.

In fact, the check-in counter even boasted a live receptionist. She was young, quite pretty, and well aware of it. Flanking her on both sides were the latest in autotellers. They did the actual work of checking people in and out. She was supposed to provide the human touch. But right now her practiced smile couldn't quite conceal her disapproval. She'd recognized Cy immediately. "Is that, er, thing yours, sir? I hope it hasn't been bothering you."

"What this?" McCade asked in mock surprise. "Certainly not. This is my portable gatzfratz. Never leave home without it. Hope you have some DC power in my room. Damned thing won't work off AC."

"Certainly not," the receptionist sniffed, appalled by McCade's obvious lie. "None of our rooms supply DC power."

"Well, mine had better supply some, and damned fast," McCade said, eyes narrowing. "I'll be happy to pay whatever costs are involved."

The receptionist gulped. "Just a moment, sir, I'll check." She didn't like this man's expression. She punched some keys on her com set and explained the situation to her supervisor.

He laughed, and said, "Sounds like Cy found himself a sucker . . . well, what the hell . . . give the man what he wants. Like Mr. Joyo says, 'The customer's always right.'"

Half an hour later McCade was thanking the maintenance tech, and showing him out. The tech had managed to run a cable from a junction box thirty feet down the hall, under McCade's door, and into his room. He closed the door and turned to see Cy extrude a power pickup and plug in. He yawned. "Enjoy, my little friend. Meanwhile I need a nap." With that he stretched out on the bed and was asleep ten seconds later.

McCade awoke to find the metal ball floating ominously over his head. In one fluid motion his gun came up and centered on Cy. "You'd better have one helluva good reason for being up there," he said levelly.

"Ooops, sorry," Cy replied, and used a squirt of compressed air to propel himself toward the far wall. "It's been a while since I could afford to run my anti-grav unit. I'm afraid I drifted off to sleep . . . and was blown over you by the air conditioning."

"No problem," McCade said, holstering his gun. He swung his feet over the side of the bed, stood, and headed for the bathroom. He stripped to the waist and smeared his face with shaving cream. It was sort of old-fashioned, but he liked the ritual. The metal sphere had followed him, and now hung suspended in the doorway. "So," he said, shaving the left side of his face, "did you get enough power?"

"Oh, yes," Cy answered eagerly. "I don't know how to thank you. It's been months since I've been able to bring storage up to max. They don't pay me much . . . so I can rarely afford more than a half charge."

"They charge you for power?"

The metal ball bobbed up and down as though nodding in agreement. "Oh, yes . . . nothing's free on Joyo's Roid."

McCade studied the hovering sphere in the mirror for a moment before starting in on the right side of his face. "No offense, but what are you anyway, some sort of advanced robot?"

A distinct sigh emanated from the silver ball. "That's what everyone thinks . . . but I'm not." Cy paused for a moment getting ready to say it. The words never came easily. Finally he steeled himself and said, "I'm a cyborg."

"Part man and part machine?" McCade asked. He'd heard of them but never met one.

"That's right," Cy replied, "although I'm mostly machine, and very little man. In fact my brain's all that's left of the man."

McCade regarded the cyborg thoughtfully as he wiped his face with a soft white towel. "So you must have a name . . . I'm Sam Lane." He'd almost said "McCade" but caught himself just in time.

"Glad to meet you, Sam. I'm Cy Borg."

"No, that's what you are . . . I asked *who* you are."

"No," Cy said stubbornly, "that's who I am too. The old me is dead."

"OK, have it your way," McCade replied, walking into the bedroom. "Mind if I ask how you wound up in your present, ah, condition?"

Cy spun back and forth as if shaking his head. "Why not? It's common knowledge. I gambled myself away."

McCade finished putting on a fresh set of leathers and zipped them up. "You what? How the hell d'you manage that?"

Cy bobbed up and down slightly as he passed through the cold air being blown out of a vent. "I'm afraid I was a very sick man. Believe it or not, I used to be wealthy. Made it all myself too. I was a whiz at electromechanical miniaturization, computers, stuff like that. In fact, I designed myself. What do you think?" Cy spun full circle like a model showing off a new gown.

"You're the best-looking metal ball I've ever seen," McCade answered dryly. "So how did you gamble yourself away?"

"Oh, that," Cy replied, as if coming back to an uncomfortable subject. "Well, I came here like most people do, just looking for a good time, you know, a little fun and relaxation. So I tried a little of this, and a little of that, and then I discovered gambling. I'd never gambled before . . . and, I loved it. I loved the risk, the excitement, the pure adventure of it. Well, to make a long story short, before I knew it I'd gambled away all my money. And when that was gone, I gambled away my business and my yacht. Then I tried to stop. But it was too late. I couldn't. So I gambled the only things I had left, my bodily organs. And I lost."

For a moment there was silence as McCade tried to imagine what it would be like. Being wheeled into surgery, knowing they were about to take your body apart, package it, and sell the pieces like so much meat. Then awaking to find they had left only your brain. It was horrible, but all too possible, since there was quite a market for organs and anything with value could be gambled away. He thought of the people cavorting around Lady Linnea's pool in their biosculpted bodies. Maybe some of them were using Cy's organs. He shuddered. "I'm sorry, Cy . . . that's a tough break. But it looks like you did a good job redesigning yourself."

"Yeah, it ain't too bad," Cy agreed, extruding a vid pickup to examine himself. "Although I should have gone for a better AC converter. But I only had a week to design and build my new body, so I had to work with what I could get. Most of me came from junked robots," Cy added proudly.

"Well, you did a damned fine job," McCade said thoughtfully as he pulled out a cigar and puffed it alight. "Now it happens that I need a guide. I don't suppose you'd have time to show me around? I'd be happy to pay you."

"Of course, Sam," Cy said eagerly. "I wish I could refuse the pay . . . but I'm afraid I need it."

"I'd insist anyway," McCade replied. "You mentioned a job earlier. Are you sure working for me won't interfere?"

Cy dropped a few inches as though hanging his head in shame. "It's not regular work, Sam. Sometimes they hire me to spy on people."

McCade raised one eyebrow. "Spy on people . . . whatever for?"

"You know," Cy said unhappily, "find out what they like, what they don't like. It helps the staff cheat them."

McCade considered the cyborg's small body and anti-grav capability. "I suppose you can go places the rest of us can't," McCade said, thinking out loud. A handy talent to have. The fact that Joyo cheated his customers didn't surprise McCade. He'd never seen an honest casino yet.

Cy bobbed in silent acknowledgment.

"Well, don't worry about it, partner," McCade said, patting Cy on his top surface. "We all survive as best we can. Let's see Joyo's Roid."

The two of them set off, and it didn't take long for McCade to discover that the asteroid was a maze of tunnels, corridors, and passageways. Some were natural and some artificial. Together they connected the countless bars, nightclubs, and casinos. Joyo knew that while all his customers wanted the same things, they didn't necessarily want them the same way. So while each area offered drugs, sex, and gambling, each made it seem like a different experience.

One area they visited was all brightly lit efficiency. Here sex and drugs were offered by wholesome-looking types, and the whole thing looked like a health-food store. At the other end of the spectrum was an area called Hell's Basement. Here everything was sleazy and decadent, dark bars harbored leather-clad deviants, and customers felt they'd stumbled into hell itself. They loved it.

McCade thought it was funny. He'd spent a lot of time in bars that really were as decadent as this one pretended to be, and knew the richly clad customers who lined the bar, and filled the tables, wouldn't last ten minutes in the real thing. But they were having a good time living out their fantasies . . . so what the hell. He ordered another whiskey from the half-naked bartender, and turned to watch the threesome on stage. They were making love, if you could call their intricate gymnastics "love," and McCade was wondering how they did it. Double-jointed perhaps? Well, it didn't matter. He had work to do. And sitting around wasn't getting it done. Cy, it turned out, was a good guide, but also attracted a lot of attention.

For one thing, all of Joyo's staff knew Cy, the same way bartenders all know the local wino. And it was quickly apparent from the comments they made, that Cy still gambled whenever he got the chance. Plus the two of them were pretty visible. A hard-eyed man dressed in black leathers with a silver ball for a sidekick is hard to miss. So much for the low-key approach. So maybe he'd try something different.

"OK, Cy . . . I think I've got a feel for the basic layout. Now let's have some fun. A friend of mine told me about a game that uses oddly marked

six-sided dice. I can't remember what he called it, but it sounded interesting."

Cy gave a metallic-sounding whistle. "Odd six-sided dice . . . your
friend must have been a high roller . . . and a bit crazy to boot. Don't tell
me, let me guess. When you talked to him he hadn't played Destiny, he was
just planning to."

McCade nodded, playing along. "I thought so," Cy said knowingly.
"Only crazies play Destiny. If they lose you never see them again. That's
part of the game. Or used to be. I heard they shut it down. The payoffs were
rare, but damned expensive when they came. Did your friend tell you how
it worked? No? Well, it was supposed to be like getting born again. You
know, sort of a second chance. An opportunity to overcome the cards dealt
you at birth. That's why it was called Destiny. First they'd have you reach
into an anti-grav cage where there were thousands of six-sided dice flying
around. You'd grab one and check it out. You'd see it had numbers on five
sides and Joyo's logo on the other. Each of the numbers would represent a
possible life outcome, like with five you might end up a millionaire, and
forty-two might mean you're a settler on some frontier planet, and so on.
So each of those five numbers became your possible destinies. Then the game
would begin. So you roll your dice. Let's say forty-two comes up, you're a
settler on some Sol-forsaken frontier planet. But that's just the beginning.
According to the rules you must roll sixty-six times. So you keep going. According to the next roll your first two crops fail, your net worth decreases,
and your family starts to starve. But you roll again, good news, you discover
rare metals on your land. However the next roll brings a pirate raid, and so
forth. Once your sixty-six rolls are up, you receive your net worth, if any.
From what I've heard most players were damned lucky to avoid slavery.
That's right, Sam . . . slavery. If you ended up with a negative net worth you
belonged to Joyo. Hey, you think I was stupid betting my organs? These
people bet the rest of their lives. So, if they're still playing Destiny, I suggest
you avoid it like the plague. Let's try mind-maze or roulette instead."

McCade groaned inwardly. Great. A game where a prince could wind
up just as miserable as everyone else. Just Alexander's cup of tea. So if he

wanted to find the prince, Destiny might be the path he'd have to follow. McCade assumed what he hoped was a nonchalant grin, and said, "Well, let's find out if they still play it, and then I'll decide."

Cy dipped in what might have been a shrug. "OK . . . it's your neck . . . but don't say I didn't warn you." With that Cy turned, and squirted himself toward the door.

McCade followed as Cy led him deeper and deeper into Hell's Basement. Finally, after what seemed like endless twistings and turnings, Cy rounded a corner and disappeared. McCade followed. But instead of another endless hallway, there was a door. Except it wasn't really a door— since only ribbons of multicolored cloth barred his way.

Brushing them aside, McCade stepped through it and into a tunnel of pink silk. A host of concealed lights made the fabric glow, and a steady breeze caused it to ripple gently, as though invested with a life of its own. Cool air touched his face with the slightest hint of perfume, and brought with it the half-heard strains of distant music. Then came the voices. There were dozens of them, all whispering, all saying the same thing. "Welcome to the Silk Road. Welcome to the Silk Road. Welcome to the Silk Road." They said it over and over, echoing each other endlessly, like ghosts speaking from beyond the grave. It sent a shiver down his spine.

As he walked down the tunnel, the whispers gradually died away, and the music grew gradually louder, its soft but insistent beat pounding with the same rhythm as his own pulse, ebbing and flowing around and through him. The Silk Road. The place the beautiful face on his com set had suggested he come. Perhaps he'd see her. He found himself walking a little faster, as the tunnel curved gently, and then emptied into a large circular room.

The walls were covered with the same pink silk which lined the tunnel. Tables circled the room, each protected by its own silk enclosure, granting those within a gauzy sort of privacy.

Dominating the center of the room was a sunken bar, also circular in shape. And there, bobbing gently in the air-conditioned breeze, was Cy. Autocarts scurried this way and that, serving their customers, and skillfully getting out of McCade's way as he headed for the bar.

The bar was practically empty, most customers evidently preferring the curtained pleasures of the surrounding tables, to the more standard liquid refreshments. Taking the empty seat next to Cy, McCade said, "Nice place, Cy . . . by far the fanciest whorehouse I've ever seen."

"Yes," Cy answered wistfully. "I can remember enjoying such things . . . but not very well." He sighed, and extruded an infrared pickup to supplement his vision. "When the bartender comes, tell him you wish to speak with Silk. She owns the place, and used to run the Destiny games. If they're still going she'll know. But I think you're crazy to even consider playing that game."

"You're probably right," McCade replied. "But I'd like to ask her a few questions." Moments later the bartender appeared from the other side of the bar, lumbered up, and ran his bar rag over the pink plastic countertop.

"Want?" His voice was a guttural rumble which sounded like distant thunder. Luminescent green eyes peered out from under craggy brows to regard McCade with generalized hostility. Like all his race, the Cellite was a humanoid mountain of muscle and bone, sculpted by the heavy gravity of his home world into a living Hercules. His oiled torso rippled when he moved.

"I'll take a whiskey and water," McCade answered. "Terran if you have it."

The bartender gave a grunt of assent, and tapped three keys on his auto-mixer. The glass emerged with a whirring sound and disappeared into the bartender's huge hand. As he set it down, McCade said, "Thanks. And I'd like to have a word with Silk when she has a moment."

The bartender eyed him appraisingly, and then grunted, "Wait." With that he lumbered away and out of sight.

McCade eyed Cy as he lit a cigar, and took a sip of his drink. He had a feeling that direct questioning wasn't going to get him much. So he needed some help, but how far could the cyborg be trusted? He wasn't sure, but decided to take a chance. That way he could pursue the gambling angle, while Cy tried other less obvious possibilities. He cleared his throat. "Cy, I'm afraid I wasn't entirely honest with you earlier."

"I know that, Sam," the cyborg replied calmly, turning a vid pickup in

McCade's direction. "Regular customers either ignore me, or just laugh at me. They'd never risk a fight with Rad. So," he added shrewdly, "since you aren't a customer, then you're after something, or somebody."

"Somebody," McCade answered evenly, blowing a thin stream of smoke toward the ceiling. "And I need your help."

"I owe you my life," Cy said simply. "If I can help you, I will."

McCade smiled. "Maybe you lost your body, Cy, but you've still got lots of guts. I'm trying to find someone who disappeared about two years ago. Here's what he looked like back then." McCade unzipped a pocket, and pulled out the vidfax of Alexander which Swanson-Pierce had supplied.

Cy extruded an articulated metal arm. He took the vidfax with his three-fingered hand, and held it up in front of a vid pickup. McCade searched for any sign of recognition. After all, Alexander's likeness had appeared on every vidcast in the Empire countless times before and after his disappearance. But either Cy didn't recognize him, or he did, and carefully concealed it. As he handed the vidfax back McCade wished Cy had a face. How the hell can you tell what a metal ball's thinking anyway? Talk about a poker face. . . .

"This is the friend you mentioned . . . the one who played Destiny?"

McCade nodded. "I'm trying to find him."

Cy bobbed his understanding. "As I explained earlier your friend could be anywhere, depending on how his game went. If he won, then perhaps he chooses to be elusive. If he lost . . . then who knows. But Joyo maintains an extensive data bank on all his customers. Since many come back again and again, the records help him keep track of what they like, what they don't, and how to maximize his take without driving them away. Anyway . . . if I'm very careful, I might be able to access his central computer."

"I was hoping for something like that," McCade admitted. "Have you got any storage compartments?"

There was a soft whirring noise as a small hatch slid aside to reveal a tiny recess in Cy's metal body. McCade reached into a pocket and pulled out the wad of expense money Walt had given him. Splitting it in two, he stuffed half into Cy's storage compartment. "There's no telling how things will go . . . so here's a little something to tide you over. If you're careful it should solve your DC problem for quite a while."

For a moment neither said anything. Finally Cy broke the silence. "This is very dangerous, Sam. Be careful what you say to Silk, she belongs to Royo mind and body. And he doesn't like people poking into his affairs."

"Thanks, Cy. I will. And the same to you. Don't take any unnecessary chances."

Cy bobbed in the affirmative. "I won't. Watch for me, Sam . . . I'll find you." And with that he was gone, sailing across the room toward the distant tunnel.

"Come."

McCade turned to find the bartender had returned. Stubbing out his cigar in an ashtray, he stood and said, "After you, gabby."

The Cellite scowled, and did an abrupt about-face. McCade grinned, and followed the huge humanoid toward the far wall. As they approached, the bartender stopped and pointed to a curtained doorway. "In."

"Somehow I knew you were going to say that," McCade said, shaking his head in disappointment. The bartender scowled even harder as he stepped aside and motioned for McCade to enter. As he stepped through the curtained entranceway, McCade saw a luxuriously furnished office, and the woman called Silk. She was sitting on the corner of a large desk. The same beautiful face, blue hair, red lips, and long straight nose. And in spite of her somewhat androgynous look, there was no longer any question of her sex. Her red silk gown managed to both reveal and conceal a spectacular female body. Unfortunately she wasn't alone. A cadaverous-looking man, dressed entirely in black, sat behind the desk, smiling a thin smile. Jerome Joyo. And on either side of him there stood a Cellite bodyguard, their huge hands dwarfing the blasters which were pointed in McCade's direction. The thin man spoke first.

"Welcome, Citizen Lane, or whatever your real name is. You are in very deep trouble."

NINE

Cy was scared. No, on second thought, he was terrified. For the last ten minutes he'd hovered in front of the open air vent, trying to work up enough courage to enter. He'd already unscrewed the grille and swung it out of the way. Now all he had to do was enter, find his way through the complex maze of ducts to Joyo's computer center, plug in, and run a high-speed data search. Not an easy task, but not all that hard either, except for the crawlies. They scared the hell out of him, and for a very good reason. If they found him in the ducts, they'd kill him. That was their job. Joyo was not a stupid man. He'd forseen that the air-conditioning ducts could be used against him. In fact, he used them himself. Cy knew, because on more than one occasion, he'd been sent into the ducts to spy on customers. For hours on end he'd waited by vents, forcing himself to listen to their boring talk, waiting for that one gem of information for which Joyo would pay. Joyo said it was cheaper than bugging all the rooms. But that was different. The crawlies had always been deactivated for his benefit. Now, however, they would be very much alive, just waiting for him.

Crawlies were rectangular in shape, and were designed so that they fit snugly inside the endless ducts supplying Joyo's Roid with warm and cool air. All four sides of their boxy bodies were equipped with traction drives, which enabled them to crawl through the ducts, and explained their name. Hollow in the middle, so they wouldn't obstruct the free flow of air through the system, crawlies were governed by a microcomputer so primitive, so simple, it was almost retarded by the normal standards of robotics. How much intelligence does it take to sense unusual amounts of heat, noise, or movement, and fire a battery of low-power lasers? Crawlies were equipped with low-power lasers so they wouldn't damage the ducts, but low power or not, they'd cook Cy in seconds.

Still, Cy thought to himself, trying to push the fear down and back, I'm smarter than they are, and that's an advantage. Plus I'm smaller, faster, and more maneuverable. He felt the fear retreat a ways, crouching like an animal in its lair, watching and waiting to see what he'd do. And there's one more thing, damnit! he thought defiantly. Sam said I've got guts. Machines don't have guts. Maybe I'm locked up in this tin can body, but by Sol I'm still a man! And with that he entered the duct, extruded an arm to pull the grille closed behind him, and squirted himself into the darkness. Let the crawlies come. . . . He'd show 'em a thing or two!

An hour later, he was still moving, but with a good deal less bravado. He sensed an intersection up ahead. As always he approached it with great care. He'd already dumped all but essential systems to minimize heat. His infrared and audio sensors were cranked up to max, and he was using his sonar to gently probe ahead. What was that? A noise. Inside the duct or out? Sometimes it was hard to tell. Nothing on sonar. Inside. Definitely inside. A slight grating of metal against metal, like a traction drive with a worn bearing, or a poorly adjusted servo. Oh, shit . . . it was just ahead . . . coming toward the intersection just like he was. Which duct? Well, it wasn't in his, so that left three possibilities. Should he just stop and hope for the best? Or should he attack? Attack? How the hell could he attack? The Sol-damned things had lasers and he didn't have shit. Oh, wait a minute . . . lasers . . . they literally cut both ways. If he could just work fast enough. . . .

Frantically he extruded three articulated arms, and went to work on his own metal housing, swearing when one screw refused to budge, then giving thanks as it finally came free. A distant part of his mind kept nagging him, pointing out he was making enough noise to raise the dead, reminding him the crawlie would reach the intersection in seconds. Then it would zap him, and a few days later the smell of his rotting brain would offend some guest, and they'd send in a maintenance bot to find him, and throw him in the recycler.

As half his housing came free, he spun it around, and sensed the flare of heat as the lasers hit. But there was no hot searing agony. No plunge into the darkness of death. Only an incandescent flash of light as the crawlie took the reflected laser blast, and died. It worked! The concave surface of his shiny metal housing had served to concentrate and reflect the lasers, turning them back against their source.

At first he couldn't believe it, and then suddenly he did, giving a whoop of joy, which scared the hell out of a couple making love in a nearby room. Pushing his way down the duct, Cy located the dead crawlie, and spent a moment gloating over his victory. Then, just as he was about to continue his journey, he remembered something. Quickly probing and touching, he found the crawlie's power pak, checked it for damage, and chuckled when he found none. Ten minutes later he'd jury-rigged a connector, plugged in, and was happily draining delicious DC from the robot's storage cell. It took some time to suck up all the crawlie's power, but eventually the task was complete, and thus refreshed, Cy continued happily on his way. Now he moved with some speed, pushing his homemade laser reflector in front of him, almost daring crawlies to attack him. One did, and quickly suffered the same fate as its predecessor. This time Cy was forced to leave the corpse only partially drained, since his own storage capacity was up to max. Great Sol, it felt good!

He was close to the computer center now . . . so all he had to do . . . Then his thoughts were shattered, as someone slammed a grille against a wall up ahead, and he heard the sound of male voices. "Shit, I don't know, Vern . . . I mean how the hell would I know what trashed the crawlies? Meg told me one went off her board, and then another one croaked too. And like she says, two in one day's no accident. Somethun's in the vents. But whatever it is ain't gonna last long. Not after the snake finds 'em. Ain't that right, snaky?"

Snaky? Cy wondered. What the hell was a snaky? He'd never heard of such a thing. Up ahead there was a metallic slithering. Suddenly Cy had a feeling he'd get to meet snaky real soon.

The Cellite hit McCade with a massive open-handed blow. Pain rolled over the considerable pain he already felt. And when he hit the wall, the impact created a whole new wave of pain, which rolled over all those which had gone before. As he slid down the wall to the floor, he could detect distinct layers of pain, sort of like an archaeologist digging down through layers of artifact-laden soil, each telling its own special story.

"Why don't you just tell us what you're doing here?" Joyo asked reasonably. "It would save you so much pain."

From his vantage point on the floor McCade could see a certain logic to the suggestion. After all pain hurt, and hurting was bad, so anything that stopped the hurting was good. No wait a minute, telling was bad, so hurting was good. Oh, to hell with it, throwing up was good, so he'd do that. By expending a little extra effort, he managed to do it on Joyo's shiny boots. He watched dully as the boot went far away, and then came straight at him with incredible speed. The resulting darkness felt good.

The snake was about six feet long. Where a real snake's head would normally be, the robosnake had a bulbous housing containing sensors and weapons. Its brain, a micro-computer only marginally more intelligent than those issued to crawlies, was located in its tail, its designer having concluded this would be a safer place for it.

Cy, however, was in no mood to appreciate the subtlety of the robosnake's design. He just wanted to kill it, and do so as quickly and simply as possible. But how? Well, first he'd try the laser trick. It had worked on the crawlies, so maybe it would work on robosnakes too. He made a little noise, and waited for the lasers to hit. Nothing. Just more metallic slithering. Faster now that the snake had a target.

"Oh, shit," Cy said to himself as he struggled back into his housing and secured it. He hated to use up precious time, but he didn't want to fight the snake bare-assed naked either. The moment his housing was back in place, he activated his anti-grav unit, and whizzed back to the next intersection. He needed time to think.

Cy's mind was racing through the possibilities. Apparently the snake wasn't equipped with lasers or projectile weapons. The fact that he was still alive seemed proof of that. So the damned thing was designed to work in close, and since he had no defenses to speak of, it would be critical to keep the snake at a distance. But how? He could keep running, but eventually he'd make a mistake, or just run out of power, and the damn thing would have him. The snake had been designed to operate in the ducts and he hadn't. But wait a minute! *Outside* the ducts the electronic reptile couldn't touch him. Not while he had power for his anti-grav unit anyway, and thanks to the crawlies, he had power to burn. Cy zipped farther down the duct until he found a grille. The room beyond the grille was dark, and Cy couldn't hear any movement or conversation. With luck it would be vacant.

The scraping of metal on metal was closer now. Working quickly he reached through the grille with two articulated arms, undid the screws holding it in place, and pushed it aside. Turning to face the snake, Cy slid a section of his housing aside to reveal a high-intensity light. He flicked it on, and damned near scared himself to death. The snake was even closer than he'd thought, its bulbous head bristling with sensors, acid jets, and power drills, its brightly scaled metal body gathering itself for an attack.

McCade was dimly aware of being scooped up by one of the enormous Cellite bodyguards, and carried like a baby down a series of hallways and corridors, before being unceremoniously dumped into a small room. He heard the door slam, and the sound of retreating footsteps. He ordered his body to get up, and swore silently when it failed to respond. He understood the problem. It had to do with dispersal. Somehow he was everywhere, and in order to accomplish things, he had to be somewhere. He'd have to gather himself in and focus his energies. Easier said than done he concluded glumly. Nonetheless he had to try. Bit by bit he gathered himself together, and as he did, he became increasingly aware of his surroundings. The cold metal deck under his cheek, the reek of strong disinfectant, the glaring light of the room's single chem strip. Eventually, in what he considered a heroic expenditure of energy, McCade managed to roll over. From there it was a simple matter to crouch, and then stand. It only took an hour.

His whole body ached and throbbed from countless bruises. A careful inventory revealed a deep cut on his face where Joyo's boot had hit him, two black eyes, a broken tooth, two broken fingers on his left hand, and a sprained right ankle. His eyes were almost swollen shut, but from what he could see, the room was entirely bare. Naturally. Cells rarely come with a lot of furniture.

Hobbling toward a corner, McCade used his good hand to pat his pockets, searching for a surviving cigar butt. He found nothing but crumbs. The bastards had taken everything: his money, cigars, lighter, and, needless to say, his gun. Slowly he lowered himself to the floor and closed his eyes. He'd had better days.

As the snake struck, Cy propelled himself sideways, and through the open vent. The robosnake followed its target, launching itself into the darkened room, and then falling like a rock. There was a loud scream as the heavy metal snake fell across the large bed. Somewhat confused, but nonetheless determined, the snake sensed a spherical source of heat and attacked. The woman continued to scream as her husband managed to flick on the lights. To his utter amazement a six-foot-long metal snake was draped across his wife and seemed intent on destroying the globular com set located on their bedside stand. Being a retired general, the man had fairly good nerves, and the presence of mind to retrieve his handgun and blow the snake's head off. Much to his surprise this did nothing to stop the snake's determined attack. Denied its primary sensors, but still possessed of its limited intelligence, the robosnake reevaluated the situation, and mistakenly decided the rather large mass of warm tissue lying under it had been the source of the attack. Quickly wrapping itself around the lump of offending tissue, the snake began to squeeze. Unable to shoot at the snake's midsection for fear of hitting his wife, and no longer calm, the General blazed away at the only available target, the snake's tail. He got two solid hits and the snake went limp. His wife continued to scream as he tried to operate the destroyed com set, and neither of them noticed as two articulated arms finished screwing the air-conditioning grille back in place, and then disappeared.

Cy zipped through the ducts racing for the computer center. Once security found the robosnake, all hell was going to break loose. The fact that the grille was screwed shut might confuse things for a while, but not for long. Moments later he was peering out of a vent into a large, brightly lit room full of humming computers. There were two people in sight. From their tool belts Cy deduced they were repair techs rather than programmers. Good, he'd give them something to repair.

Seconds later he was at the far end of the computer center undoing a grille. Spying a likely printer, he squirted himself over, and started pulling a plastic print fax out of its box. Looping it around and around the printer he built quite a pile. Then, extruding a tiny arc welder, he lit the pile of plastic. Though not highly flammable, the stuff did manage to burn, giving off clouds of horrible-smelling smoke. Cy had no more than ducked back into the duct when the automatic alarms went off.

Both repair techs were up and running for the other end of the room seconds after the alarm went off. So, they failed to see the grille over their table swing open, and a metallic ball squirt out, heading for the control console. Cy extruded two articulated arms, both of which ended in three-fingered hands. As he hovered over the control board his fingers moved with blinding speed, first entering the access code which he'd seen and memorized while working for Joyo, and then setting up the program he wanted the computer to run. It was a large computer, but since it was early morning cycle on Joyo's Roid, largely unused at the moment. It ran Cy's program in forty-three seconds, and spit out three feet of print fax from the nearest printer when it was finished. Cy didn't take the time to look at it. He just rolled it up and clamped it to his side. Then working quickly, he dumped the program he'd set up, and cleared out. If they really checked, they'd find about a minute of unauthorized computer use, but since they had no reason to check, chances were they wouldn't.

As soon as the grille was screwed shut, he took off down the duct at high speed, before suddenly coming to an abrupt stop. What the hell was he doing? He didn't know where Sam was, and he could run into a crawlie anytime. Mentally gritting teeth he no longer had, he undid half his housing, and pushed it ahead of him as he moved through the maze of ducts at a more moderate pace.

A quick check of Sam's room found nothing. Literally nothing. Even his carryall was gone. Had he checked out? Not likely . . . no, this looked like Joyo's work.

Grimly Cy headed for the Silk Road. Along the way another crawlie attacked and fried itself. Cy didn't even pause. Finally he drifted silently along the duct which ran around the circumference of the silk-lined brothel. Each time he came to a grille he took a look. There were lots of people, doing some fairly amazing things, but none of them was Sam.

Damn! Sam could be anywhere. Cy racked his brain trying to think of some way to locate his friend. Nothing came. But chances were, if he waited by Joyo's office long enough, he'd hear something that would tell him what he needed to know. So he scooted over there and settled down to wait.

Cy awoke with a jerk. He heard voices. One he immediately recognized as Joyo's; the other, softer voice belonged to Silk. Extending a vid pickup, Cy peeked through the grille. Joyo was behind the desk, seated in his high-backed leather chair, speaking to Silk who was just out of sight.

". . . The man's nothing more than another two-bit chiseler. We'll turn his absurd lifeboat into scrap, and send him to Worm. As usual Torb's complaining about a shortage of slaves. I swear the ugly bastard uses them up like there's an endless supply."

"Maybe that's because you raise his production quota four times a year," Silk replied softly.

Cy couldn't see Joyo's face, but he sensed the scowl on it when he replied. "Don't lay that crap on me, lady. I don't see you turning down the flow of credits coming in from Worm."

"Granted," she said placatingly. "And I want that flow to continue. Which is why I wonder if we're doing the right thing. This Sam Lane smells like trouble. What about his lifeboat, for example? A lifeboat implies a larger ship. Where is it? Who's on it? There's too many unanswered questions." Her voice was so soft Cy had difficulty hearing it. He cranked up the gain on his audio pickups.

Joyo shrugged. "Maybe, but my people on Terra weren't able to come up with anything, except that there's no Sam Lane matching his description. Now we could take his retinals, cut a voiceprint, map his dentition, and send the whole mess to the Earth Central mainframe. Chances are it could tell us who he is, what he does, and the kind of cereal he likes for breakfast. But that could create as many problems as it solves. Asking Earth Central mainframe for information cuts both ways. You get it, but you also provide it. So, if he's wanted we could have bounty hunters all over the place, or if he's got powerful friends, they might give us trouble, or what, God forbid, if he's a pirate? That kind of trouble we don't need. No, a call to Rad and his lifeboat disappears, then a little trip to Worm, and the problem's solved."

Silk moved into sight and sat on Joyo's lap. She smiled. "Well, you're the boss . . . boss."

McCade heard the grille squeak open and looked up through bleary eyes. As Cy squirted himself into the room he tried to speak but only produced a croaking noise.

"Great Sol, Sam, are you all right? Ooops, stupid question, of course you aren't." Cy spun around helplessly, looking for some way to help.

McCade cleared his throat. "I'll be okay, Cy . . . just need some R & R, that's all. How'd it go? But before you answer . . . check to see if this cell's bugged. If it is . . . you better haul ass."

"Nah, it ain't bugged," Cy replied loftily. "I checked before I came in. As for how it went, I've got some good news and some bad news."

"Give me the good news first," McCade croaked, trying to find a more comfortable position against the hard wall.

"I got into Joyo's computer," Cy said proudly, "and here's what it coughed up." Cy unclipped the roll of print fax, and used an articulated arm to hand it to McCade.

As McCade accepted it he did his best to grin. It hurt. "You're quite a guy, Cy . . . nobody else could have done it."

Cy felt a pleasurable warmth inside at the praise, and a renewed determination to help Sam any way he could.

McCade unrolled the print-out, and scanned it through his blurred vision. His eyes were so swollen he could hardly get them open, plus his two broken fingers kept getting in the way. The computer had used the matrix of information supplied by Cy to search for men who'd played Destiny and matched Alexander's general description. McCade's heart sank as a quick scan failed to turn up a perfect match. Maybe Lady Linnea had tricked him, or maybe Alexander really was dead, or maybe a hundred different possibilities.

Nonetheless he turned his attention to those who most closely matched the prince's description. One caught his eye time after time. A man calling himself Idono H. Farigo. He'd arrived about the right time, played Destiny, and lost. The only trouble was that Joyo's computer placed him at only a ninety percent match for Alexander's physical description. Examining the detailed analysis which followed Farigo's summary, McCade noticed some interesting facts. First, Farigo's race and age matched Alexander's perfectly. Second, both men were exactly six feet one inch in height, and both weighed 178 pounds. And third, they both had blue eyes. However, where Alexander had light brown hair, Farigo's was black, and though both had even features, Farigo's were rougher and less refined.

As McCade leaned back to think, he ignored the pain of his various injuries, and wished he had a cigar. Forcing his mind, to the task at hand, he considered the facts. On second thought, maybe a ninety percent match was pretty good. Especially when the two men were a one hundred percent perfect match in everything but facial appearance. And from years of bounty hunting, McCade knew how unimportant facial characteristics could be in tracking someone down. Given enough credits, a new face was as close as the nearest biosculptor, and the prince certainly had enough credits. What if he'd visited a biosculptor before coming to Joyo's Roid? And from what Lady Linnea had told him, it would be just like the prince to roughen, rather than refine his features. That way he'd have a face more in keeping with the common herd. Then, disguised as Farigo, he'd arrived on Joyo's Roid, played Destiny, lost as he'd no doubt hoped he would, and been sent to some miserable planet as a slave. It all made a crazy sort of sense . . . but what if he was wrong?

"Can I see that?" Cy asked, hovering in front of McCade.

McCade nodded and handed over the print-out. "As a matter of fact you can keep it. Otherwise I'd have a hell of a time explaining where I got it."

Cy bobbed in agreement. "Did you find anything?"

"I think so," McCade replied doubtfully. "Take a look at that Farigo guy. He seems like my best bet, but if I'm wrong I could waste a lot of time and energy on him."

Cy found Farigo's name on the print-out, and sounded it out, "I-do-no-H-Far-I-go . . . that's a weird name."

McCade sat up straight, and then wished he hadn't. Everything hurt. "Well, I'll be damned . . . at least the bastard has a sense of humor. How much you want to bet the 'H' stands for 'how.' 'I don't know how far I go.' That's got to be him. Thanks, Cy, now I'm sure Alexander and Farigo are the same man. You've been a big help. OK . . . you said there was some bad news . . . I guess I'm as ready for it as I'll ever be."

Cy felt happy and sad at the same time. He'd been able to help, but it wasn't going to do any good. "They're sending you to a slave planet called Worm," Cy replied sadly. "And they don't plan on you coming back."

To Cy's amazement, McCade broke into gales of laughter, grimacing at the pain it caused him, and pointing at the print-out clutched in Cy's metal fingers. Cy aimed a vid pickup at Farigo's entry, and there under "disposition," it said, "Manual labor, ten years, the planet Worm."

T E N

In some ways, McCade actually enjoyed the trip to Worm. While his quarters aboard Joyo's supply ship were something less than luxurious, the chow wasn't bad, and the ship's engineer was also a damned fine medic. She was middle-aged, homely, and gruff. Though far from sweet, even as a baby, hopeful parents had blessed her with the somewhat unlikely name of Candy. But McCade liked her nonetheless. And not just because she patched him up, and brought his food each day. Behind Candy's rough facade there was a quick mind, and a sharp wit. Plus she'd knocked around the Empire even more than he had, and when properly coaxed, knew how to spin a good yarn. So, over time, he'd come to view her as more friend than jailer, and suspected that, deep down, she felt the same way about him. Of course both knew the trip would soon end, and with it, their friendship. So McCade continued to act out his role as miserable prisoner, while Candy did her best to play the heartless jailer. Then they were in orbit around Worm, and Candy was giving him one last examination.

"Flex your fingers," she said curtly. McCade obeyed, flexing all his fingers. They worked perfectly, including the two which Joyo's bodyguard had broken. The ship had been in transit for about three standard weeks, having come out of hyperspace just the cycle before, and the passage of time, plus the attentions of the ship's automedic, had healed his fractured bones. Now only the faintest shadow marked where his black eyes had once been, and Candy had closed the cut on his face so skillfully the scar was almost invisible. She grunted her approval.

"You're healthy as a horse. Might even last a month or so down there." McCade would've sworn he saw a trace of sadness in her eyes.

As the hatch clanged shut and locked behind her, McCade leaned back to stare at the overhead. He hoped her sadness was unnecessary. By now Cy should have delivered his message to Rico and Phil. If so, they'd soon drop out of hyperspace, and take up position a few lights out. Meanwhile he'd go dirtside. There he'd find the prince, signal his friends, and escape. Nice and simple. Sure, there were a few problems to iron out, like what if Cy hadn't delivered his message, or what if he couldn't figure out a way to signal Rico and Phil? But these were mere details, he told himself, in all other respects the plan was perfect. Then why was he so worried?

A few hours later McCade had been transferred to the freighter's shuttle, and was trying to cooperate as Candy ordered him to move this way and that. First she secured his nerve shackles. If he strained against them they'd deliver a powerful shock to his nervous system. Like most bounty hunters he'd used them on fugitives once or twice, so he knew what they could do, and had no desire to experience it himself. Especially since he wanted to go where they were taking him.

Once the nerve shackles were secure, Candy strapped him into the acceleration couch. As she double-checked his harness, she glanced forward to make sure the pilot and copilot weren't looking, and shoved a flat rectangle into the waistband of his pants. It felt cold against his back. "Cigars," she said gruffly. "Don't know why you insist on smoking the damned things. Go easy on 'em. You'll see why."

A few minutes later the pilot goosed the power, and nosed the shuttle down toward the surface of Worm. It was a smooth trip. After a flawless landing the copilot came back to release his harness, and lead him to the lock. She was young, badly in need of a bath, and amused by his condition. The inner and outer doors cycled open in turn, and McCade stepped out into hard yellow light. The heat hit him like a sledgehammer.

Seeing his reaction, the copilot grinned and said, "Welcome to Worm." Once the lock had closed behind them, she touched his nerve shackles with a small black wand, and they fell away. "Go ahead," she said. "You can run but you can't hide." Then she broke into peals of laughter as she strode off toward the distant complex. As he followed, McCade saw what she meant. Except for the shabby dome up ahead, the terrain was flat, only occasionally broken by spires of jagged rock. Heat waves shimmered in the distance, and he was already sweating like a pig. The copilot was right. You could run . . . but there was no place to hide.

A few more steps and he realized he was short of breath. Worm's atmosphere was low on oxygen. Plus, each step stirred up a small cloud of dust, and that made it even harder to get enough air. The copilot turned to hurry him up. Now he noticed the small canister she wore on the back of her belt, and the single tube leading up and over her left shoulder fed a nostril plug. No wonder she was so peppy. She was using supplemental oxygen. McCade offered her an ancient gesture which she returned with a smile.

By the time they reached the dome, McCade was out of breath, and very tired. The approach was littered with huge pieces of scrap metal, worn-out machinery, and other less identifiable junk. A well worn track wove its way between the larger obstacles and disappeared under a huge pair of sliding doors. Judging from the patterns they'd left behind, McCade guessed the vehicles were fairly large, and equipped with tracks. A smaller personnel entry whirred open at their approach, releasing a blast of cool air.

McCade followed the copilot inside, and heard the door close behind him. He saw sudden movement out of the corner of his eye, but moved way too late. A massive fist hit the side of his head and he fell like a rock. From his position on the ground, he decided someone was going to pay. And that meant getting up. Slowly, painfully, McCade made it to his knees and was about to stand when a huge boot kicked him in the side. The blow rolled him over so that he landed on his back.

He found himself looking up at one of the ugliest human beings he'd ever seen. Fire had twisted the man's features into a mass of ridged scar tissue. An intricate tattoo decorated his bald head, a gleaming ruby replaced his right eye, and his left ear sported an earring made of bone. At first McCade couldn't figure out why the bone looked so familiar, until he realized it was really three bones wired together, all of which had once been part of a human finger. A quick glance at the big man's hands confirmed an intuitive guess. The little finger on his left hand was missing. "Well, scum . . . what the hell are you staring at?"

Raising himself on one elbow, McCade shook his head tentatively to make sure it was still connected, and said, "Beats the hell out of me . . . but whatever it is . . . I like it."

The man threw back his head and roared out his laughter, then he reached down to offer McCade a hand. McCade took it, and was effortlessly jerked to his feet. The big man looked him up and down as though inspecting a side of beef. "Well, you've got balls—even if you won't be needin' 'em—and I like that. Name's Torb. Do what you're told and you'll live. Go against me and you're dead. It's as simple as that. Hey, Whitey, fresh meat . . . come'n get it." With that Torb put a massive arm around the copilot, and together they marched off toward a distant door.

Meanwhile a skinny man, with a shock of white hair, had appeared at McCade's side. In spite of his white hair he wasn't more than twenty-five. He had pale skin, pink eyes, and a very nasty smile. "Gotcha, Torb. Come on, meat, I haven't got all day." Whitey gave him a shove, and when McCade started to turn produced a nerve lash. "Come on, meat, you wanta taste of this?" For a long moment Whitey looked into hard gray eyes, and suddenly wished he was somewhere else. This was one of the crazy ones, the kind that didn't care, the kind that would take a nerve lash just to get their hands on you. "Move it." He did his best to sound hard, but even as the other man obeyed, Whitey knew he'd lost.

Now that he was inside the dome McCade found the air was cool and rich with oxygen. Overhead, the dome's armored plastic was so scratched from the abrasive action of wind and sand that it did little more than admit a hazy half light. Large crawlers were parked here and there in haphazard fashion, scarred flanks and worn tracks suggesting hard use, energy cannon hinting at hidden dangers. Except for the huge double doors somewhere behind him, the circumference of the dome was taken up by what he supposed were enclosed sleeping quarters, office space, and maintenance shops. As they walked along, McCade felt the box of cigars dig into his skin, and wondered why he hadn't been searched. They probably assumed there wouldn't be much point. He'd been a prisoner aboard the freighter, hadn't he? As he approached the far side of the dome, a door slid open to admit them, and then closed behind them, as they moved down a dimly lit hall. It ended in front of a lift tube. McCade looked at Whitey and lifted an eyebrow.

The guard threw him a metal disk on a plastic loop. "Put it around your neck if you wanta eat." McCade caught it and did as he was told. "Now, meat, into the tube." McCade obeyed, turning to see Whitey aim a remote control unit in his direction. The door whined shut on Whitey's nasty smile. "Sleep tight, meat. I'll see you in the morning."

There was a short drop before the doors hissed open. McCade stepped out into a huge underground cavern. Smoke filled the air, occasional lights cast deep shadows, and hundreds of men moved aimlessly this way and that, talking, gambling, or just killing time. The loud hum of their conversation suddenly stopped as the doors of the lift tube closed behind him.

"How many came with you?" The voice was strident, demanding. McCade scanned the faces nearby, searching for the one which went with the voice. With the exception of the occasional black or brown face, they were pale, like the grubs which inhabit the under surface of things, an army of zombies risen from the dead. Then he found two bright glowing eyes, which locked with his, and McCade knew he had the right man. His face was drawn and haggard, his clothes little more than rags.

"None," McCade replied. "I came alone."

"Shit." The other man turned away, and the hum of conversation returned to its previous level.

"We were hoping for more. The more men we've got, the easier it is to meet Torb's next quota." This voice came from slightly behind and to the right. McCade turned to find a wrinkled-up prune of a man, grinning a toothless smile. Bright little eyes regarded him with amusement. "They call me Spigot."

McCade accepted the little man's extended hand and found a grip as hard as durasteel. "Glad to meet you, Spigot, I'm Sam Lane." It seemed wise to stick with the name he'd arrived under. "How long have you been on this dirtball?"

Spigot's eyes seemed to go slightly out of focus as he thought back. "That's a tough one, Sam. It's hard to keep track . . . about twelve local years, I reckon . . . give or take one or two."

McCade nodded. "Then you're the man I'm looking for. I need someone who can give me the straight scoop, you know, who to look out for, how to avoid the worst work, that kind of stuff."

"You've been locked up before," Spigot observed slyly.

"A time or two," McCade agreed wryly. "But nothing like this." As he looked around he noticed a number of men eyeing him in a speculative fashion. They all wanted something. It might be his boots, his body, or just a new fund of dirty jokes, but each was a survivor, and saw McCade as something to be used.

"Let's find a place where we can sit and talk," McCade suggested.

Spigot grinned. "Make you nervous, do they? Sure, why not. But I'm no different. A man's gotta live, and what you want's worth something."

McCade felt the box of cigars pressing against his back. God bless Candy . . . properly used the cigars could make a big difference. "Damned right, Spigot, and pay I shall. How 'bout the next meal?" McCade saw no reason to let anyone know about his cigars until he'd found a good place to hide them. Otherwise they'd jump him the minute he fell asleep. Besides, he felt sure he could pass up one chance at whatever slop they were serving, without missing much.

Spigot pretended to consider McCade's proposal, finally nodding his agreement. "Normally I'd insist on two meals, but you seem like a regular guy, and there's no reason to take advantage."

McCade smiled. "Thanks, Spigot, I appreciate that." He'd obviously overpaid. Nonetheless a little goodwill wouldn't hurt.

"Think nothing of it," Spigot said generously. "Follow me. I know a place where we can talk without those bone pickers staring at us." With that the little man moved off, his oversized rags swirling around his knobby knees, his feet moving among the litter of rocks with a sureness born of long experience.

As they wound their way between small clumps of men, McCade saw hard faces, and tough leathery bodies from which all but the essential juices had been evaporated out. These were the survivors. The ones, who'd arrived with nothing, and still managed to live, not because they hoped to escape, but because they didn't know how to give up. Did one of those faces belong to Prince Alexander? Did he have the strength and the guts to survive in a place like this? McCade tried to find the face described on Joyo's print-out but failed. It was a big cavern. And life here could change the way a man looked. Finding the prince might take a while.

Now they'd left the open cavern far behind. Spigot led him around a rock pillar, and through a small opening in the rock, before climbing up and out of sight. McCade followed, and soon found himself sitting on a rock ledge overlooking the distant cavern, protected from observation by a low rock wall. "This is it," Spigot said proudly. "Home sweet home. I've never showed it to anyone else."

For some strange reason McCade believed him. A bundle of rags in one corner had the look of a crude bed, and a litter of empty meal paks and other junk testified to extended use. "Thanks, Spigot, I won't show it to anyone without asking you first."

Spigot nodded his approval. "OK, Sam, a deal's a deal. Shoot." As McCade asked questions, and the other man answered them, it quickly became apparent that Spigot liked to talk. Fortunately, he was pretty good at it, and had something worthwhile to say. There was a good sharp brain at work behind those bright eyes, and it had managed to integrate twelve years of experience and observation into a useful body of knowledge. So as Spigot talked, an overall picture of life on Worm quickly emerged.

The planet itself had very little going for it. While it did have some arable latitudes, these could not support Terran crops due to the low levels of CO_2 in the atmosphere, and a shortage of certain minerals. And while the planet did have large deposits of iron ore, and certain other metals, these were also available elsewhere closer in toward the heart of the Empire. So all activity centered around the rockworms which had given the planet its name. The rockworms were huge, leathery gray tubes, averaging some thirty feet in length, and six feet in diameter. As far as McCade could gather they spent all their waking hours eating their way through solid rock. Each had a circular mouth boasting thousands of grinding teeth. The worms cut their way through the rock by rotating their teeth back and forth in a half circle. Then some sort of strong acidlike substance secreted by glands in the worm's mouth went to work, gradually turning the loosened rock into a thick jelly, which they promptly ingested. From there the jelly went through a series of five different stomachs, each serving to further digest the rock, each responsible for leaching out certain minerals.

The result was an incredible labyrinth of tunnels through the solid bedrock which overlaid much of the planet. And the way Spigot explained it, when the worms weren't eating, they were screwing, a life-style which he clearly envied. The results of these amorous encounters were small clutches of two or three eggs. These were deposited in small rock alcoves created by the female worms. Then it was the male's responsibility to fertilize the now-dormant eggs, and seal them into the alcove with partially digested rock. In due time the infant worms would hatch, eat their way out, and the whole cycle would start over again. But every once in a while a clutch of eggs would escape fertilization. For years they would sit there, slowly crystallizing, their internal chemicals gradually recombining, changing consistency and color, until finally they became rock hard. Then careful cleaning in a series of chemical baths would reveal iridescent jewels, each different from every other, each invested with a brilliant fire deep in its center. Properly cleaned each would be worth a million credits or more. These were the fabulous Fire Eggs so sought after by the wealthy of many races. McCade had heard of them but never seen one.

But the worms didn't give up their unborn young easily. First you had to find them, and that meant venturing into their subterranean maze of endless tunnels, where your life expectancy was measured by your luck, and the amount of oxygen and power you had left. But even worse than the possibility of becoming lost, or dropping into the occasional vertical shafts created where tunnels crossed paths, were the worms themselves. It seemed the planet was calcium poor, and while the worms needed a certain amount of calcium to survive, it was very hard to come by. Which explained why the worms loved the rare, but calcium-rich limestone deposits that dotted the planet, and were equally fond of human bones. Where calcium was concerned, the worms had some very fine senses indeed, and the amount of calcium present in the human skeleton was sufficient to bring them galloping from miles away. "So," Spigot said succinctly, "the trick is to find their eggs without becoming a vitamin supplement."

McCade shifted position trying to find a more comfortable way to sit on the hard rock. Having a box of cigars shoved down his pants was damned uncomfortable. "Why not use robots?"

Spigot spat, the glob of spittle easily clearing the low rock wall, to splatter somewhere below. "Cause we're cheaper. How much did they pay for you?"

McCade thought for a second, and said, "Outside of transportation . . . nothing."

"I rest my case," Spigot said with a grin.

"Still," McCade countered, "how do they make you work? Surely they can't send a guard along with each prisoner."

"Simple," Spigot replied. "There's a bonus for any man who finds an egg, extra food usually, and a penalty for the whole group if we don't make Torb's quota. And since we all want to stay alive, it works real well."

"OK," McCade said thoughtfully, "I've got the big picture. Now, how about people. Who's the top dog around here?"

Spigot eyed him sharply. "You don't miss much, Sam. I'll have to keep an eye on you. Well, topside Torb's the big cheese, but I suppose you already figured that out."

McCade rubbed the side of his jaw. It still hurt. "Yeah, he certainly has a way with words."

Spigot chuckled "That's Torb . . . he believes in making an impression on the new meat right away. Anyhow he's the boss, and under him there's a whole bunch of guards, nasty bastards most of them, though one or two are halfway human. Then there's our own pecking order to consider. Course it keeps changing as people buy the farm."

McCade nodded in sympathy. "Who's top man right now?"

"That'd be 'The Animal.' Of course that's just his nickname."

"Glad to hear it," McCade answered dryly. "I'd hate to think his parents named him that."

"Well, knowing him, it probably fit," Spigot replied with a shake of his head. "The Animal is not a nice man. But you'll find out soon enough. Just like Torb . . . he likes to make an impression on new meat."

"I can hardly wait," McCade answered dryly. "By the way, I haven't seen any women, what's the deal?"

Spigot looked wistful for a moment, and then shook his head sadly. "We had women up till about six years ago, but there wasn't enough, so Torb took 'em all away. Said there were too many fights."

Suddenly a klaxon went off, and Spigot stood up, all business. "Meal time," he said, and held out his hand. McCade removed the loop of plastic from around his neck and handed it over.

"Thanks," Spigot said. "I'll return it right after I eat. Be nice to feel full for once. Where shall we meet?"

"How about right here?" McCade asked. "If you don't mind."

"Nah, that's fine," Spigot answered as he started climbing down to the floor of the cavern. "Just don't let anyone see you coming or going. I like my privacy."

"You've got it," Sam promised, and followed the other man down. With a wave of a hand, Spigot disappeared into the maze of rock passageways which led back toward the open cavern. McCade waited a full five minutes, making sure the little man hadn't doubled back to spy on him, and climbed back up to the balcony. After a bit of exploration, he found a small dead-end tunnel, toward the rear of Spigot's living area, and a tiny niche high in its darkest corner. Removing the cigars from the waistband of his pants, he opened the box, withdrew a handful, closed the container, and slid it into the niche. As he retired to the balcony, he stuck one cigar in his mouth, and tucked the rest into an inner pocket. Selecting a comfortable seat, he puffed the self-igniting cigar into life, and took a long satisfying drag. There was plenty to think about.

ELEVEN

One look at the man in front of him, and McCade knew Animal's nickname fit like a glove. And not because of the way he looked. Animal was a lot better-looking than Torb. No, it was his eyes. They were hard black lumps of coal, dead things, empty of all feeling, set in a face of pallid white flesh. And he was tough. Not big, not muscular, just tough. It showed in the way he moved and held himself. McCade sighed. Animal held his position through physical force. That meant each new man had to be beaten into submission. And because he was a sadist, and enjoyed inflicting pain, no matter what McCade did or said, Animal would insist on a fight. So, it was a no-win situation. If McCade fought Animal and lost, he might be seriously injured, and if he won, he'd have a powerful enemy. Either way he was in trouble.

Six hours had passed since McCade's arrival. Spigot had returned from his double meal, belched a couple of times, and offered to take McCade on a tour of the cavern. McCade had accepted, welcoming an opportunity to search for the prince among his fellow prisoners, and eager to learn the ropes. As they wandered through the cavern, McCade encouraged Spigot to introduce him to the men they ran into along the way, but none were Alexander.

So while McCade made no progress in his search for the prince, he found the cavern itself quite interesting. Thousands of years before, the huge subterranean vault had served as a sort of a natural terminal for the worms, providing them with a place to meet, and mate. At one time hundreds of their tunnels had branched off in all directions, but Torb and his guards had sealed the passageways with explosives, creating the perfect underground prison.

"Have the worms ever tried to tunnel in?" McCade asked.

Spigot looked surprised. The thought had never occurred to him. "Not that I ever heard of, Sam. Who knows, maybe they ate all the good rock way back then."

McCade nodded agreeably. "You're probably right, Spigot. Anyway, I'm glad they won't be interrupting our dinner." Thanks to Spigot's built-in timer, they had arrived in front of the lift tube just as the klaxon sounded and the next meal arrived. This, the little man explained, was breakfast. Not to be confused with the identical meal paks which were called dinner. Lunch didn't exist.

After breakfast they'd go to work. It would be dark outside in an hour or so, and it seemed the worms were less active at night, making it safer to enter the tunnels. It was a sensible policy, since it was always pitch-black in the worm tunnels anyway, and it did serve to reduce casualties. It didn't eliminate them entirely however, because there always seemed to be a few worms who liked to wander around at night. Anyway, no one wanted to eat in the tunnels, so "dinner" would be served when they returned from work. If they'd made the week's quota that is. Otherwise it was one meal a day. Eat, grab a few hours of sleep, and then do it all over again. It wasn't much of a career, although McCade imagined that it would beat the hell out of working for Swanson-Pierce full-time.

So they got in line, displayed their disks to a bored guard, grabbed one of the identical meal paks, and headed for the open area where most of the men ate their meals. They were halfway there when Animal and two of his henchmen stepped into their path.

Although Animal directed his comments to Spigot, his dead eyes were on McCade. "So, Spigot, what's this piece of garbage you've been dragging around?" Spigot didn't answer. He just looked down and shuffled his feet.

McCade put down his meal pak and turned toward Animal: The facial tic which plagued him during moments of stress was twitching like crazy.

He hoped Animal wouldn't notice it. "OK, you want to fight . . . so why don't we dispense with the preliminary bullshit and get on with it. Spigot, what's the penalty if I kill this sonovabitch?"

Spigot looked at him in openmouthed amazement, as did Animal's two toadies. Sensing entertainment, a crowd began to gather. Animal's eyes were unreadable, but a slight sheen of perspiration had appeared on his forehead. This wasn't the way things were supposed to work. He forced a grin. "That's big talk, meat, but talk's cheap. Try it."

McCade ignored him and turned to Spigot. "Well?" he demanded.

Spigot gulped, and said, "A day outside with no supplemental O_2."

McCade looked Animal up and down as though examining a new disease. He smiled. "It'll be worth it."

Over the years Animal had found that a sudden and unexpected attack often gave him the advantage. So, with a roar of self-induced rage, he charged straight at his opponent. Forcing himself to wait until the last second, McCade stood his ground. And then, when Animal was only inches away, McCade drove the six-inch piece of sharpened steel straight into Animal's heart. Animal jerked, gurgled, and then fell.

McCade wiped his slippery hands on his pants and picked up his meal pak. "Spigot, if you'd be so kind as to notify the guards of Animal's much deserved demise, I'd like to eat my dinner. I don't suppose there's much room service outside."

The crowd laughed, some stopping to slap him on the back, others shaking his hand, already ingratiating themselves with the new boss. Then they drifted away, talking excitedly among themselves. Who'd have thought someone could walk in and take Animal like that? What kind of taxes will he levy? Who is this guy anyway?

Meanwhile McCade pretended to eat his meal. But as soon as the crowd was gone, he stood and sauntered over toward the rocks surrounding the open latrine. Having made sure no one else was there, he promptly threw up. It was partly nervous reaction, and partly revulsion at what he'd done. He'd killed many times, but never so coldly, so calculatedly. The whole thing had gone exactly as planned.

First he'd pumped Spigot about Animal, then he'd verified the little man's observations with others, and finally he'd slipped away to buy the knife. Naturally Animal had lots of enemies, it showed in their eyes whenever his name was mentioned, and McCade had spotted one honing a handmade knife. He's spent half his cigars to get it. After that it was simply a matter of time. Animal wasn't all that bright and, being a creature of habit, used the same insults time after time to pick his fights, following up with his predictable charge. In a way the poor bastard had killed himself. McCade straightened up, wiped his mouth, and left the latrine. By the time he emerged he had a grin plastered on his face, and was pretending to zip his pants.

"I did like you told me, and they're waiting for you, Sam," Spigot said, nodding toward the lift tube.

"Thanks, Spigot," McCade replied. "You've been a big help. See you in . . . how many hours does it take this crudball to rotate anyway?"

"About twenty."

"OK, see you in twenty hours then." With that McCade walked over, and presented himself to Whitey. Taking no chances, the albino had armed himself with an ugly-looking riot gun, and his nasty smile made it clear he'd love an excuse to use it.

"So, meat, it didn't take you long to get your ass in trouble, did it? Well, get in, Torb wants to see you." McCade noticed that in spite of Whitey's tough talk, both he and the hulking neanderthal he'd brought with him kept their distance. Apparently anyone who could take out Animal deserved a certain amount of respect. McCade grinned as he stepped into the tube.

"You know, Whitey, it doesn't seem possible, but I'd swear you're even uglier now than you were six hours ago. What is it . . . some sort of makeup?"

The neanderthal took a moment to process this, and then broke into deep grunting laughter. Whitey scowled at him and said, "Shut up, stupid. That goes for you too, meat. You're in enough trouble as it is."

McCade smiled, and they finished the ride in silence. When the door hissed open, Whitey motioned McCade out first. Together they marched across the center of the dome toward a door on the far side. Now it was dark outside and therefore cooler inside. When they reached the door Whitey gave a nod of approval, so McCade palmed it, and stepped through when it slid open.

He found himself in a surprisingly nice office. Though not fancy, it was clean and well furnished. Torb dominated the room. He was seated behind a large metal desk, his huge boots propped up on its bare surface. From what McCade could see he was surprisingly calm. Or at least that's the way it seemed, though with all that scar tissue it was hard to tell. Torb's ruby eye remained motionless, reflecting light, while his good eye looked McCade up and down. A full minute passed before he spoke.

"So, Animal's dead. Well, you certainly didn't waste any time." He paused reflectively, like a judge considering the merits of a difficult case. "On the one hand that really pisses me off, cause we're always short of meat, but on the other hand I kinda like it, cause that's the way I'd do it myself. My guess is you outsmarted him, which sure as hell didn't take much, and now you're king o' the heap." Suddenly Torb's single eye locked onto McCade like a tractor beam. "Well, that's just fine . . . but you'd better remember that it's my heap that you're king of . . . and when I say 'shit,' you'd better ask 'how high.' Do you hear me, meat?"

McCade nodded. "Loud and clear."

Torb nodded and seemed to relax a bit. "Good. You might be interested to know that the Animal and me had us a little understanding. He ran things down there, and I ran 'em up here. And between the two of us, we never let the meat get outta line. I ain't got time for riots and that kinda crap. So you run it the same way, and you can pick up where Animal left off. You know what this is?" Torb threw a rectangle of plastic on the top of his desk. McCade picked it up and looked at it.

"It's an account card drawn on Terra's Imperial Bank," McCade said, handing the card back.

Torb nodded approvingly. "That's right, meat. And there's about thirty thousand credits stashed in there that used to belong to Animal. You keep 'em in line and it's yours. Plus a tenth of one percent of what they find. That's how Animal made his. So whadaya say?"

"I'd say you can count on a very cooperative labor force," McCade answered with a grin.

Torb got up, came around to the other side of his desk, and brought his face within an inch of McCade's. Besides being ugly he had very bad breath. McCade struggled not to back away, and only barely succeeded. "Good," Torb said. "Now I'm gonna have Whitey take you outside and leave you for one rotation. And while you're out there . . . suckin' what little air there is . . . sweatin' . . . and wishin' to God you were dead, remember this: hit 'em, kick 'em, but don't ever kill 'em. You got it?"

"I've got it," McCade answered, willing to agree to anything that would put some distance between him and Torb's breath.

"Take him away," Torb told Whitey, and minutes later McCade was being marched out of the dome.

So when the big tracked carriers rumbled out into the night, Spigot and all the rest crowded over to see where McCade had been staked out. Whitey had an eye for the dramatic, and had therefore chosen a slight rise, and even rigged a battery-powered light to ensure a good view. Although his ankles and wrists were chained to deeply driven stakes, McCade managed to wave one hand, and a cheer went up from the carriers. For the moment he was their hero.

As the crawlers disappeared over a rise, and the sound of their engines slowly dwindled away to nothing, McCade set to work testing his chains, and the stakes they were connected to. They didn't budge an inch. But his efforts used a lot of oxygen, and all of McCade's attention was soon focused on the simple act of breathing, and the searing pain which went with it.

It took half an hour to get rid of the pain, and achieve some sort of equilibrium. He found that by remaining absolutely motionless, and breathing slow deep breaths, he could just barely take in enough oxygen. After that, it wasn't too unpleasant. The night was cool, but not cold, and he even managed a few short naps. Twice he was awakened by a small animal that scurried over him, dashing this way and that in search of food.

And the crew woke him a third time, as they returned from the tunnels, and yelled their encouragement.

Once again McCade waved a hand, and again they cheered, though less enthusiastically now that they were tired. And no matter how hard they tried to forget, many of them couldn't rid themselves of Samms' screams. Somehow a male worm had sensed him, and trapped him against a rockfall. The debris had completely blocked the tunnel, and Samms died trying to remove tons of fallen rock with his bare hands. Those working nearby tunnels had been forced to listen to his screams for a full five minutes. The worm had slowly ingested him, feet first, chewing carefully, savoring each milligram of calcium.

Not long after the crawlers had disappeared into the dome, Worm's sun poked its orange-yellow head over the far horizon, spearing McCade with its first rays. It was still cool at first, but as time passed he began to sweat, and before long trickles of precious moisture were vanishing into the dirt around him. One by one, the hours slowly dragged by, the sun doing its best to burn its way through the thin tissue of his eyelids, while he turned this way and that trying to escape. But there was no escape. Whichever way he turned the sun was there, anticipating his every move, trying to beat him into submission.

Eventually he began to slip in and out of consciousness. Pieces of his life seemed to come and go, an endless parade of old friends, enemies, and jumbled events. McCade allowed himself to drift with the flow, preferring it to reality, and hoping that when he came to, the torture would be over. Eventually he began to enjoy the visions, and became annoyed when a strange face appeared. It was a man's face, young and rather pleasant. But he'd never seen it before, and tried to get rid of it, preferring instead the jumbled flow of familiar people and places which had preceded it. But in spite of his efforts the face always came back. Cool green eyes regarded him with amusement, as though aware of his efforts, yet not offended by them.

Frustrated, McCade decided on direct confrontation. "OK, who the hell are you and what are you doing in my hallucinations? I don't remember meeting anyone like you."

The face smiled. "I'm the one they call Walker, and you're quite correct, we've never met."

"OK," McCade responded, doing his best to sound reasonable, "then why now? I'm kind of busy at the moment, and no offense, but you aren't as entertaining as some of my other hallucinations."

Walker laughed. "Sorry about that, but I thought that perhaps I could help, and besides, what makes you think I'm a hallucination?"

McCade considered that for a moment. It was hard to think without becoming conscious, and he wanted to avoid that at all costs. Perhaps if he humored this hallucination it would go away and be replaced by something more interesting, like naked women for example. McCade tried to grin. "Well, if you're not a hallucination, then you're damned stupid to be hanging around out here in the sun. Hey, if you want to help, how about some O_2 and water?"

Walker shook his head sadly. "Sorry, Sam, I wish I could, but that's not the kind of help I can offer."

"Terrific," McCade replied sarcastically. "So what kind of help *can* you offer?"

The other man grinned. "I thought you'd never ask. I can help you find the one you're looking for."

Suddenly McCade was completely conscious. The sun still seared his face, but now it was past its zenith, and already dipping toward the west. In a few hours it would set, and the torture would be over. McCade forced himself to look around. He saw nothing but hot emptiness. He felt strangely disappointed. Walker had seemed very real somehow, but apparently he was just another hallucination. Not that hallucinations were bad. In fact they beat the hell out of reality. He tried to slip into the half-conscious state he'd been in before, but found he couldn't.

So he just lay there, sweating out the minutes and hours until the sun finally set and twinkling stars filled the sky. As he watched them pop out one after another, he wondered if Rico and Phil were out there somewhere, drinking his booze, and breathing his nice clean oxygen. Silly question. Of course they were. The bastards.

By the time Whitey and the neanderthal came to release him, McCade was somehow floating above the pain and discomfort. It seemed as though he was a sponge which had absorbed all the pain and discomfort it could hold, and was therefore impervious to more. He even managed a grin and a croaked greeting. "Well, if it isn't Snow White and one of the seven dwarfs. It's amazing what crawls out at night."

Much to his amazement they didn't even hit him. They just looked at each other and shook their heads in amazement. First Whitey lifted his head and gave him a tiny sip of water. It was cold and tasted better than the finest wine. Then the neanderthal put a mask over his face, and his grateful lungs sucked in pure sweet oxygen. First it seemed to revive him, then it seemed to let him go, dropping him into a deep dreamless sleep.

"Wake up, Sam. Damnit, we gotta eat and go to work." Slowly McCade swam up out of comfortable darkness to feel a body which ached all over, and see a toothless grin which could only belong to Spigot. The little man waved a warm meal pak under his nose, and McCade felt an answering growl from his stomach.

Slowly he sat up, accepted the meal pak, and then leaned against a rock. He dimly remembered coming to, for short periods of time, someone holding water to his parched lips, and then more blissful sleep.

"Welcome back, boss," a voice said. "We missed ya." Now he saw there was a whole circle of faces beyond Spigot's. There was general laughter and someone said, "Let him eat. The poor bastard's about to meet the worms . . . and they like 'em fat and sassy." There was more laughter, and the crowd moved away.

McCade peeled the cover of the meal pak back, and dug in. For once the bland stuff actually tasted good. Between mouthfuls McCade said, "Thanks, Spigot, I owe you. How long was I out?"

"A full rotation," the little man answered, "and that's all Torb allows. That's why I had to wake you up."

McCade nodded. "And I certainly wouldn't want to disappoint old Torb. Did you know that bastard and Animal were working together to keep you guys in line?"

Spigot shrugged. "I didn't know, but it doesn't surprise me. Did he offer you the same deal?"

McCade finished off the meal pak and threw it toward a pile of empties. "Yup, one tenth of one percent of whatever you guys find."

Spigot gave a low whistle. "You'd better keep that under your hat, Sam, the guys wouldn't like it."

"I will for the moment," McCade agreed. "And then we'll see what the future brings. Meanwhile, Spigot old friend, an excellent meal like that calls for a good smoke. Do you indulge?"

"I used to, Sam," Spigot said piously, "but my stay on Worm has cured me of the nasty habit."

"Ah," McCade said understandingly. "Well, it happens that I have a secret stash of cigars, and if you'd be so kind as to go get one for me, I would be happy to help you reinitiate the disgusting habit."

Spigot's eyes lit up. "Really? I swear I won't tell anyone where they are."

"And I believe you," McCade assured him. The little man listened carefully as McCade explained where the cigars were hidden, and then scurried away to get them. A few minutes later he was back, cigars in hand. Together they puffed the cigars into life, and then settled back to enjoy them. They were still smoking when the klaxon sounded again, and the men gathered in front of the lift tube.

There were quite a few envious looks as Spigot strutted importantly back and forth, emitting puffs of smoke like a runaway steam locomotive. But no one laughed when he got dizzy and almost fell down. Spigot was under McCade's protection, and therefore immune to the ribbing he'd once accepted as a matter of course. McCade didn't care for the dictatorial aspects of the situation, but he knew they were a natural outgrowth of the conditions the men lived under, and just might come in handy. So he did his best to play the part, waving his cigar expansively, and cracking jokes until the lift tube hissed open.

It took a number of trips for the lift to transport all of them to the surface. Once there, they stood in a sullen mob, each thinking about what lay ahead, each dealing with it in their own way. McCade did his best to scan their faces, and while there were a few possibles, none provided a perfect match with Alexander's latest looks.

Then the carriers coughed into life, and the guards herded them aboard. McCade crushed his cigar butt under a boot, and then followed the crowd as they moved up a ramp, and into one of the big tracked vehicles. Inside there were hard bench seats, one along each side, and one down the middle. McCade took a seat on the right side, and a moment later Spigot plopped down beside him. The little man had two five-gallon water containers with him. Each was equipped with a spigot and a cup on a string. "It's why they call me Spigot," the little man whispered cheerfully. "I bring the water. And that means I don't have to explore any tunnels by myself."

"Good thinking, Spigot," McCade said. And it was. Somehow he'd managed to stay alive for twelve years under appalling conditions.

McCade's thoughts were interrupted as two more prisoners appeared, each carrying a box. One passed out oxygen canisters with nostril plugs, while the other handed out headlamps. McCade watched the others as they hooked the oxygen canister to the back of their belts, and brought the small plastic hose up and over one shoulder. He did the same. "Don't turn on your O$_2$ till we're outside," Spigot advised. "You want all the margin you can get."

McCade nodded his agreement, and pulled the headlamp's elastic band down over his head. "Test it," Spigot suggested. "If the bastards forget to recharge one, you're shit out of luck.

McCade switched it on and off and found that it worked perfectly.

"Good," Spigot said approvingly. "Now whatever you do . . . don't lose it. There's a locater beacon built into the light. That way they can find you if you get lost or trapped by a rockfall."

"Now that's a cheerful thought," McCade said. "I notice the only way to get rid of the beacon is to throw away the light."

Spigot gave him a toothless grin. "You're catching on, Sam."

A few moments later, the vehicle jerked into motion, and headed outside. As the doors of the dome slid shut behind them, the men activated their oxygen canisters, and slipped in their nostril plugs. McCade did likewise. After a full rotation outside without it, the trickle of O_2 was quite comforting.

The crawler turned this way and that, following a twisted course between the huge spires of dark rock which punched their way up through the planet's skin. But they hadn't gone far when the vehicle suddenly slowed and came to a halt. The men all looked at the guard, but she pressed on her earplug for a second, and then shook her head. The ramp went down with a whine of hydraulics and then came right back up. A man came with it. McCade couldn't see what he looked like in the dim half light of the vehicle's interior, but whoever he was, he belonged somehow, because everyone greeted him as he moved down the aisle. Except the guards. They seemed to ignore him. So the man wasn't part of Torb's organization. Then why had they stopped for him?

McCade watched with interest as he felt the crawler jerk into motion, and the man continued to move up the aisle, stopping every now and then to talk with one of the men. Finally he dropped onto the center seat across from McCade, and a slash of light fell across his face. Their eyes made contact, and suddenly McCade found himself looking at a hallucination. The man smiled and stuck out his hand. "You remember me, I hope? The name's Walker. It's good to see you again, Sam."

TWELVE

McCade shook Walker's extended hand. The other man had a firm grip, kind of surprising in a hallucination, but then McCade had very little experience in such matters. "And it's good to see you too," McCade said wryly, "or at least I assume it is. How do you do that?"

"What?" Walker asked innocently, his cool green eyes laughing merrily.

McCade looked around, wondering if his fellow prisoners were paying any attention to this somewhat bizarre conversation, but all the others were busy talking among themselves. "You know, appearing in someone's head like that. What is it, telepathy?"

Walker shook his head. "Nope. Physical bodies aren't everything, Sam. There's lots of other ways to get around." He gestured vaguely. "If you read Terran religious history you'll find all sorts of theories. Some of 'em are even true." He laughed.

"So you won't tell?"

Walker shrugged. "I can't. Not in the amount of time we've got anyway. But it's not magic, it's a skill, something you learn. Some people are better at that sort of stuff than others. I'm among the worst."

McCade lifted one eyebrow, and started to reply, but the crawler jerked to a halt and the guard said, "All right, worm meat, hit the ramp. This ain't no excursion bus." She ignored the prisoners' rude gestures, and motioned with her riot gun. The men obeyed.

As McCade stood, Walker said, "I'll catch up with you later."

"Terrific," McCade said dryly. "Be sure to bring your body."

"If you insist," Walker countered, and vanished into the crowd as the men surged forward and down the ramp.

As McCade emerged, he was almost blinded by the hot white glare from the powerful floodlights mounted on each crawler. Gradually his eyes began to adjust, and before long he could make out the other crawlers a short distance away, and the men which surrounded them.

A few hundred yards to the north, there was a low hill with an ominous-looking hole in its side. McCade didn't need a road map to know where they were going. The hole practically screamed, "I'm dangerous, don't come in here." So naturally that's where they'd have to go.

The land surrounding the hill faded off into soft darkness, interrupted here and there by rocky spires of denser black. After a brief moment of confusion, the guards herded the men into a single line, and then watched impassively as they shuffled by a large open box. "That's the tool line," Spigot said, appearing at his elbow. "Go ahead and I'll meet you at the other end."

McCade followed the little man's suggestion. The line moved quickly, and a few minutes later a bored-looking guard handed him a tool, before ordering him to move along. McCade examined it as he left the other end of the line. It was a durasteel rod, about two inches thick, and four feet long. One end was pointed for use as a pry bar, and the other was flattened out and bent at a right angle, kind of like a pickax. It had seen hard use and showed it. Which made sense, because you had to shift a lot of rock, and then break through the solidified goo the male worms used for a sealer, before you could get at the eggs. Or at least that's what he'd heard. Not something you'd want to do with your bare hands. He tried swinging the tool around. Not a bad weapon in a pinch, which explained why they were collected at the end of each shift. Torb didn't want the prisoners digging their way out of the dome's underground prison, or taking a swing at the guards.

"All right, meat, this ain't no damned picnic. Get your butts down there and find some eggs. Torb's offering five extra meal paks per egg, so keep your eyes open." The voice belonged to the same female guard who had been on the crawler. She wore her hair in a short crewcut, and her face was thin and bony. "If you don't," she cautioned, "you're all going on short rations. We're behind quota."

Her speech was met with mixed jeers and grumbling. One voice said, "Yeah? So what else is new?" Another said, "If you're so hot for worm eggs, then get your skinny ass down there and find 'em yourself." But in spite of their brave talk, no one wanted to charge the guard's riot gun, so slowly but surely they shuffled their way toward the dark mouth of the cave.

The path was quite worn, suggesting that they'd been coming here for quite some time. McCade wondered how long it took to exhaust a particular area. Or did the worms lay eggs so fast it didn't make any difference? But if that were true the eggs would be easier to find. Well, it made little difference to him. He was looking for something else, and making damn little progress. He'd spotted a couple of possibilities, but deep down in his gut he knew they weren't Alexander. No, so far his only lead was Walker. The man was strange, but apparently quite real, and seemed to know all about McCade's mission. How and why? McCade swiveled his head right and left, but Walker was nowhere to be seen. He'd promised to catch up. How would he manage that down in the tunnels? But that thought, and all others vanished as they entered the dark opening in the hillside.

It was cold inside and McCade shivered. A slight breeze blew from somewhere up ahead, hinting at other openings, and bringing with it the smell of things long dead. McCade was one of the few who still hadn't turned on his headlamp. Now he did so, adding still another bobbing blob of light to the hundreds which already splashed the tunnel walls. Some of the men were grimly silent, others engaged in forced banter. "Sure hope we don't walk right up a worm's rear end," someone said. "Hell, you are a worm's rear end," another voice replied. "Nah, I've seen a worm's rear end, and it's better-lookin' than Frank is," a different voice said. There was general laughter which quickly died away as they entered a dimly lit open area. Countless tunnels branched off from all sides. The cavern apparently served the worms as a hub, much as the large subterranean vault under Torb's dome once had. Tilting his head back, McCade's light was quickly lost in the darkness above.

"All right, meat, listen up. I'm only gonna give it to you once." McCade recognized Whitey's voice right away. By standing on a small rock, he could see over the men in front of him, and sure enough there was Whitey, seated at some sort of makeshift console, peering into a portable terminal. The wash of light from the VDT gave Whitey's skin a sickly green appearance. The neanderthal, plus a mean-looking black man in worn leathers, stood to either side of him, their riot guns resting in the crook of their arms. "All right. Mendez, tunnel four. Riker, tunnel two. Mugabe, tunnel twenty . . ."

As Whitey read off their names and tunnel assignments, the men reluctantly trudged off, presumably heading for their particular tunnels. McCade had no idea how they knew which tunnel was which. "McCade, tunnel thirty-four."

"Just follow me, Sam." It was Spigot. He had a water container in each hand but no tool. McCade followed, as Spigot wound his way around piles of fallen rock and pools of water, to the far side of the cavern. As they approached the dark mouth of a tunnel, McCade saw there was a small sign over the entrance, and sure enough, it read "34."

"They're numbered one through one hundred and forty-six, starting back where the entrance meets the cavern, and moving from left to right," Spigot explained.

He stepped into the tunnel, and motioned for McCade to follow. As McCade stepped inside, the walls seemed to close in on him, and suddenly he could feel the tons of rock pressing down on him. The passageway was barely six feet tall, and in places he had to stoop to pass. He knew it shouldn't bother him, after all he'd spent months at a time in some very small ships, but that was different somehow. Outside there had been the vast emptiness of space, not ton after ton of solid rock, and while that shouldn't make a difference, it did. Taking a deep breath, he forced the fear into the back of his mind, and followed Spigot's bobbing light.

Suddenly he slipped and almost fell down. Tilting his head forward to throw some light on the tunnel's floor he saw some sort of glistening substance. "Hey, Spigot, what's this stuff?" he asked, pointing down.

Spigot turned to see what McCade was referring to. "Worm slime," he answered matter-of-factly. "Some say they use it to lubricate their way through the tunnels." He smiled a toothless smile. "Others say it's how they shit. Personally I figure it don't make much difference."

McCade nodded at Spigot's obvious wisdom, and they moved farther into the stygian blackness. Every now and then, Spigot would stop to explain a fine point of egg hunting, or tunnel survival. Once he pointed out a small hollowed-out space just off the tunnel, and declared that a prisoner named Hagiwara had found two prime eggs in it. Scooping up what looked like crumbled rock, he held it out for McCade's inspection. It had a slightly reddish hue. "That's what you look for, Sam. It's what their sealer looks like when it's all dried out. As you can see it's a different color than most of this rock."

And about ten minutes later, Spigot stopped again, to point out the side tunnel in which Samms had died. McCade shuddered as Spigot described Samms' death, how the worm had taken him feet first, and how he'd screamed forever.

"But," Spigot added cheerfully, "don't let it worry you, Sam. It actually improves your odds some. I can't remember the last time we lost two in a row in the same tunnel. Anyway, this is where I leave you. Gotta make my rounds. It's all virgin territory from here out. Keep an eye out for color changes in the rock and watch for worms. There's a buzzer built into your headlamp. When you hear it, head back." And with that the little man was gone.

The next four hours were very strange. McCade had decided to approach the situation systematically. For the first four hours he would examine the right wall, and then he'd turn around, and spend the next four hours on the left wall. That should put him back at his starting point with only an hour or so left to kill. As he moved cautiously down the tunnel, there was an eerie silence, broken only by the sound of his own footsteps and the occasional dripping of water. Every now and then, he came to intersections where other worm tunnels crossed his, or passageways had been carved out of solid rock by a thousand years of running water. He ignored them. One tunnel was plenty, without adding the additional hazards of more. More than once he slipped in the worm slime, and almost fell. Twice, he spotted reddish places in the tunnel wall, and attacked them with his tool. But all he found was solid rock. Apparently there was some reddish rock around. Finally, after what seemed like an eternity of darkness, the four hours were up. He had just turned around, and started back up the tunnel, when he heard someone call his name and saw a distant light. It bobbed closer and closer, until it was only feet away, casting long shadows down across Walker's face. He smiled.

"We've got to stop meeting like this."

McCade laughed in spite of himself. Then he said, "I suppose you used some more of whatever it is you do to find me."

Walker grinned and shook his head. "Nope. It seemed a lot simpler just to peek in Whitey's holo tank. There you were, checking out tunnel number thirty four, just like an old pro. Whitey was very impressed."

Of course. McCade wondered why he hadn't thought of it earlier. They'd be able to track all the prisoners via the beacons built into their headlamps. That way if someone decided to take a nap, or tried to take off, they'd know about it. Although there'd be damn little chance of that, since anyone who tried to escape would run out of oxygen a few hours later.

Walker looked around, selected a likely looking boulder, and sat down. He reached into an inner pocket and pulled something out. He handed it to McCade as he said, "I understand you like these things, so here's a little present."

As McCade accepted it he saw it was a cigar. "It may be a bit stale," Walker said apologetically. "I don't smoke. My predecessor did though, and left it behind."

McCade thanked him, and eyed the other man thoughtfully as he puffed the cigar into life and took a seat opposite Walker. "Your predecessor?"

"Yes," Walker answered. "We keep a one-man station on Worm. That's how we found out about the prince."

McCade felt his pulse quicken as he blew out a thin stream of gray smoke. Maybe he was about to get somewhere. "No offense, but it would really help if you could start at the beginning. First of all, who's *we*?"

Walker looked surprised. "You mean you don't know? I'm sorry, I guess I just assumed you did. I'm a Walker of The Way. That's why they call me Walker. Have you ever heard of us?"

McCade shook his head.

"Well, that's not too surprising," Walker said. "We avoid publicity. Simply stated we're a loosely knit group of sentients who follow The Way."

"It's a religion then," McCade suggested.

"No, not in the conventional sense," Walker replied. "For example, The Way isn't written down anywhere, it's discovered through the process of living and therefore accessible to all. We have no rites, no layers of priesthood to separate us from the truth, and we don't attempt to proselytize. In fact, we don't interfere with those around us unless asked, and even then there are severe limits on what we can do. That's why Torb and his guards tolerate me. Besides, I suspect he thinks I'm a useful figure, sort of a priest, or father confessor figure for the men. Frankly, I've encouraged them to view me that way . . . even though our organization doesn't have priests."

McCade shrugged. "Sounds good to me . . . although I've got enough problems in the here and now, without worrying about the hereafter. You said you maintain a station on Worm? Whatever for? Especially if you're not trying to convert the prisoners."

Walker smiled. "There was a need. I told you earlier that others have abilities far beyond my own. Well, some of them can read what they call the flux, which is simply the ebb and flow of cause and effect. I won't attempt to describe how they do it, because I don't understand it myself, but basically it amounts to a heightened form of meditation. Somehow they momentarily step out of their bodies and can see the complex patterns and relationships which flow out of all that we do. By studying these patterns they can predict trends and probabilities as to what may come. And sometimes, not often, but sometimes, we can use that knowledge for the greater good."

McCade tapped the ash off his cigar, and resisted the temptation to ask how they knew what the "greater good" was. Historically mankind had used religion, and the concept of "the greater good," to perform unspeakable acts of cruelty and barbarism on each other, usually because their leaders got their own personal "good" all mixed up with everyone else's.

Unaware of McCade's skepticism, Walker continued to speak. "Many years ago, one such read the flux, and discovered that Worm would eventually become a significant place in human events. So a call went out for volunteers to sit on Worm and wait. Each had the same orders. 'Watch, wait, help to whatever extent you can, but do nothing to change the status quo.'" Walker smiled. "That last order was necessary, for slavery offends all of us, and the temptation to interfere had been very strong. But to do so would change the flux, and that might erase our chance to accomplish an even greater good, so we have obeyed. And it's good that we did, because during my predecessor's stay the prince arrived, and suddenly we understood. Eventually the emperor would die, and if Alexander was allowed to die on Worm, his sister would inherit the throne. And given her beliefs, Claudia might start a war which could swallow all sentient life in this part of the universe."

There was silence for a moment, and then McCade cleared his throat. "How did your predecessor know Alexander's true identity? He didn't announce it, did he?"

Walker laughed. "No, he didn't. He arrived calling himself Idono H. Farigo, like 'I don't know how far I go.' Get it?"

"Yeah, I've got it," McCade acknowledged dryly. "The prince is a thousand laughs. Then I suppose he did his 'I'm just one of the guys routine.'"

Walker shrugged philosophically. "Alexander was determined to live through the experience without recourse to either his father's power or position. But his actions quickly separated him from the rest—just as yours did—and my predecessor gradually learned the truth."

"Well," McCade said, watching his cigar smoke curl up through the light of Walker's lamp, "if it's any comfort, Naval Intelligence agrees with the conclusions of your flux readers. But since Naval Intelligence is usually wrong, that doesn't mean much. Nonetheless, just to be on the safe side, we might as well grab the prince and get out of here."

Walker only smiled.

McCade said, "Uh-oh, I've got a feeling I'm not going to like this."

Walker looked at him sympathetically. "The prince has been gone for some time I'm afraid."

McCade groaned. "Then why are you still here?"

"That's simple," Walker responded earnestly. "I've been waiting for you."

"Come on," McCade insisted. "I'll give you people credit for predicting something important would happen here on Worm, your presence seems to prove it, but there's no way you could've known I was coming."

Walker smiled patiently. "Not *you* personally. I was waiting for someone *like* you. No offense, but if it wasn't you it would've been someone else. Just as the flux predicted Alexander's coming, it also foretold your arrival. That's how I know the Emperor is dead. Only his death would force those who oppose Claudia to find out if the prince is still alive, and if he is, to place him on the throne. You were picked for the mission, and the trail led you here."

The way Walker put it, everything sounded so simple, and lacking any other way to explain the man's presence and knowledge, McCade was forced to believe him. At least until a better explanation came along.

"So where is he?" McCade asked.

"On a planet called the Wind World," Walker replied. "My organization has a monastery there. Alexander spent a great deal of time talking with my predecessor and, after a good deal of soul searching, asked permission to go there and study. His request was approved."

McCade dropped his cigar into some worm slime where it hissed and went out. "Aren't you leaving something out? Like how Alexander managed to get off this pus ball?"

Walker grinned. "That was quite simple actually. One day Alexander went into the tunnels and was eaten by a worm. He's a bit of a ham, you know, and his screams sounded quite realistic. Afterward they found only his headlamp and one boot. Very touching, and very convincing, since no one willingly parts with their headlamp."

"And then you got him off-planet," McCade finished. "Very slick. And that brings us to the present. Are you willing to give me some help as well?"

Walker's light bobbed up and down. "That's why I'm here. Now that his father's dead, it's imperative that you reach Alexander and convince him to accept the throne."

McCade frowned. "Why me? He obviously respects you and your organization. Why not convince him yourselves?"

Walker shrugged and spread his hands. "We cannot interfere without risking negative changes in the flux. Besides, our role is to facilitate, not control. And while his father lived, there was no reason to force the issue. Now we can only hope that when you tell him of his father's death, he will see the need to assume the throne, and do so of his own free will. But the decision is his. We will not try to force him."

"Terrific," McCade responded sourly. "Thanks a lot. Well, let's get on with it. Have you got a radio?"

"A good one," Walker replied, "though I have to be careful how often I use it. Torb's under the impression that I rely on his."

"Good," McCade said. "I've got some friends and a ship just off-planet. At least I hope I do. If you'll call them they'll come and pick me up. First, however, we'll have to stage my death like you did Alexander's."

Walker agreed, producing a stylus and a small notebook into which he wrote the frequency and code words which would allow him to contact Rico and Phil on *Pegasus*.

"Just let me know a time and where to meet," McCade added.

"No problem," Walker said, getting to his feet. "I'll try to set it up for to-morrow or the next day. Meanwhile you'd better start working your way back, before Whitey decides you're taking a nap."

McCade stood, and the two men shook hands. "See you soon," Walker promised, and hurried up the tunnel. McCade watched until his bobbing light disappeared around a gradual curve.

With almost half the shift still left to go, McCade took his time working his way back up the tunnel, swearing when he lost his footing on the slippery floor, and watching the wall for color changes. But he felt good knowing that Alexander was still alive, and apparently living like a monk on some backward planet. It was just his style. Gambler, slave, and now a reclusive mystic. The guy never quit.

If he hadn't been thinking about Alexander, McCade might have noticed a liquid grinding noise, or felt a slight vibration in the surrounding rock, but he didn't. Therefore it scared the hell out of him when solid rock parted with a loud crack, and the right side of the tunnel caved in. As the hole appeared, it was filled with an obscene bulge of glistening gray flesh, and McCade felt a lead weight drop into the pit of his stomach.

THIRTEEN

More and more rock continued to fall, and McCade knew if he didn't move soon, he'd be trapped. Fortunately this section of the tunnel was larger than most, so the initial cave-in had failed to completely block it. He eyed the narrowing gap between the top of the rockfall and the ceiling. If he was fast enough, he just might make it. Forcing himself to ignore the loop of slimy gray flesh which now protruded out into the tunnel, he backed off a few feet, and then ran full tilt toward the pile of rocks. A series of quick leaps carried him to the top, and a shallow dive took him through the small opening. He fell head over heels down the other side, hitting and bouncing off a variety of rocks, before finally coming to rest at the bottom. With a roar of falling rock, the rest of the ceiling caved in, and the small opening disappeared.

His right knee hurt like hell, and he didn't feel like getting up, but the large rocks which continued to roll down and crash around him suggested that he should. Besides, at any moment the worm might decide to join him. Forcing himself to his feet, he limped up the tunnel, trying to put as much distance between himself and the worm as possible. After about fifty feet or so, he was suddenly short of breath, and noticed that his oxygen hose had pulled loose from his nostril plug. As he stopped to fix it, he glanced back over his shoulder, half expecting to see the worm in hot pursuit. It wasn't. Maybe the rockfall had slowed it down, if so, good. Apparently the blasted thing had been busy creating another tunnel parallel to his own, when the thin rock wall separating the two tunnels had collapsed, causing the roof to cave-in as well.

By the time he emerged from tunnel thirty-four, McCade's right knee felt better, and his limp was almost gone. Making his way between the large rocks which littered the floor of the cavern, McCade caught occasional glimpses of the guards gathered around the makeshift console. When he got there, they would probably chew him out, and send him into another tunnel. After all, there were more than two hours left in the shift. But what the hell, maybe he could talk Whitey into giving him a break. It was worth a try. Either way, he'd soon be off Worm, and having a good meal aboard his own ship. Assuming of course that Phil and Rico had left anything edible in the galley. In the meantime he would do his best to take it easy, and avoid worms.

McCade put on his best hangdog expression as he approached the guards, and prepared to tell them a somewhat exaggerated version of his encounter with the worm. But much to McCade's surprise, all three ignored him in favor of Whitey's VDT. They glanced his way, but continued to talk excitedly among themselves, even allowing him to walk up and peek over their shoulders. Apparently his position as unofficial enforcer granted him a certain amount of privilege.

"Looks like the little creep's luck finally ran out," the black man said cheerfully. "I'll bet you ten Imperials he doesn't last another ten minutes."

The neanderthal grunted his agreement.

McCade saw that the object of their discussion was a flashing green dot in tunnel seventeen. Whitey was tracing its progress with an electronic arrow. Strangely enough the dot seemed to be moving down the tunnel away from the safety of the cavern.

"You're on, sucker," Whitey sneered, without taking his eyes off the screen. "Ten Imperials it is. Spigot's got a lot of tunnel savvy so I say he's good for twenty minutes easy. See . . . I figure the worm's right here"— Whitey pointed the red arrow at a spot just behind the green dot—"and Spigot's trying for this side passage down here." He pointed to a small tunnel which branched off from the larger one. "In fact, he might even loop in behind the worm and get clean away. How 'bout a side bet?"

But the black man didn't reply, because McCade chose that particular moment to crush his skull with a large rock. As the riot gun fell from the guard's lifeless fingers, McCade caught it and brought it to bear on the neanderthal. It pays to take out the worst of the opposition first. The big man wasn't too bright, but his reactions were just fine, and as his partner fell the neanderthal was already spinning in McCade's direction. But he was too late. His huge torso jerked three times, and fell over backward as McCade squeezed the trigger, and felt the heavy weapon buck in his hands. The sound was still echoing off the cavern walls as Whitey clawed for his sidearm with one hand, and tried to stop the slugs with the other. It didn't work. The automatic shotgun roared twice, taking his hand off at the wrist, and erasing his face. His body toppled sideways out of his chair and crashed to the ground.

"If it's any comfort, Whitey, you look better this way," McCade said as he rolled the corpse over and undid the gunbelt which circled its waist. McCade was strapping Whitey's gun on, when three other prisoners ran up.

"Shit, boss, you don't mess around," a short blocky man called Fesker said. "God, look at that, he took all three of 'em."

"I'm glad you men showed up," McCade said. "I could use a little help. Are you with me?"

"You bet we are, boss," Fesker said, picking up a riot gun. "Right, Mendez? Right, Hawkins?"

"Count me in," Mendez agreed calmly, kneeling to strip off the neanderthal's gunbelt.

Hawkins just nodded solemnly, and ran his hand lovingly along the length of the second riot gun. He had even features, bright blue eyes and long brown hair, which hung down his back in two braids.

"All right," McCade said. "Now listen carefully . . . and do this exactly the way I tell you to. As the men come out of the tunnels, hold them right here. Whatever you do, don't let them leave the cavern. Otherwise the guards on the crawlers will know something's fishy, and mow you down before you even get close. The time to take them is at the end of the shift, when they expect us to come out."

"Right, boss," Fesker agreed enthusiastically. "It'll be just the way you said."

"Good," McCade replied. "How about radio? Do you know if Whitey had some way to communicate with the crawlers?"

Fesker shook his head. "Naw, the rock's too thick."

"Excellent," McCade replied. "At least there's one problem we don't have to worry about. Now, Hawkins, give me a hand with one of these bodies. Spigot's in a tight spot, but there's a chance we can pull him out." McCade bent over, struggled to get a hold on Whitey's body, and only barely managed to pick it up. It was damned heavy. Doing his best to ignore the nature of his burden, McCade headed for tunnel seventeen.

Hawkins slung the riot gun across his back, eyeing first the black man, and then the massive form of the neanderthal. He quickly chose the black man. With one smooth motion, he lifted the corpse, and threw it over his right shoulder. Then, carefully picking his way through the rocks, Hawkins hurried to catch up.

As he entered the tunnel, McCade had only the vaguest of plans. But if Spigot was as elusive as Whitey gave him credit for, it might even work. Even so, speed was of the essence. It wasn't easy to jog with a dead body in his arms, so McCade was forced to stop, and sling it over one shoulder as Hawkins had. Having done so, he made much better time.

Finally he saw it, a narrow slitlike crevice in the rock, cut by running water rather than worms. The opening was a tight fit, but he forced his way through it, with Hawkins right behind him. They couldn't run in the narrow passageway, but they still made fairly good time, splashing through the shallow water until suddenly a rock wall barred their way. At the base of it there was a small hole through which the water gushed into the open space beyond. They could make it, but they'd have to lay down in the water to do so, and there was no guarantee as to what they'd find on the other side.

McCade dumped Whitey's body into the water. "You first," he said, pushing the guard's body down, and into the hole. It was quickly sucked out of sight. McCade motioned to Hawkins. "Your friend's next."

Hawkins grinned, and followed McCade's example.

As soon as the other body had disappeared, McCade gave Hawkins what he hoped was a confident smile as he lay down in the water, and shot through the hole feet first. First he felt bitter cold as the water hit his skin, and then pure terror, as the current grabbed him and pulled him through the opening. Suddenly he was falling, wondering if this was how he would die, and then he hit, plunging deep under the surface of the water. Kicking upward, he wondered why everything was black, and then realized his eyes were closed. He opened them to crystal-clear water, his headlamp shining up toward the surface, bubbles dancing in and out of the light. Then he was through the surface, splashing water against a rock wall, and gulping down air. He cursed himself for never wondering if the light was waterproof, and gave thanks that it was.

He heard a tremendous splash behind him, jerked around, almost laughing when he realized it was just Hawkins, shooting through the opening and into the pool. Turning his head McCade's light fell across a steeply shelving beach. He gave a kick and stroked toward it, almost screaming when he hit something soft, and Whitey's faceless corpse popped up in front of him. Forcing himself to push it in front of him, he heard Hawkins surface, coughing up water.

"Over here!" McCade shouted, and splashed the water to attract the other man's attention.

Hawkins coughed in reply, and began swimming toward the beach.

McCade felt his feet touch bottom, scooped up Whitey's body, and stumbled up and out of the water. Suddenly he froze. What the hell was that? Some sort of a noise. Then he heard it again and saw a flash of light over to his right.

"Take that, you big turd. I hope you choke on me and die." It was Spigot!

"He's somewhere to the right!" McCade yelled, lunging toward the flashing light. After a few steps, he came to a place where the wall opened to the main tunnel, and there was Spigot, one leg twisted awkwardly under his body, his headlamp swinging wildly this way and that, as he threw both rocks and insults at the worm.

The worm was by far the ugliest thing McCade had ever seen and, considering its size, moved with surprising speed. It made a sort of sloshing sound as it surged forward, its circular pink maw opening to reveal thousands of black teeth. As it moved, it belched out waves of rotten acidic breath. McCade felt the hair on the back of his neck stand on end. A primitive part of him started to gibber and scream deep in the back of his mind. He pushed it down and pretended not to hear it. Twenty-five more feet and the worm would have Spigot.

Hawkins appeared at his side, riot gun at the ready, reminding McCade of the task at hand. Apparently the other guard's body was still somewhere in the pool. "Well, I guess it's up to you, Whitey," he said to the corpse. Turning to Hawkins he said, "Grab Spigot, and get him out of there!"

Seconds later, Hawkins was dragging a surprised Spigot back away from the oncoming worm. Meanwhile, McCade forced himself to move toward the undulating monster. When he was about ten feet away, he dumped Whitey's corpse unceremoniously on the ground, and quickly backed up. As he did so, McCade drew Whitey's handgun, and Hawkins pumped a round into the chamber of his riot gun. For the first time since they'd met Hawkins spoke, "*Bon Appétit,* you sonovabitch." Spigot cackled gleefully from his position on the ground.

Then all three watched in horrified fascination as the Worm reached Whitey's body, delicately sucked the corpse into its mouth, and began to chew. The sound of Whitey's bones being ground into a fine paste sent chills up McCade's spine, but at least they'd bought some time, now all he had to do was find a way to use it.

"So far so good," McCade observed, turning to the others. "Now if there's only some way to get past the damned thing."

"This is no time to kid around, Sam," Spigot said. "The minute that thing's done with Whitey, it'll come for us. Let's leave the same way you came in."

"I'd like to, Spigot, but I'm afraid that's out." McCade quickly described the passageway, the fall into the pool, and their subsequent arrival.

Much to McCade's surprise, Spigot laughed. "That's a new one on me, Sam. No wonder you're wet. I assumed you came through the side passage, that hits the main tunnel about twenty yards behind us. That's where I was headed when I slipped in the slime and broke my leg."

McCade looked at Hawkins, and they both laughed. "All right, Spigot," McCade said. "Let's get out of here." Carrying Spigot between them, McCade and Hawkins made their way down the tunnel. They went about twenty yards, and sure enough, there was the passageway, right where Spigot said it would be. It took a good twenty minutes of hard work to carry the little man through the passageway and out of the tunnel. As they emerged, McCade wasn't ready for the crowd of men, or their applause. The shift was about to end, and true to his word, Fesker had held all the men inside the cavern. He and Mendez were standing at the front of the crowd, having appointed themselves as McCade's assistants.

Turning to the crowd Fesker yelled, "There he is, men, he just snatched Spigot from a worm, and now he's gonna kick Torb's ass, are you with him?"

As the crowd roared their approval, Spigot grinned, and waved, as though they were cheering him. Suddenly McCade realized that things had gotten out of hand. What started as an effort to help a friend had somehow turned into a full-scale revolt. The men expected him to lead them against Torb, and having killed three guards, McCade realized he didn't have much choice.

As the crowd calmed down, two men took Spigot aside, and applied some rough and ready first aid. There wasn't much time, so McCade jumped up on a rock and motioned for silence. "Thank you, men. Now listen carefully, because if we don't do this right, the guards are going to cut us up into very small pieces." For the next few minutes McCade outlined his plan, assigned responsibilities, and answered questions. Then it was time to move.

McCade nodded. "All right then . . . let's do it." There was a sense of subdued excitement, as the men walked out of the cavern, and into the early dawn light. They were different somehow, backs straight, heads erect, they no longer moved like slaves. McCade worried that the distant guards would notice the difference. If they did, the whole thing could turn into a terrible slaughter. They had to get close enough to take over the crawlers. Once they accomplished that, they'd have powerful weapons, plus a way to crack the dome itself. The chances were good that Torb would receive some sort of warning, and unless they had the means to break in, he could lock them outside the dome until they simply ran out of oxygen.

But his fears were groundless, because as they approached the crawlers, the guards regarded them with the same bored disdain they always did. McCade, Fesker, Hawkins, and Mendez were each leading a contingent of men toward one of the four crawlers. They had the only weapons, so it would be up to them to neutralize the guards, and McCade knew that even with surprise on their side, it wouldn't be easy. The guards were tough, and many were professional killers.

As the men lined up to throw their tools in an open box, McCade was watching both of his guards. The driver was sitting on the bow of the crawler, completely oblivious to his surroundings, reading a skin mag. The other guard was the same woman they'd had on the way out, and one glance told McCade she was suspicious. Her features were locked into a rigid frown, and her glittering eyes scanned the crowd, searching for something to confirm the feeling in her gut. She knew something was wrong . . . she just couldn't figure out what it was. Then McCade saw her eyes widen as she realized that Whitey and the other two guards were nowhere in sight. Her lips moved, and her hand dived for her sidearm, but the only sound was the roar of McCade's gun. The heavy slug hit her in the left thigh, and she went down hard, the gun spinning from her hand to land in the dirt. The driver was fast. He was up and scrambling toward the weapon turret so quickly that McCade fired three times before a slug finally caught him and threw him off the far side of the crawler.

McCade pointed at three of the nearest men. "You . . . you . . . and you. Get the men aboard and secure this rig. Find somebody who knows how to run it. And not some bozo either . . . our lives are going to depend on him in a few minutes. And get that guard some first aid. Watch her though, she's down, but she isn't out. Got it?" They nodded and scrambled off to obey his orders.

Suddenly Fesker appeared at his side. "Trouble, boss. We got two of em, but the guards on the fourth killed Mendez, and managed to button it up."

As if to punctuate Fesker's words, there was the whine of a starter, followed by a stuttering roar as the last machine in line started up, and then jerked into motion. "Hit the dirt!" McCade shouted, and promptly followed his own advice.

Incandescent pulses of blue light flashed and rippled toward them, slagging everything they touched, as the crawler gradually built up speed and rumbled away. Men ran screaming in every direction as the turret-mounted energy cannon cut them down in swathes. But suddenly two of the captured machines began to return fire, scoring at least one clean hit, before the escaping crawler disappeared around a spire of rock. "Damn," Fesker said as he got to his feet. "Sorry, boss."

McCade did likewise and shrugged. "Couldn't be helped. We were lucky it wasn't worse. Well, let's see to the wounded, and get organized. There's no reason to give Torb any more time than we have to."

An hour later they'd done what they could for the wounded, passed out what weapons there were, and assigned the most experienced drivers and gunners to the three remaining crawlers. As they neared the dome, Mc-Cade was worried. They had an hour, two at the most, before they ran out of oxygen. Torb knew that, and therefore knew exactly how long he had to hold out to win the battle. An advantage to say the least.

McCade ran a critical eye over the outside of the dome and didn't like what he saw. First, the base of the dome was made out of durasteel reinforced permacrete; second, the bubble was constructed of forty ply armaplast; and third, the damned thing had four weapons emplacements, one for each point of the compass. Bad—but not hopeless. By the look of them, the multibarreled energy weapons were intended for anti-aircraft use, and not for defense against a ground attack. Since he had Worm to himself, Torb had assumed that an attack would come from space. McCade grinned as he remembered what they'd taught him at the Academy. The first role of warfare is, don't assume anything. Spread out the way they were, McCade figured he could neutralize two of the gun emplacements by attacking just one side of the dome. While that would leave only two emplacements to deal with, they would be able to support each other, and place his forces in a cross fire.

The only other thing going for him was Torb's sloppy housekeeping. The junkyard of rusting metal surrounding the dome would provide his crawlers with some cover. Lacking heavy weapons, or specialized explosives, he figured the main door was his best bet. It should be the weakest point in the dome's structure. For a moment he considered calling for Torb's surrender, but quickly rejected the idea as a waste of time. Torb had both time and oxygen to burn. He'd never surrender in a situation like that.

McCade picked up the mic and keyed it open. He smiled as he imagined Torb listening inside the dome. "All right, men, let's do it by the numbers. Remember the signals we agreed on, remember your individual missions, and remember what an asshole Torb is. All right, let's go!"

As his crawlers jerked into sudden motion, McCade grabbed the twin grips of his energy cannon, and waited for the range to close. His job was to engage the left weapons emplacement. Meanwhile the second crawler would attack the door, and the third would tackle the right weapons emplacement. His head hit the side of the turret, as his driver made a hard right, and then a left, starting the evasive maneuvers they'd agreed upon. Ignoring the pain McCade concentrated on his target. Meanwhile the range was closing . . . closing . . . closing. At the precise moment when McCade squeezed his triggers, pulses of blue light also stuttered out from the weapons emplacements, trying to lock onto the swerving crawlers and destroy them.

As far as McCade could tell, both emplacements were firing independently of each other. Good. Tied together under computer control, Torb's weapons would be even more lethal.

Meanwhile, the third crawler, with Hawkins in command, had taken refuge behind a pile of rusty plating, and was doing battle with the right emplacement, while Fesker led crawler two against the doors. The metal was already glowing cherry-red under the determined assault of his energy weapon, but his machine was terribly exposed, and would soon draw fire from both emplacements. McCade doubled his efforts to hit the left emplacement, swearing when it suddenly ignored him, and went for Fesker. Seconds later the other emplacement did likewise. Torb was finally exercising some fire control.

As he glanced from one emplacement to the other, something kept bothering McCade, but he couldn't figure out what. Then he had it. Torb's forces couldn't depress their weapons any farther than they already were! Because they were intended for anti-aircraft use, their mounts limited how far down the barrels could be depressed. So, if Fesker moved in even closer, they wouldn't be able to hit him.

McCade keyed his mic on, and brought it up to his lips, just as Fesker's crawler took a combined hit. Flames poured out of the engine compartment as the driver spun the big machine around and ran for the shelter of a junked fuel tank. McCade and Hawkins provided covering fire as men poured out of the damaged machine and ran for cover. Most had escaped by the time the crawler blew up a few seconds later.

Then, much to McCade's surprise, both weapons emplacements fell suddenly silent, and Torb's voice crackled over his radio. "Sam Lane, you out there?"

McCade keyed his mic open. "I'm here, Torb, what's for lunch? We thought we'd join you."

"You can't win, Lane," Torb said reasonably, "you're running out of oxygen . . . and there's no way you're gonna break into the dome to get more. Give it up. I promise you won't be punished. We'll just chalk it up to experience . . . and then go back to the way things were."

McCade squinted against the glare, and smiled grimly. "Screw you, Torb."

There was a moment of silence, and there was fury in Torb's voice when he answered. "Then you're dead, Lane. Good-bye."

Suddenly both emplacements opened up with renewed fury, and McCade wondered if Torb was right . . . maybe they were dead.

Inside the dome's com center, Walker conscientiously powered the equipment down, and returned all major systems to standby. Things were going fairly well. He had managed to reach McCade's friends aboard *Pegasus*, and they were on the way, ETA, about six hours. He had also programmed and activated one of the three message torps his organization kept in parking orbit around Worm. Within minutes it would break out of orbit, accelerate away from Worm, and go hyper. Eventually it would emerge near the Wind World, and play back its coded message. Then his superiors would know the Emperor was dead, and that McCade was on the way. He sighed. He'd also done his best to send the message in another way, but had apparently failed, since there'd been no acknowledgment. It seemed as though he'd never get the hang of that stuff. But at least the torp, would get through. Now there was only one problem left to solve.

Walker stood, and turned out the lights as he left the room. He knew that outside the dome the battle still raged, and unless McCade won, the prince wouldn't take the throne, and a terrible war could result. And it didn't take a genius to see that McCade was going to lose. He wondered if the flux readers had known it would end up like this, although it didn't matter much. He knew what to do, but it scared him. What if his brothers and sisters were wrong? What if there was no life after death? He shrugged. Then that's just the way it goes, he decided.

Torb's guards ignored Walker as he strolled across the center of the dome. Most of their attention was directed outside, and besides, everyone knows a Walker doesn't take sides. As Walker approached the dome's huge doors, he was praying in a tongue no longer heard on Terra, and hoping that his action would be in concert with the flux. He was only feet from the control box when a guard shouted, "Hey, you! Walker! Get away from those doors!"

The guard was fast, but Walker was just a little faster, diving for the box, touching the controls just as the bullets hit him. Even as the slugs tore him apart, Walker held the button down, smiling because he'd fooled the silly bastards, and was far, far away.

FOURTEEN

McCade gritted his teeth, and ordered his crawler forward. With Fesker's rig out of action, someone had to tackle the doors, even though it seemed hopeless.

McCade was thrown in one direction, and then another, as his driver, Freak, did his best to avoid the flashing blue beams that stuttered out from Torb's weapons. Hawkins tried to provide covering fire, but Torb's gunners ignored him, throwing everything they had at the crawler racing toward them.

Then their port engine took a direct hit, and McCade was half blinded by the flash, and almost deafened by the loud explosion. An energy beam sliced through the right track, and the crawler slewed left as Freak dumped power and thumbed the intercom. "OK, people, this is the end of the line. Please pay the driver as you disembark. All gratuities will be appreciated."

As men tumbled out of the crawler and ran for cover, McCade did his best to cover them, but here and there they jerked and fell, as a hail of lead and lethal energy tossed them about like so many rag dolls. He felt sick. Now they were well and truly screwed. The whole thing was a complete disaster. It was time to surrender and save as many lives as he could. He was reaching for his mic when the radio squawked into life, and Hawkins said, "Damn! Look at that, boss! They're opening the doors!"

McCade looked, and sure enough, the huge double doors were slowly sliding upward. He couldn't be sure, but it looked like there was some kind of a fight going on inside the dome. It didn't make sense, but what the hell, some chance was better than none. He keyed his mic and said, "Go, Hawkins! Get the hell in there and secure the dome!"

Hawkins didn't reply. He didn't have to. His crawler spewed gravel, and threw up a cloud of dust as it swept around a big pile of empty cargo pods and roared toward the dome. McCade swore under his breath as he saw the doors reverse direction and start downward. Whatever the problem was, Torb's men had it under control, but could they close the doors in time? Hawkins was close, closer, through! The doors closed behind him.

Once inside the dome Torb's guards didn't stand a chance. Hawkins had a field day, grinning as he cut down the running guards, using the crawler to grind them into paste.

Ten minutes later the battle was over, and ten hours later, McCade was ready to lift off Worm. The dome had been secured, Torb and his guards were safely locked into their own underground prison, and the dead had been buried.

One grave stood above all the rest. It was located on top of the little hill where McCade had been tortured, and where the man with the cool green eyes had invaded his dreams. Walker was dead, and McCade didn't know how to mark his grave, or say good-bye. So he gave up, figuring that if Walker was still around, then he knew how McCade felt, and if he wasn't, then it didn't matter.

Turning, he walked down the slope, and headed for *Pegasus*. Her slender shape was a black silhouette against the last rays of the setting sun. Off to the right the glow of cargo lights revealed a small crowd. Some of the men had come to say good-bye. As he headed their way, he thought how good it would feel to leave Worm's eternal heat for the cool darkness of space. He threw the shovel toward the nearest pile of junk and quickened his pace.

A cheer went up as he approached. As McCade tried to quiet the crowd, Phil's shaggy form materialized beside him. The big variant shook his head in disbelief. "It's obvious they don't know you the way we do," he growled.

McCade laughed. "Unlike you, these men appreciate my finer qualities."

"And what finer qualities might those be, ol' sport?" Rico asked, appearing on his other side. "I'll bet the list ain't very long."

But before McCade could answer the crowd grew silent. Fesker stepped forward with Spigot and Hawkins by his side. Clearing his throat importantly, Fesker said, "Well, boss, with you liftin' an all, me and the boys thought we oughta come and say good-bye."

"I'm glad you did," McCade replied solemnly. "I've never served with a finer group of slaves."

They all laughed, shouted friendly insults, and congratulated each other on their wit. Fesker waited until they'd quieted down, and then cleared his throat once more. "As you know, boss, we found Torb's stash of Fire Eggs, and we figure to share and share alike. Well, the way we see it, if it wasn't for you we'd still be slaves. So we all voted, and everyone agreed to give you this."

With that, Spigot hopped forward on a single crutch, and proudly handed McCade a small package.

As the men looked on expectantly, McCade carefully unwrapped the package to reveal a glorious Fire Egg. The very last rays of the sun hit the egg, exploding within to create a ruby red blaze of fire, shot through with iridescent sparks of blue and green. It was the most beautiful thing he'd ever seen.

Rico gave a low whistle. "Now that's some play pretty."

McCade looked up from the fiery egg to the waiting crowd. "Thanks, men, this means a lot. I won't forget you."

They laughed and joked, but as they waved and turned to go, he could see that they were pleased.

Spigot remained after the rest had gone. He grinned his toothless grin. "Thanks, Sam." He glanced at *Pegasus* and back, clearly curious, but too polite to ask. "It's been good knowing you."

"And you too, Spigot," McCade replied. "What's your real name anyway?"

Spigot blushed, looked over his shoulder to make sure the others couldn't hear, and then spoke in a secretive whisper. "You promise not to tell anyone?"

McCade nodded his agreement.

"Alfonso Esteverra Maxwell-Smith."

"It's a good name," McCade said solemnly. Spigot grinned his thanks, they shook hands, and the little man hopped off to catch up with the rest of the group. Occasionally one or two paused to look back and wave.

McCade waved back, and then, with Rico and Phil at his side, he turned and walked toward *Pegasus*.

"So what're they gonna do now?" Rico inquired.

McCade grinned. "Well, about half of them plan to stay awhile, and teach Torb and his guards how to find Fire Eggs."

Phil made a deep rumbling noise which was actually laughter. "And the rest?"

McCade shrugged. "They're happy with the Fire Eggs they've got, and plan to take over the next supply ship Joyo sends out. There should be one in a couple of weeks." The thought reminded him of Candy. Fesker had promised to watch out for her, and make sure she didn't get hurt.

A few minutes later, the lock had cycled closed behind them, and McCade was taking one last look at the Fire Egg, before locking the ship's safe. The jewel's internal fire lit up the inside of the armored durasteel box. It was probably worth more than the ship itself. For one brief moment, he considered quitting, hanging it up. After all, why keep going, keep risking it all, when he had enough for the rest of his days right here in front of him? As quickly as the thought came, it disappeared, pushed aside by Sara's trusting eyes, and Walker's bullet-ridden body.

Turning to Rico, McCade said, "Let's take a look at those coordinates Walker fed you."

Rico's large fingers flew over the keyboard with surprising delicacy, and while most of the computer continued its pre-flight check, a small subprocessor turned its attention to this new request. A second later the words "Wind World" appeared on the master screen, followed by a long list of numbers. McCade grinned. There it was, the end of the search. The numbers were coordinates for the Wind World, and the Wind World was where they'd find the prince.

"There they are," Rico said, pointing a stubby finger at the screen. "Just like your friend sent 'em."

"Speaking o' your friends," Rico continued, "that Cy's quite a character."

McCade laughed. "Yeah, he's definitely one of a kind. Obviously he made it or you wouldn't be here."

Rico nodded. "There we were playin' cards, killin' time, 'n' waitin' for you to get tired o' the bright lights and come back, when suddenly the chime for the main lock goes off. You shoulda seen Phil, he damn near had a heart attack; I mean, who the hell could it be? None o' the detectors had gone off. He didn't pack enough mass or velocity. So we looked at the vid pickup for the main lock, and there's this metal ball floatin' there, and it comes over the ship-ta-ship freq and says, 'Hello, could I borrow a cup of DC?'"

"I almost had a heart attack, did I?" Phil said. "Well, you might ask Rico who spilled the full cup of coffee in his lap."

McCade laughed. "That sounds like Cy all right. How did he manage to reach *Pegasus*?"

"Said there wasn't anything to it," Rico replied. "Bein' a cyborg, all he needs is a little O_2 for his brain, and he's got that in a tank, so vacuum don't bother him a bit. He just locked onto a departing yacht, waited till they were free of Joyo's Roid, and squirted himself in our direction. It took him a few days . . . but he made it."

McCade tried to imagine what that would be like, launching yourself on a one-way trip toward a target you couldn't see, days passing as your precious reserve of power slowly dwindled away, knowing if you didn't find the ship you'd never make it back. It would take an incredible amount of guts.

McCade looked around. "So where's Cy?"

Rico shrugged. "We offered to bring him along, but he said he had unfinished business on Joyo's Roid, something about beating the odds. So as we headed this way, we dropped him off real close to the Roid. Last we saw him he was lockin' onta an incoming yacht. Crazy little beggar."

McCade shook his head sadly. Like most inveterate gamblers Cy just couldn't quit. Well, maybe one day he'd win really big. McCade hoped so.

His thoughts were interrupted as the computer announced the ship was ready to lift and started a countdown. All three men checked to make sure their harnesses were secure, and then someone dumped a couple of anvils onto McCade's chest, and *Pegasus* roared toward the sky, riding a lance of orange-red flame.

They hadn't even cleared Worm's thin atmosphere when every proximity alarm on the ship started hooting, buzzing, or flashing. Someone was waiting for them in space, and when it comes to unexpected visitors, it's always best to assume the worst. Pinned to his chair by the ship's acceleration, McCade armed all weapons systems verbally, and struggled to see through blurred vision.

As *Pegasus* broke free of Worm's gravity the ship's computer quickly scanned the immediate area, evaluated the available data, and gave itself permission to use emergency voice simulation. "Prepare to surrender or abandon ship. Estimated time to total annihilation is one minute 43.2 seconds. Enemy forces include one major warship, cruiser or better, two lesser vessels, and a full wing of Interceptors. All ships provide a 99.9 percent match to Imperial design. Probability for successful engagement, none. Probability for successful escape, none. The autobar and showers will be closed until further notice. This ship's manufacturer will not be held responsible for damage incurred during contra-indicated combat."

"You'd better get that thing fixed, Sam, or I swear I'm gonna rip out its mother board, and dance on it," Phil growled as he unsnapped his harness, and half floated, half climbed up and into the top weapons turret. If they decided to fight, the computer would control the ship's main armament, since no mere human could track and hit multiple targets traveling at thousands of miles per hour. Not unless they got very close. That's when the ship's secondary armament could make the difference.

"Damn," Rico said in amazement as he scanned all the blips on their detector screens. "Where the hell did *they* come from? We weren't followed from Joyo's Roid, and they weren't here when we went dirtside."

Rico's questions went unanswered. Then the com set buzzed, and McCade flicked it on. The screen faded up from black to reveal a stern-looking naval officer. Her black hair was heavily streaked with gray, her eyebrows met just above her hooked nose, and her mouth was a hard straight line. "I'm Captain Edith Queet, commanding officer of the Imperial Cruiser *Neptune*. Cut your drives and prepare to be boarded."

McCade tapped a few keys, and *Pegasus* went into a series of stomach-wrenching evasive maneuvers, only barely escaping the massive tractor beams which lashed out from *Neptune*. In fact one came so close to lock-on that it rattled McCade's teeth.

Doing his best to assume a nonchalant expression, McCade switched the com set to send. "Captain, I'm afraid you're mistaken regarding your current tactical situation. It is you, not I, who should cut your drives and prepare for boarding. Otherwise I shall be forced to destroy your entire fleet."

Rico made a choking noise, and Phil shook his head in pained amusement.

Suddenly Queet's face disappeared to be replaced by Claudia's. There was no mistaking her blond hair, cold blue eyes, and bad temper. "Cut the crap, McCade, or we'll turn your pathetic little ship into so much free metal."

"My, but we're a bit testy lately," McCade replied, his eyes narrowing. "It must be a rough day for the royal retinue. As for blasting my ship . . . go right ahead. But keep in mind that your brother might be aboard, and then again, he might not. That's why you haven't blasted us already, isn't it? You don't mind killing him, but what if he's still out there somewhere? What if I'm going after him right now?"

"Cut your drives, McCade, or I swear I'll blast you, and sift the pieces for my beloved brother."

McCade's eyes flicked to his readouts and back to the screen. Just a little more time. *Pegasus* needed more velocity before she could go hyper. "Right . . . just give me a minute here . . . one of your tractor beams came damn close, and I'm having control problems. How the hell did you find us anyway?"

To his surprise she took the bait. "When you started barging around Joyo's Roid, Joyo tried to check you out with his operatives on Earth, and one of them works for me. I sent Major Tellor to check it out; he ran a check on Joyo's computer, found the glitch where you accessed it, and the rest was easy. Knowing my brother's pathetic sense of humor, it didn't take long to see through his Idono H. Farigo nonsense."

Suddenly a computer-coordinated net of tractor beams flashed out from Claudia's fleet, just as McCade's fingers danced over the control board. She'd been stalling too, and had almost succeeded, but the tractor beams fell slightly short. *Pegasus* leapt outward, still steadily picking up speed.

"Damn you, McCade! I'll triple whatever they're paying you!"

"Thanks, your imperial wonderfulness, but no thanks. I'll see you around." And with that, McCade's stomach lurched, and he felt a brief moment of disorientation. *Pegasus* had entered hyperspace. Outside, the stars suddenly disappeared. Inside the ship's screens showed computer simulations of how the stars should look, would look, if the *Pegasus* wasn't traveling faster than the speed of light.

McCade lit a cigar, and leaned back, slowly allowing his muscles to relax. They were safe for the moment. Without the coordinates for their destination, Claudia couldn't follow, and by the time she did, he'd have the prince and heading for Terra.

"Is the bar open?" he demanded.

"Affirmative," the computer replied. Was it McCade's imagination, or was there a grudging tone to the machine's reply?

McCade shrugged off his harness and headed for the tiny lounge. Phil and Rico were right behind. "It would appear our troubles are over, gentlemen. The last one into the lounge cooks dinner!"

As she watched *Pegasus* disappear off her screens into hyperspace, Claudia swore and clenched her fists. "Damn that man. When I catch him he'll die by inches. Captain Queet, I want a report on that message torp, and I want it now."

Captain Queet nodded, and spoke softly into her headset. Around her the bridge crew literally sat at attention, eyes locked on their screens and multicolored indicator lights. By remaining perfectly still, and performing flawlessly, each hoped to avoid being singled out for one of Claudia's caustic remarks.

Lady Linnea stood toward the rear of the cavernous bridge, doing her best to maintain an expression of aristocratic superiority, while inwardly giving thanks that McCade had escaped. Had Alexander been with him? There was no way to tell, but she knew that if Claudia caught him, he'd soon be dead. Over the last month she'd become more and more obsessed with taking the throne, and now Linnea was convinced she'd stop at nothing to get it. She shivered, praying that wherever Alexander was, he'd never fall into his sister's hands.

Linnea's thoughts were interrupted as Captain Queet looked up, and smiled. "Crypto's very close, Your Highness. They're having trouble with the message, but they've got the coordinates."

"Excellent!" Claudia snapped, eyes gleaming. "Tell them I'm coming down." She spun on her heel, and marched off the bridge. Linnea reluctantly followed. Lately Claudia insisted she stay nearby. The more dictatorial Claudia became, the more she seemed to need Linnea's reassurance, and the harder it was to give.

When they entered the corridor, Major Tellor, plus a full squad of marines, snapped to attention. As Claudia and Linnea passed, they fell in behind, their heavy boots hitting the deck in perfect cadence. Claudia rarely went anywhere without her bodyguard anymore. Maybe her own treachery led her to expect it from others. The thought made a hollow space in the pit of Linnea's stomach. Could she know?

When Claudia and her party entered the crypto lab, Lieutenant Chang barely glanced up from his work. Anyone else would have been dressed down, or even disciplined for such a breach of etiquette, but not Chang. At twenty-five, he was already a legendary genius and eccentric. A long series of frustrated instructors and commanding officers had finally given up, realizing that in order to exploit his brilliance, they'd have to put up with his personality. It was a high price for a military organization to pay, but Chang was worth it, because when it came to cryptology he was the very best. His long lank hair hung down into the inner workings of the long slender torpedo while smoke, from a non-reg dope stick, curled up and around his head. Long slender fingers made a final adjustment, and then he straightened up, wiping his hands on an already filthy uniform. Chang's almond-shaped eyes regarded Claudia with the same friendly enthusiasm he offered the lowliest ratings. "Hi, Princess, step right over here and I'll print out what we've got so far."

Claudia struggled mightily, and just barely managed to ignore Chang's familiarity.

At the cryptologist's touch, a printer began to whir, and while it spit out plastic fax, Chang provided a cheerful stream of conversation. "She's a beaut, isn't she?" he asked, indicating the torpedo. Its long black hull rested on four supports. Claudia knew it consisted of a drive, hyperdrive, and mega-memory. A minicomputer provided guidance and control. It was the mega-memory that held whatever secrets had been entrusted to it. At the moment, a maze of multicolored wires led from the mega-memory's circuitry to some specialized crypto equipment, which in turn was linked to the ship's main computer. Blithely ignoring Claudia's pained expression, Chang continued his monologue.

"I guess she gave our Interceptor jockeys a real run for their money. She was just about to go hyper when they threw some light tractors on her. I figure somebody's got something real important to say, because unlike our converted jobs, this baby was really designed to carry the mail. Someday we'll figure out how to punch com messages through hyperspace and these suckers will become so much scrap. Don't get me wrong though, you can't get anything better than a torp from Techno. I mean that sucker's built. It took me two hours to defeat the electromechanical traps, and another three to get around all the stuff hidden in the programming. Still," he added happily, "I showed those Techno types a thing or two."

The printer stopped whirring, and Chang ripped off the fax. Proudly he handed it to Claudia. She found herself looking at the words "Wind

World," and a long string of numbers. "There you go, Princess, that's where the torp was headed, and although we haven't broken their message code yet, you'll notice they didn't try to encode proper names. For example, 'Mc-Cade,' and 'Farigo,' appear more than once. Does that help?"

Claudia's face broke into a rare smile. "It certainly does, Lieutenant, no, make that Lieutenant Commander, Chang. You've been a very big help indeed! Please feed those coordinates to the bridge, and tell Captain Queet I want to reach the Wind World in record time."

Claudia watched Chang as he called the bridge, and neither saw Lady Linnea as she slipped away on an errand of her own.

McCade had never liked hyperspace shifts in general. The whole concept of leaving normal space for some other reality, which only a few mathematicians understood, bothered him. But to do it without nav beacons seemed especially stupid. Oh, he'd done it often enough, one didn't have much choice out along the frontier, but he didn't like it. He preferred the situation in toward the Empire, where nav beacons marked all the major trade routes, and were taken for granted. Once each sixty seconds the beacons automatically shunted from normal, to hyperspace, then back. Meanwhile each nav beacon broadcast its own distinctive signal, thereby marking a proven entry and exit point. It was a very useful system. Unfortunately this was the rim, and one helluva a long way from any trade route, so they weren't going to run into any nav beacons. Of course as long as you had good coordinates you didn't really need a beacon. And they had the coordinates provided by Walker. "Which means we're in good shape," the optimistic McCade told himself.

"Sure," the pessimistic McCade answered, "but Walker was under a lot of pressure when he sent Rico those coordinates. What if he made a mistake? What if he transposed two digits for example? You might come out of hyperspace right in the middle of a sun . . . and that could be a tad uncomfortable. So why not just forget the whole thing and go home?"

The discussion was suddenly rendered academic, as the computer cut the ship's hyperdrive, and slipped *Pegasus* into normal space. There was a brief moment of nausea, followed by subtle changes in all the viewscreens as they switched from simulated to real space.

Rico gave a low whistle. "Well, ol' sport, your friend certainly liked 'em tight."

McCade nodded his agreement. They'd come out of hyperspace so close to the planet they were damned near in orbit. Walker liked them close indeed. Most pilots considered it prudent to leave a little more leeway, even if it meant a day's travel in normal space. It might be slower, but it was a lot safer.

McCade tapped some keys, and the ship's computer obeyed, taking *Pegasus* down into a high orbit. He wanted to look things over before trying to put the ship down. There was nothing in the ship's data bank on a planet called Wind World, and Walker had mentioned something about high winds.

"Well, Rico, let's see if anybody's home," McCade said. "Try all the standard freqs."

Rico ran through the most commonly used frequencies as McCade studied the fleecy ball below. It wasn't hard to see why they called it the Wind World. Here and there the clouds were shaped into huge whorls, and as he watched, he could actually see them move, driven no doubt by some very strong winds. It didn't take a degree in meteorology to see landing could be very dangerous indeed.

"Here we go, Sam, I've got somebody," Rico said. He flipped a switch, allowing a cultured male voice to come over the control room's speakers. Cultured or not, it was clearly synthetic.

"Greetings, gentle beings. I am a weather and communications satellite known as FG65, in geosynchronous orbit above a settlement known as Deadeye, which also happens to be this planet's only spaceport. At this particular moment surface weather conditions are such that radio communications with Deadeye are somewhat intermittent. Perhaps I could be of help."

"This is the ship *Pegasus*," McCade replied, "requesting permission to land, and instructions on how to do so."

"Permission granted," the satellite responded gravely. "I have scanned your ship for illegal weapons and technology, and have found none. Providing that you agree to obey the laws and customs of our planet, you are welcome."

"We agree," McCade said solemnly.

"Excellent. Now, if you will put your computer on line," the satellite continued, "I will send it Deadeye's position, some basics on the planet's atmosphere, ecology, laws, and so forth, plus the relevant meteorological information regarding current conditions."

McCade tapped a quick sequence of keys, and said, "Our computer's on line."

Three seconds later, the satellite was back. "Please review the information I've provided, and prepare to land in approximately one half standard hour, on my command. Current conditions suggest a brief period of calm at that time. Until then, remember, 'Those who ride the wind must accept where it goes.'" Then there was a click, followed by static.

McCade looked at Rico with a lifted eyebrow, and the other man shrugged his massive shoulders. "I've seen everything now, ol' sport, includin' a philosophical satellite."

For the next half hour they studied the information the satellite had sent them. It quickly became clear that the winds which whipped across the surface of the planet below were not all that random. In fact most were quite predictable. Which explained why the spaceport was located at the very center of a large, circular, semipermanent storm. Although the storm occasionally shifted a little from north to south, and from east to west, it didn't go far. In fact, according to the information supplied by FG65, it stayed right where it was most of the time. Once in a while it would vanish for a time, but it always returned to take up the same position.

The com set buzzed, and satellite FG65 said, "Please initiate your descent. Based on past weather patterns, a brief period of relative calm should prevail in all layers of the atmosphere above Deadeye during the next hour or so."

"Understood," McCade replied. And while one didn't usually thank computers, in FG65's case, it seemed quite natural to say "thank you."

McCade assumed control from the ship's computer as *Pegasus* entered the planet's atmosphere. Tricky atmospheric landings were one of the few things human pilots usually did better than computers. Lots of research had been done trying to figure out why, since logic seemed to suggest it should work the other way around, but no one had come up with any really believable answers. The best they could do was suggest that sentients were capable of something called kinesthetic intuition, which meant human pilots could "feel" subtle things computers couldn't, and could then "guess" what to do about them.

The ship shuddered as the wind hit and shoved it sideways. McCade corrected, and then swore when the wind suddenly fell off, forcing him to compensate.

"If this is 'relative calm,' then I'm a Tobarian Zerk monkey," Rico said, frowning at his instruments.

"Now that you mention it, I do see a certain family resemblance," Phil growled.

McCade grinned, but quickly lost track of their friendly insults as he fought his way down through layer after layer of disturbed air. Finally, after a braking orbit which seemed years long, they came in on final approach. Below, the storm which surrounded Deadeye raged on as it had for more than a thousand years. Ahead, clouds swirled around a vertical tube of calm air which marked the eye of the storm. All he had to do was stop *Pegasus* in midair and drop her straight down that tube. "Nothing to it," he told himself. "Child's play for a pilot of my experience." But as the critical moment approached, sweat trickled down his spine, and the tic in his left cheek locked into permanent spasm. Then it was too late to worry. He killed power, kicked the nose up, felt her drop, goosed the drives to slow their descent. Now all he could do was sit back and hope for the best.

And much to his surprise he got it. *Pegasus* dropped as smoothly as a lift tube in an expensive hotel, giving him a chance to grab a quick look at the planet's surface. Where the rest of the surface was hidden by wind-driven sand and dust, the area directly below was clear. The first thing he noticed was the relative sameness of the land. Yes, he could see distant mountains poking their peaks above the roiling storms, but directly below the land was flat, ridged here and there where the eternal hand of the wind had carved topsoil away from solid rock, but otherwise smooth and featureless. He saw nothing resembling vegetation, and quickly checked the computer to confirm a breathable atmosphere. Sure enough, the atmosphere was within a couple of points of Earth normal, so there was some biomass somewhere even if he couldn't see it at the moment.

His thoughts were interrupted by the buzzing of a proximity alarm as the ground rose to meet them. He turned his attention back to the controls, and a few minutes later felt a gentle thump as the ship settled onto its landing jacks.

He was still congratulating himself when the com set buzzed. This voice was real, somewhat nasal, and belonged to a fat woman. Her hair had been braided and then piled on top of her head. She had laughing eyes, a button nose, and at least four chins. Due to where the viewscreen cut her off, McCade couldn't see below the level of her chest, but if her enormous bosom was any indication, she was very, very large. "Hey, good lookin', unless you plan to stay here the rest of your life, you'd better move that toy. The winds'll shift soon, and when they do, that little thing's goin' bye-bye. So follow the red drone, and then come on down to Momma's Saloon for a drink." She winked a tiny eye, and then disappeared.

McCade had dropped into some pretty casual spaceports in his time, but this was the first time he'd run into a combination air traffic controller-saloon keeper. He checked the main viewscreen, and found a large red sphere had indeed appeared, and was waiting for them to move. The words "follow me" flashed on and off across the front of it, and as a small gust of wind hit, the drone bobbed slightly.

McCade fired his repellors, lifted the ship off the ground, and danced her toward the red ball. The drone drifted left and he followed. As *Pegasus* moved, her repellors cut shallow trails through the dirt, throwing up rooster tails of dust, which were quickly blown away by the light breeze.

There wasn't much to look at, and what there was didn't qualify as works of art. To the right, a heavily reinforced, all-purpose antenna housing pointed a dark finger toward the sky, looking like some sort of primitive obelisk. And to the left, a pylon shaped like a vertical airplane wing soared upward, ending in a sleek housing, and a slowly turning propeller. When the wind was blowing full force, the aero-dynamically shaped pylon would rotate to meet it, and the propeller would turn at incredible speeds. Wind power made practical. So, while the surrounding countryside looked a bit bleak, at least the locals had plenty of cheap nonpolluting power.

And things did look bleak. The sky, the ground, and the rocks were all done in different shades of gray. As a result, the red ball seemed even brighter than it was. It stopped, and McCade did likewise, noticing that the ground below had given way to a huge durasteel plate. Now the words "follow me" disappeared, and were replaced by "cut repellors." McCade obeyed, dropping *Pegasus* gently onto the scarred metal surface.

Moments later he felt a slight jerk, and the metal plate, ship and all, began to sink underground. It didn't surprise him, since the arrangement was quite similar to the underground hangars on Alice, which also served to get ships down and out of the weather.

The rock walls which slid upward around them were as smooth and uniform as duracrete. Suddenly the walls vanished, giving way to a large, brightly lit open space, rectangular in shape, and quite uniform in construction. This was no work of nature but a well-executed creation of man.

The red ball had dropped with them, and now its "follow me" sign reappeared. McCade fired his repellors again, lifting *Pegasus* only inches off the deck, and followed the sphere into a rather generous berth. Once in place, he killed the drives, and delegated control to the ship's computer. It began a post-flight diagnostic check on all systems. When McCade looked up he found the red ball had disappeared.

"Well, gentlemen," McCade said, releasing his harness, "the lady said we should have a drink, and I think it would be rude to ignore her invitation."

"Hear, hear," Phil said. "Never let it be said that we were rude."

"I wouldn't think o' such a thing," Rico agreed solemnly, heading for the lock.

thigh, the other in a shoulder holster under her left arm. Except for a round island of kinky black hair on the very top of her skull, her head was shaved, and she was very beautiful. Her eyes flashed when she spoke. "Either get out of my way . . . or make your move." Her fingers hung just above the butt of her blaster.

The three hardcases just stood there, fingers twitching, trying to decide. They'd seen her in action, and knew that even with the odds on their side, the outcome was still in doubt. Even if they won it would be a close thing.

As the seconds ticked slowly by, McCade blew smoke at the mirror, and allowed his left hand to drift down toward his handgun. Finally, when the moment was stretched thin, one of the men said, "This isn't over, Mara."

"Thanks for the warning," she replied calmly. "I'll watch my back." Then she walked straight toward them, showing no surprise when they parted to let her through.

She seemed to take the bar in with one sweeping glance, her eyes stopping on McCade as she headed for the bar. McCade turned in time to see the hardcases leave the bar, and to accept her out-thrust hand.

She had a strong grip and a low melodious voice. "Welcome to Wind World. I'm Mara, the Walkers of The Way sent me to meet you." She looked from one to another. "Which one of you is Sam McCade?"

"I am," McCade replied, "and I'd like you to meet my friends, Rico and Phil." As Rico and Phil said their hellos, McCade had already taken a liking to her, and knew his friends had too. Rico insisted on giving her his seat, while Phil kissed her hand, something most men couldn't do gracefully, but which worked somehow when the big variant did it.

Then a brief battle was fought to see who would buy her a drink, with Rico emerging the winner, and Mara laughing at the competition. "Really, gentlemen, this will never do. I'm supposed to guide you to Chimehome, not sit around while you buy me drinks."

"Chimehome?" McCade asked.

Mara threw her drink back and nodded. "Chimehome's the name of the Walker monastery. Say, where's my old friend Pollard? Isn't he with you?"

At first McCade didn't understand, then he realized that "Pollard" must be Walker's real name. For a moment he said nothing, stubbing out his cigar, and stalling for time. Finally he looked up into deep brown eyes.

"I'm sorry, Mara, but Pollard's dead. Right after he programmed that message torp and sent it your way he was killed. He saved my life, along with quite a few others."

He saw his words hit Mara like physical blows. She looked down at the surface of the bar and closed her eyes. It didn't take a genius to see that Mara and Pollard had been more than just friends. They sat that way for a couple of minutes, Mara silent and withdrawn, the three men awkward and embarrassed. Then she looked up and smiled, twin tracks marking the path of the tears which had trickled down her cheeks. "This round is on me."

As if by magic, Momma appeared with a new round of drinks, and then waddled away to serve other customers. Mara raised her glass. "To one helluva man."

"To one helluva man," the others echoed, and drained their glasses.

"Tell me about Pollard," Mara asked softly.

So McCade told her: how they'd met, the plan they'd agreed on, and how her friend had died. To his surprise she showed no further signs of grief as he spoke. She laughed when he described how Pollard invaded his hallucinations, nodded while he explained their plan, and winced when he told her about the door. But she didn't cry, and remembering his own farewell at Pollard's grave, McCade knew that at least for the moment, she too had found a way to deal with his death.

When he'd finished both were silent for a moment. Hoping to take her mind off Pollard, and genuinely curious, McCade cleared his throat. "Now it's your turn. Tell me all about a beautiful lady who packs two blasters . . . and doesn't step aside for anyone."

Mara laughed. "You make me sound so dangerous! There isn't much to tell. I was born on an ag planet called Weller's World. Ever heard of it?"

McCade nodded. "I've been there."

"You're one of the few," Mara replied with a grin. "Anyway, my mother died while I was still quite young, and my father raised me. He's the one who taught me how to fight. 'When it's you or them, honey,' he used to say, 'make damn sure it's them.'"

"Words to live by," McCade agreed solemnly, sipping his drink.

"Ain't it the truth," Mara said, her face softening. "He never told me everything, but I suspect he was a soldier of fortune . . . or maybe something worse before settling on Weller's World. I know this for a fact, during my childhood he never worked a single day on-planet, yet we lived quite well. Once each year he always went off-planet saying, 'I've got some business to take care of, honey . . . I'll be back in a few weeks.' And sure enough, a few weeks later he'd be back, wearing a big smile and loaded down with presents."

Mara frowned. "I didn't think anything of it, back then, but now I believe those trips were somehow connected with money, and whatever he did to get it. Anyway the years passed, and as my father grew older, he became increasingly interested in religion. He was never willing to admit it, but I suspect the prospect of death scared him, and like many others, he hoped to find some guarantee of continued existence. Yes, please."

Mara paused while Momma freshened her drink, and then picked up where she'd left off. "During his research, Father came across occasional mention of the Walkers and their philosophy. For some reason it fascinated him. The funny thing was he didn't know that much about them or 'The Way,' but nonetheless he became certain they were right. Somewhere he learned of the monastery here on Wind World, and decided to come." Mara smiled as she remembered. "Frankly I opposed it, but his mind was made up, and he was determined to go, with or without me."

Mara looked up into McCade's eyes. "By this time Father was quite elderly. I couldn't let him go alone. So we sold our place on Weller's World, and hopped a series of freighters, eventually landing here. During the trip, Father's health deteriorated, and by the time we arrived was quite bad. At his insistence we finished the trip to Chimehome, and he died a month later. His last words to me were, 'Take care, honey, I'll be around.' And you know what?"

McCade shook his head.

"Every now and then I think he is . . . although maybe it's just my memories of him. Anyway, after Father's death, the Walkers invited me to stay and I accepted. I've learned a lot . . . and used some of the things Father taught me to help out." Her right hand strayed to the butt of a blaster. "Meeting you is a good example."

McCade smiled. "We can sure use the help."

Mara looked thoughtful for a moment. "And that brings us back to the present. Something you said is bothering me. Something about Pollard launching a message torp. What message did he send?"

McCade lifted one eyebrow in surprise. "Beats me. I just assumed it was his way of letting you know about us. You mean the torp never arrived?"

Mara smiled and shook her head.

"Then how did you know we were coming?"

She laughed. "How did Pollard get inside your head?"

McCade looked her right in the eye, and knew she wasn't kidding. "I don't believe it."

"The facts speak for themselves," she replied lightly. "We haven't received a torp, but I knew your name, your mission, and approximate time of arrival. All were given to me before I left Chimehome." She chuckled. "It sure sounds like Pollard. Like you, he always had trouble believing in anything beyond the physical, and therefore doubted his own abilities. It would be just like him to use a message torp as a backup."

It all seemed pretty strange to McCade, but as Mara pointed out, the facts seemed to support her contention that Pollard had used nonphysical means to send his superiors a message. If so, what had happened to the torp? They weren't infallible, but they were fairly reliable, and it seemed strange that it hadn't shown up. He felt a cold hand grab his stomach. What if Claudia had managed to intercept the damned thing? It would be just like the miserable bitch. He picked up his glass and finished off his drink. As he turned toward the others, he wiped his mouth with the back of his hand and plastered a grin on his face. "Well, here's to a quick and successful journey."

SIXTEEN

The Nuags filled the dimly lit staging area with their bad-tempered grunting and the stench of their excrement. Tons of flesh pushed and shoved, eager to reach the succulent roller bushes just dumped into their pen. The smaller animals, males mostly, were quickly pushed toward the rear while the dominant cows took their rightful positions in the front. Like pink snakes their long, greedy feeding tentacles slithered out from under leathery gray armor, to snatch up prickly round balls of vegetation and pull them back toward hungry mouths. It wasn't a pretty sight. The sounds that went with it weren't all that great either, McCade decided, as the nearest cow put away another roller bush, slurping and gurgling with happiness. In addition to their other unpleasant traits, Mara informed him Nuags were also lazy, stubborn, and not very bright. In other words they'd make outstanding admirals, McCade thought.

"So why keep them around?" he asked.

"Because," she answered, "they are also big, strong, and perfectly happy to spend the night in the middle of a storm which would kill us. All of which makes them perfect for hauling you around."

"Couldn't we use a nice cozy crawler instead?" McCade asked wistfully, imagining one equipped with a small, but serviceable bar, and some comfortable bunks.

"Because," Mara replied patiently, "our storms tend to pick up crawlers, and toss them around like feathers, something which rarely happens to Nuags. Follow me and you'll see why."

So he followed her down to the staging area where the Nuag convoys were loaded and unloaded. It was a huge man-made cave which served as both a barn and warehouse. At the moment the place was packed with milling Nuags. Mara was forced to shout over her noisy subjects.

"Look at how they're shaped!" Mara shouted. McCade looked, and saw that most Nuags were about thirty feet high, and forty feet long. Their smoothly rounded gray armor made them look like huge beetles. Only beetles have heads and Nuags don't. In fact, with the exception of some narrow breathing vents, their exterior coverings were completely smooth. "The wind just flows over and around them," Mara yelled. "They can travel during even the worst storms."

McCade nodded his understanding, and followed as she waded into their midst, kicking, pushing, and swearing. Much to McCade's surprise, the Nuags did what Mara told them, albeit reluctantly, as if respecting anyone as mean and crotchety as they were. As she shoved her way through the crowd, McCade did his best to avoid their prodigious droppings, making a face at her when she turned and laughed.

"They may be ugly, Sam, but once you've tried getting somewhere without them, they start looking a lot better. Besides," she shouted, adopting a professional air, "each one is a masterpiece of evolutionary engineering. Take those breathing vents for example." She pointed toward the nearest Nuag. "Each one is protected by a flap which closes automatically when the wind hits it. Meanwhile the ones on the opposite slope of the mantle remain open, allowing the Nuag to breathe. Neat, huh?"

"Incredible," McCade agreed, ducking as one of the miserable beasts relieved itself of sufficient gas to power a small city.

Mara laughed. "It's a good thing you weren't smoking a cigar. Now, take a look at this." She hammered her fist on the side of the nearest animal. Its armor started to flex, and then curled slowly upward, until it was about four feet off the ground. "After you," she said politely, delivering a formal bow.

"You're too kind," McCade replied dryly, ducking under the edge of the raised armor. She followed, the Nuag's protective covering dropping into place behind her.

To McCade's surprise, he found the interior to be well lit, and rather spacious. The light originated from some chem strips fastened to the animal's belly with some sort of adhesive. But even more interesting was the large gondola suspended below the Nuag's midsection by a massive harness. The gondola was made of light plastic boasting both windows and a door. Taking a peek inside McCade saw comfortable seats, an array of darkened viewscreens, and even a tiny galley. He groaned.

"Don't tell me, let me guess. We get to travel in this thing."

Mara shook her head in pretended amazement. "Amazing. It'll be tough putting anything over on you."

McCade decided to ignore her sarcasm. "How the hell do these things see anyway? I didn't notice anything resembling eyes out there."

Mara nodded. "Right, there weren't any. Follow me."

McCade followed her toward the front of the animal. He noticed it had no head to speak of, just a rounded area above its chest, which was mostly mouth. At the moment two feeding tentacles were busily stuffing a gray roller bush into the large pink maw. Mara pointed, and McCade saw there was a single eye located just below the Nuag's mouth, right in the middle of its massive chest. The eye was red in color, and seemed to regard McCade with considerable hostility. "Their eyes are located down here," Mara said, "safe from windblown dust and sand."

McCade looked up from the Nuag's baleful red eye, and into her pretty brown ones. "Kind of a limited point of view, isn't it?"

She shook her head. "Not really. First you must realize that because of the frequent storms, the surface visibility is often zero. And second, it happens that Nuags have no natural predators other than man. And, since they navigate using some sort of biological direction finder we haven't figured out yet, all they have to see is the next few feet of trail."

"Very impressive," McCade said politely, eyeing the gondola dubiously. "How far did you say it was to this Chimehome place?"

"I didn't," Mara replied, grinning. "But you'll be pleased to know that it's only a hundred miles or so."

Six hours later, McCade tried to ignore the swaying motion of the gondola, and convince himself that a hundred miles was no big deal. Uncomfortable though it was, he consoled himself with the thought that if the viewscreens meant anything, it was much worse outside. Before departing Deadeye, Mara had placed heavy-duty vid pickups on the outer surface of the Nuag's armor. During the early part of the trip the pickups had provided a somewhat monotonous view of windswept plains. Now even that would be welcome. For the last hour or so all he'd seen was a brown mist of windblown dirt and sand.

Even though he couldn't see it, McCade knew Rico and Phil's Nuag was close behind, with still another animal bringing up the rear. In fact, he could have called them on the radio had he wished to. Although the storms made long-distance communication difficult, short-range stuff worked just fine. Nonetheless he resisted the temptation. They were probably sacked out. That was the weird part of traveling by Nuag. You didn't have anything to do.

Apparently early settlers had wasted a great deal of time and energy trying to train the Nuags like horses or other domesticated riding animals. Eventually, however, they noticed that each group had its own migratory paths, and that animals from a particular herd refused to walk any paths except their own. They also observed that Nuag herds were fairly well distributed across the surface of the planet. So, knowing when they were beat, the colonists quit trying to train the Nuags to go everywhere, and took advantage of the places they went on their own. Research stations and mines were placed along secondary paths, while major settlements were generally located where a number of primary walks came together.

Deadeye was a good example. Approximately one third of all ancestral routes passed through Deadeye. This was due to the plentiful supply of roller bushes pushed there by the circulating winds. It seemed all the Nuag walks had evolved from the eternal search for food. Like the Nuags themselves, their food also roamed around, searching for windblown nutrients. And because the major weather patterns were quite repetitive, the windblown food tended to end up in certain places, at certain times of the year.

So, while the colonists hadn't managed to train the Nuags, they had found ways to use them.

McCade had to admit that the system seemed to work. For hours their Nuags had trudged along without any sort of guidance. Still, he thought Mara's attitude a bit too relaxed, and was determined to keep a careful eye on the viewscreens. So he scanned them one after another, fighting the hypnotizing movement of the brown mist, completely unaware when he drifted off to sleep.

He awoke with a guilty jerk. The horrible swaying motion had stopped, Mara was no longer asleep beside him, and the door to the gondola was wide open. Glancing at the viewscreens he saw that either the storm had stopped, or they had moved out of it, and into an area of momentary calm.

He climbed down from the gondola, and thumped his fist against the inside of the Nuag's armor, just as he'd seen Mara do. The beast uttered a grunt of protest at this unreasonable demand, but grudgingly lifted its armor, allowing McCade to duck under and out.

Outside, a chill breeze tried to penetrate the stiff fabric of his seamless one-piece windsuit, failed, and whistled past, searching for easier victims. The sky was a dark gray color, and McCade imagined that somewhere above the clouds, the sun was nearing the horizon. About fifteen or twenty other Nuags dotted the area. Most were motionless, resting or asleep, almost covered by windblown sand. But others were awake, and pulling restlessly against whatever held them in place, eager to socialize with the newcomers. McCade looked around but there was no one in sight.

Hearing a noise, he walked around the nearest animal to see Mara feeding the third, with Rico and Phil looking on. The Nuag was grunting contentedly, as Mara pushed a roller bush under its mantle with the help of a short pole.

"So, sleeping beauty awakens," Phil said cheerfully. "It's about time." McCade noticed that due to his thick fur, Phil had seen fit to dispense with a windsuit, and wore only his traditional kilt.

"Hello to you too," McCade replied good-naturedly. "Where are we anyway? And why?"

Mara wrestled the pole away from a playful feeding tentacle, and gave McCade a smile. "We're at Thirty Mile Inn, which is where we're staying tonight."

McCade lifted one eyebrow as he pretended to scan the horizon. "I don't want to seem ungrateful, but at first glance the accommodations seem somewhat spartan."

In response, Mara reached into the cargo pocket on her right thigh, and pulled out a small black box. It had only two buttons and a short antenna. She thumbed the top button, and McCade heard a crunching sound to his right, as a thin crust of dirt and rock parted, making way for a metal shaft. It rose from the ground with a whine of hidden hydraulics. The shaft was about six feet square, had one large door, a lot of smaller hatches, and a pointed top. A number of cables led out of the smaller hatches to disappear under the sand. As it ground to a halt, a sign lit up above the door, WELCOME TO THE THI TY MILE INN.

"Don't tell me, let me guess," McCade said. "The Nuags always stop here for the night . . . so this is where they built the inn."

"Like I said before," Mara grinned. "There's no fooling you. Now, if you gentlemen would give me a hand, I'd sure appreciate it."

She led them over to the metal shaft and opened three small hatches. Behind each door was a power lead. Pulling one out, she handed it to Rico. "If you'd be so kind, sir. You'll find a connector mounted on the rear of your gondola. Just plug it in and flick the mode switch to charge. That way your gondola will have a full charge by morning . . . plus your Nuag will still be here. They tend to drift a bit if you don't tether them, and I don't know about you, but I don't need a mile hike first thing in the morning."

"Yes, ma'am," Rico replied cheerfully. He trudged off toward his Nuag, dragging the power lead behind him. McCade did likewise, quickly discovering that after a few feet the cable got damn heavy.

Meanwhile Mara and Phil headed for the third beast, which though equipped with a cargo gondola, still required power for various passive systems. The big variant used only his thumb and two fingers to haul the heavy cable. It was hard to tell if Mara was impressed or simply amused.

A few minutes later they all met in front of the metal shaft. Mara palmed the lock and the door whined open. A gentle blast of warm air hit them, bringing with it the faint smell of cooking, and the less pleasant odors of stale smoke and beer.

It was crowded inside the small elevator, but their journey was soon over. Apparently the inn was just deep enough to keep it out of the wind. After all, McCade thought to himself, why dig any deeper than necessary?

As they got off the elevator, it became quickly apparent that the management of the Thirty Mile Inn never did anything they didn't have to. Where Momma's place was squeakily clean, and therefore the exception to rim world bars, this one was all too typical. The metal grating under McCade's boots just barely managed to keep him up out of the muck below. The walls of the corridor were bare earth, and what little light there was came from some tired chem strips dangling from the ceiling.

"How quaint," Phil growled. "Sam always takes us to the nicest places."

"Yeah," Rico agreed, "I wonder what time the string quartet performs."

Just then the corridor opened into a large open room and McCade knew they were in trouble. As they entered, the normal buzz of conversation suddenly stopped, leaving an unnatural silence broken only by the steady drip of a leaking faucet. Tension drifted with the floating smoke to fill the room and dim the light.

Nine heavily armed people stood with their backs to the bar. None of them looked too friendly. Especially the three hardcases Mara had faced down back in Deadeye. They stood at the very center of the semicircle. One of them, a weasel-faced man with short black hair, wore a shit-eating grin. When he spoke there was a general scraping of chairs as noncombatants scrambled to get out of the way. "Well, bitch, say whatever prayers the Walkers taught you, cause you're about to die."

McCade couldn't believe it. The idiot was a talker. One of the stupid-scared ones that always have to explain how tough they are before they beat up some old geek, and take his drinking money. After a while they get in the habit, and eventually they wind up talking when they should be shooting. Weasel face died getting his next sentence ready. Mara's blaster bolt drilled a neat hole through his chest, hit the full tankard of beer behind him, and turned it to steam. Suddenly all hell broke loose.

Rico and Phil had already spread out right and left. Phil went into full augmentation ripping off the first burst from his machine pistol before McCade had even pulled his slug gun. Two men were still falling, their bodies riddled with Phil's bullets, when McCade's gun leaped into his hand and roared four times. His first shot kicked a leg out from under the woman in the middle, the other three punched black holes through the guy on her right, slowly climbing until the last one erased his face.

Out of the corner of his eye, McCade saw Mara stagger and spin as she took a hit, and saw Rico nail the man who'd shot her. Then death plucked at McCade's sleeve as someone opened up with a flechette gun. Picking them out of the crowd, Phil roared with rage, and leaped across the intervening space to bang two heads together, dropping the limp bodies like so much dead meat. Limp fingers released the flechette gun and it clattered to the floor.

That's when the man on Phil's right brought out a ten-inch blade and prepared to ram it into the variant's back. McCade fired twice and the man toppled backward, landing in a pile on his own guts.

For a long moment there was silence in the bar, interrupted only by the groaning of a wounded man, and the whimpering of a female bystander. Then, as though coming out of a trance, the room gradually came back to life. Rico and Phil gave Mara some first aid, simultaneously chewing her out for scaring them half to death. Phil breathed a sigh of relief when he found the slug had only creased her side.

Meanwhile McCade methodically searched the room. Others' eyes met his, but saw only death, and slipped away to look at something else. Satisfied that the immediate danger was past, McCade felt the adrenaline start to ebb away, and cursed the twitching in his check.

Thirty minutes later the bodies had been hauled away, and the worst of the gore had been mopped up. At Mara's insistence they took seats at a circular table, and waited while a nervous old man placed drinks in front of them.

McCade watched Mara as he slowly rotated a cigar over his lighter. "Maybe you'd better tell us what this is all about."

She shook her head regretfully. "I'm really sorry you got caught in the middle of it. I didn't think they'd make a move this soon. The three in the center were Wind Riders; the rest were just local muscle, waiting for the next caravan out, and eager to make an easy credit."

"Who are these Wind Riders?" McCade asked.

"Basically they're bandits. The name stems from the powered hang gliders they use to attack settlers."

"Wait a minute," McCade interjected with a wave of his cigar, "I thought atmospheric flight was supposed to be impossible here."

"Dangerous and inefficient, yes," Mara replied, "but not impossible. Although long-distance point-to-point flight is so difficult, it's just about impossible. However, that still leaves localized flight outside the storm zones, or on the edge of them, and that's what the Wind Riders specialize in. They use ultra-light aircraft to make aerial attacks on Nuag caravans or settlements. They take great pride in their skill, and rightfully so, because they're very good at it."

McCade sighed. Great. Now in addition to Claudia, they had a bunch of flying bandits to contend with. He tapped his cigar in the general direction of the floor, and said, "OK, the Wind Riders are in the robbery business, but why are they so fond of you in particular?"

Mara shrugged, and then winced slightly as the motion pulled on her wound. "It's not me so much as it is the Walkers. As a group we oppose the Wind Riders, and encourage the settlers to do likewise. So, when I'm not running supply convoys in from Deadeye, I spend a lot of time helping the locals fortify their homes, and organize commandos."

Phil nodded proudly. "That would piss 'em off all right. No wonder they tried to take you out." Then he turned to McCade with an expression which seemed to say, "So there. You were wrong. The woman's a saint."

"Excuse me, noble ones . . ." The shaky voice belonged to the old man who had served them earlier. He'd watched the fight from the safety of a dark corner, and now he was scared, positive that the people sitting at this table must be even worse than the Wind Riders. His rheumy eyes darted this way and that, like frightened animals trying to escape a trap. "Is one of you noble gentlemen named Sam McCade?"

"Yup," Rico answered, waving his drink in McCade's general direction. "Sam's the ugly one."

Terrified that McCade might resent Rico's joke and take it out on him, the old man began to shake. "I . . . have a message for you . . . you, sir. It . . . It just came in from Deadeye. They picked it up from a ship . . . ship in orbit."

"Once in a while Deadeye can use high-speed transmission to squirt something through during a moment of calm," Mara explained. "They never know exactly when that moment will come, so they record the message, and if it's important enough, broadcast it for days at a time." She turned to the old man. "Take it easy, old one, we won't hurt you. What was the message?"

Relief washed over the old man's face as he fumbled a piece of fax out of his pocket, and read it in a quavering voice. "'An open message to the citizens of Wind World, from Her Royal Highness, Princess Claudia, Empress pro tem of the human empire. Greetings. It is my unpleasant duty to inform you that a fugitive from Imperial justice has taken shelter among you. Do not believe his lies. Aid him at your peril. He is guilty of murder, treason, and flight from Imperial justice. His name is Sam McCade. I will pay fifty thousand credits for his body—dead or alive—no questions asked.'"

SEVENTEEN

The tiny grains of sand flew across the plain like miniature bullets. They stung McCade's cheeks and hands and splattered against his goggles. Sand was everywhere. It had worked its way past the seals of his windsuit, sifted through his underclothes, and was gradually filling his boots. For hours he'd labored in a windblown hell, where everything was gray-brown, and nothing came easily.

Standing only three feet tall, the wall represented hours of back-breaking work, and didn't deserve the title "fort." But a fort it would have to be when the Wind Riders attacked, as Mara assured them they would. At Mara's insistence they had left the questionable hospitality of Thirty Mile Inn, and resumed their journey. Before long the Wind Riders would hear of Claudia's offer and come after them. The opportunity to get Mara, plus the bounty for McCade, would make it irresistible.

Meanwhile, the fugitives decided to make as much progress as possible. It wasn't easy to convince the Nuags to move at night, and they didn't move fast, but every mile would put them that much closer to their goal and safety. So they left the inn hoping to reach the protection of the next way station before dawn.

They hadn't even come close. A storm came up slowing the Nuags to a crawl. All through the long hours of the night, the Nuags struggled against the wind. Even with their streamlined bodies and phenomenal strength, the big animals were unable to do more than about two miles an hour.

Finally, with dawn only hours away, Mara ordered a halt, pointing out that when the storm cleared, they'd be sitting ducks. And due to the Nuags' predictability, the bandits would know exactly where to find them. They'd simply cruise along the appropriate Nuag path from Deadeye to Chimehome, and bingo, there they'd be, easy targets.

Soon the air would become warmer, creating thermals, and helping the Wind Riders into the air. Shortly thereafter the bandits would locate their prey.

Suddenly Phil appeared at McCade's side, touching his arm, and pointing to the right. Turning, he saw Mara as a black silhouette against the gray dawn. Beneath her feet was the rounded shape of a Nuag. Most of the sound was whipped away by the wind, so McCade heard only a dull thump as she fired Rico's heavy slug gun. The animal's legs collapsed and the poor beast slumped to the ground. It was the last. In spite of his distaste for the animals, McCade couldn't help but feel sorry for them, and for Mara. Tears had streamed down her face as she killed the first two. The Wind Riders would have killed them anyway, and by positioning them evenly around the perimeter of their makeshift fort, she'd at least put their bodies to good use.

The bandits made it a practice to kill Nuags first. Doing so prevented any possibility of escape, immobilized their loot, and demoralized their opponents all in one easy step. Besides, they couldn't carry the animals on their ultra-light aircraft. Even if they could, the Nuags refused to deviate from their ancestral paths and were therefore useless to the bandits.

McCade slumped down in the shelter of the stone wall. By connecting the three Nuags it created a large triangle. Its main purpose was to provide cover for anyone moving between the three strongpoints, and for use in the case of a ground attack. According to Mara, the Wind Riders often ran short on fuel, forcing them to land and attack on foot.

Reaching inside his windsuit, McCade found a cigar, and used the protection of the rock wall to light it. Moments later Mara and Phil joined him.

"You might as well grab some shut-eye, Sam. They won't be coming until the storm's over, so jump in the nearest gondola and get some rest.

There's enough juice left in the storage cells to keep it warm for a while. Rico volunteered to take the first watch."

"How 'bout you two?"

Mara smiled while Phil tried to look innocent. "We're going to talk for a while . . . and then we'll get some sleep too."

McCade nodded and got to his feet. More power to them. Grab a little happiness when you can. Maybe Mara was reacting to Pollard's death . . . and maybe not. Either way it was none of his business.

A few minutes later he'd managed to pry up a section of Nuag shell and was stretched out in a nice warm gondola under several tons of dead Nuag. It seemed sleeping under dead bodies was getting to be a habit. Sara wouldn't approve. As he drifted off to sleep, he held a picture of her in his mind, and wondered if he'd ever see her again.

He tried to lose himself in total darkness, but found he couldn't. A jumbled montage of thoughts and pictures floated by. A strange face kept inserting itself between them. This had happened once before, but he couldn't remember why, or when. It was a woman's face, pleasant, but somehow concerned. She felt good. Like peace and warmth and comfort. He liked her. She was talking, but he couldn't make out what she was saying.

"I can't hear you," he shouted, his words echoing endlessly back.

She frowned. Her lips moved once more, and this time there was sound, but it was slow and distorted, like a tape playing at half speed.

"Faster," he shouted. "I can't understand you!"

"How's this?" she asked, her voice soft and melodic.

"Much better," McCade sighed, feeling the tension flow away.

"Good," she replied. "By the way, I know the answer to your question."

"I'm glad," McCade said happily. "What was the question?"

"You wondered if you'd ever see her again," the woman replied patiently.

"I did? Oh, yes, I did." McCade thought of Sara and suddenly a lump of fear filled his gut. What if the answer was no?

"Shall I tell you what I see in the flux?" the woman asked.

"Thanks, but no thanks," McCade replied. "I couldn't stand it if the answer was no."

"Very wise," the woman said, nodding her agreement. "Now there is something you must remember when you awake."

"Something I must remember," McCade agreed stupidly.

"Yes," she said. "There will be a fight."

"A fight," McCade agreed.

"Do not kill the blue one."

"No," McCade said, "I won't kill the blue one. . . . What blue one?"

But she was gone, leaving only darkness in her place. "What blue one?" McCade demanded, feeling silly when he realized he was sitting upright inside the gondola talking to himself.

Having people messing around with your dreams can be a bit unnerving, and having dealt with Walker, scratch that, Pollard, he felt sure that someone new had just gone for a stroll through his head. He shrugged and glanced at his wrist term. It was time to relieve Rico. He opened the door to the gondola and crawled out into the morning light.

Jubal stepped out of the shabby dome and finished zipping up his bulky flight suit. It seemed to get tighter every time he put it on. He wasn't tall, and he'd always been beefy, only now some of the beef was turning to lard. "Still," he assured himself, "there's plenty of muscle under the fat, and my reactions are still good."

He closed the final zipper and sniffed the morning breeze. It smelled like easy pickings. Thanks to Princess Claudia, there was a rich prize out there, just waiting to be claimed. Having the Emperor's daughter drop in out of nowhere was a bit weird, but the timing couldn't have been better. The strategy meeting the night before had almost turned into a disaster. He'd barely gaveled the meeting to order when word arrived from Thirty Mile Inn that the bitch Mara had not only escaped, she'd completely wiped out the team he'd sent to kill her as well. Damned embarrassing, and potentially dangerous, when there were scumbags like Yako around just waiting for a sign of weakness. Oh, how that scrawny little runt would like to take over leadership of the Wind Riders! And he might too—if there were any more disasters like the Thirty Mile Inn episode. Stupid buggers.

As Jubal strolled between the low domes, skirting the junk and piles of garbage, a big smile creased his puffy, unshaven face. Children scurried to get out of his way, their parents shouted greetings, and he lifted a noble hand in reply. "Maybe we aren't rich," he told himself, "but we're a damned sight better off than most of the dirt-scratching settlers." Yes, all things considered, the Wind Riders had prospered under his leadership. Under his predecessor, ol' one-eyed Pete, they'd been living in caves. He grinned wolfishly. It was too bad the way ol' Pete just disappeared like that. He wouldn't let the same thing happen to him.

As Jubal approached the flight line, Yako was already sitting in the seat of his tiny aircraft, running a pre-flight check. Where Jubal was beefy, Yako was wire-thin, having both a body and a personality like a ferret. As Jubal approached, Yako watched him out of the corner of his eye, while pretending to check out the twin energy weapons mounted on either side of the cockpit.

"Good morning, Yako," Jubal said cheerfully as he passed. "Should be a good day for you youngsters to gain some experience."

Yako knew the older man was needling him, and it made him mad, but he managed to swallow his pride and smile. "Good morning, Jubal. I hope you're right."

The other man waved nonchalantly and continued on his way.

Good luck on getting your fat ass off the ground, Yako thought after him.

Two-faced bastard, Jubal thought to himself as he nodded to his ground crew and heaved himself into the seat. There was a provision for a rear seat, but at the moment the space was occupied by a reserve fuel tank. Like all their aircraft, Jubal's was little more than an alloy frame partially covered with thin duraplast. The cockpit was completely open. Above it, the wing itself was surprisingly long, and mounted a tiny engine. The engine was used primarily for gaining altitude and for flying against the prevailing wind. When possible the engine was shut off, and the plane was flown like a glider, explaining its considerable wingspan, and the light-weight construction.

Unlike many of the Wind Riders Jubal found no joy in gliding. Given the choice he would have used his engine constantly. Unfortunately that wasn't possible. Since the Wind World didn't have any oil reserves, all petrochemicals had to be imported, and that made gasoline a very valuable commodity indeed. Outside of expensive anti-grav technology, gasoline engines were the only thing light enough to do the job.

Having completed his perfunctory pre-flight check, Jubal used a thick finger to stab the starter button, and smiled his satisfaction as the engine stuttered into life. Just one of the many benefits of leadership. His plane always got the best maintenance. Glancing to the left and right, he saw all five members of his wing were ready. They were older men like him, veterans of many raids, and getting a bit long of tooth. Nonetheless he preferred them to the greenies in Yako's wing. At least you knew what they'd do when the poop hit the fan. They weren't in any particular formation. He didn't go in for all that precision crap like Yako and his flying fruitcakes. "Get your ass in the air and the job done." That was Jubal's motto.

Yako watched Jubal's wing stagger into the air with open contempt. The whole bunch of them should be in a museum somewhere. They'd simply been at it too long. Gone were the days of easy pickings. Thanks to the Walkers the settlers had started to fight back. Hell, they'd started using surface to air missiles for God's sake! When was Jubal going to wake up and see that the old ways weren't good enough anymore? When the wind stops blowing, that's when.

Glancing right and left, Yako saw his own wing was ready to go. There were three ultra lights to either side, each perfectly aligned with his own, each awaiting his command. His pilots were young, eager, and impatient to make their mark. Yako chinned over to his wing frequency. "All right, let's show the old farts how to do it right."

All seven pilots revved their tiny engines, the sounds merging into a single high-pitched scream. "Hold . . . hold . . . get ready . . . now!" As each pilot released their brakes, the tiny planes surged forward, springing into the air a few feet later.

Suddenly Jubal's cheerful voice crackled over Yako's headset. "Tally ho! Last one there's a Nuag's rear end!"

Sure, now that you've got a five-minute head start, Yako thought to himself, putting his plane into a climbing turn. The old clown was obviously in a good mood. And why not? The miserable bastard was about to wiggle out of the trap he'd put himself in. Assuming things went well, they'd punch Mara's ticket, and pick up a nice little bonus from Princess Claudia in the bargain. A success like that could keep Jubal in the driver's seat for some time to come. It was a depressing thought.

The distant planes sounded like angry insects. Even standing on top of a dead Nuag, McCade still couldn't see them yet. Nonetheless, he checked the energy rifle Mara had given him. The power Pak registered a full charge, plus he had a pak in reserve. Wind Worlders favored energy weapons because they were equally effective in all kinds of weather. Heavy winds can play hell with a projectile, but they don't affect an energy beam in the least. Phil and Rico had energy rifles too and were dug in near the other Nuags. Between the three of them they hoped to catch the Wind Riders in a cross fire.

Mara however was their secret weapon. In spite of Phil's repeated objections she had insisted on hiding in a pit about five hundred yards out from their make-shift fort. They'd used a roller bush to disguise the opening, and tied some more down as well, since they were usually found in groups. Nonetheless it was a dangerous place to be. Once they located her, the bandits could easily cut her off. On the other hand they wouldn't expect her to be outside the fort, and the combination of surprise, plus her mini-launcher might just do the trick. "Well, it oughta scare the hell out of them anyway," McCade told himself.

Jubal grinned. There they were, just waiting for him to come along and scoop 'em up. How considerate! He pushed the stick forward, putting the plane into a long shallow dive. Up ahead he saw three dots which quickly grew into Nuags. They were spaced out to form the three points of a triangle. At first he thought they'd been hobbled that way. Then he realized they were dead. And someone had built a low wall between them too. Smart. But it wouldn't do any good. Flipping a switch on his instrument panel he activated both energy weapons. There was no point in getting tricky. Just strafe the area until everything was dead. Simple and effective. He grinned. Given the chance, Yako would no doubt waste a lot of time creating some fancy strategy to accomplish the same thing. Silly bastard. Now the ground was rushing up fast. Jubal released the safety and pushed the red button mounted on the top of his stick. Twin beams of lethal energy lanced down to cut parallel black lines across the ground below.

The little plane came in much faster than McCade had expected. Instead of shooting back, he found himself diving for the ground, hoping he wouldn't get his ass shot off. The energy beams sizzled as they cut a deep trench through the Nuag's corpse. McCade spit sand and swore. At this rate their fort wasn't going to last very long.

One after another the planes screamed over, their energy beams crisscrossing the compound, quickly reducing the Nuags to large lumps of charred meat. Try as they might, the three men found they could do little more than snap off an occasional shot. The little planes were just too fast and maneuverable.

Yako kicked his right rudder pedal and banked left. By now both wings had made two or three passes apiece, and as far as he could see, all they'd done was cook a few Nuags, and waste a lot of gas. At this rate they'd soon be forced to land and fight on foot, something which not only reduced their advantage, but seemed somehow demeaning. Pilots should fly, not slog around on the ground. As usual Jubal was using brute force instead of brains. Of course you can't use what you don't have. Down below he saw the occasional wink of an energy weapon, but thus far their fire had been completely ineffectual. He'd counted three defenders so far. Yako frowned. Shouldn't there be four? According to the messenger, two men and some sort of an alien had been with Mara at Thirty Mile Inn. So where was number four?

Mara peeked out from under the roller bush to see the planes buzzing and diving over the fort like motorized birds of prey. It was time to make her move. She'd forced herself to wait until the bandits were completely occupied with the fort. Ignoring the pain in her side, she eased the launcher up, until it was just barely sticking out from under the prickly vegetation. As she peered into the tiny sight the planes suddenly grew larger. She noticed half were red and the other half bright blue. Each had a number painted on its wing. A blue plane with the number one inscribed on its wings was circling the compound, apparently looking the situation over. "Good, number one. You can be the first to die." She squeezed the trigger, and there was a whoosh of displaced air as the heat-seeking missile went on its way.

McCade looked up at the blue plane with the number one painted on its wings. The "blue one"! The one he shouldn't kill! And he hadn't told the others. They'd maintained radio silence for fear the Wind Riders would monitor their frequency, but McCade felt sure this was important, so he touched his throat mike. "The blue plane with the number one—whatever you do—don't shoot it down!"

"What?" Mara demanded. "Why? Not that it matters because I just . . ."

She never finished her sentence because at that moment the missile hit and exploded. Hot shrapnel flew in every direction, and by chance, a chunk of hot metal hit another plane's fuel tank and blew it out of the air as well.

Chunks of wreckage crashed all around the fort sending up a cloud of billowing black smoke. Mara was still reloading when the blue plane with the number one painted on its wings dove out of the smoke and came her way. She hadn't hit it after all! Not that she could see why it made a difference. One of the other blue planes must have swung in front of it and been hit instead. Oh, well, better late than never, she'd nail him now. The plane quickly filled her sight, and her finger was resting on the trigger, when McCade said, "Don't fire, Mara! Let him go!"

She dived for the bottom of her hole and swore when an energy beam sliced along one side of her hole splattering her with globs of melted sand. Suddenly her side began to hurt even more. Reaching down, Mara found her wound had opened up. She fumbled out a self-sealing battle dressing and slapped it on. "Damn you, McCade, you'd better have one helluva good reason for this!"

"I do," McCade replied, "at least I think I do. I'll explain it later, when you're in a better mood. In the meantime perhaps you'd oblige us by cooking a few more of these bastards. Just leave number one alone."

Twisting herself around in the small hole, Mara managed to gain her feet once more. Picking up the launcher she aimed it toward the wheeling planes and picked out another blue target. "All right, I'll try." She saw movement out of the corner of her eye. The bastard in the "blue one" had located her, and was coming in for the kill. She forced him out of her mind as she picked a target.

Yako was shaking with rage. Two planes! Two pilots! He'd kill her for that. He could see her clearly. Her damned launcher was aimed toward the other planes. Why not him? Surely she must see him coming. Well, never mind. All he had to do was hold it steady and then fire. There was a puff of vapor, and he knew another missile was on its way. He knew he shouldn't look, but found he couldn't resist. Damn! The miserable bitch had done it again! Another blue plane exploded into a thousand pieces. Why didn't she aim at one of Jubal's planes? Suddenly he realized he'd already passed over Mara's hiding place, and there, right in front of him, flying like he didn't have a care in the world, was Jubal. Something deep inside Yako suddenly snapped. A wave of anger and resentment flooded through him. When he squeezed the trigger he did it without conscious thought. The twin beams of blue energy cut Jubal's plane in half. Both pieces spun into the ground with tremendous force and burst into flames. For a moment there was silence, as they worked to absorb what they'd just seen, and then there was chaos, as everyone tried to talk at once.

"Did you see that? Yako just killed the boss! Let's nail the bastard."

"Try it and you're dead meat," a blue pilot replied.

"Oh, yeah?"

And suddenly the sky was full of dueling planes. McCade looked on with amazement as the ultra lights wheeled, soared, and dived in a clumsy parody of air combat. In spite of the way the blue plane had blown the red plane out of the air, the dueling pilots didn't seem to be doing much damage to each other, although they were putting on a spectacular show. Even though McCade didn't have the slightest idea why the two groups were fighting, he felt sure it had something to do with the woman in his dream, and what she'd told him. And he knew it was going to save their lives. As the Sky Riders fought each other, they moved farther and farther away, until finally disappearing toward the west.

Mara walked in, and one by one the exhausted defenders emerged from their hiding places to sit slumped in the shelter of a half-burned Nuag. McCade told them about the dream, and though Mara had seen the Walkers do even stranger things, she was still amazed, and said, "Then help is probably on the way."

They all nodded, just happy to be alive, too tired to worry about the future.

EIGHTEEN

McCade rubbed a bleary, bloodshot eye, and looked again. It was still there. Maybe he wasn't hallucinating after all. Maybe there really was a big yellow sail coming his way. He'd been watching it for some time now. It had gradually grown from a drifting dot to a large splash of color. The sail was triangular in shape like those used on any planet with enough water to float a boat. But according to Mara's maps they weren't near any water, so the sail must belong to something else. The sail suddenly flip-flopped. Whatever it was had just tacked, and was now headed directly at him. The Wind Riders again? Coming to finish them off? Or some of Mara's friends—coming to the rescue. Which? There was no way to tell.

They had discussed the possibility of hiking to the next way station, but Mara had objected. She felt they were better off staying where they were. In her opinion McCade's dream proved that the Walkers knew where they were, and knew they needed help. Something about the way she said it made McCade wonder if she wasn't just a bit jealous. After all, she was a Walker herself, but for some reason he'd had the dream. Anyway they'd agreed to wait for a while and see if some help came along. Now somebody was coming . . . and the question was who.

He pulled back the corner of the emergency tarp and touched Mara's shoulder. Rico woke in midsnore, and jumped to his feet, while the other two were still untangling themselves. "What's up, sport?"

McCade nodded toward the plain. "We've got company."

"Bandits?"

McCade shrugged. "Maybe . . . maybe not. Let's see what Mara thinks."

Mara had overheard, and wasted no time scrambling up onto the Nuag. She gave a whoop of excitement, turned, and slid to the ground. "I told you they'd help us! They sent a wind wagon. Grab your stuff and let's go. We'll have to jump it on the run. Once they stop it takes 'em forever to get going again."

Each grabbed their weapon and a pack prepared earlier, slipping their arms through the straps as they followed Mara out onto the plain. In spite of her wound, Mara was way ahead of them. Phil had given her some kind of a painkiller and apparently it was working.

The sail was closer now, and McCade saw it was supported by a metal mast, which jutted upward from a low boxy platform. Since the wind wagon was coming straight at them it was hard to see much more, but it was certainly fast, bearing down on them at twenty or thirty miles an hour.

Phil frowned. "Aren't they going to slow down?"

Mara laughed. "'They' are an 'it,' and the answer is 'not much.' Come on!" And with that she started running again.

There was little the others could do but follow. As he broke into a run McCade decided he'd finally lost his mind. What a silly way to die. Run over by a landlocked sailboat on some rim world! Claudia would love it. She wouldn't even pay a bounty on him. That at least would have cost her something. It was close now, so close he could see the welds holding it together, and hear the big sail slapping against a stay. Just as he decided his only chance lay in falling flat and letting it roll over him, he heard a klaxon go off, and the machine began to turn. It was starting to tack!

"Now!" Mara yelled, leaping for the short ladder which was welded to the hull. Three quick steps and she was over the top, turning to shout encouragement at the others. Phil went into partial augmentation. He took three giant strides and jumped. Huge paws caught the top edge of the hull, while powerful muscles pulled him up, and over. Rico, meanwhile, had managed to jump onto the lowest step of the ladder. He hung on with one hand, stretching the other out towards McCade.

"Come on, ol' sport, you can make it."

But McCade knew Rico was wrong. He was running as fast as he could, and he still wasn't going to make it. Bit by bit the distance between him and Rico's outstretched hand grew larger. Then he heard a crack of sound, and the sail started to flap as it lost the wind. Out of the corner of his eye he saw the heavy boom swinging toward him. He jumped, wrapped his arms around the boom as it passed overhead, and swore as it picked up speed. He'd have to drop off when it passed over the hull, otherwise it would throw him off when it crossed over the far side and was jerked to a halt. Everything was a blur, so he closed his eyes, let go, and hoped for the best.

He landed on his pack. It broke his fall but knocked the wind out of him. The part of his mind not occupied with obtaining more oxygen suddenly realized that he'd lost his energy rifle. That wasn't exactly good news, but it was better than lying in the dirt, watching the wind wagon race away. He opened his eyes to find himself looking up at Rico. The wind tugged at Rico's hair and ruffled his beard. He wore a big grin. "Always showin' off. Maybe if you'd cut back on them cigars you could run a bit faster."

Still unable to speak due to a lack of oxygen, McCade offered the other man an ancient gesture. Rico laughed and helped him up.

The wind wagon had come about, and was making good time back across the plain. Now that he was on his feet McCade saw the hull was a large metal triangle. The sides were low but strong. The mast was made of metal, and was located about halfway down the wagon's length. A quick glance over the side confirmed his original impression that it was equipped with three wheels. Two were located on either side of the stern, and one in the bow, which was used for steering. The hull was about fifty feet across at its widest point, and seventy or eighty feet long. A network of wire stays supported the mast, while a host of lines snaked down through pulleys and power winches, to disappear into a sealed metal box. Since there was no crew in sight, and nowhere for them to hide, McCade assumed the metal box housed some sort of a computer, which controlled the ship via sensors and servo motors. The whole thing was scarred and pitted from countless collisions with windborne debris. Almost every square foot of sail showed signs of repair. The whole thing worked nonetheless.

"Well, what do you think?" Mara asked, gesturing toward the rest of the machine. McCade's reply was forestalled when a sudden gust of wind hit the sail, causing the left rear wheel to leave the ground, and throwing them off their feet. A few seconds later the computer made a minute correction and the wheel thumped back down.

McCade looked at Mara, and they both laughed until Mara grabbed her side, and said, "Enough . . . it hurts when I laugh."

As they helped each other up McCade said, "It's a bit treacherous, but it sure beats walking."

"Or watching Nuags rot in the sun," Mara agreed, brushing herself off. "Apparently this was the best the Walkers could come up with on short notice."

"I won't even ask how they knew we needed it," McCade said, looking around. "What are these rigs normally used for anyway?"

"Ore carriers," she replied, gesturing toward the bow. "And," she continued, "once you've built a wind wagon it's cheap to run. As you can see, they don't need any crew, and the computer's solar powered. Besides catching the wind, the sail also acts as a solar collector and, even with all our clouds, puts out more power than the computer can use."

"So why the Nuags then?" McCade asked, leaning back to look at the huge sail. "Why not use these babies instead?"

Mara smiled. "They're great out on the plains, but completely worthless in the hills and mountains. Which by the way is where we're headed." She pointed toward the distant horizon.

By squinting his eyes, McCade could just barely make out a dark smear above the plains, and beyond that a vague darkness that might have been mountains.

Hours passed, interrupted only by the hooting of the klaxon each time they tacked, and a somewhat spartan meal of emergency rations. Like the others, McCade passed the time by taking short naps, and then getting up to see how much progress they'd made since the last time he'd looked. Finally he stood to find that what had once been a dark smear had now resolved into low rolling foothills, and the darkness beyond them had indeed turned into mountains, which though rounded off by a million years of wind and rain, still reached up to hide their peaks in lowlying clouds. Now the sun was low in the sky, throwing softly rounded shadows out beyond the foothills, making even the Wind World's harsh landscape seem pretty.

"Is that smoke?" It was Rico, pointing off to the right.

McCade looked out beyond the bow, and sure enough, smoke was pouring up from the edge of the plain. Now Mara joined them and eyed the column of smoke with obvious concern. "It's coming from Trailhead, a small settlement, which also happens to be our destination. I can't imagine what's burning. The whole place is made out of shaped earth, reinforced with rock."

McCade noticed the smoke went straight up for several hundred feet before strong winds whipped it away. He had a pretty good idea what could have caused the smoke, but he hoped he was wrong. He'd seen smoke like that before. A glance in Rico's direction told him the other man had similar thoughts. They'd know soon enough.

Twenty minutes later the wind wagon's klaxon sounded three short blasts. There was a whine of servo motors and the clacking of winches as the computer started to lower the sail. At the same time the boom began to rotate, winding the sail around itself, creating a neat cylinder of fabric. Meanwhile the wagon slowly coasted to a stop. There were three similar craft moored a short distance away, and beyond them McCade could see the outskirts of the settlement. Low rounded warehouses and the like mostly, the kind of buildings that go with light industry. Behind them smoke billowed up to fill the sky and the crackle of flames was clearly heard. Now McCade was almost certain this was no ordinary fire.

They climbed over the side and helped Mara snap the mooring lines to the large eyebolts sunk into the plain for that purpose. Otherwise the large vehicle could be blown away by a sudden storm. Once the wagon was secure they followed her toward town. The sun was dipping behind the horizon, now, soon to disappear.

The flatness of the plain quickly gave way to a gentle slope. Their path was wide and unpaved but rock hard from constant use. Up ahead McCade could see the dim shapes of the outlying domes and hear the shouts of those fighting the fires. Smoke swirled everywhere, irritating his eyes and making it hard to breathe. They came to a stop when a middle-aged man with a blackened face and a grim expression appeared out of the smoke. He nodded in Mara's direction.

"Hello, Mara. So you're here. The Walkers sent word to expect you." There was no welcome in his voice or his eyes. They were angry and resentful. He turned to the others. "My name's Nick. Welcome to Trailhead . . . or what's left of it. I don't know what this is all about, but I sure hope it's worth it." And with that he turned his back on them and started back up the trail.

McCade looked at Mara and she shrugged. Silently they followed Nick up the trail. It didn't take long to see why he felt the way he did. For all practical purposes Trailhead was a memory. Many of the low earthen domes had been crushed. Others were surrounded by flames fed by some sort of liquid that burned with intense heat. As they reached the top of the low hill Nick stopped and pointed wordlessly down into the center of the settlement below. McCade looked and found his worst fears had come true.

Sprawled across the small valley was the long broken shape of an Imperial Intruder. There was no mistaking the ship's lethal ugliness. Intruders were specifically designed for landings under combat conditions, but the Wind World had turned this one into a pile of useless scrap. The fires which burned around it, and reflected off its polished surface, made it look like a vision from hell. Muffled explosions could be heard as internal fires found and set off stored explosives. Rivers of flame were born deep inside the ship to flow out and between the domes. Here and there figures darted through the flames, searching for survivors, salvaging what they could.

Mara turned away from the destruction and placed a hand on Nick's shoulder. "I'm sorry, Nick. I know that doesn't help, but please believe me, it's more important than you can imagine." She hesitated for a moment as if considering her options, and then spoke in a low, urgent voice, quickly outlining what was happening and why.

When she'd finished, much of the anger had disappeared from Nick's eyes, leaving only sadness behind. He nodded. "Yes, I'll do what I can. You'll have to catch those bastards before they can reach Chimehome."

"Catch them?" McCade and Mara asked together.

"Yes," Nick replied, anger flooding his features once more. "Right after the ship crashed, a hatch opened and an armed crawler rolled out. An officer, Major Tell, Tellor—something like that—asked me for directions to Chimehome, and like an idiot I told him. Then they took off. Didn't even try to help their own . . . much less ours."

The three men looked at each other. Major Tellor! Here. It certainly sounded like him. All three remembered the enjoyment in his eyes as he'd left them to die in the coliseum. Their situation had just gone from bad to worse.

"All right," McCade said grimly. "They've got a head start . . . and we've got to stop them before they reach Chimehome. Is there anything around here which can match that crawler for speed?"

Nick thought for a moment, and then shook his head. "No, we've got a few tractors for pushing ore around, but nothing to match that military job."

Mara shook her head. "Even if there was, we'd be crazy to race them, that crawler won't make it even halfway to Chimehome."

Nick nodded his agreement.

Seeing the doubt in McCade's eyes Mara said, "The planet will stop them. That's why we don't use crawlers ourselves. This world turns unprotected machinery into junk faster than you can bring it in. All we have to do is grab a couple of Nuags and plod along. They'll be waiting for us."

McCade had his doubts, but Mara seemed certain, and from what Nick said there wasn't much choice. Of greater concern was what lay ahead. Assuming Mara was correct, something nasty would eventually happen to the Imperial crawler, and as a result, they would run into Major Tellor and an undetermined number of marines. And knowing Tellor, his troops wouldn't be sitting around reading poetry to each other. They'd either be hiking toward Chimehome on foot, a less than pleasant experience on the Wind World, or, more likely, laying in ambush, hoping to acquire some new transportation. Like a couple of Nuags for example. With us thrown in as a bonus, McCade thought to himself. It wasn't a very pleasant thought.

NINETEEN

At some time during his long career Tellor had probably been more uncomfortable than he was right now, but he couldn't remember when. For almost half a day he'd been waiting. It was the sound that bothered him most: a low rumble, which rose and fell endlessly. Try as he might he couldn't get rid of it. He'd tried ignoring it, accepting it, and humming over it. Nothing worked.

Gritting his teeth, he stared at the point where the path disappeared around the bend, and willed some sort of transportation to appear. Anything. Anything that would get him up the path to Chimehome. Sweeping his powerful glasses across the land his eyes confirmed what his mind already knew. Had known even in orbit. Out here it was a long way between bars.

The space jockeys had provided a fairly decent aerial survey map showing all the major roads, settlements, and ground features for the area. The cloud cover had obscured a few areas, Chimehome among them, but all things considered it was a good map. One glance told him: One, this was wide open country with very little vegetation or other natural obstacles, in other words, tank country, and two, for some stupid reason all the roads meandered from place to place. Solution, ignore 'em. The quickest way from point to point is always a straight line. So Tellor laid his plans accordingly, but instead of a nice neat landing, the damn winds had smeared the Intruder all over the landscape.

Luckily, about ten percent of his insertion team survived the crash, as did one of his five armored vehicles. Not good, but not bad all things considered. The idea of aborting his mission never even occurred to him. Duty first.

They had made pretty good time at first, slowed by the wind, but still burning up the miles. As the only surviving driver, Blenko had the con. He was a homely man, with raw asymmetrical features, stooped shoulders, and tiny little white hands. As he drove they darted here and there, uncertain and afraid.

The road was not a road in the conventional sense. No intelligence had planned and then paved it. It went where Nuags had gone for thousands of years.

Seeing no reason to follow the road's meandering course, Tellor ordered Blenko to ignore it. So the crawler cut across great loops of road doing in minutes what it took Nuags hours to do. It looked like they'd reach the settlement in time for lunch the next day. And then, just when things were going so well, it all came apart. They were rolling across the floor of a valley, heading toward the far slope, when disaster struck.

Looking left, Blenko saw a brown wall of wind-borne sand scudding toward them, and shrugged. No big deal he told himself, just another dust storm. Since leaving the ship they'd rolled through three or four small ones without a hitch, and no wonder, it takes a lot to stop an armored crawler. Blenko's flat brown eyes flicked over the gauges. All four intake filters looked good, both engines, okay, all systems go. Satisfied there was nothing to fear, Blenko slumped back, returning his attention to a well-worn fantasy concerning Sergeant Okada.

At first Tellor agreed with Blenko's superficial assessment of the storm, but as he watched it race toward them, he began to wonder, and wonder turned to doubt, and then doubt to certainty. Punching the port screens up to full mag he felt the bottom drop out of his stomach. Sol! That thing was carrying more than just sand! It was picking up boulders and tossing them around like feathers! Other shapes were dimly visible within the brown mist too, including something which looked a lot like one of those big animals the local colonists used, and other stuff as well. Now the brown wall was only a mile away and moving with incredible speed. They'd never out-run it, and if the storm hit them broadside, those rocks would pound the crawler into pieces.

"Turn into the storm, Blenko! Turn left, damnit!"

Tellor could still see the vacant look in Blenko's eyes as the marine slowly turned his attention from a vision of Okada's naked buttocks to his commanding officer's urgent voice. Finally Tellor's words seemed to regis-ter, and Blenko's tiny white hands fluttered from one control to the next, slowly turning the crawler into the storm. Had he reacted faster they might have made it.

Thunderclaps of sound came at them as the storm beat the crawler like a gong, pushing it higher and higher, finally flipping it over altogether, and exposing its vulnerable underside to the full fury of the storm. Within sec-onds the rock bombardment had destroyed the crawler's drive-train, ripped off a track, and holed the main fuel tank. Ten minutes later the storm was gone, leaving three dead marines, a wrecked crawler, and a furi-ous Major in its wake. Once he realized the storm was over Tellor grabbed Blenko from behind, with every intention of killing him. Unfortunately his hands encountered no resistance. The driver was already dead.

Salvaging what they could from the wreckage, the marines trudged to the nearest loop of road, and dug in. Tellor sighed. So instead of rolling into Chimehome, he was lying on some very uncomfortable rocks, trying to shut out the sound of the blasted wind. Even if the interference suddenly disappeared, their remaining com set wasn't powerful enough to reach into space, so help was out of the question, and the storms made continuing on foot impossible. So, all he could do was wait, and hope some transporta-tion would come along and fall into his trap.

And then, as if in answer to his prayers, something moved in the far distance. Whipping the binocam left, he stopped, hitting the autofocus button, and marveling at his good luck. He certainly deserved some, and there it was, one, no, two of those beetlelike animals. Where were their heads anyway? They'd been included in the pre-drop briefing, but he hadn't paid much attention. Nugs? No, Nuags. All he remembered was people rode under them, instead of on top, and that Nuags refused to deviate from their ancestral paths. Well, it didn't matter. A ride's a ride. Carefully chinning his mic on he whispered, "Objective in sight. Range, two thousand yards. Hold for my signal."

Eight double clicks echoed in Tellor's ear as each member of his team flicked their mic on and off twice. Good. Everyone was awake and paying attention.

The Nuags were closer now. Just a few more minutes and he'd spring the trap. His troops would slip out of their hiding places quickly surrounding the animals. They'd call for the passengers to surrender, and if they refused, go in after them. Either way they'd have to die. On a mission like this one it's a mistake to leave enemies or witnesses behind you. Those were the rules—good rules—rules which had protected him for many years. After all, what if by some twist of fate Claudia lost her bid for the throne? His sponsor would be gone, along with her the legal protection he presently enjoyed.

Suddenly something hard and cold was jammed into Tellor's right ear. He knew what it was. A gun barrel. The damned wind had allowed someone to sneak up on him unheard.

"Move and you're dead." For a split second Tellor considered going for his blaster but didn't. The voice was as hard and as cold as the steel in his ear. He felt an expert hand remove his sidearm, combat knife, and the tiny backup needler strapped to his ankle. He still had a small knife concealed in his belt, but that wasn't going to accomplish much against someone with a gun. Best to wait, and see how things went.

"OK, you can turn . . . slowly." A chill ran down Tellor's spine. There was something familiar about that voice. It couldn't be. Nobody could have luck that bad. As the gun barrel left his ear he slowly turned his head. Shit! It was Sam McCade.

McCade grinned. "Hello, Major, fancy meeting you here." He placed a finger over his lips. "Mum's the word though. We wouldn't want to distract your team with our idle chatter."

McCade used his left hand to remove the binocam from Tellor's unresisting fingers. He used his left hand to sweep it across the hillside below, while his right hand kept the slug gun centered on the marine's spine. Tellor didn't even consider testing McCade's reflexes. Not after seeing tapes of the battle in the Imperial Coliseum.

McCade saw that the Nuags were almost in position. "All right, Major, in a moment I'm going to say 'now.' When I do, give your team the go ahead. Get fancy and you're dead. It's up to you. OK . . . ready . . . now."

Tellor chinned his mic switch, and said, "The objective is in position . . . go!"

And they went. Rising from the ground like ghosts they swept down the hillside to surround the Nuags below. The moment they were in position, Sergeant Okada bellowed, "You're surrounded. In the name of the Emperor, throw down your weapons and come out!"

For a moment nothing happened. Then, just as Okada started to order the team in, the lead animal gave a snort of protest, and grudgingly lifted an armored skirt. An attractive black woman emerged. As she straightened up, Okada saw both her hip and shoulder holsters were empty. "Where's the rest?" Okada demanded.

The black woman smiled. "Behind you. Throw down your weapons and surrender."

But Okada was having none of that. She knew what her job was, and it didn't include dropping her weapon for some unarmed colonial. Her blast rifle was already spitting blue energy as she spun around. Her dying brain barely registered the flash of light that killed her before a wave of darkness snuffed her out. Two more marines fell to Rico's and Phil's markmanship, before the rest gave up, and threw down their weapons. As Rico and Phil made their way down from their hiding places at the top of the hill, Mara forced the marines to sit on their hands, while she gathered their weapons into a pile.

As McCade followed Tellor down the hill, he gave thanks the plan had worked. About a hundred things could have gone wrong but didn't. They'd been very lucky to spot the marines while they were too busy carving hiding places to notice.

After forcing the Nuags out of sight down the trail and sneaking up to the crest of the hill, they'd watched the marines for a while, counting the opposition, mapping their locations, and planning their counterambush. Unfortunately the Nuags wouldn't leave their ancestral path, so there was no way to circle around the ambush. After that, it was a matter of creeping into position, and hoping for the best.

As McCade and Tellor reached the bottom of the slope, Phil said, "Welcome, Major, if you'd just step over there." He pointed to the group of angry-looking marines.

Tellor did as he was told. Rico turned to McCade. "What's the plan, sport, we can't take 'em with us."

McCade ran his eyes over the marines. They were a bedraggled bunch, but far from beaten, and even unarmed they were dangerous as hell. He hated to leave them behind, but Rico was right, they didn't have room for prisoners. If the positions were reversed, McCade knew what Tellor would do. But McCade had no stomach for cold-blooded murder. They'd have to leave the marines behind and hope for the best.

Tellor sneered, as if able to read his thoughts, and amused by his weakness. McCade ignored him as they made ready to depart. They left the marines their food and medical kits, nothing more.

Thirty minutes later they were on their way. Mara and Phil rode together, suspended under the first Nuag, while McCade and Rico followed along behind.

The marines were just a dwindling image on the rear screens. They stood in a clump apparently listening to Major Tellor. A little pep talk perhaps, or maybe a major ass chewing, with the Major doing the chewing.

Hours passed and it seemed as if their luck had taken a turn for the better. The wind died down, the clouds vanished, and the Nuags walked along under blue skies. Soon they were out of the foothills and working their way up into the mountains beyond.

Occasionally they took turns walking beside the Nuags, enjoying the fresh air and the exercise. There were lots of things to look at. Rocks shimmered and sparkled in the sun. Flowers shaped like dinner plates, which turned toward the sun and shook off layers of windblown dust to reveal their brilliant colors. Small animals scurried here and there, largely ignoring human and Nuag alike, intent on their various errands. Mara told them that while the clear weather wouldn't last long, it arrived with a certain regularity, and played an important part in the local ecology. Each period of clear weather functioned like a Terran spring, setting off a frenzy of feeding, mating, and other behaviors. As a result, many life forms had very short birth to death cycles, though some—the Nuags were a good example—had evolved adaptations allowing them to live to a ripe old age.

Once, McCade sighted a distant speck in the sky. It moved in wide lazy circles, riding the thermals upward. Thinking it a bird, he pointed, and asked Mara what kind it was. She took one glance and swore. "Wind Riders." She spat the words out one at a time. Moments later the speck disappeared into the distant haze. There was no way to tell if they'd been spotted, but the incident worked to dampen their spirits, and Mara urged the Nuags to move faster.

Night had come and gone, and all were walking in the early morning light when McCade heard the music. At first it seemed part of the gently rising wind. However, when the wind dropped off for a moment, and the music continued, he knew it was real. It had a strange haunting quality, quite unlike anything he'd heard before, yet familiar somehow. It managed to make him both happy and sad at the same time. Looking at the others McCade saw they heard it too. Their expressions reflected mixed emotions. Except for Mara. Her expression was different. She was happy—like someone greeting an old friend too long absent.

Now the wind reasserted itself, and as they walked the music became louder and louder, until the air seemed saturated with it, driving McCade's emotions up until he thought they could go no farther, and then releasing them to slide quickly downward, to start all over again.

A few minutes later they rounded a bend, and there, spread out below them, was Chimehome. The village was nestled in a small valley between twin mountain peaks. The valley served to protect the small collection of white domes from storms, and also acted as an acoustic enclosure for the huge wind chimes, which gave the place its name.

A single glance told McCade the chimes were a work of nature. Eons ago a spire of volcanic rock had been upthrust from the planet's molten core. Millions of years came and went. By now the rock had cooled, and the winds had come to rule the planet, bringing their endless cycles of good and bad weather. With them came the countless snows which blanketed the surrounding peaks with white, melted during brief periods of sunny weather, to run gurgling and splashing down into the valley below. As it passed, the water pushed and tugged at the small spire of rock, as though considering the various uses to which it might be put. Then, as if decided, it went to work. With eternal patience, the water probed and pulled, carving soft material away from hard, smoothing here, and shaping there. As the water dug deeper the spire grew taller, until finally it stood like a sentinel, guarding the valley from harm. And then one day, long before Nuags evolved from small animals which burrowed in the earth, the water cut one last tendon of volcanic flesh, and a large plate of delicately balanced rock broke free. For a moment it hung there, twisting slightly back and forth as the wind played with its new toy. Then a sudden gust pushed it sideways to strike a hard surface and the first note rang out. At first the chimes had only that single note to play, but as the years passed, and the water continued its marvelous work, other notes were added, until finally an intricate maze of delicately balanced rock produced an endless symphony of sound.

As they followed the path down into the valley below, McCade was amazed at how quickly his mind accepted the music produced by the chimes. Somehow it flowed in and around him without dominating his emotions or interfering with his thoughts. As they drew closer to the whitewashed domes which nestled together on the valley floor, he realized the whole place felt right somehow, as if expressing some internal harmony. Was that an expression of the Walkers and their philosophy? Or a manifestation of the place itself? There was no way to know, but the name Chimehome certainly fit, and the village seemed the perfect place for a monastery.

They had almost reached the village when a small group of people started up the path to meet them. They wore a variety of clothing, ranging from the somber to the gay, but all were smiling, and the young man leading them looked familiar somehow. Then McCade had it. The biosculptors had roughened his features slightly, but he was still tall, handsome, and blond like his sister. There was laughter in his sparkling blue eyes. As they shook hands the blond man smiled. "You must be Sam McCade. My name's Alex. I understand you've been looking for me."

TWENTY

McCade was alone in the observatory. Outside, the storm still raged, though more slowly now, much of its energy expended during the night. The rising sun was a dusty glow in the distance, still barely visible through the curtain of windblown sand. Eventually the wind would die away, but until then they were prisoners of the storm.

McCade lit another in a long series of cigars, blowing the blue smoke upward, to gather toward the top of the transparent duraplast dome. It swirled there for a moment, until the nearest exhaust vent sucked it away to become part of the storm. The last day and a half had left him with mixed emotions. On the one hand there was the satisfaction of finding Prince Alexander, and on the other, there was the growing fear of losing him. The longer the storm kept them captive, the more time Claudia had to find them. And that would be very bad, not just for them personally, but for the Empire as a whole.

Reluctantly, and against his better judgment, McCade had come to admire Prince Alexander, or Alex, as he preferred to be called. This was no spoiled princeling, insulated from the real world, and demanding respect he didn't deserve. No, there was a quality to the man. A questioning spirit, which had caused him to gamble his inheritance, plus a wealth of intelligence and courage which had seen him through when he'd lost. Those qualities, combined with a self-deprecating wit, made the prince hard to resist. It was as if Alexander had inherited his father's pragmatisim, but invested it with a genuine concern for other people. They had talked for many hours, waiting for the storm to pass. Alexander had put him immediately at ease by saying, "I already know about my father's death, Sam, and have for weeks."

Seeing McCade's confusion, the prince smiled. "I know all this must seem very strange to you, Sam—Chimehome, the Walkers, and the rest. Believe me, I felt the same way at first, but it's all quite real, and very useful. My father's death is a good example. You've heard about what the Walkers call the flux? Good. Well, the concept fascinated me from the start. However, the elders were reluctant to provide me with instruction. They are rightfully wary of novices who care little about learning The Way, and seek instead special powers with which to elevate their own egos, or gain advantage over others. But I argued long and hard, worked to understand the principles which light The Way, and finally received their permission. I was taught to meditate, to work through a variety of exercises, and, most of all, to consider what good I might accomplish if I succeeded. For as the elders pointed out, such abilities are nothing but tools, worthless unless applied to some purpose.

"So one day, there I was, working my way through a series of exercises, and not making much progress, when suddenly I was somewhere else, standing in a matrix of multicolored energy. It pulsed and flowed all around me, and somehow in its movement I saw shapes and patterns, people and events, all moving and interacting in accordance with their own free will, and the immutable laws of the universe. Millions and billions of variables forming to create endless combinations of cause and effect. It was incredible, Sam."

As Alexander spoke, his eyes glowed, and his whole face seemed to light up. "For one splendid moment it all made sense. Each life seemingly isolated, but part of the whole, just as each drop forms part of the ocean. At first I couldn't understand what I saw, overwhelmed by the sheer size and complexity of it all, but eventually I began to focus on smaller areas, and things began to have meaning. Here and there I saw patterns emerge, saw energies gather, build, and then release themselves to create what we know as reality. It was then that I saw my father's death, knew it had already taken place, and understood the forces it had set in motion."

For the first time since they'd met, McCade saw Alexander's face darken, as if a cloud had just passed between him and the sun. "Up ahead, I saw a branching, a division of energies which I somehow knew represented two possible futures, each equally possible based on past events, each dependent on the free will of certain individuals. In one case Claudia took the throne, and the tendril of energy which symbolized her rule led off into what seemed like a final darkness. The other path was mine. It was weaker, less likely, but led to a future which seemed to swirl and shift with many possibilities, some good, some bad. And then it was over, and I've never managed to duplicate the experience since." Here Alexander laughed. "So beware, Sam, even if I take the throne, the Empire's problems aren't over."

McCade half smiled, and flicked some cigar ash toward a nearby receptacle. "I'm glad you said that, Alex. Otherwise it would be tempting to shoot you here and now. One Claudia's enough."

For a moment the prince frowned, as if thinking McCade's comment through, and then he laughed uproariously, almost falling out of his chair. "And you would too! By God, if we get out of here alive, remind me to surround myself with people like you. In fact, how would you like a job? I could use you on my staff."

McCade smiled. "Thanks, but no thanks, Alex. I don't think I'd fit in around the palace."

"Well, at least consider it," the other man replied seriously as he leaned back in his chair. "Anyway, after my experience with the flux, I approached the elders, and they confirmed what I'd seen. At first I was angry—why hadn't they told me? Then as I began to calm down I was glad they hadn't. My experience with the flux was something special, something I'll never forget, and all the more valuable because I'd experienced it firsthand. So I spent a couple of days thinking about it, and although I still wasn't thrilled with the idea, it seemed as if I should return and, God willing, take the throne. In fact, I was preparing to leave when word came through that you were on your way. All things considered, it seemed wise to wait for some help. I understand Claudia is trying to find and kill me." He shrugged sadly. "It pains me that she would do that, but doesn't especially surprise me. Looking back I realize she's got a lot of her grandfather in her. Whatever it takes to get the job done. Well, anyway, now you've heard my story, so let's hear yours."

So McCade recounted the adventures leading up to his arrival at Chimehome. Every now and then Alex interrupted with a question. The first concerned Swanson-Pierce. "This Rear Admiral who engaged your services, what was his name again?" As McCade answered he realized he was probably doing Swanson-Pierce an enormous favor. Damn! Walt was bad enough as a rear admiral; if he made full admiral he'd be completely insufferable. Chances were, Alex was putting together a mental list of those deserving a reward after he took the throne.

Having explained who Walt was, and how they happened to know each other, McCade continued his story. It went smoothly until he reached the meeting with Lady Linnea. Then the prince stopped him again, his expression was one of eagerness mixed with suspicion. "How did she look?"

McCade repressed a smile as his mind conjured up an image of Lady Linnea in the nude. "Very beautiful. As a matter of fact she sent you a message."

Alexander became suddenly impatient and annoyed, providing McCade with a glimpse of his royal upbringing. Alex might be a regular guy in some respects, but deep down he was still a prince. "Well, man, out with it. What did she say?"

"She said I should tell you she loves you, and that the Empire needs you."

For a moment Alexander's face softened, and McCade was reminded of the holo showing the two of them in the garden. There seemed little doubt that he loved her, yet his face hardened as he asked, "But what of her friendship with my sister?"

McCade shrugged. The conversation was becoming distinctly uncomfortable. "I'd say she's on your side. Apparently she's forced to maintain the appearance of friendship with your sister."

Alexander nodded thoughtfully as if the whole thing made perfect sense. "Yes, otherwise my sister might destroy Linnea's father . . ." For a moment he seemed lost in thought, then he motioned for McCade to continue.

As McCade did so, he felt that more and more of plain old Alex was dropping away, gradually revealing something that looked a lot like an Emperor. A nice Emperor . . . but an Emperor nonetheless. Well, it made sense. After all, he'd been born and raised to the job.

From that point on, the prince restricted himself to an occasional chuckle, or a spontaneous "well done," making no other comment until McCade reached Pollard's death. As McCade described how the Walker had died letting them into the dome, a great sadness came over Alexander's face, and he looked down toward the floor. They were both silent for a moment, and when Alexander finally looked up, tears were running down his cheeks. He made no effort to wipe them away. "I lost a good friend, Sam, but my tears are for myself, not Pollard. He's where no one can hurt him."

McCade had never been able to decide about the question of life after death, but he nodded his agreement anyway, hoping it was true. They drank a series of toasts to Pollard, and by the time McCade finished his story, they were both slightly drunk. "To you, Sam McCade," Alex said, forming each word carefully, and holding his glass up high, "to one helluva bounty hunter. No, let me rephrase that, to the best damn bounty hunter in the Empire! Nobody else could've done it."

"Thank you," McCade replied, trying not to slop any of his drink on his lap. "And here's to you, the only Emperor stupid enough to give it up, and smart enough to get it back!"

Alex roared with laughter, and the two of them proceeded to drink and tell lies, until McCade began falling asleep. Tactfully suggesting they both needed some sleep, Alexander had gone to bed, allowing McCade to do the same.

Now, nine hours later, McCade felt slightly hung over, and wished the

storm would abate, allowing them to head for Deadeye and *Pegasus*. Fortunately they wouldn't have to spend days riding under a Nuag. Instead, they
would use some large gliders which belonged to the Walkers, and could be
launched from high in the mountains. Weather and thermals allowing, the
gliders could make it to Deadeye in just a few hours. Later they would be
torn down, and brought back to Chimehome by Nuag caravan. It was a lot
of work, and therefore something the Walkers seldom did, but this was an
emergency, and they had gladly offered McCade and Alex use of the system.

Of course, once they made it to Deadeye, there was still the matter of
getting safely off-planet, and finding a way to slip through Claudia's blockade undetected. McCade stubbed out his cigar and stared out into the
storm. They had a long way to go.

Twenty miles to the north, the storm continued to blow, but more gently
now, as it gradually lost its strength. Yako completed his inspection of the
ultra lights, located the flashing blue beacon marking his survival shelter,
and struggled toward it through a brown mist of windblown dirt and sand.
Other identical shelters surrounded his, each housing two members of his
wing, and each having its own colored beacon. It wasn't a pleasant place to
camp, but it was close to Chimehome, and when the storm died down, that
might become important. Getting down onto his hands and knees, he
wriggled his way through the low entrance into the relative comfort of the
interior.

"Welcome home," Major Tellor said with only a trace of sarcasm. He
was sitting with his back against a pile of equipment, an open meal pak
steaming beside him. The light suspended from the roof reflected off his
recently shaven head, and cast deep pools of shadow beneath his eyes.
"Everything all right?"

"Good enough," Yako grunted as he found a place to sit. "The storm's
dying. In four or five hours we'll be able to fly."

"And so will they. That's when they'll try the gliders." Tellor made it
more a statement than a question.

Yako shrugged. They'd been over this many times and the marine never seemed to listen. What the hell did he want? A gold-plated guarantee? "There's no way to be sure, Major. If they're in a hurry, the gliders are the fastest way to reach Deadeye. On the other hand, the Walkers rarely use them, partly because of us, and partly because of all the work involved in carting them back. So this McCade guy might opt for ground travel instead."

"In which case he'll run right into my team . . . and this time he won't be so lucky," Tellor said thoughtfully. "My people have orders to blast anything that comes down that path."

"Right," Yako said reassuringly, remembering the weapons he'd sold to the marines at incredibly inflated prices. "No matter what they do, you've got 'em."

"Why gliders anyway?" Tellor asked.

"Beats me," Yako replied. "Someone told me it's part of their harmony with the planet thing, but you'd have to ask them." Asshole, Yako added silently.

Tellor nodded, and proceeded to eat his food, chewing each bite with military precision. He was staring off into space, as though he could see right through the wall of the shelter, all the way back to Terra.

Happy to end the conversation, Yako fumbled around inside an open duffle bag until he found a meal pak. Damn. Pseudo meat again. Yako ripped off the tab and waited for the contents to warm up. He didn't like Tellor much and was doing his best to hide the fact. First because the Major had promised him enough credits to last the Wind Riders for a long, long time, and second, because the marine scared the hell out of him. After all, it sounded like half the Imperial fleet was in orbit around the Wind World. Something like that could be real bad for business. But it wasn't. In fact he'd had a lot of good luck lately. Take Jubal's untimely demise for example. Sure, he'd lost some good people in the brawl with Jubal's wing, but he'd also wound up in command, something which had seemed hopeless just a few days before. Then, just to put the icing on the cake, one of his scouts had stumbled across Tellor and his marines. The scout had been looking for Mara and McCade; after all, Jubal or no Jubal, they had a score to settle with those bastards. So here comes a pack of marines willing to pay him for doing exactly what he wanted to do anyway! What could be better? Yako chuckled deep inside. In spite of Tellor's efforts to gloss it over, you didn't have to be a military genius to see that he'd been ambushed, stripped of all his weapons, and left to make his way on foot. If Tellor failed to find McCade and kill him, Claudia would have his ass. Yako found the prospect quite appealing.

"What's so funny?"

Yako looked up, startled. He wasn't sure that he'd laughed out loud. Tellor's eyes were narrowed, as if he somehow knew the laughter was directed at him. "Nothing special, Major," Yako replied. "Just a joke someone told me earlier today."

Tellor nodded, but continued to watch Yako suspiciously, until the little man grew so uncomfortable he decided to take a nap. Anything was better than Tellor's unwavering gaze. A few minutes later Yako was asleep, dreaming about a monster who wouldn't stop staring at him, and a man named McCade who was supposed to die but wouldn't.

McCade watched the preparations with a jaundiced eye. He'd flown gliders before, but usually they were towed into the air behind an aircar, not launched off the side of a seven-hundred-foot cliff. In front of him two skeletal-looking ramps swooped down the steep hillside to end at the edge of the abyss. People were climbing all over the durasteel structures making sure that recent storms hadn't damaged them. Meanwhile a white glider sat poised at the top of each ramp. They were pretty craft, made out of light-weight duraplast, and gracefully shaped. So much so that the energy weapons mounted under the long slender wings and behind the canopy looked foreign and out of place. McCade prayed they wouldn't need the weapons. Flying a glider after so many years without practice was bad enough, but having people shoot at you while you did it, well, that was just too much. However, it seemed like he didn't have much choice. It turned out the gliders were two-place craft, which meant they'd have to leave Mara behind, and do their own flying. And while Alexander had flown just about everything else, he'd missed gliders, and Phil's experience was limited to aircars. So McCade and Rico would have to get behind the controls and hope for the best. He looked up toward the sky. At least the weather was right. The wind had died down to a gentle breeze, and here and there, the sun peeked through the eternal overcast.

There was the shrill sound of a whistle, and turning toward the sound McCade saw the inspectors had scrambled down off the ramps, and were gathering around the gliders. Rico waved in his direction and shouted, "Come on, ol' sport, all aboard the Deadeye express!" With a jaunty wave Rico climbed into his glider, settling himself behind the controls.

Forcing a grin McCade climbed up the path leading to the launching platform. Off to one side he saw Phil give Mara one last bear hug, before lumbering over, and climbing in behind Rico. Earlier, while saying his good-byes, McCade had noticed Mara's eyes were red. Phil hadn't said anything, but apparently there'd been a parting of the ways, and not at his request. If so, McCade wasn't too surprised. In order for the relationship to succeed, one of them would have to make a very large sacrifice. While he hadn't complained, Phil's variant physiology made life on anything but an iceworld distinctly uncomfortable. And, in her own way, Mara was just as tied to her world. She had an almost mystical understanding of it. Besides, she clearly wished to continue her studies with the Walkers, and that would be impossible if she left.

As he climbed onto the platform Alex was there, shaking hands and exchanging hugs with various friends, turning mischievously as McCade arrived. "Oh, driver, do try to be more prompt in the future. Imperial affairs await, you know."

"A thousand pardons, Your Supreme Effluence," McCade replied, bowing deeply. "If you would be so kind as to lower your Imperial posterior into the cockpit, we can depart posthaste."

"It's so hard to find good help these days," Alex confided to an amused woman with long black hair. "One must put up with the most outrageous incompetence." With a grin and a wave, Alexander followed McCade into the cockpit, and helped slide the canopy closed over their heads.

McCade put on the pilot's helmet and chinned his mic. "Rico? Do you read me?"

"Loud and clear, Sam," Rico answered from the other glider, grinning from behind his plastic canopy.

McCade quickly scanned the simple instrument panel. With no engine to worry about, there weren't many instruments, and very little which could go wrong. Except getting our rear ends blown off, he thought to himself. However, due to the height of their launching platform the altimeter already showed 725 feet, and that made him feel better. At least they wouldn't have to go through a long vulnerable climb up from the ground.

"All set, Alex?"

"Ready when you are, Sam."

"OK, the last one to Deadeye buys the beer!" And with that McCade hit the lever marked release, and felt his stomach lurch, as the glider slid downward. The aircraft quickly picked up speed, moving faster and faster, until they shot off the end of the ramp and their wings cut into the air. Pulling the stick back, McCade started looking for more altitude. In spite of the seven hundred feet they already had, it wasn't nearly enough to reach Deadeye. Because a glider has no engine, it spends a great deal of its time falling. Glider pilots like to call this part gliding, but in reality it's nothing more than controlled falling, which accounts for the sport's relative lack of popularity, and also explains why gliders aren't used for serious transportation. "Except on this stupid planet," McCade said through gritted teeth as he felt the nose drop and the glider start downward.

Banking to the right, McCade tried to find some warmer air which would buoy them upward. Meanwhile the altimeter continued to unwind. Six hundred and fifty, then six hundred and twenty-five, and finally six hundred feet came and went, before he cut across a thermal and felt it lift his wings. Circling to stay with the warm air, the glider soared upward, first regaining the lost altitude, and then picking up even more, until the thermal disappeared, and McCade leveled out at eight hundred and seventy feet. A glance to the right confirmed that Rico was still with him. The other pilot gave him a cheerful thumbs-up, and McCade waved in return. Then he checked his course to make sure they were headed for Deadeye, and allowed himself a smile of satisfaction. They still had a long way to go, but it was a pretty good start.

Then Alex's voice came over the intercom. It was tense and concerned. "Looks like we've got company, Sam, behind us about eight o'clock high."

McCade craned his neck to see, and swore softly when his eyes confirmed Alexander's report. They were just black specks for the moment, gradually climbing, but there was no doubt as to who they were. The Wind Riders had found them.

TWENTY-ONE

The Wind Riders were steadily gaining on them. Each time McCade lost altitude, and was forced to circle searching for a thermal, the bandits got closer, their engines buzzing like a flight of angry bees. Then, just when the bandits got close enough to fire, the gliders had always managed to find an updraft warm air, allowing them to soar up and away. However the Wind Riders knew how to use the thermals too, and were in fact better at it than either McCade or Rico, and that had allowed them to slowly close the gap. It was just a matter of time before they caught up.

Nevertheless, McCade was determined to stretch that time out as long as he could. The chase was more than an hour old, and they had already covered more than half the distance between Chimehome and Deadeye. It was funny in a way. On any other planet a hundred miles would have seemed insignificant. A fifteen-minute ride in an aircar. But not here. Here one hundred miles was an eternity, a long passage requiring days of grueling travel in a Nuag caravan, or in the case of air travel, hours of fear, wondering if at any moment unpredictable gusts of wind might reach out and smash you into the ground.

There was a burst of static over McCade's headphones. "They're closin', Sam. Looks like a fight comin' up."

"I'm afraid so, Rico. But let's drag it out as long as we can. Since they've got powered aircraft they'll have the advantage. The most important thing is to reach *Pegasus* and lift. So don't let 'em sucker you into mixing it up. Dodge and duck, but keep your nose lined up on Deadeye."

"Roger," Rico replied.

Suddenly laughter cut through the light static. "You call that a plan?" Both the laughter and the voice belonged to the same man. Major Nolan Tellor. McCade felt the muscle in his left cheek begin to twitch. Somehow the miserable bastard had hooked up with the Wind Riders . . . and was still on their trail. He should have shot the sonovabitch when he had the chance.

"Why, Major, I see you've found some new recruits for the Imperial air force. A scruffy lot, I must say. Still, I suppose this beats lying around in the dirt waiting for a Nuag caravan to happen by, doesn't it?"

For a moment the Wind Riders filled the air with mixed laughter. None of them liked Tellor, and they all knew McCade and his friends had ambushed the officer and his team, stripping them of their weapons. So in spite of McCade's reference to them as being "scruffy," they still had a good laugh. Then Yako's voice cut in. "Shut up, you idiots. So far the joke's been on you. So save the laughs for later."

After that both sides maintained radio silence. McCade and Rico concentrated on eating up as much distance as possible, while the bandits held on, throttles full out, grimly watching as their fuel gauges steadily dropped toward empty.

Then everything seemed to happen at once. McCade spotted the heavy-duty antenna and pylon which marked Deadeye's location up ahead, and hit a pocket of cold air at the same moment. Even though he put the glider into a shallow dive, it seemed to fall like a rock, and he had to either find a thermal or put it down miles short of Deadeye. Recognizing the problem, Yako's pilots began to shout with excitement. By God, the quarry wouldn't escape this time!

As luck would have it, McCade and Rico found a thermal rather quickly, but were still fighting for altitude when the Wind Riders attacked. The first energy beam was just a hair off, but close enough to leave a black line across the top surface of McCade's port wing. "Try and keep their heads down, Alex!" McCade yelled over the intercom. "Make 'em keep their distance."

Alexander didn't answer. He was lining up his first target. By working two foot pedals he could swing his seat and the gun mount 360 degrees. Twin pistol grips were built into the arms of his chair, and by squeezing them he could fire one, or both, of his two energy weapons. As the ultra lights swarmed after them, he smiled a predatory smile. He didn't know it, but it was the same smile his grandfather, the first emperor, had smiled as he led his fleet into battle. And it expressed similar feelings. He'd found their weakness. Although the Wind Riders were excellent pilots, they didn't know a damned thing about air combat! With the single exception of their fight with Jubal, they'd always attacked ground targets prior to this, so instead of coming up under the gliders, and attacking their most vulnerable point, the bandits were coming in from above, exposing their own bellies. Though not a professional like his sister, Alexander had served in air reserves, and had a reputation as something of a jet jockey. Aerial gunnery had been one of his favorite exercises. So he waited until two of the blue machines were hanging just above him, spitting out lethal bursts of energy, and missing as McCade dodged back and forth. Having never practiced aerial combat before this, their markmanship was very poor. But Alexander's wasn't. He squeezed both grips, literally cutting one ultra light in two, and blowing the second out of the air.

As the wreckage of Alexander's kills went tumbling toward the ground, Phil took out a third, and suddenly Yako's force of eight aircraft was almost cut in half. Yako was stunned, scared, and secretly glad to be alive. He forced himself to think. What the hell was going on? We're better pilots than they are, so how come they're winning? Because they know some tricks we don't, he realized. What are we doing wrong?

"What are you idiots doing?" The voice came from Major Tellor in the backseat. "You call yourselves pilots? Go for their bellies for God's sake. My grandmother could outfly you."

Yako instinctively knew Tellor was right. They'd been attacking from above, right into those rear turrets. He banked right and dove, pulling back on his stick, and sliding up under the nearest glider.

Glancing left, McCade saw one trying to come in from below. The bastards were learning fast! Slamming the glider into a barrel roll he lost some precious altitude but did manage to come out below the attacking ultra light. Seeing the opportunity, Alex squeezed both pistol grips, and flamed Yako's starboard wing.

As the ultra light tipped, and went into a final spin, Yako closed his eyes, and wished he could listen to something besides Tellor's enraged swearing. What a miserable way to die.

McCade tried to look everywhere at once. As the burning ultra light smashed into the ground, he turned to see smoke streaming from a dark hole in the side of Rico's glider, and the brown smear of ground beyond. However, both men seemed to be okay, Rico giving a cheerful thumbs-up, and Phil waving an empty fire extinguisher. What's more, Rico had apparently scored another kill, because only three Wind Riders remained. And they seemed to suddenly think better of it, banking right, and circling down to search the ground for survivors. Looking forward, he saw Deadeye's antenna and pylon just ahead.

Both gliders made decent landings, were taken in tow by a couple of the now-familiar red drones, and were soon lowered into the underground hangar. As the elevator moved smoothly downward they climbed out of the gliders and brought their energy rifles with them. The underground hangar would make a perfect place for an ambush. So when the walls dropped away they were crouched behind the gliders ready for anything. Anything except total silence. No energy beams screamed around them. No Imperial marines rushed forward to kill them. Nothing happened at all. In fact, except for an old man and a teenaged boy working on the wrecked ship in one corner, the place was empty of all life.

As they stepped off the elevator, the boy eyed them with open curiosity but, after a whispered word from the old man, turned back to his work. McCade noticed that the freighter which had been there earlier had disappeared, and been replaced by a beat-up old tug, but the old lifeboat was still there, and still for sale.

Pegasus was just as they'd left her. McCade palmed the main lock, entered, and initiated a pre-flight check. The computer assured him no one had attempted to enter, or had disturbed the ship in any way. Nonetheless, he left via the main lock to perform a visual inspection of the entire ship. It always pays to be careful . . . especially when you've been away for a while. Just because the computer said no one had bothered the ship didn't make it necessarily true. What if Claudia's people had found a way to fool his sensors? Attached some sort of explosive device to the hull, for example? As he ran his eyes over the ship, McCade wondered why Claudia's forces hadn't tried to ambush them inside the hangar. Maybe Claudia had that much faith in Tellor. Or maybe she had something even worse up her sleeve. Time would tell.

Rico and Phil had gone off to pay Momma for their berth. When they returned both wore big smiles. McCade suspected they'd found time to put away a beer or two. "We're cleared for take-off, Sam," Rico said. "By the way, Momma says an Imperial Intruder put down here about two days back. Some second louie and half a section searched the place, warned her how evil ya are, and lifted. Kinda makes ya wonder, don't it?"

"It sure does," McCade answered grimly. "Why leave *Pegasus*? Why not take her? Or disable her? It doesn't make sense."

"Oh, but it does," Alex answered, joining them under a stubby wing. "I overheard the last part of that, and it's exactly what Claudia would do. She *wants* us to lift. Chasing us all over the planet isn't working, so she'll allow us to lift, and then grab us in space."

McCade reluctantly nodded his agreement. "Viewed that way it does make a twisted sort of sense. So what do we do? We can't sit here forever."

"True," Alexander agreed. "And time's running out. How long before she takes the throne by default?"

"Three standard months from your father's death," McCade said. "And there's about a week of that time left."

"Just enough to reach Terra if I start now," Alexander mused.

"So," Rico said, "we have ta lift . . ."

". . . but if we do she'll nail us," McCade finished.

Phil had remained silent so far. Now he cleared his throat with a deep growl. "True . . . but maybe we can at least give ourselves something to negotiate with."

The other three turned to look at him. "I'm all ears," McCade said.

"Well," Phil said thoughtfully, "seeing that lifeboat over there gave me an idea." He pointed to the decrepit-looking boat with the FOR SALE sign scrawled across its hull. "We could have used yours, but you left it on Joyo's Roid."

"I'll try to be more considerate next time," McCade said dryly.

Phil ignored McCade's comment. "We buy the lifeboat and load it aboard *Pegasus*. Then we have Alex here dump the full story of what's happened into the boat's vocorder, preset its course for Earth, and dump it the second we clear atmosphere. Maybe we find a way through Claudia's blockade, and maybe we don't, but even if she grabs us it's too late. No matter what she does the lifeboat's gonna show up in Earth orbit and spill the beans. Knowing that, she lets us go!"

McCade lit a cigar, took a deep drag, and blew a column of blue smoke toward the floor. There were a number of holes in Phil's plan. The largest and most obvious was that the lifeboat in question wasn't equipped with hyperdrive. A single glance told him that. So, by the time the boat arrived in Earth orbit and delivered its message, Claudia would have been dead for hundreds of years. Assuming the old tub didn't fall apart along the way. Not much of a threat. While Phil was an excellent biologist, he didn't know much about ships. Nonetheless, maybe there was another way to use the lifeboat to their advantage.

"With a couple of slight alterations, your idea might give us an edge, Phil. Now here's what I have in mind . . ." After McCade presented his idea, a lengthy technical discussion ensued, eventually ending with general agreement that while the plan might work, chances were it wouldn't.

"Nevertheless," Rico summarized, "Sam's had even worse ideas than this one, and some of those worked, so why not give it a try?"

"Thanks for the overwhelming vote of confidence, Rico," McCade said.

The others laughed, and split up to handle their individual assignments. Rico and Alex took off to acquire the lifeboat, and program its vocorder, while McCade and Phil raided the supply lockers aboard *Pegasus*. A short time later they started the alterations to the lifeboat's tiny drive.

About four hours later the alterations were complete, the lifeboat had been loaded aboard *Pegasus*, and they were ready to lift. McCade fired his repellors, and carefully danced his ship out of her berth, and over to the elevator. There was the hum of hidden machinery as they rose toward the surface and emerged into the beginnings of a storm.

"It's a good thing we're liftin' now," Rico said from the copilot's position. "Another hour and this place'll be socked in but good."

McCade looked out at the swirling dust and nodded his agreement. Apparently the perpetual storm which usually surrounded Deadeye was about to reassert its authority. With a gentle touch on the controls he slid *Pegasus* off the elevator. "Stand by to lift. Five from now."

As he spoke, his eyes scanned the banks of indicators, and his hands moved over the controls with the surety born of long patience. Then with a final glance at the viewscreens, his right hand came to rest on the red knob located just over his head. "Hang on, gentlemen, here goes." And with that he gave the knob one turn to the right and pushed it in. The ship vibrated for a moment as her engines built thrust, and then she was gone, a momentary pinpoint of light high in the sky, glowing for a moment, and then gone.

As they cleared the atmosphere, McCade felt the weight come off his chest, and shook his head to clear his vision. "OK, Rico, stand by to eject the boat. On five. One . . . two . . . three . . . four . . . five."

Rico touched a key on the panel in front of him, flipped up a hinged cover, and flicked the switch it protected. Halfway down the hull a hatch slid open and the lifeboat shot out. Seconds later its drive kicked in, and it swung off on a course which would eventually take it to Earth, about three or four hundred years hence.

Hitting the power, McCade accelerated away as fast as possible, but he didn't get far. Suddenly all sorts of proximity alarms went off. Lights flashed, buzzers buzzed, and klaxons hooted. And before he could do much more than swear under his breath, *Pegasus* was locked in a matrix of Imperial tractor beams. They had obviously tracked him from lift-off. Claudia didn't even bother to call them up and gloat. She just reeled them in.

Locked in the embrace of the tractor beams, there was no reason to remain at the controls so McCade and Rico released their harnesses, joining the other two in the ship's small lounge. Dropping into a chair, McCade lit a cigar, and watched the main screen. The Imperial Cruiser *Neptune* got larger and larger, until it blocked out the star field beyond it, and *Pegasus* was pulled through an enormous hatch and into a brightly lit launching bay. McCade saw Claudia had turned out an entire section of marines to welcome them. They wore full space armor.

"It appears my sister has sent an honor guard," Alex said dryly. "How considerate."

McCade laughed. "Your sister is quite generous with honor guards. We always get one, isn't that right, gentlemen?"

"Absolutely," Rico said, eyes twinkling.

"Every time," Phil growled.

The com set buzzed and lit up to reveal Captain Edith Queet. She looked very, very tired. "I will say this once, and once only. After the bay has been pressurized, open your main hatch. Come out unarmed, with your hands behind your heads. Failure to obey my orders will result in death." Then she was gone.

Time passed as *Pegasus* was maneuvered into a berth next to a supply shuttle, the huge launching bay doors were cycled closed, and a thin atmosphere was pumped in to replace vacuum. "The Captain seems a bit testy," Alex observed, releasing his gunbelt and throwing it onto a chair.

"No offense," Phil growled, "but your sister does that to people."

Alex grinned. "Ain't it the truth!"

McCade activated the main hatch, and they left the ship as ordered, unarmed, and with hands behind their heads. They were quickly surrounded by ominous-looking marines. The marines' features were hidden by reflective visors and their actions were hard and jerky in the bulky armor. McCade couldn't hear what they said via their suit radios, so they seemed to move silently, in perfect harmony. It made them look even more menacing.

Working quickly and efficiently, the marines shackled their hands behind them, using two sets of restraints on Phil instead of one. Apparently someone remembered his performance in the coliseum.

Then they were shoved and pushed into a single file, herded through an inner airlock, and marched down a gleaming corridor. After what seemed like miles of corridors, they were ordered to halt, and forced to wait outside the ship's wardroom. Whether the wait was intended as a psychological device, or simply meant Claudia wasn't ready, McCade couldn't tell. Either way he was sure that she had caused it. After about thirty minutes they were finally ushered in.

The wardroom was large and spacious, boasting a long bar against one bulkhead, with a mirror behind. Claudia had staged the scene very carefully, using the bar and mirror as a backdrop. She sat in a chair on a raised platform, which though not a throne gave that impression. She was dressed in a simple white gown. Her blond hair was draped over her left shoulder, her hard blue eyes sparkled with excitement, and her lips were curved upward in a smile of triumph. Her personal bodyguard stood in a semicircle behind her looking ominous in their reflective visors and black armor. However, what grabbed and held McCade's eyes were the two people standing to Claudia's right. Rear Admiral Walter Swanson-Pierce and Lady Linnea Forbes-Smith stood there with hands shackled, and under guard.

Alex surged forward only to be knocked down by a rifle butt. Claudia laughed, and said, "Welcome aboard, dear brother. I see you're still alive. Well, that's easily remedied."

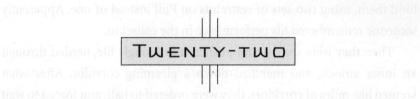

TWENTY-TWO

Things were not looking good. As a marine jerked Alex to his feet, McCade felt his spirits fall. Things were a lot worse than he'd expected. Deep down he'd hoped for a last-minute rescue by Swanson-Pierce, or maybe some secret assistance from Lady Linnea, and those possibilities were now eliminated. Both his rescuers needed rescuing themselves. Neither looked very good. Their clothes were soiled and ripped, and they swayed, as if barely able to stand. Swanson-Pierce kept trying to jerk his head up, but each time he tried it seemed to weigh too much, and it fell back to his chest.

As though reading McCade's mind, Claudia's eyes flicked over to the prisoners, and then back to him. "Well, we meet again, Citizen McCade." She nodded toward the two prisoners. "Pathetic, aren't they? Good examples of what happens to those who would betray me. You at least fight your battles directly. These," she said disdainfully, "cower in the shadows, too scared to come out and fight.

That one"—she pointed at Lady Linnea—"pretended to be my friend, while behind my back she sent secret messages to him." She indicated Swanson-Pierce.

The naval officer tried to bring his head up to respond, but failed once again.

Claudia laughed. "He actually tried to sneak aboard, from a supply ship, disguised as a Chief Petty Officer." She shook her head in amusement. "Who knows what kind of absurd plan he intended to carry out. As you can see we've been asking him a few questions, but so far he's proved quite stubborn. A credit to the Academy."

To McCade's amazement there was pride in her voice. Even as she tried to break Swanson-Pierce, she took pride in the fact that she couldn't, and credited the Naval Academy for his strength. She was even more bizarre than she'd been the first time they'd met. Still, he'd learned something valuable. She didn't know why Swanson-Pierce had tried to slip aboard. Good for you, Walt, McCade thought to himself. Now I wonder what you had up your sleeve, and if it's still operational.

"But wait!" Claudia said, her face lighting up with sudden understanding. "You graduated from the Academy too, didn't you, McCade? Of course! That explains why you've been so effective."

Alex and McCade exchanged glances. Claudia was obviously a few planets short of a full system. Somehow, in her mind, the Naval Academy had become elevated to the status of something very special, something with the power to confer unusual strength and power in its graduates.

Meanwhile Claudia continued to talk, apparently oblivious to their reaction. "Fortunately I'd been on to Linnea's treachery for months, and when she went sneaking off to meet Swanson-Pierce, I had her followed. It was as easy as that.

"Which brings us to you and my dear brother," Claudia said thoughtfully, fastening Alex with a hostile stare. "The Academy wasn't good enough for you, was it?" Apparently she didn't expect an answer, because she kept right on talking. "We found the lifeboat, you know, and I must say, as ideas go it was just as inferior as you are. By the time it reached Terra and delivered your pathetic message, we would've all been dead. Not a very good idea, was it, McCade?"

McCade felt his heart begin to beat faster. They'd fallen for it! Part of it anyway. Now, if only the lifeboat was aboard *Neptune.* If they'd put it aboard some other ship, or simply blasted it, then this was the end of the road. But at least there was still hope. And with Swanson-Pierce and Linnea out of action it was their only hope. He slapped a confident grin on his face. "You can't win 'em all."

"How profound," Claudia observed dryly. "I'd forgotten what a brilliant conversationalist you are."

"Claudia, why don't you just cut the crap and get on with it," Alex said wearily. "You've got what you want, so do your worst, and let's get it over with."

"Why, Alex," Claudia said in mock surprise, "whatever do you mean? I wouldn't dream of hurting my own brother. In fact, I'm going to turn you loose." She paused for a moment to run her tongue over thin lips, enjoying her power over them, intentionally dragging out the suspense. "Yes, I'm going to turn you loose . . . in your own lifeboat."

She laughed as she saw their expressions. "Don't blame me, I got the idea from you. After I listened to your message on the lifeboat's vocorder, I thought, how dramatic! Hundreds of years after the fact, a message arrives from the long-lost prince, describing how his evil sister robbed him of the throne! The public would love it! The historians would go crazy! I'd be even more famous! In fact, the idea was so appealing, I almost let the boat go, message and all."

Claudia paused, assuming a look of pained regret. "But then I realized how selfish that would be. Surely you would prefer to deliver your message in person! True, the trip would last hundreds of years, but I knew you wouldn't mind. A message is always so much more personal if you deliver it yourself!"

Alex shook his head sadly. "No wonder Father wanted me to assume the throne. You're sick."

Claudia's eyes flashed a brilliant blue, all color draining from her face. "Sick? You call me sick? Why you . . ."

Suddenly there was the muted thump of a distant explosion. The whole ship shook like a thing possessed, and since McCade was expecting it, even hoping for it, he was ready. As he fell he managed to take two marines with him. A distant part of his mind heard the emergency klaxons going off, knew the exploding lifeboat must have done a lot of damage to Neptune's launching bay, and hoped it would keep the crew busy for a while. The lifeboat's drive had gone critical and blown up a full half hour later than he'd originally estimated. But, he thought as he hit the deck and managed to kick one of the marines in the head, sabotaging drives is not an exact science.

McCade looked up just in time to see Rico put his head down, run full tilt into a marine's stomach, and fall as a vicious blow from a rifle butt brought him down.

Phil had already gone into full augmentation, snapping his durasteel shackles as if they were made of cheap plastic, and charging Claudia's bodyguard all in one continuous blur of motion.

Already confused by the explosion, and safe inside their armor, the guards saw Phil coming but didn't take him seriously. After all, what could a shaggy-looking freak do to them? By the time they found out, it was way too late. Phil peeled their armor off like tin foil. Then he went to work with razor-sharp durasteel claws, slicing through flesh and bone, killing anything that moved. As the marines tried to fight back, they found themselves slipping and sliding in their own blood. And as they died, they couldn't believe what was happening. How could this be? What kind of creature can tear armor apart with its bare hands?

However, Phil didn't escape untouched. He was soon bleeding from a dozen wounds, adding his blood to that of the marines.

Claudia tried to run. As she launched herself toward the open hatch her face was frozen in a mask of terrified desperation. She had thought herself invulnerable, absolutely inviolate, and the ease with which Phil had decimated her bodyguard had shaken her to the core.

McCade swore. She was going to escape! Desperately he slammed the heel of his hand into the marine's nose, pushing the cartilage up into his brain, killing him instantly. Then he tried to get up, knowing he'd never make it in time. By now the only obstacle between Claudia and the hatch was the swaying figure of Swanson-Pierce. The explosion had knocked Lady Linnea to the floor, but by virtue of some miracle, or just his own stubborn pride, the naval officer still stood. With a tremendous effort of will, Swanson-Pierce managed to bring his sagging head up, and smiled at Claudia as he toppled forward into her path.

She tripped over the officer's body, skidded across the slick floor, and crashed into a console. Before she could recover, her brother had rolled over to lock powerful legs around her neck, squeezing until her eyes bulged and her face turned blue.

McCade yelled, "Alex!" but the other man was already releasing her.

"Freeze!" McCade's heart sank as Captain Queet stepped through the hatch, a blaster in each hand, and a squad of heavily armed navy ratings right behind her. Seconds later a doctor and a number of medics rushed in and began to tend the wounded.

Phil froze as ordered, but it didn't make much difference, because every marine in the room was either dead or wounded.

"On your feet!" Queet ordered. McCade struggled to comply, and then realized the naval officer wasn't even looking in his direction. Instead her blasters were pointed at Claudia.

Claudia's face registered disbelief as she stood with help from one of the medics. Her hands went up to touch her bruised throat as she croaked, "What's the meaning of this, Captain Queet? How dare you give me orders!"

"You!" Claudia pointed a trembling hand at a Chief Petty Officer who stood just behind Queet. "I order you to arrest Captain Queet for insubordination. Lock her in her quarters."

The Chief, a slender man named Lister, didn't move an inch. His blaster remained where it was, lined up on Claudia's chest. For a moment there was complete silence, and then Claudia seemed to slump inward, her eyes on the floor, her lips a hard thin line.

Queet turned to Alexander with a questioning look. "Sir?"

Alex nodded.

Turning to Lister, Queet said, "Lock her in her quarters, Chief. No one comes or goes without my permission."

The Petty Officer nodded, and motioned with his blaster. Claudia obeyed, stepping through the hatch without a word. As the last of Claudia's escort disappeared from sight, Queet turned, and snapped to attention. "Captain Edith Queet, commanding the Imperial Cruiser *Neptune,* at your service, sir."

Alex smiled. "At ease, Captain. Thank you."

She obeyed, already liking his style better than Claudia's. For months she'd been working with Swanson-Pierce, feeding him information, but hoping she would never have to come into direct conflict with Claudia. They'd agreed to move against her only if Alexander were found. But eventually it became clear that Claudia would do anything to take the throne. Then Claudia had discovered Swanson-Pierce and Lady Linnea, leaving only Captain Queet to make the final decision. Strangely enough, when Swanson-Pierce was no longer there to guide her, the same Academy training Claudia was so fixated on provided Queet with the answer. Ironically it was in the form of a maxim originating with Claudia's own grandfather, and drummed into every cadet: "An officer's ultimate duty is to the good of the Empire regardless of personal cost." Thinking about that made her feel better as she moved off to restore order to her ship. The damage was considerable, and that made her mad, but what could she do? Chewing out the Emperor didn't seem like a good career move. As she strode down the corridor Queet allowed herself a rare smile, much to the shock of a passing tech, who wondered if she'd smiled at him.

For a moment Alexander allowed his eyes to rove the wardroom. The price of victory had been very high indeed. It looked like a butcher's shop. Mangled bodies lay everywhere. Sadly enough the marines had died defending the Empire. His empire now. His marines. Knowing nothing of the issues involved, the marines had simply done their duty for Claudia, as they would for him. Of course, if it hadn't been for Phil, Rico, and McCade, those same marines would have happily sealed him into an old lifeboat and sent him off to die in space. He sighed. It didn't make much sense.

Over to one side, McCade and Rico were helping two medics load Phil on a stretcher. The big variant had collapsed. As always, full augmentation had left him drained, plus he'd lost a lot of blood. He'd probably sleep for about sixteen hours. Meanwhile, the rest of the wounded had been loaded onto auto stretchers, and the worst cases were already headed for sick bay. As they took Phil away, Rico went along to make sure his friend received good treatment, and McCade watched them go. He knew he should feel bad about the marines, but he didn't. He was just damned glad his friends were alive.

As the last of the stretchers were rolling out, Alex spotted Linnea. Her auto stretcher was gliding toward the hatch under the control of a rather plump young doctor. "Linnea!" He rushed to her side. Looking down, he felt heartsick. "My God, what have they done to you?"

Her beautiful face was pale and drawn. Her eyes fluttered open and she managed a weak smile. "Welcome home, Alex, we need you." Then her eyes closed again and her head fell to the side.

Alex looked up at the doctor, who smiled nervously, and shook his head. "She'll be just fine, sir." Under Claudia's orders the doctor had been present during Linnea's interrogation. Now it appeared her brother was suddenly in charge, and he was obviously concerned about Lady Linnea's health. What would she tell him? The doctor felt himself start to sweat.

Alex found he had to clear a lump from his throat before he could speak. "Good. Lady Linnea is to receive your personal attention. God help you if anything happens to her."

The doctor nodded, and started toward the door, jerking to a stop when Alex held up a restraining hand. Whirling around Alex said, "The naval officer who was with Lady Linnea, Swanson-Pierce, where is he?"

"Over here," McCade answered. "At the moment he's out of it, but I suspect he'll survive to make my life miserable."

"Him as well," Alexander admonished the doctor. "I want reports on their condition every four hours."

By now the doctor was quite pale. He nodded nervously, steering Linnea's auto stretcher himself, and urging the medic in control of Swanson-Pierce's stretcher to hurry up. He didn't understand what was going on and didn't want to. Safety lay in the direction of sick bay, and he unconsciously urged Linnea's stretcher to greater speed.

McCade was lighting a cigar when the Emperor walked over to join him. "Well, Alex, or should I say 'Your Highness'? The empire is yours. Wear it in good health."

The Emperor laughed. "It may be mine, but I don't think it's possible for you to say 'Your Highness' and mean it. So let's agree that you'll always call me Alex instead." And with that the Emperor held out his hand to the bounty hunter.

McCade stuck his cigar between his teeth and shook the Emperor's hand. "It's a deal, Alex."

The Emperor looked serious for a moment. "I'd say 'thanks,' but thanks isn't good enough, Sam."

"Then just make sure Swanson-Pierce comes through with my bounty," McCade answered with a grin. "He may be an Admiral, but he's still a bastard."

"The empire could use more bastards like him," the Emperor countered. "Which brings me back to my earlier offer. I could use you, Sam. I know you don't trust the Imperial government, so why not become part of it? I'll give you any job you want. That way you make sure we don't screw up."

McCade blew a stream of gray smoke toward the overhead. "Thanks, Alex, but I wouldn't fit in."

The Emperor shrugged. "All right, Sam, I respect your wishes. Nonetheless, I owe you one. Don't hesitate to call it in."

"I won't," McCade assured him. "Just out of curiosity, what will you do with Claudia?"

The Emperor smiled as his grandfather and father had before him. "Why, turn her loose, of course. All my opposition will flock to her, and then I'll be able to keep an eye on all of them at once."

McCade shook his head in amazement. "It's obvious you're the right man for the job."

"It's in the genes. Well, I'm heading down to sick bay. You coming?"

"In a few minutes. I'll catch up."

"See you there." And, with a cheerful wave, the Emperor was gone.

McCade stepped over to the bar and punched in a request for a Terran whiskey. While he waited, he took a deep drag on his cigar and then crushed it out. He knew, deep down, that in spite of everything, all they'd managed to do was buy a little time. Under Alexander's leadership, war with the Il Ronn would be delayed, but not prevented. The forces pushing both sides toward it were just too powerful.

With a gentle hum the autobar produced his drink. Turning his back to the rest of the room, he faced the mirror and lifted his glass. The man he saw there looked older but not, he decided, that much wiser. Nonetheless he was alive. Thanks to some very good luck and some very good people. "To you, Cy, may you always win. To you, Spigot. And to, you, Pollard, wherever you are. And, finally, to you, Sara, I'm coming home." And with that he drained the glass to the very last drop.